JUSTIN JORDAN
ELEONORA CARLINI

BACKWAYS ™

VOLUME
1

ALL THE FORGOTTEN THINGS

SILVIA TIDEI

MARSHALL DILLON

AFTERSHOCK

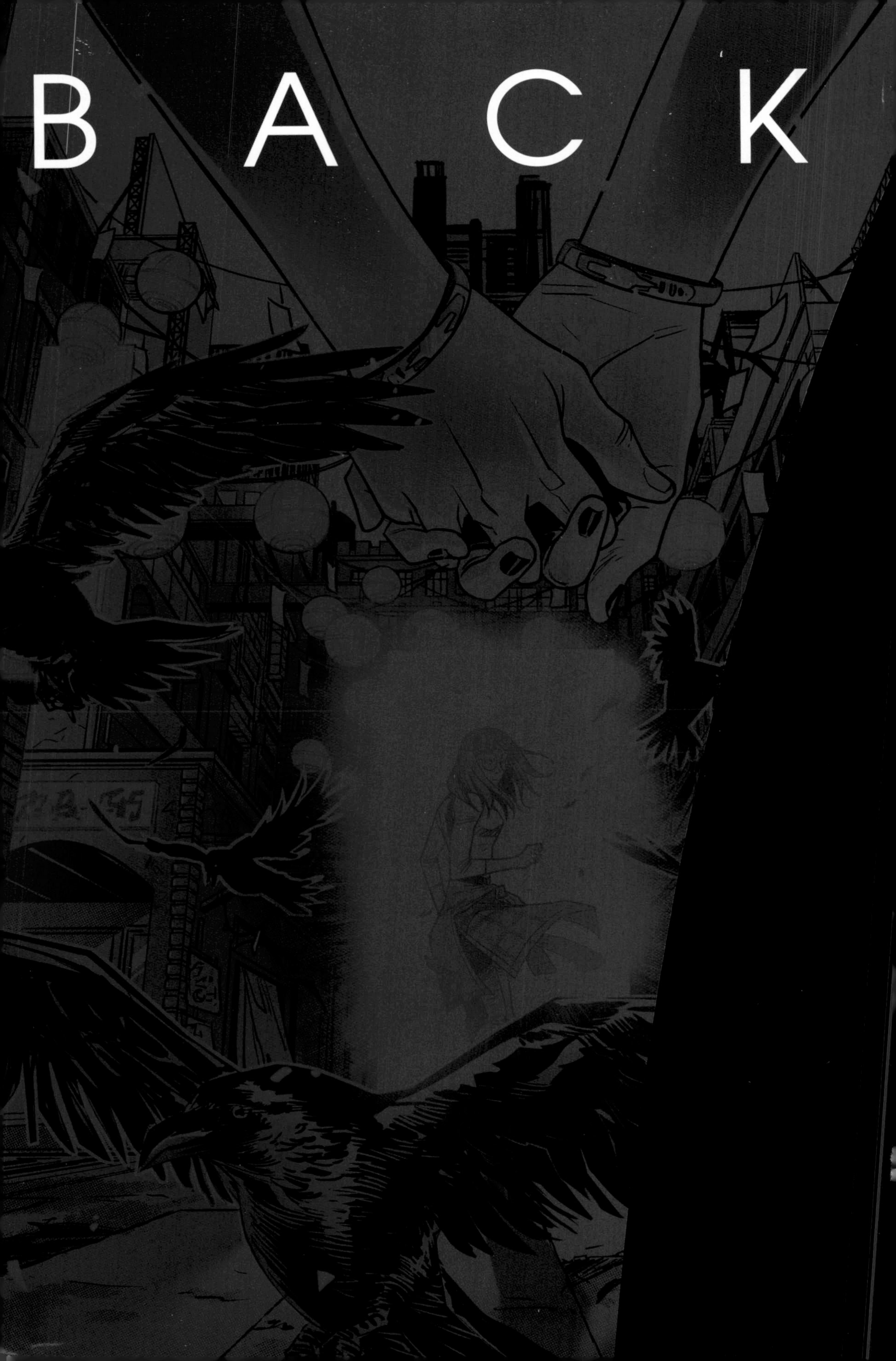
BACK

WAYS

VOLUME 1

ALL THE FORGOTTEN THINGS

JUSTIN JORDAN creator & writer

ELEONORA CARLINI artist

SILVIA TIDEI colorist

MARSHALL DILLON letterer

ELEONORA CARLINI w/ **SILVIA TIDEI** front & original covers

GEORGES JEANTY w/ **ANDRE SZYMANOWICZ**, **ERIKA ROOTH**, **MIKE ROOTH** & **BEN TEMPLESMITH** variant covers

COREY BREEN book designer

JOHN J. HILL logo designer

MIKE MARTS editor

AFTERSHOCK™

MIKE MARTS - Editor-in-Chief • JOE PRUETT - Publisher/ Chief Creative Officer • LEE KRAMER - President
JON KRAMER - Chief Executive Officer • STEVE ROTTERDAM - SVP, Sales & Marketing • LISA Y. WU - Retailer/Fan Relations Manager
CHRISTINA HARRINGTON - Managing Editor • JAY BEHLING - Chief Financial Officer • JAWAD QURESHI - SVP, Investor Relations
AARON MARION - Publicist • CHRIS LA TORRE - Sales Associate • KIM PAGNOTTA - Sales Associate • LISA MOODY - Finance
CHARLES PRITCHETT - Comics Production • COREY BREEN - Collections Production • TEDDY LEO - Editorial Assistant
SIMON WHITE - Proofreader

AfterShock Trade Dress and Interior Design by JOHN J. HILL • AfterShock Logo Design by COMICRAFT
Publicity: contact AARON MARION (aaron@publichausagency.com) & RYAN CROY (ryan@publichausagency.com) at PUBLICHAUS
Special thanks to: IRA KURGAN, STEPHAN NILSON and JULIE PIFHER and SARAH PRUETT

BACKWAYS VOL.1: ALL THE FORGOTTEN THINGS Published by AfterShock Comics, LLC, 15300 Ventura Boulevard Suite 507, Sherman Oaks, CA 91403. Originally published as Backways #1-5. PRINTED IN KOREA.
First Printing: July 2018. 10 9 8 7 6 5 4 3 2 1

AFTERSHOCKCOMICS.COM Follow us on social media

I N T R O D U C T I O N

Magic and madness.

Classically, these things have always been intertwined in myth and legend. And it makes a lot of sense, I think, because in order to do magic, you have to believe it's possible...and that requires madness.

Or at least you risk being perceived that way.

The Backways is a place where magic is real. A hidden realm created from all the forgotten spaces. And it's a place where people who have never felt at home—the mad, the strange and the desperate—can find a place to belong.

It's also a place where stories happen. Growing up I loved things like *Return to Oz*, *Labyrinth* and *The Dark Crystal*, and I think you can see them in this comic book. I wanted to create a place to tell that kind of story, about the weird and the odd that's all around, all the time, unseen and unknown.

Fortunately, I was lucky enough to have Eleonora Carlini and Silvia Tidei to actually bring this place to life. The book is infinitely weirder and more wonderful because of what they did with it.

Magic and madness. You'll find both in The Backways, and so much more.

JUSTIN JORDAN
June 2018

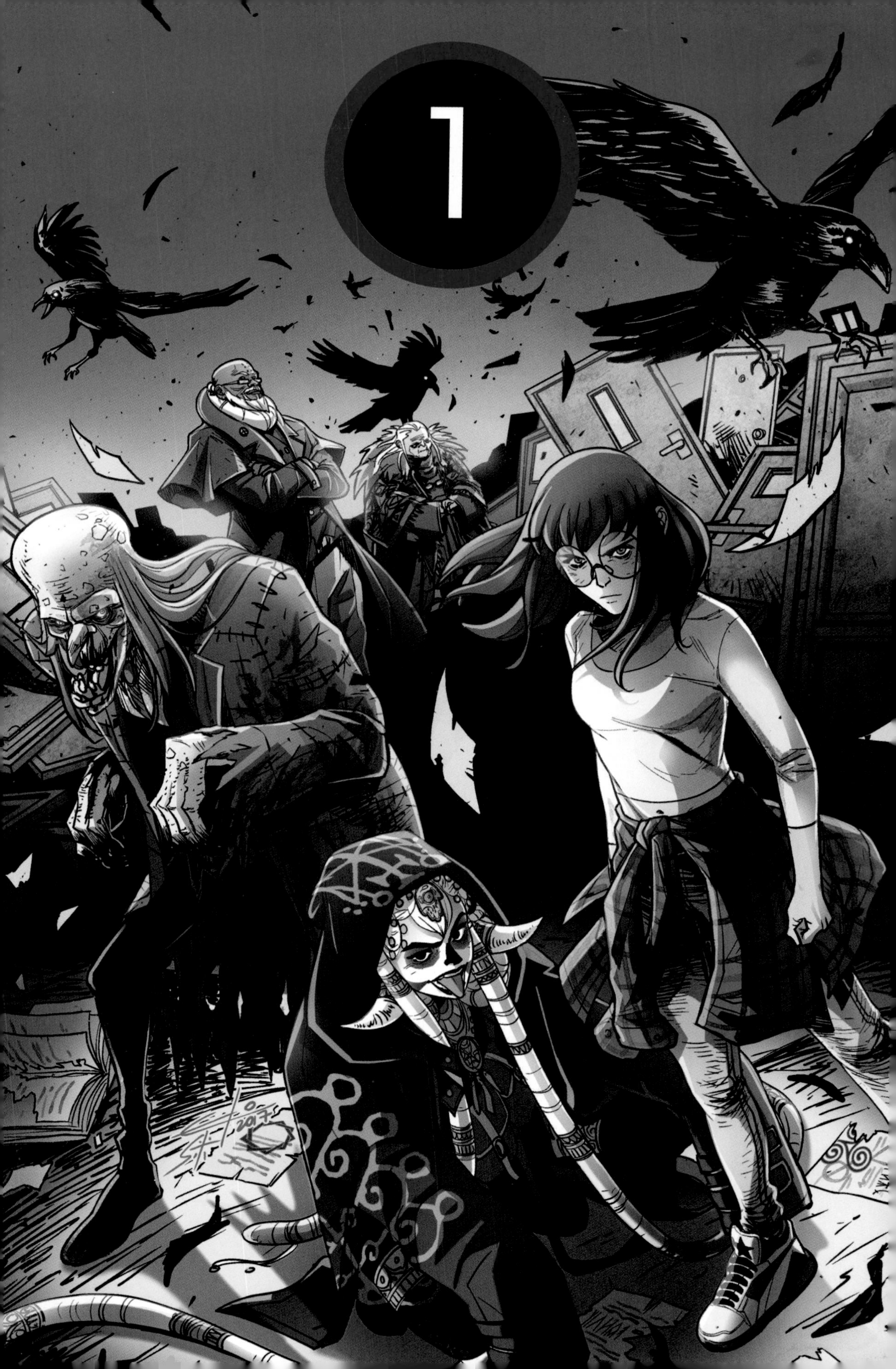
1

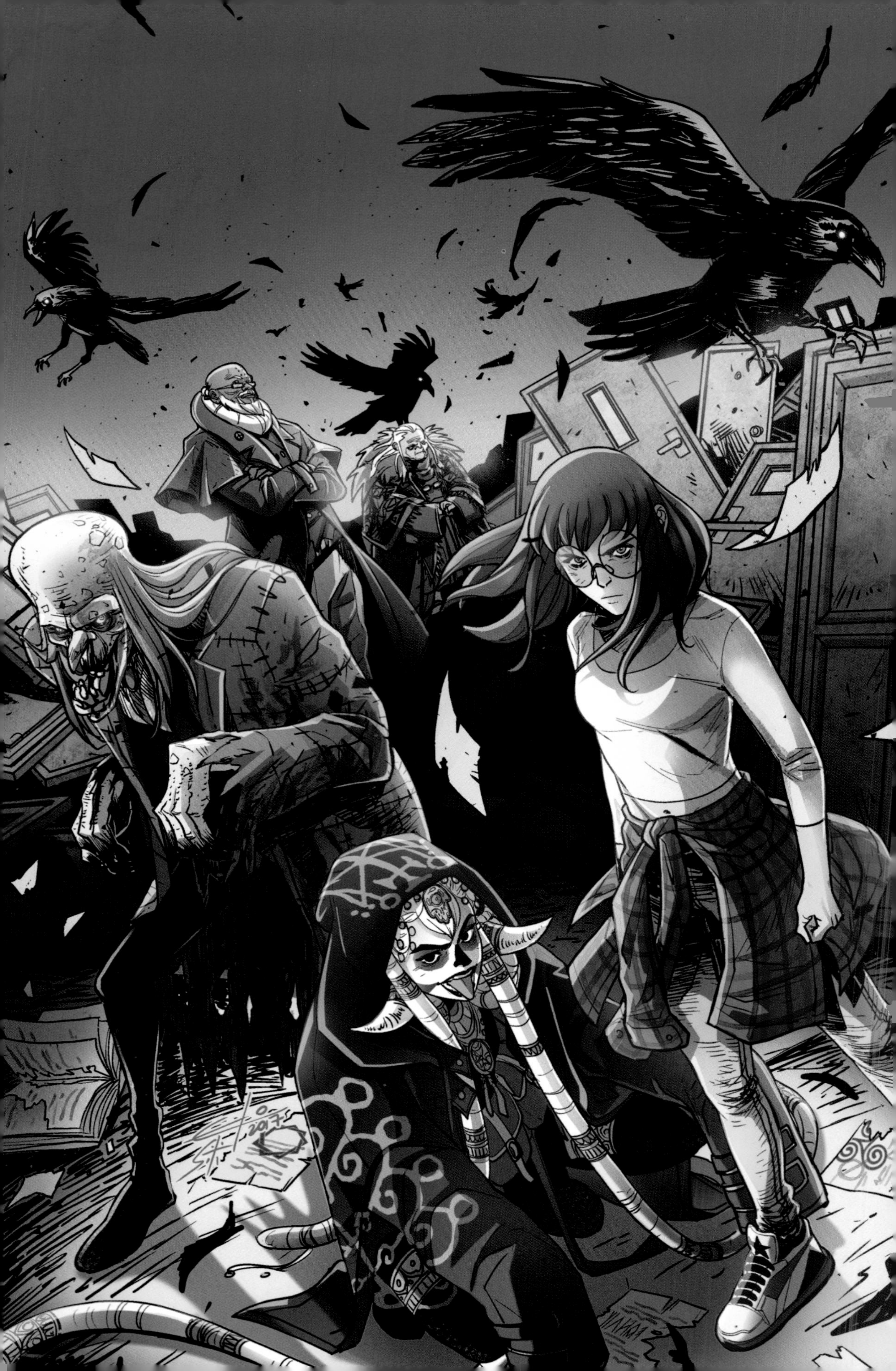

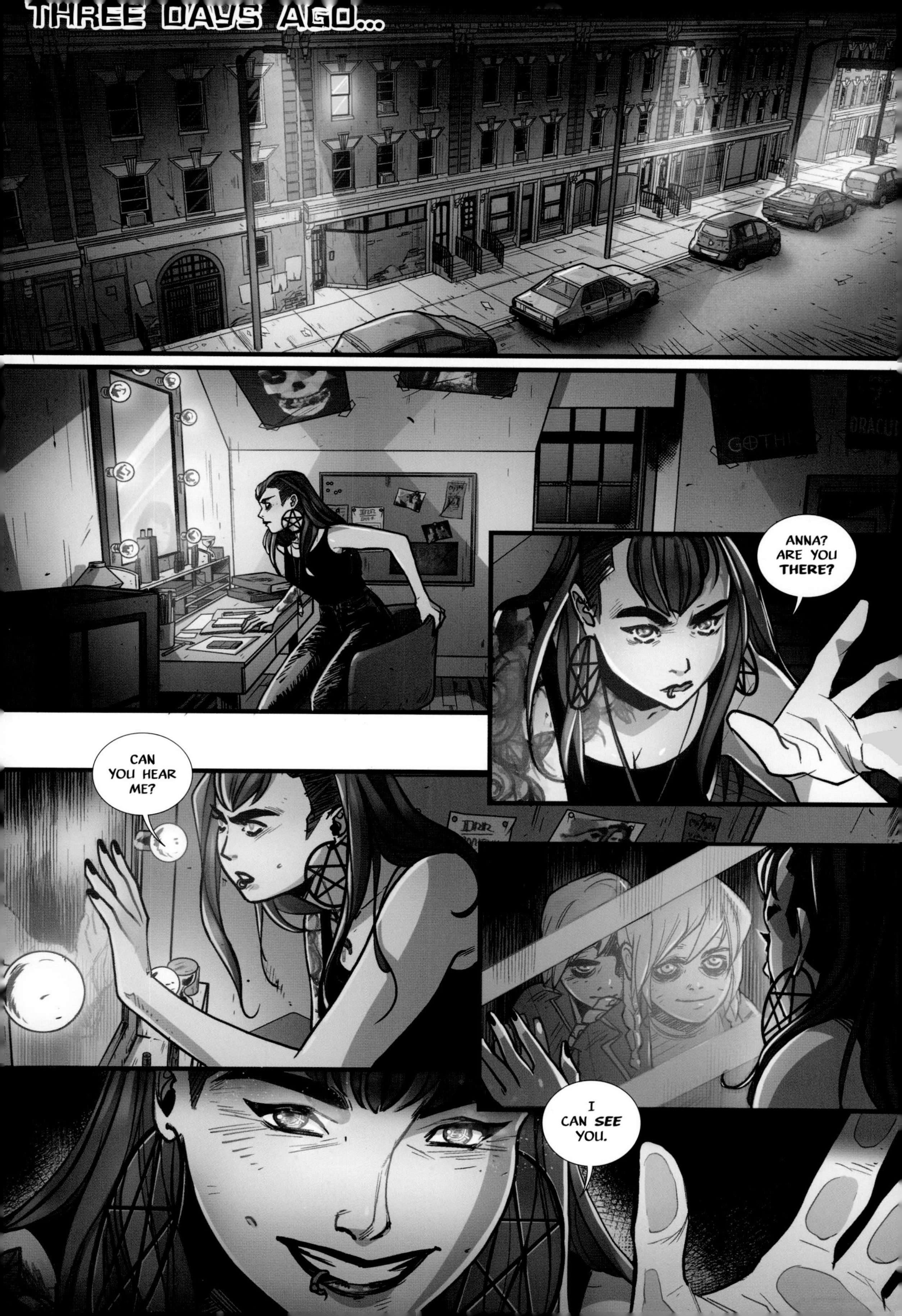
THREE DAYS AGO...
GOTHI
DRACU
ANNA? ARE YOU THERE?
CAN YOU HEAR ME?
I CAN SEE YOU.

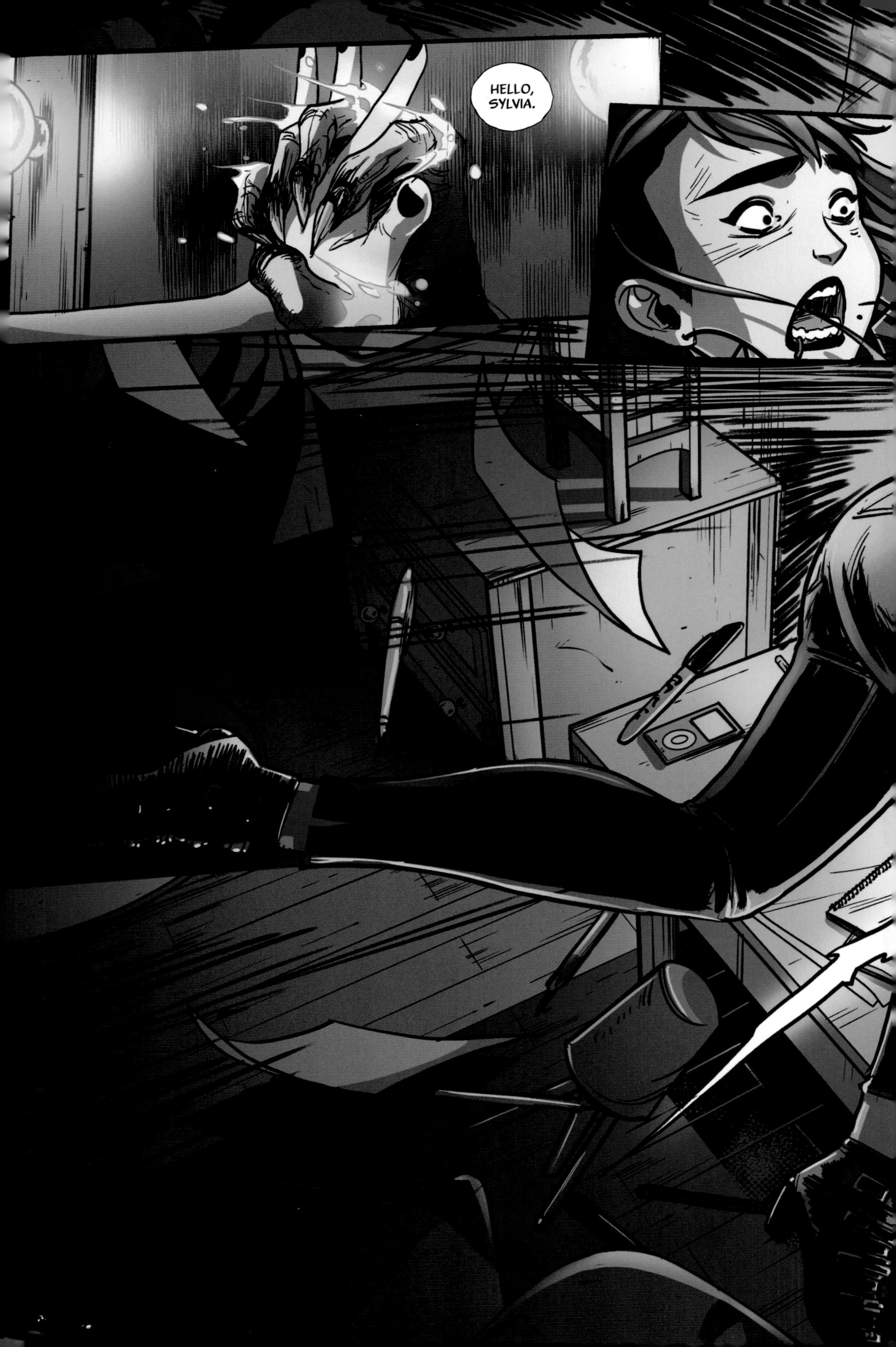
HELLO, SYLVIA.

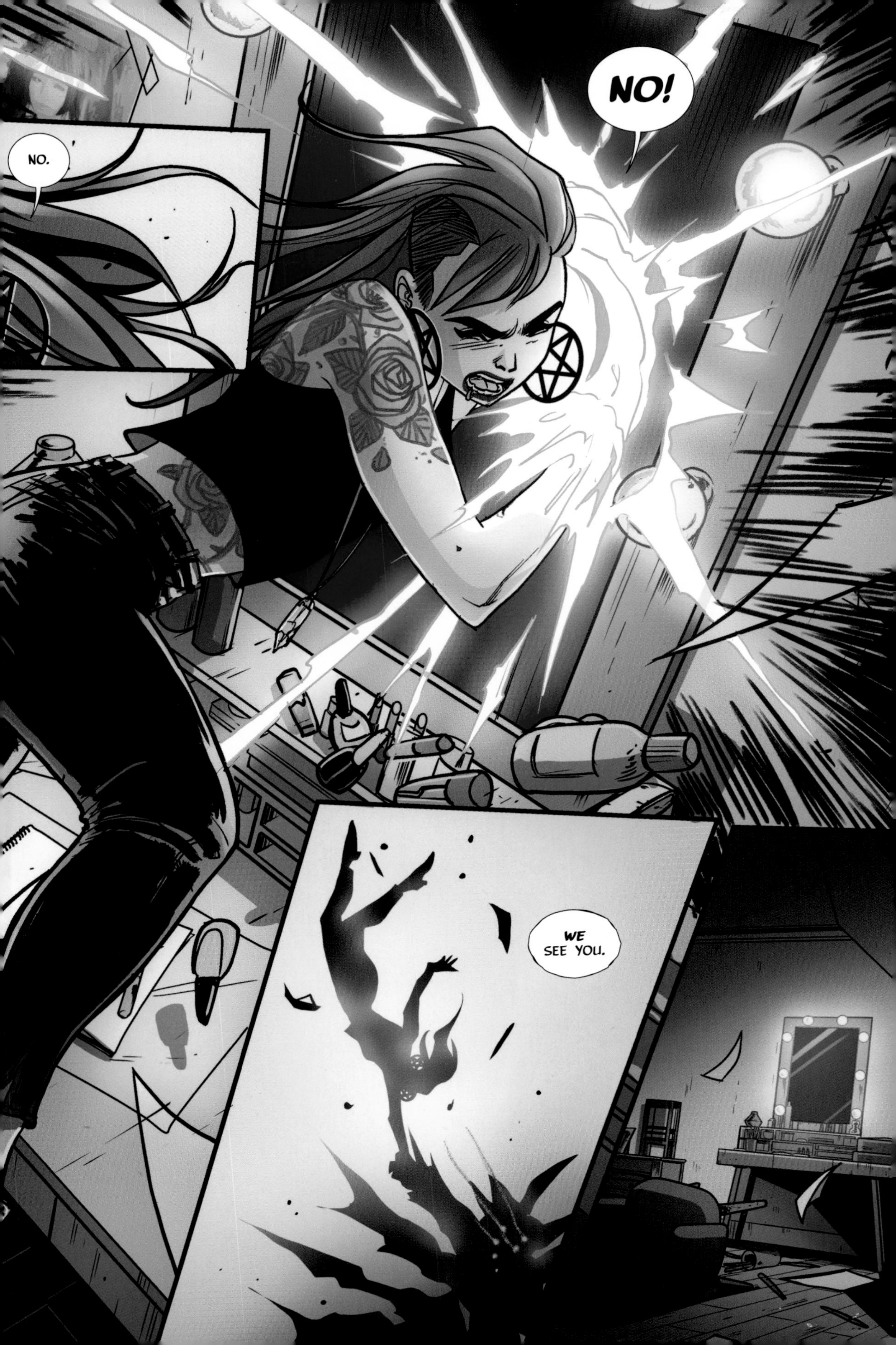
NO.
NO!
WE SEE YOU.

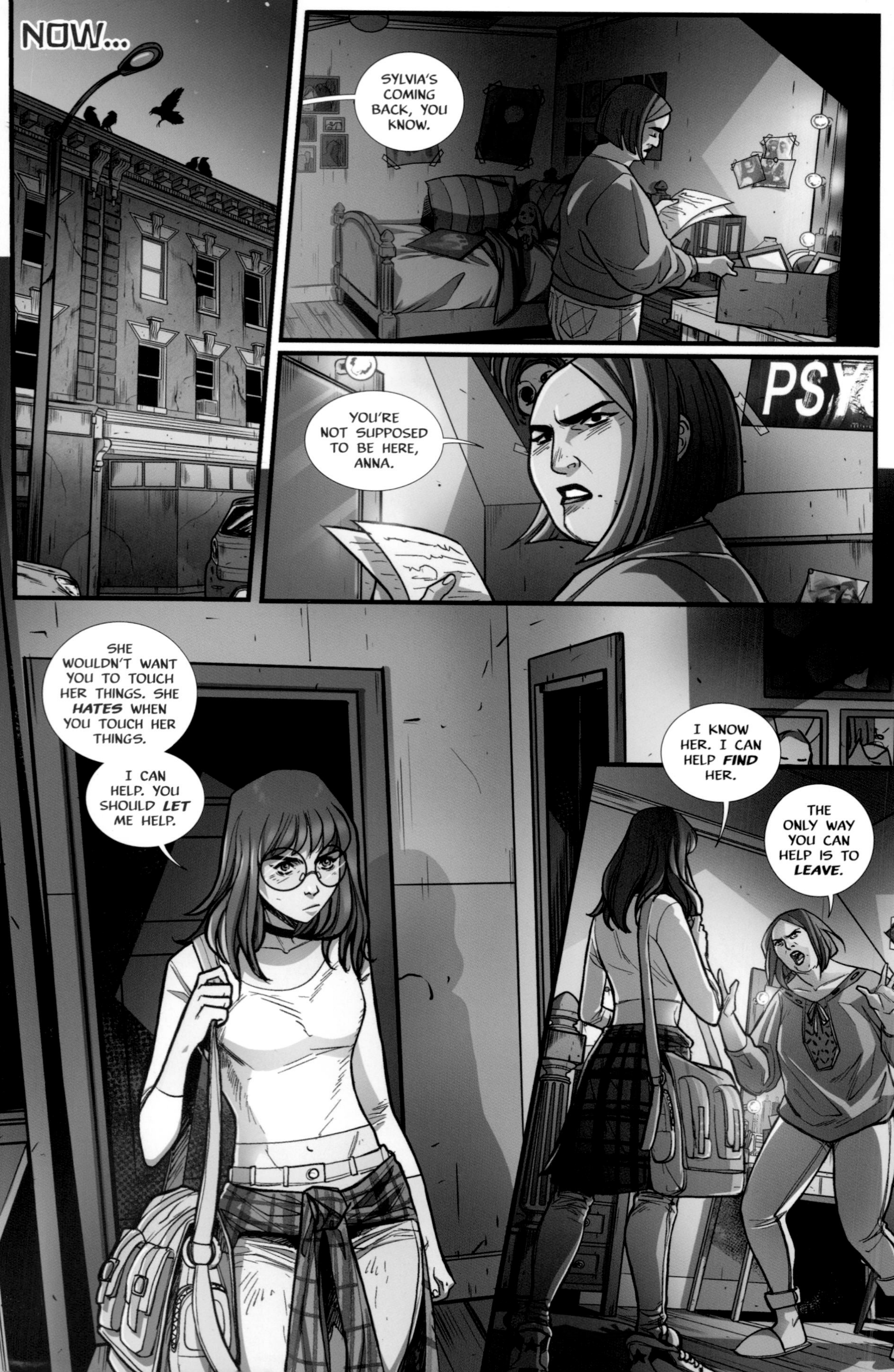
NOW...
SYLVIA'S COMING BACK, YOU KNOW.
YOU'RE NOT SUPPOSED TO BE HERE, ANNA.
PSY
SHE WOULDN'T WANT YOU TO TOUCH HER THINGS. SHE HATES WHEN YOU TOUCH HER THINGS.
I CAN HELP. YOU SHOULD LET ME HELP.
I KNOW HER. I CAN HELP FIND HER.
THE ONLY WAY YOU CAN HELP IS TO LEAVE.

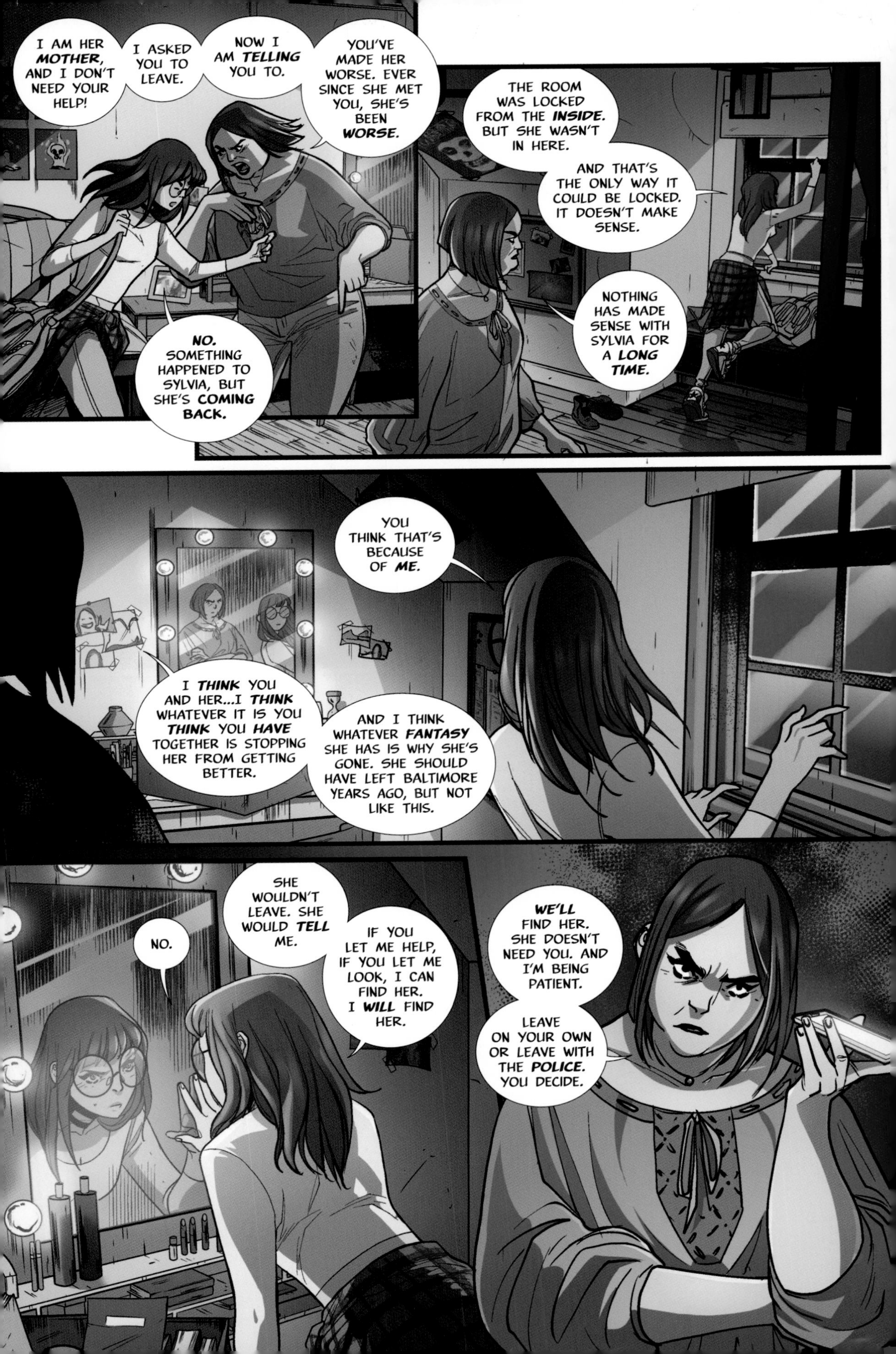
I AM HER MOTHER, AND I DON'T NEED YOUR HELP!
I ASKED YOU TO LEAVE.
NOW I AM TELLING YOU TO.
YOU'VE MADE HER WORSE. EVER SINCE SHE MET YOU, SHE'S BEEN WORSE.
NO. SOMETHING HAPPENED TO SYLVIA, BUT SHE'S COMING BACK.
THE ROOM WAS LOCKED FROM THE INSIDE. BUT SHE WASN'T IN HERE.
AND THAT'S THE ONLY WAY IT COULD BE LOCKED. IT DOESN'T MAKE SENSE.
NOTHING HAS MADE SENSE WITH SYLVIA FOR A LONG TIME.
YOU THINK THAT'S BECAUSE OF ME.
I THINK YOU AND HER...I THINK WHATEVER IT IS YOU THINK YOU HAVE TOGETHER IS STOPPING HER FROM GETTING BETTER.
AND I THINK WHATEVER FANTASY SHE HAS IS WHY SHE'S GONE. SHE SHOULD HAVE LEFT BALTIMORE YEARS AGO, BUT NOT LIKE THIS.
NO.
SHE WOULDN'T LEAVE. SHE WOULD TELL ME.
IF YOU LET ME HELP, IF YOU LET ME LOOK, I CAN FIND HER. I WILL FIND HER.
WE'LL FIND HER. SHE DOESN'T NEED YOU. AND I'M BEING PATIENT.
LEAVE ON YOUR OWN OR LEAVE WITH THE POLICE. YOU DECIDE.

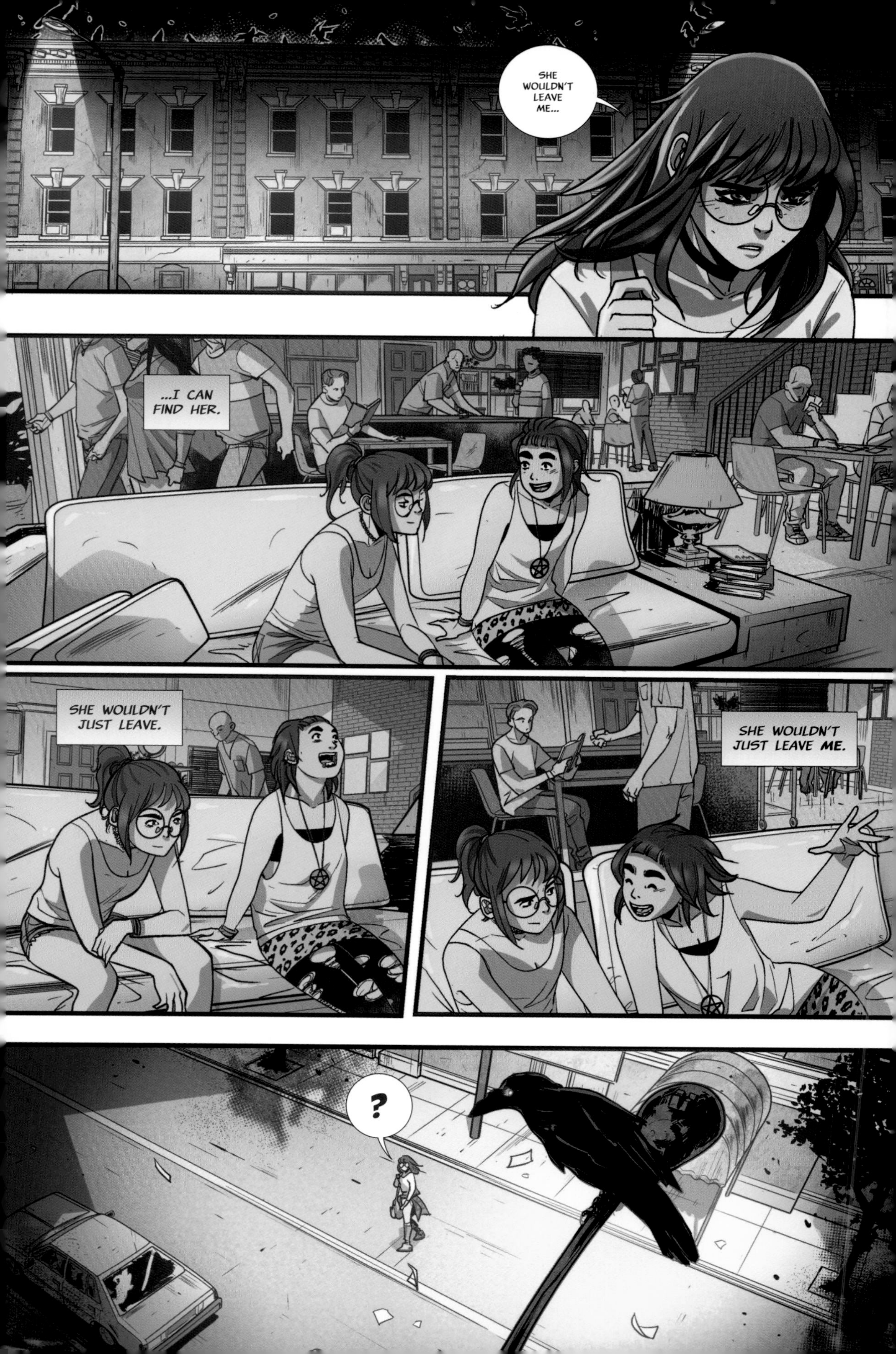
SHE WOULDN'T LEAVE ME...
...I CAN FIND HER.
SHE WOULDN'T JUST LEAVE.
SHE WOULDN'T JUST LEAVE ME.
?

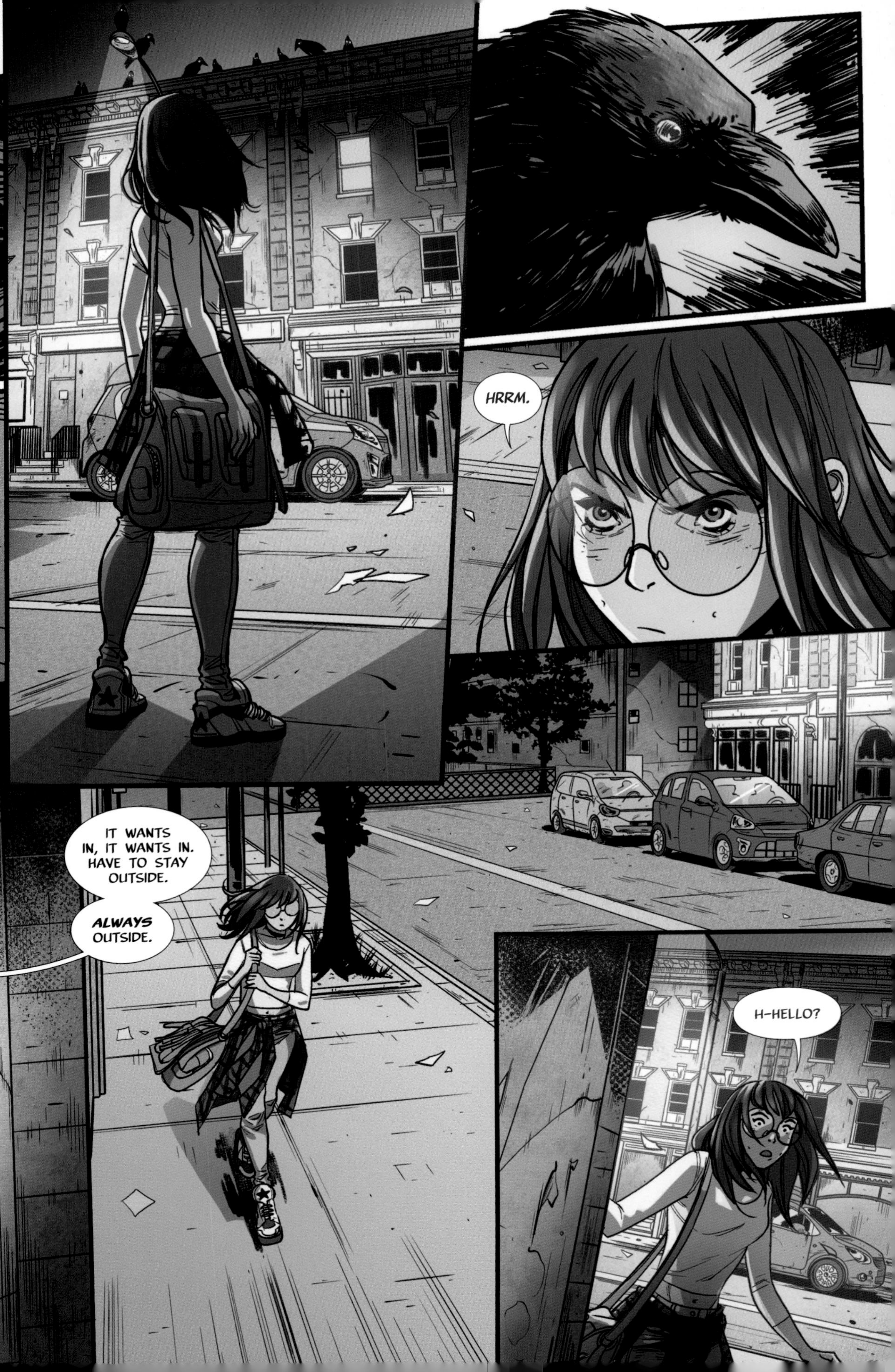
HRRM.
IT WANTS IN, IT WANTS IN. HAVE TO STAY OUTSIDE.
ALWAYS OUTSIDE.
H-HELLO?

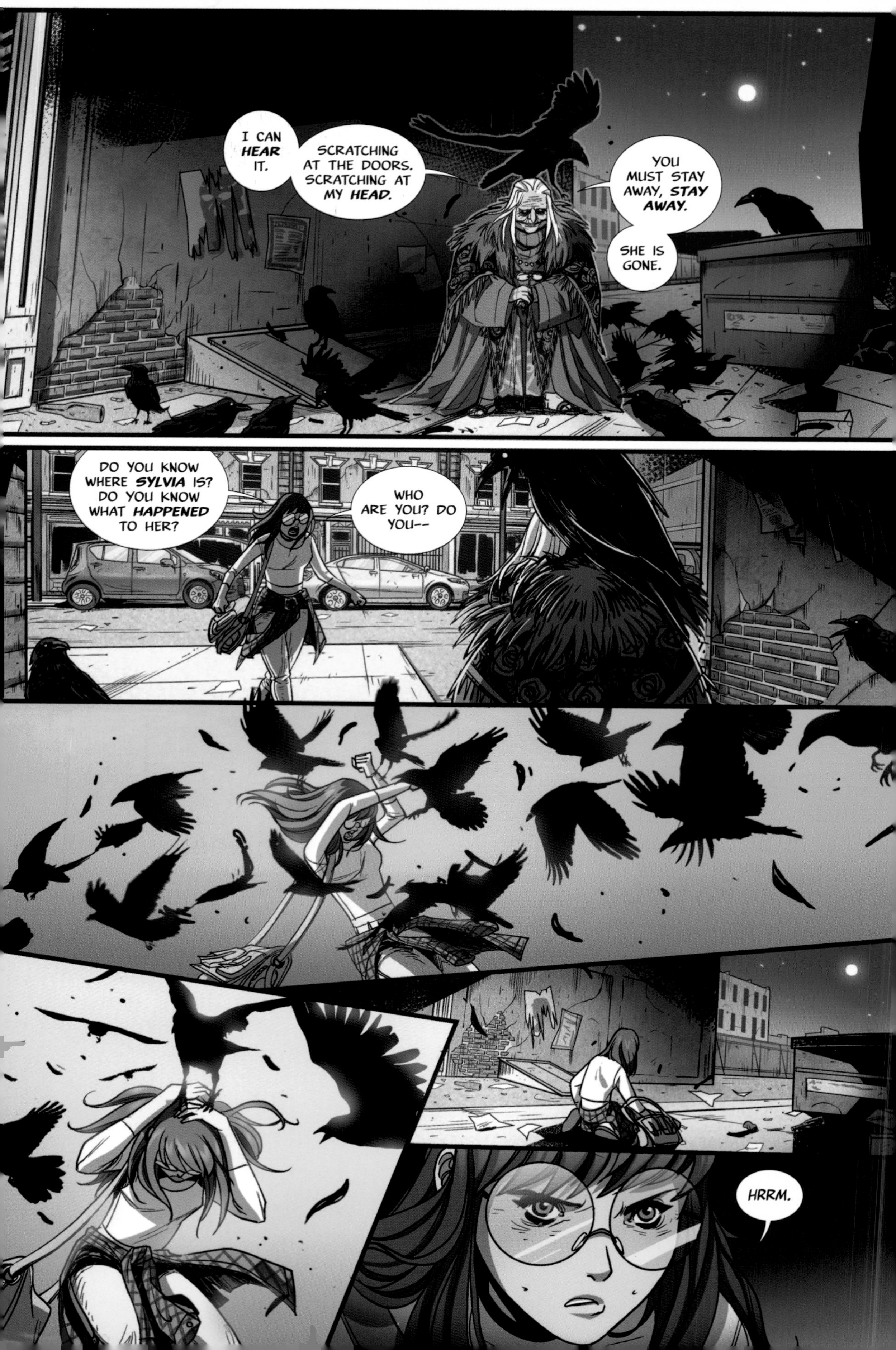

I CAN HEAR IT.
SCRATCHING AT THE DOORS. SCRATCHING AT MY HEAD.
YOU MUST STAY AWAY, STAY AWAY.
SHE IS GONE.
DO YOU KNOW WHERE SYLVIA IS? DO YOU KNOW WHAT HAPPENED TO HER?
WHO ARE YOU? DO YOU--
HRRM.

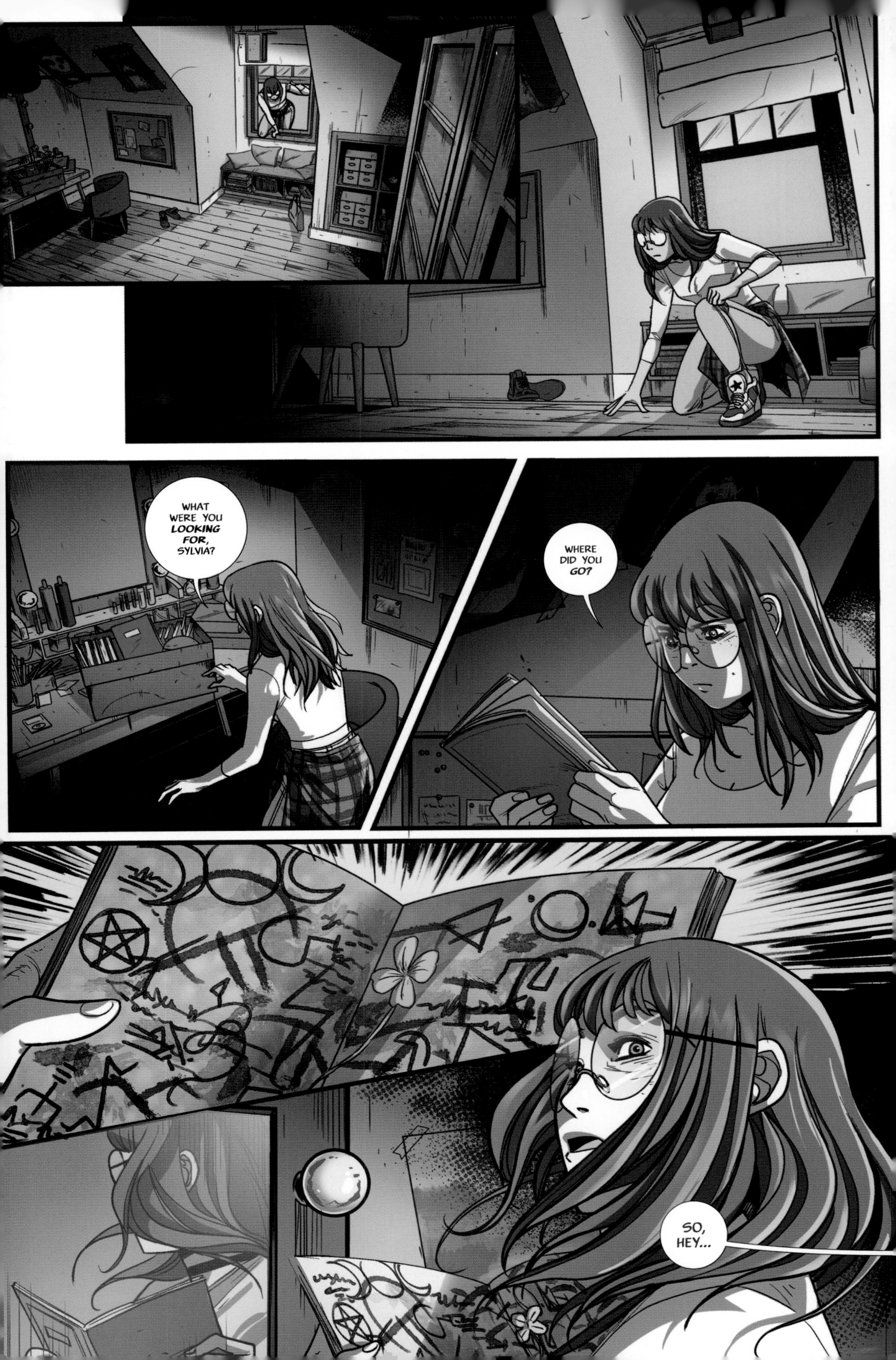
WHAT WERE YOU LOOKING FOR, SYLVIA?
WHERE DID YOU GO?
SO, HEY...

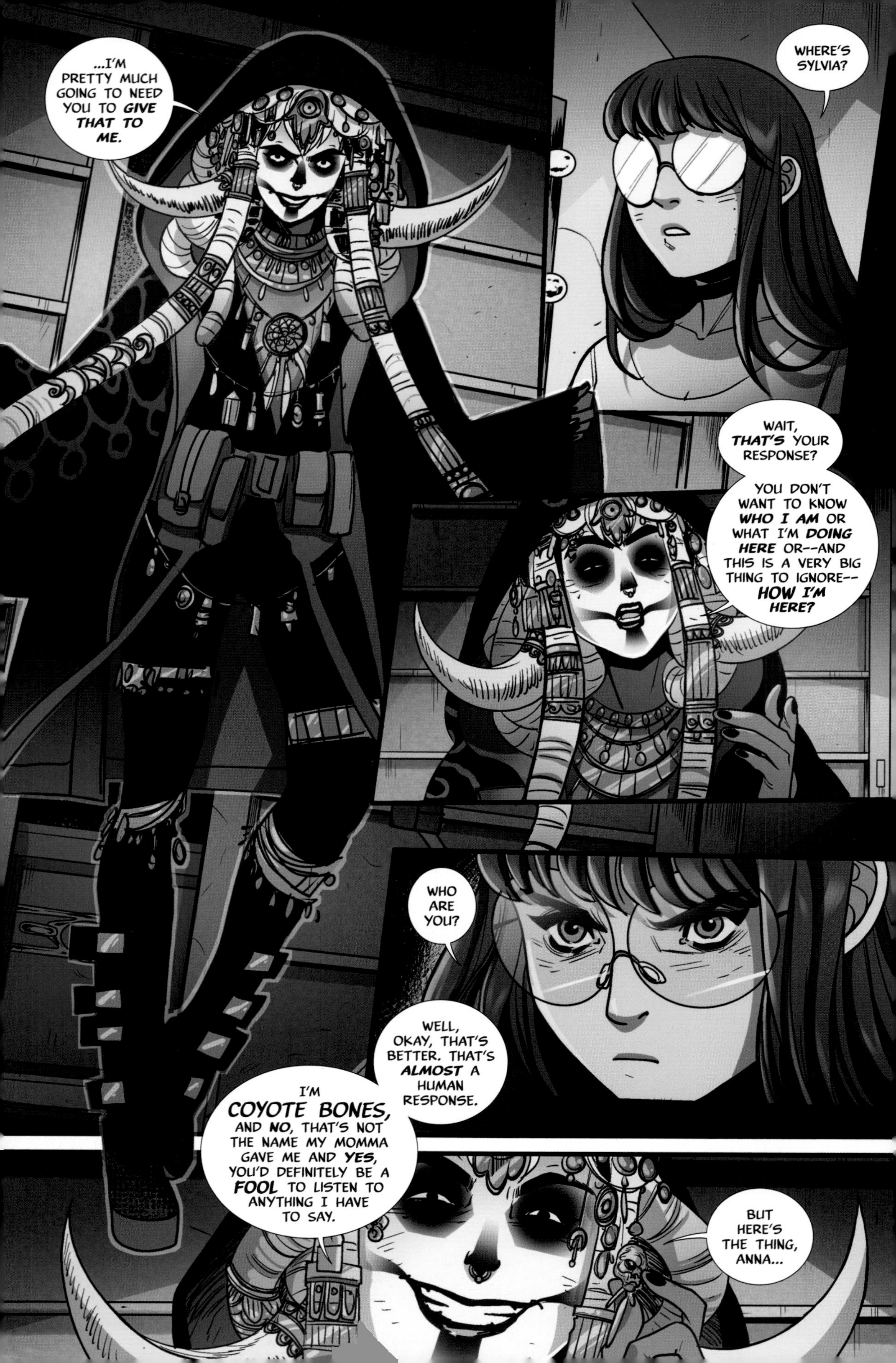

...I'M PRETTY MUCH GOING TO NEED YOU TO GIVE THAT TO ME.
WHERE'S SYLVIA?
WAIT, THAT'S YOUR RESPONSE?
YOU DON'T WANT TO KNOW WHO I AM OR WHAT I'M DOING HERE OR--AND THIS IS A VERY BIG THING TO IGNORE--HOW I'M HERE?
WHO ARE YOU?
WELL, OKAY, THAT'S BETTER. THAT'S ALMOST A HUMAN RESPONSE.
I'M COYOTE BONES, AND NO, THAT'S NOT THE NAME MY MOMMA GAVE ME AND YES, YOU'D DEFINITELY BE A FOOL TO LISTEN TO ANYTHING I HAVE TO SAY.
BUT HERE'S THE THING, ANNA...

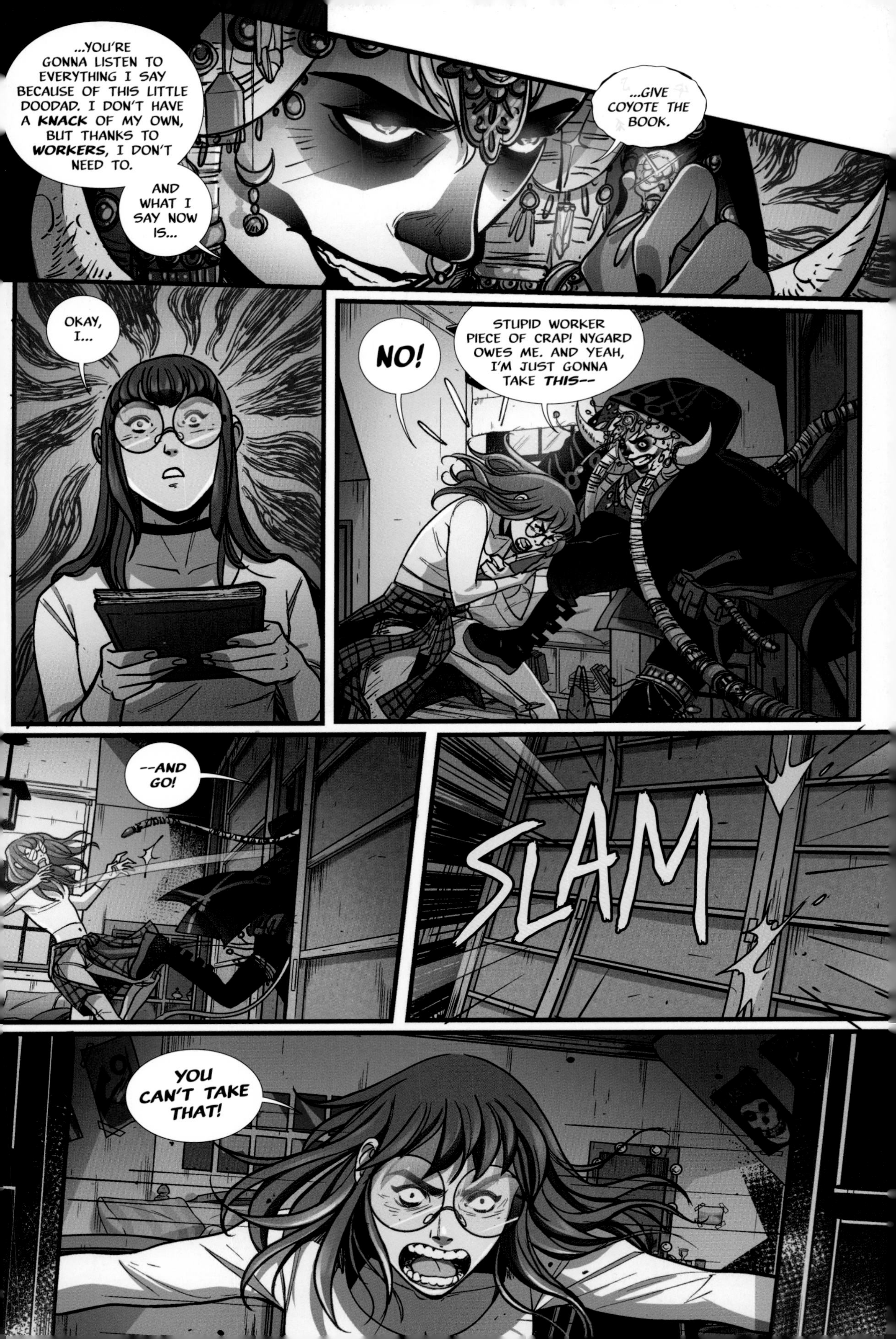
...YOU'RE GONNA LISTEN TO EVERYTHING I SAY BECAUSE OF THIS LITTLE DOODAD. I DON'T HAVE A KNACK OF MY OWN, BUT THANKS TO WORKERS, I DON'T NEED TO.
AND WHAT I SAY NOW IS...
...GIVE COYOTE THE BOOK.
OKAY, I...
NO!
STUPID WORKER PIECE OF CRAP! NYGARD OWES ME. AND YEAH, I'M JUST GONNA TAKE THIS--
--AND GO!
SLAM
YOU CAN'T TAKE THAT!

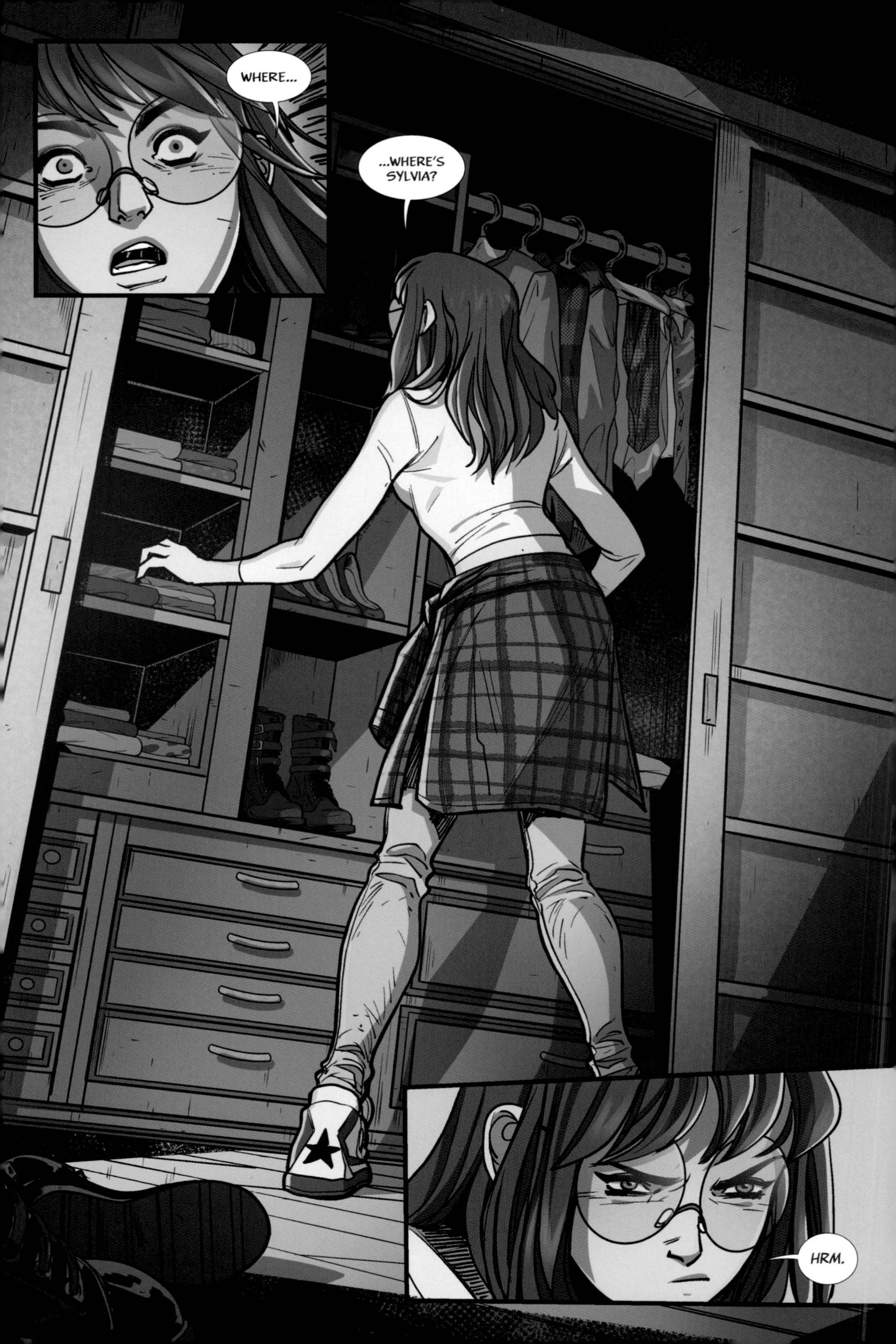
WHERE...
...WHERE'S SYLVIA?
HRM.

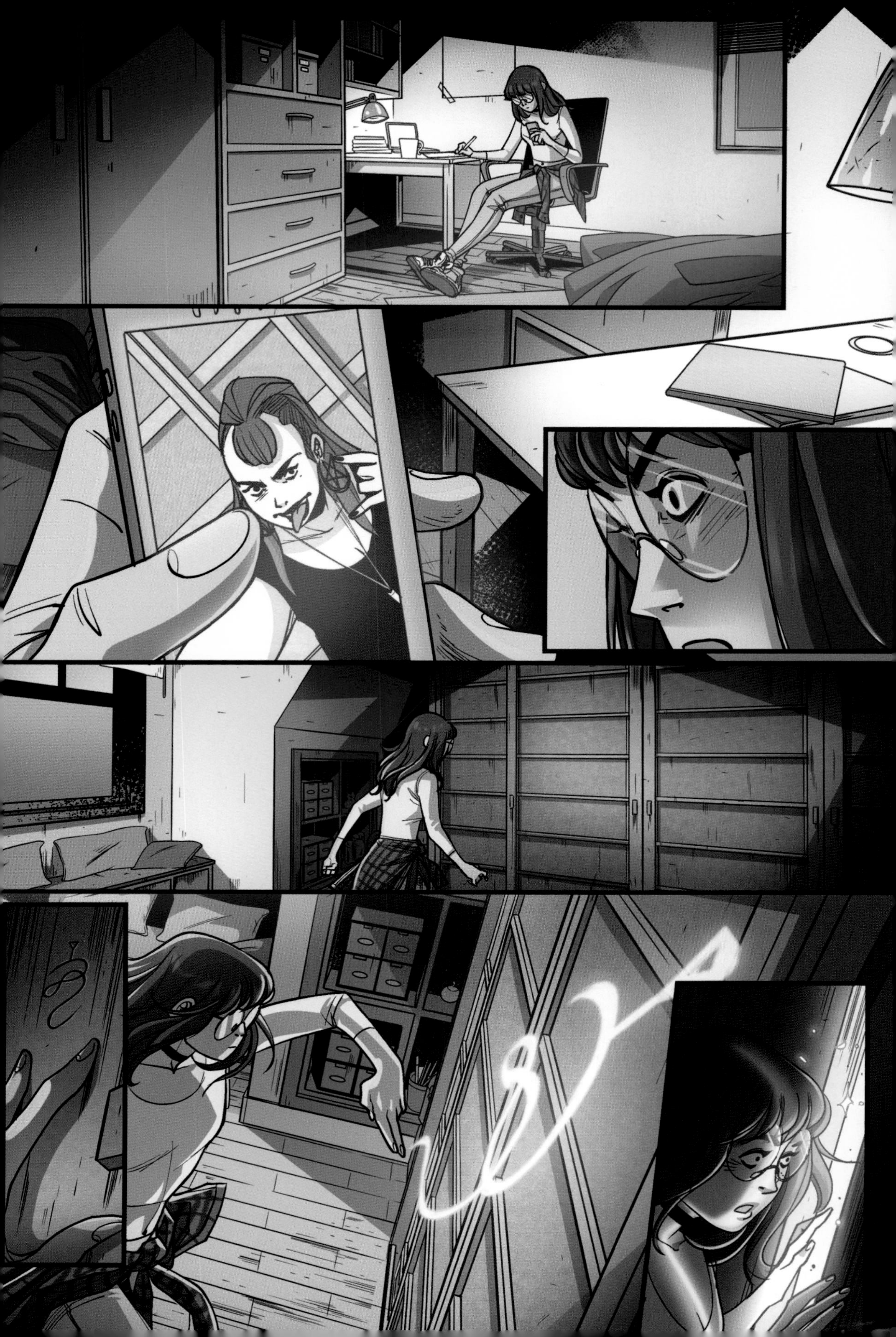

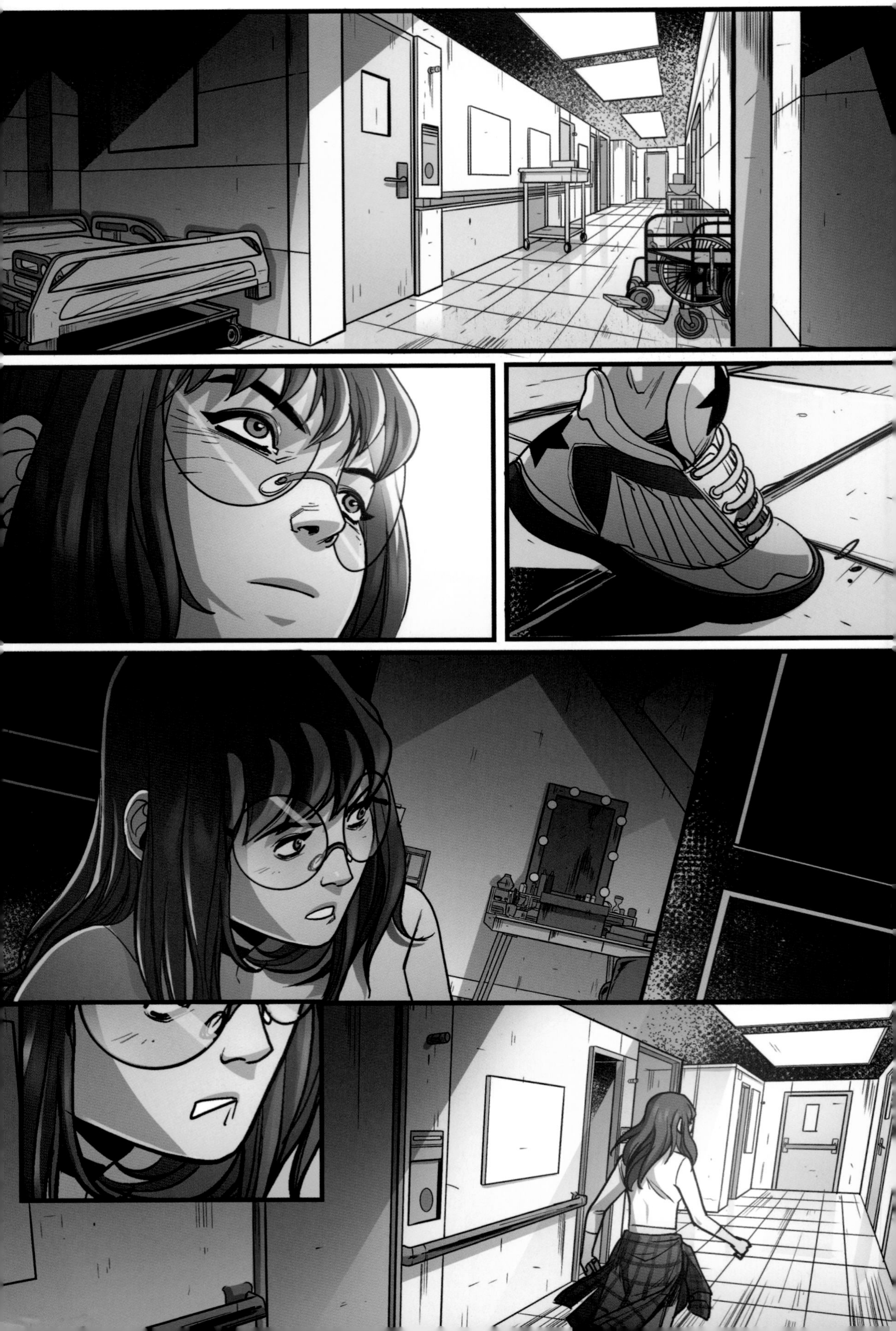

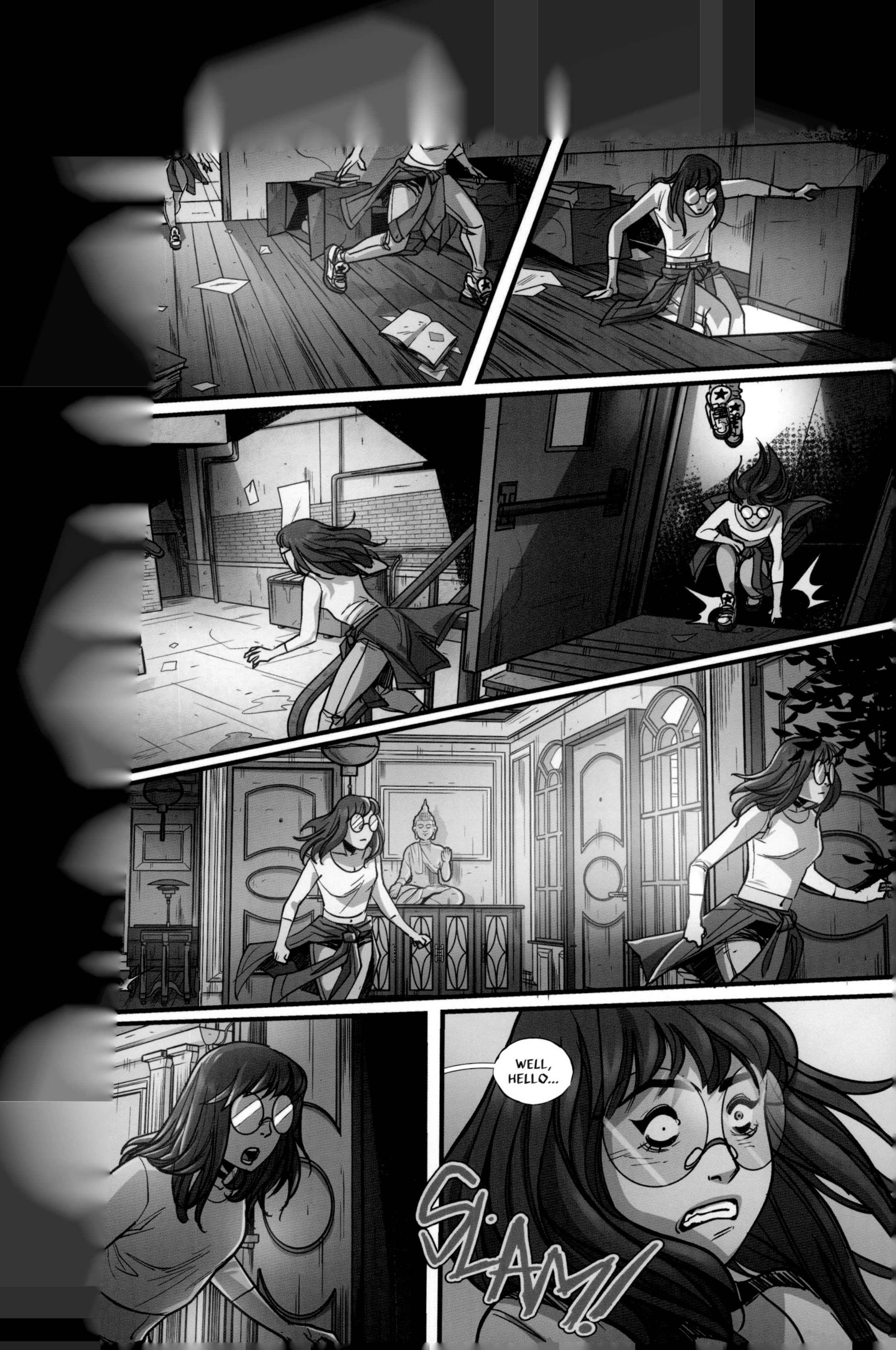
WELL, HELLO...
SLAM!

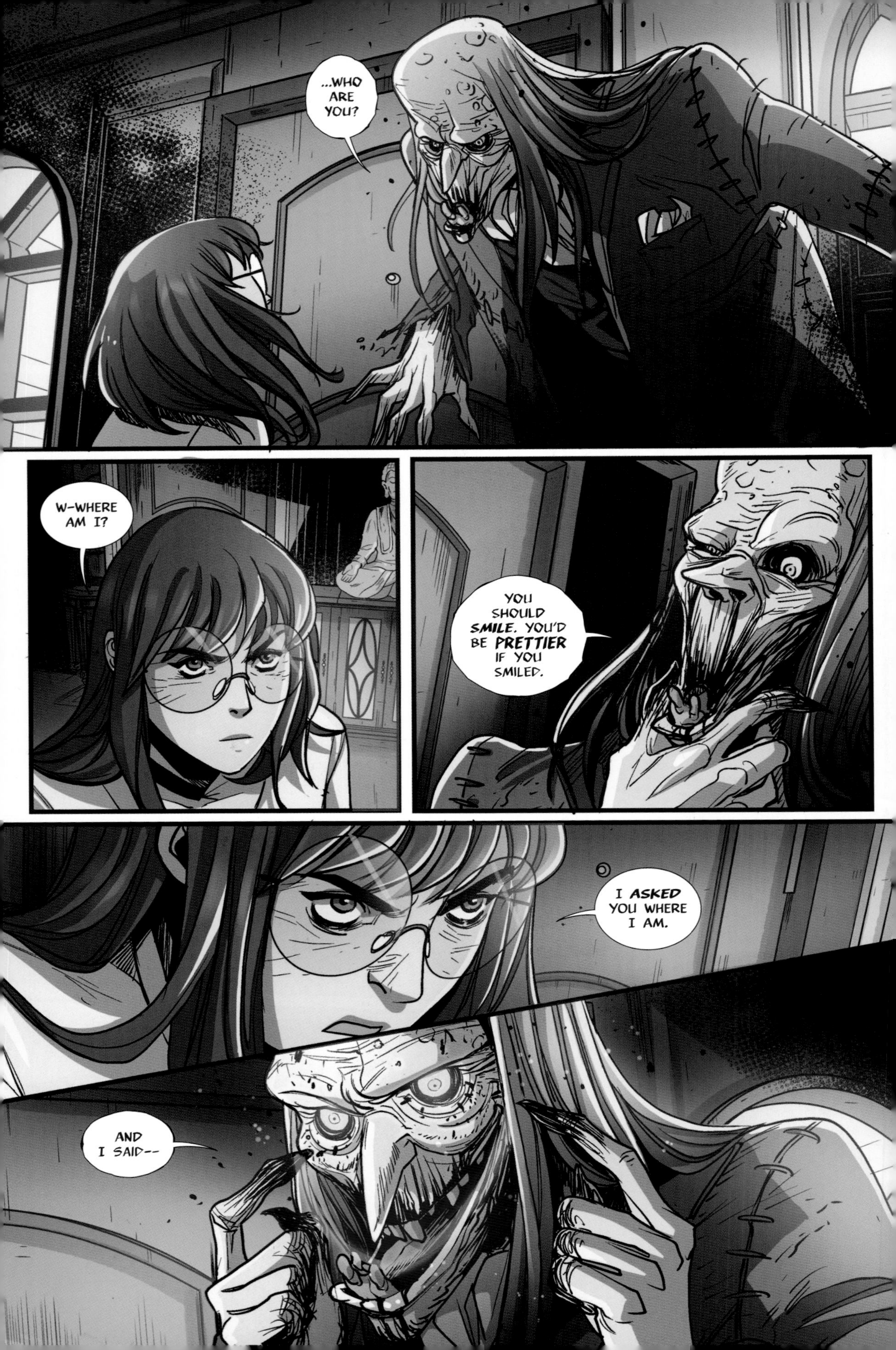
...WHO ARE YOU?
W-WHERE AM I?
YOU SHOULD SMILE. YOU'D BE PRETTIER IF YOU SMILED.
I ASKED YOU WHERE I AM.
AND I SAID--

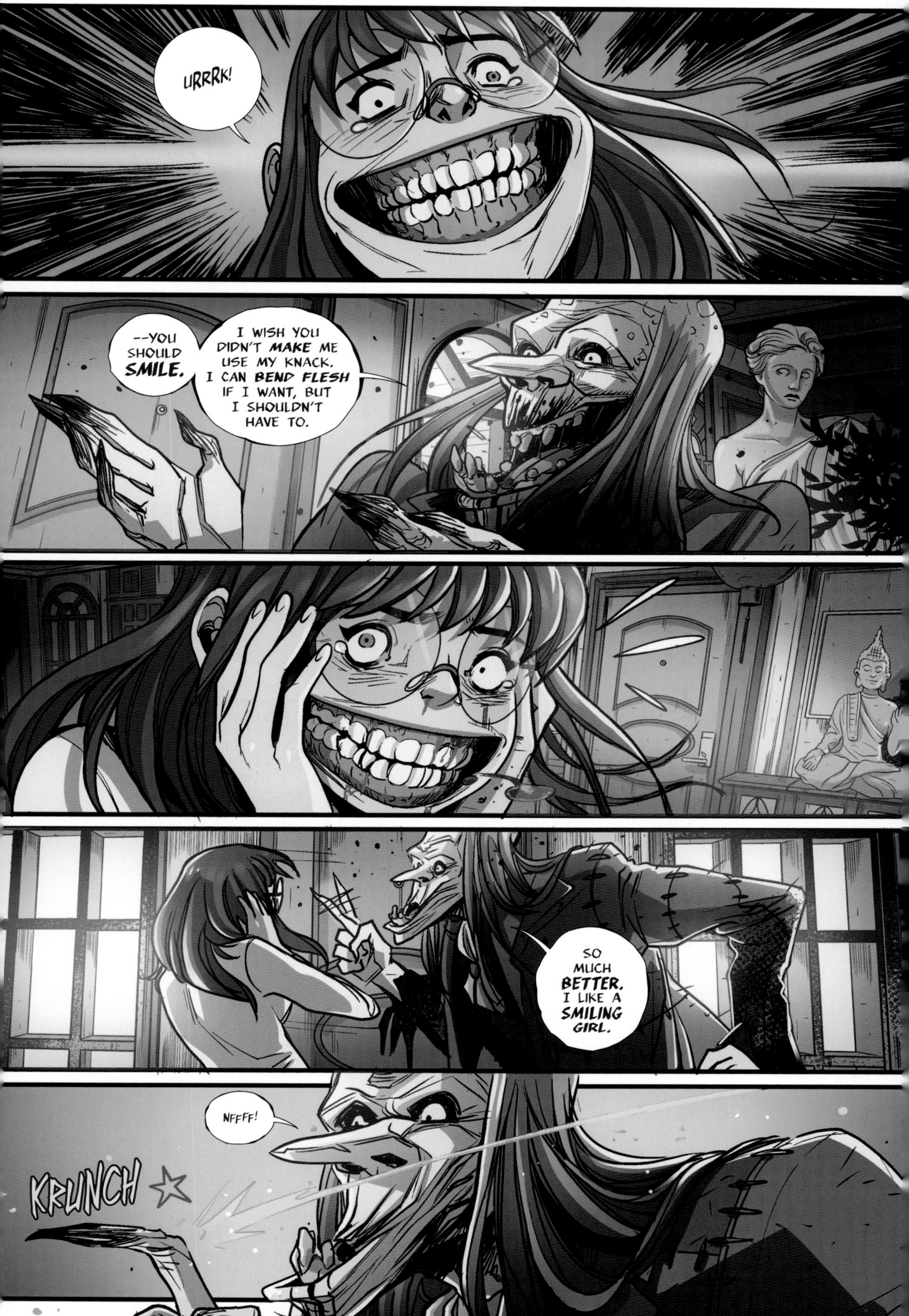
URRRK!
--YOU SHOULD SMILE.
I WISH YOU DIDN'T MAKE ME USE MY KNACK. I CAN BEND FLESH IF I WANT, BUT I SHOULDN'T HAVE TO.
SO MUCH BETTER. I LIKE A SMILING GIRL.
NFFFF!
KRUNCH

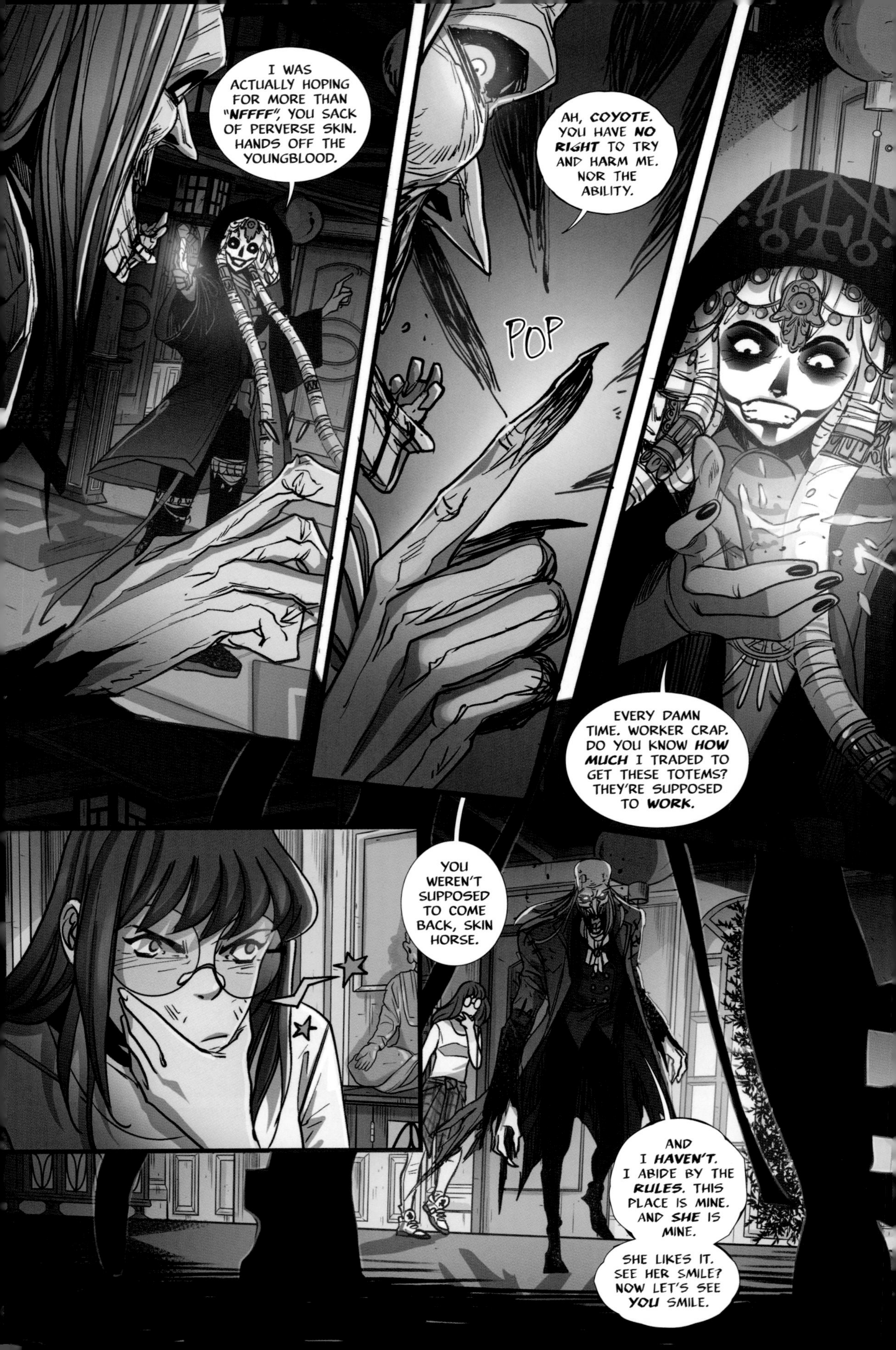

I WAS ACTUALLY HOPING FOR MORE THAN "NFFFF", YOU SACK OF PERVERSE SKIN. HANDS OFF THE YOUNGBLOOD.
AH, COYOTE. YOU HAVE NO RIGHT TO TRY AND HARM ME. NOR THE ABILITY.
POP
EVERY DAMN TIME. WORKER CRAP. DO YOU KNOW HOW MUCH I TRADED TO GET THESE TOTEMS? THEY'RE SUPPOSED TO WORK.
YOU WEREN'T SUPPOSED TO COME BACK, SKIN HORSE.
AND I HAVEN'T. I ABIDE BY THE RULES. THIS PLACE IS MINE. AND SHE IS MINE.
SHE LIKES IT. SEE HER SMILE? NOW LET'S SEE YOU SMILE.

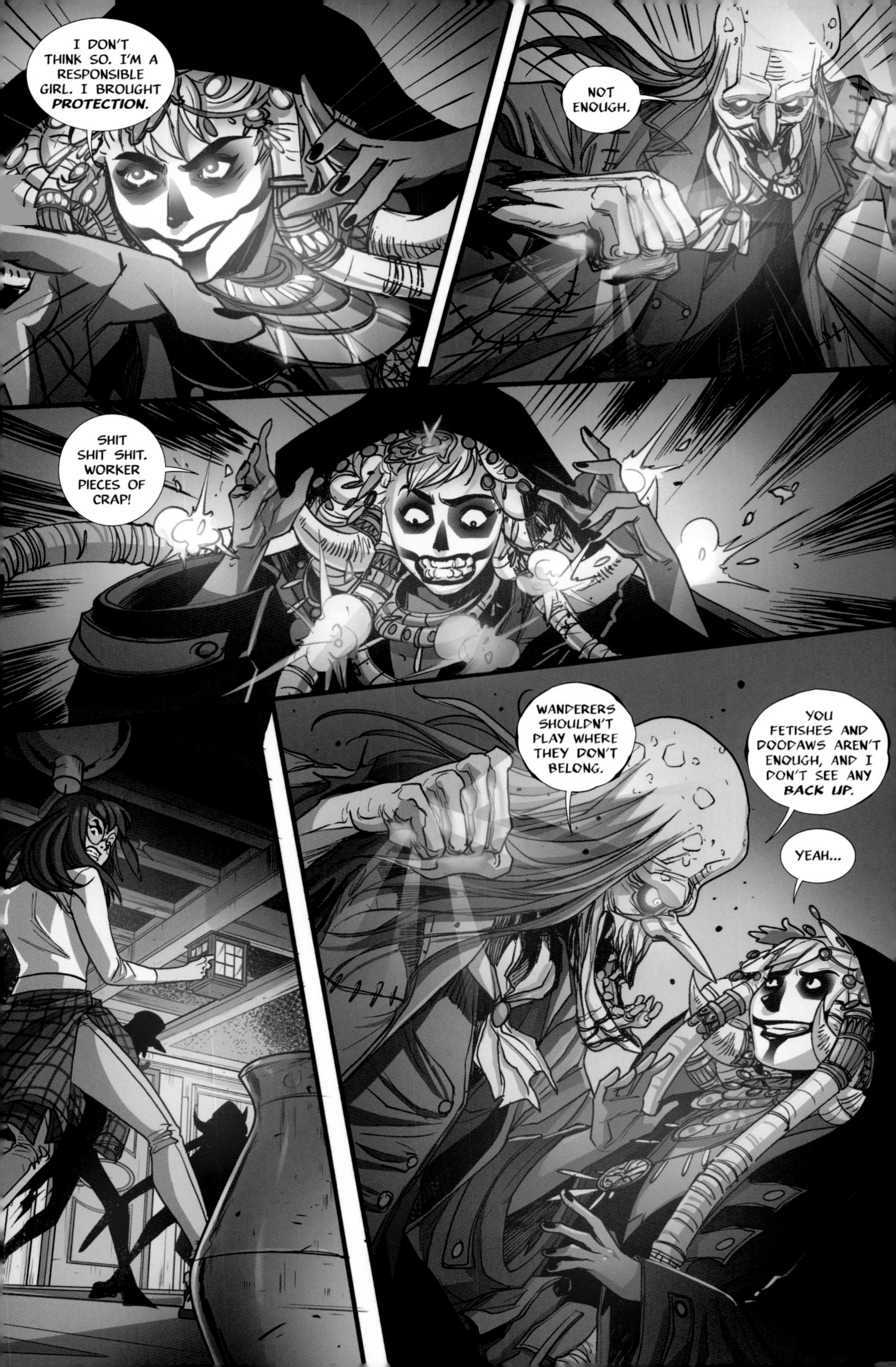
I DON'T THINK SO. I'M A RESPONSIBLE GIRL. I BROUGHT *PROTECTION.*
NOT ENOUGH.
SHIT SHIT SHIT. WORKER PIECES OF CRAP!
WANDERERS SHOULDN'T PLAY WHERE THEY DON'T BELONG.
YOU FETISHES AND DOODAWS AREN'T ENOUGH, AND I DON'T SEE ANY **BACK UP.**
YEAH...

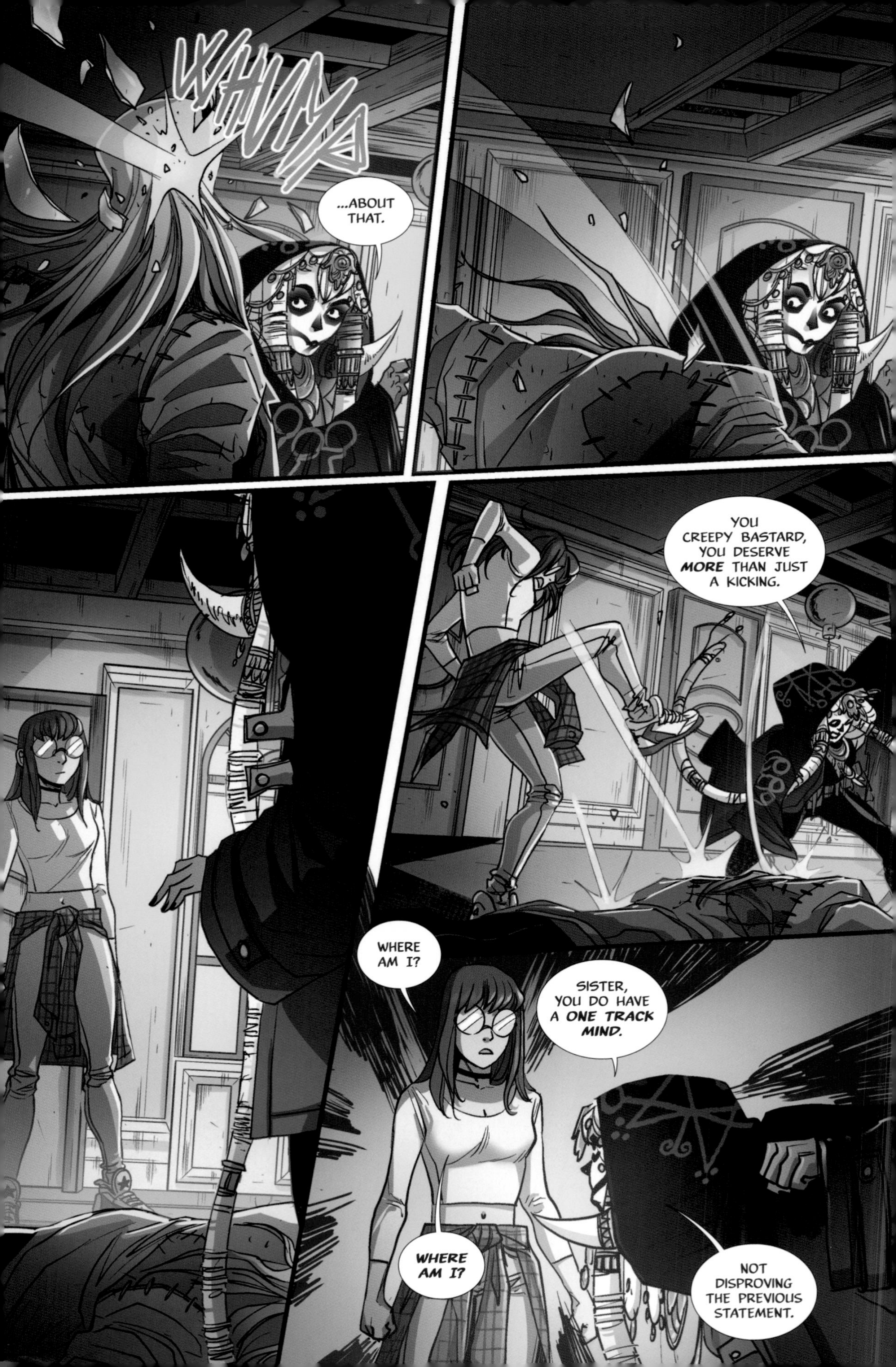
WHUMP
...ABOUT THAT.
YOU CREEPY BASTARD, YOU DESERVE MORE THAN JUST A KICKING.
WHERE AM I?
SISTER, YOU DO HAVE A ONE TRACK MIND.
WHERE AM I?
NOT DISPROVING THE PREVIOUS STATEMENT.

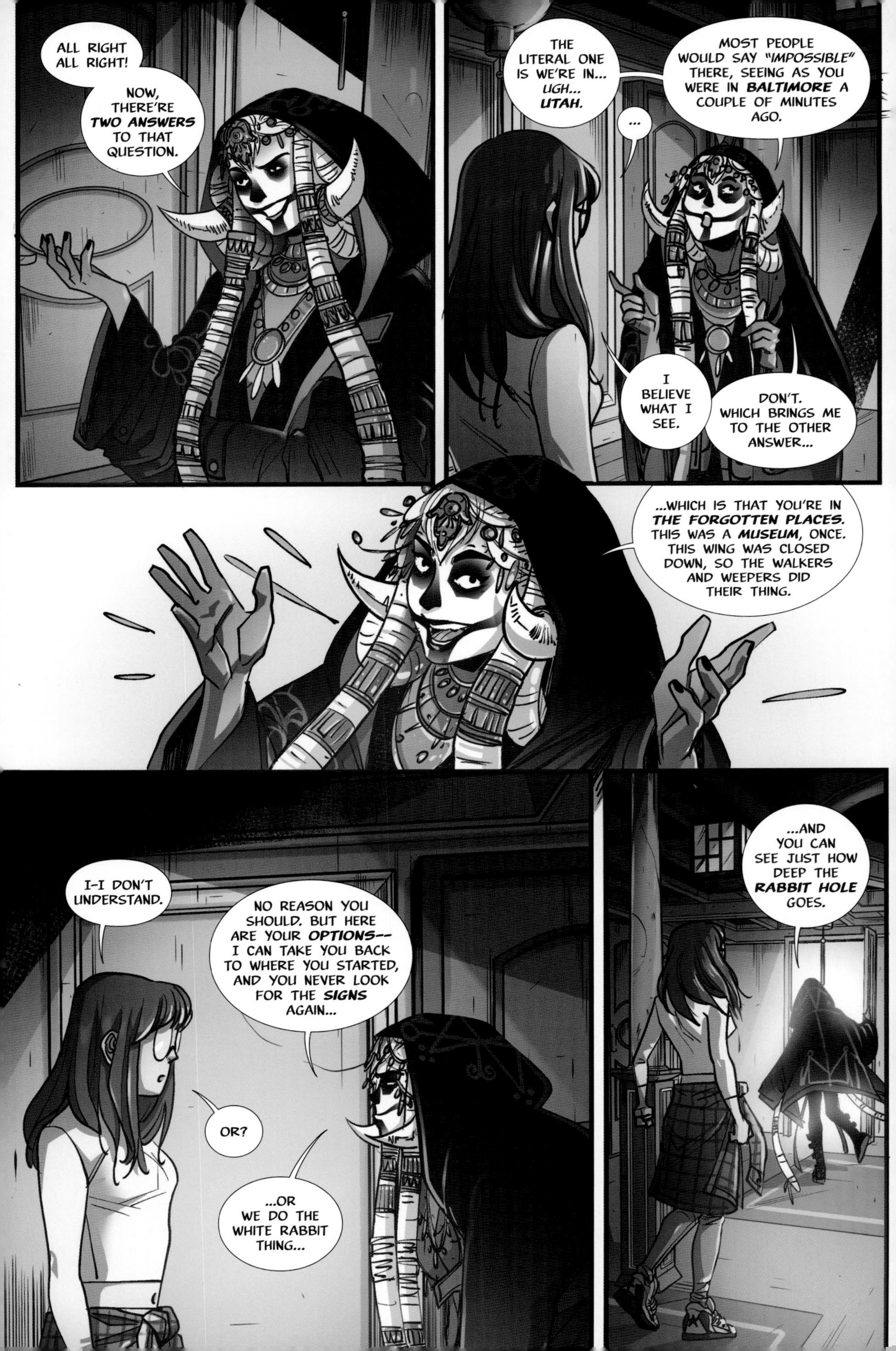
ALL RIGHT ALL RIGHT!
NOW, THERE'RE TWO ANSWERS TO THAT QUESTION.
THE LITERAL ONE IS WE'RE IN... UGH... UTAH.
MOST PEOPLE WOULD SAY "IMPOSSIBLE" THERE, SEEING AS YOU WERE IN BALTIMORE A COUPLE OF MINUTES AGO.
...
I BELIEVE WHAT I SEE.
DON'T. WHICH BRINGS ME TO THE OTHER ANSWER...
...WHICH IS THAT YOU'RE IN THE FORGOTTEN PLACES. THIS WAS A MUSEUM, ONCE. THIS WING WAS CLOSED DOWN, SO THE WALKERS AND WEEPERS DID THEIR THING.
I-I DON'T UNDERSTAND.
NO REASON YOU SHOULD. BUT HERE ARE YOUR OPTIONS-- I CAN TAKE YOU BACK TO WHERE YOU STARTED, AND YOU NEVER LOOK FOR THE SIGNS AGAIN...
OR?
...OR WE DO THE WHITE RABBIT THING...
...AND YOU CAN SEE JUST HOW DEEP THE RABBIT HOLE GOES.

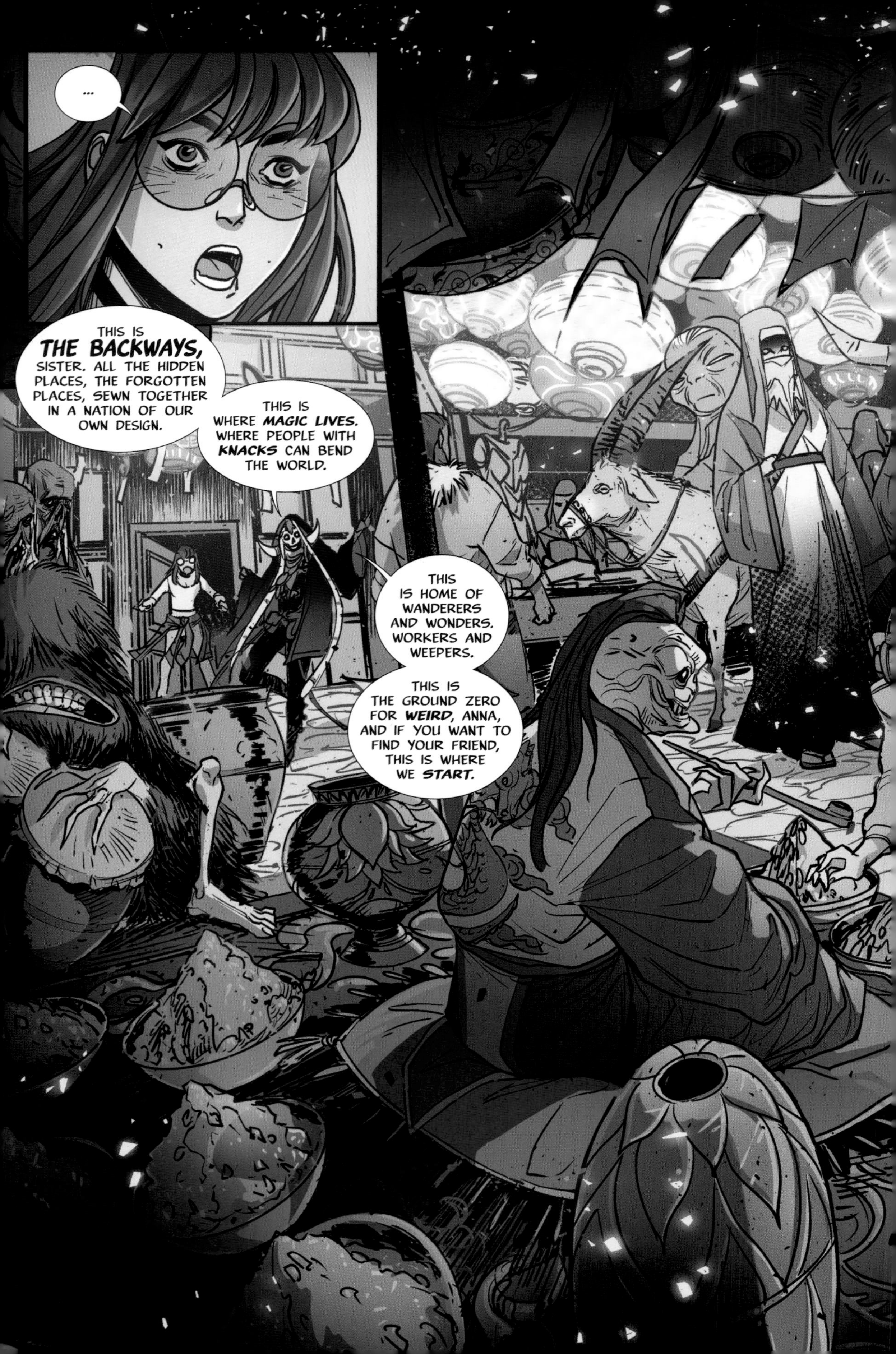
...
THIS IS THE BACKWAYS, SISTER. ALL THE HIDDEN PLACES, THE FORGOTTEN PLACES, SEWN TOGETHER IN A NATION OF OUR OWN DESIGN.
THIS IS WHERE MAGIC LIVES. WHERE PEOPLE WITH KNACKS CAN BEND THE WORLD.
THIS IS HOME OF WANDERERS AND WONDERS. WORKERS AND WEEPERS.
THIS IS THE GROUND ZERO FOR WEIRD, ANNA, AND IF YOU WANT TO FIND YOUR FRIEND, THIS IS WHERE WE START.

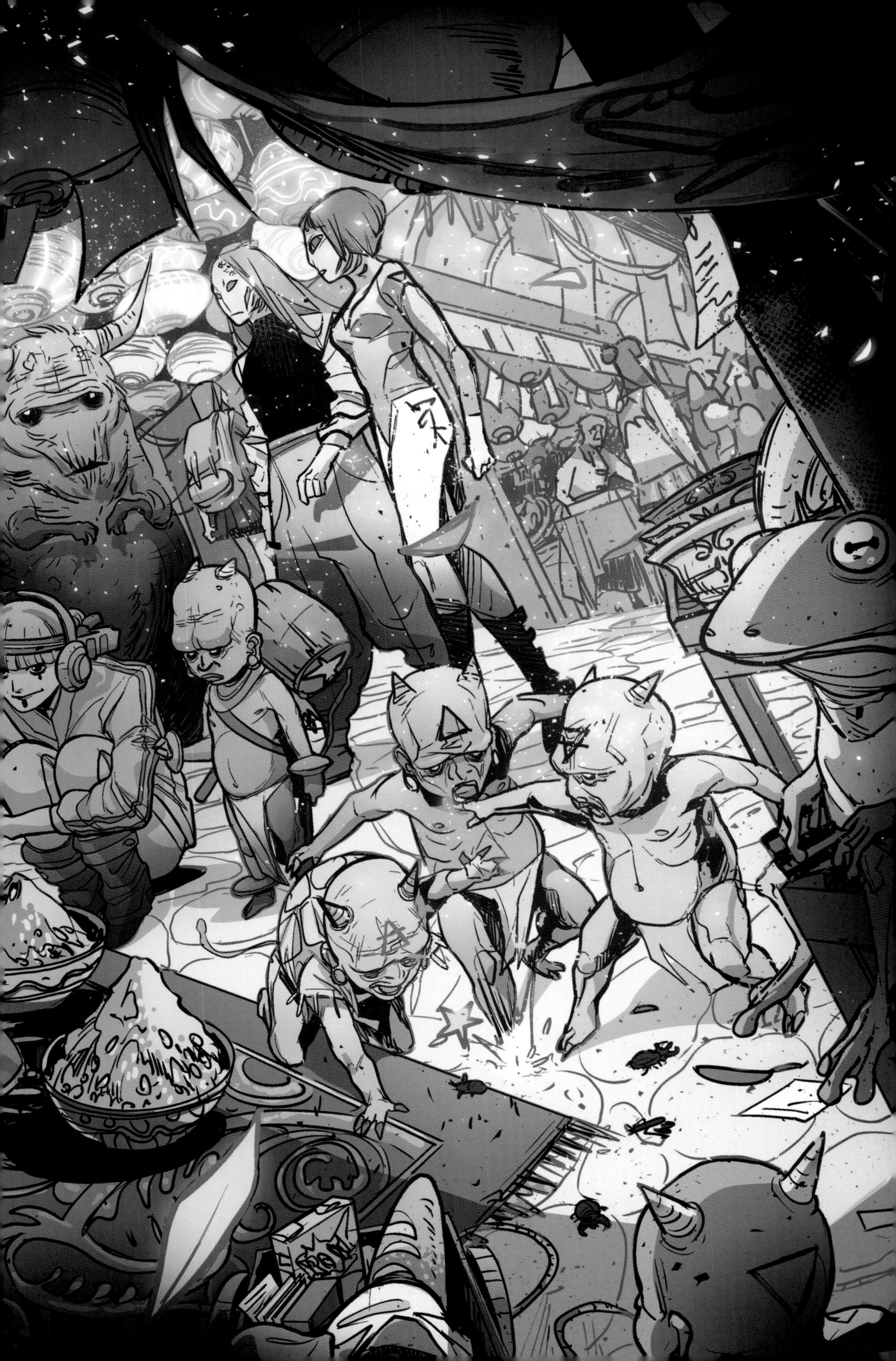

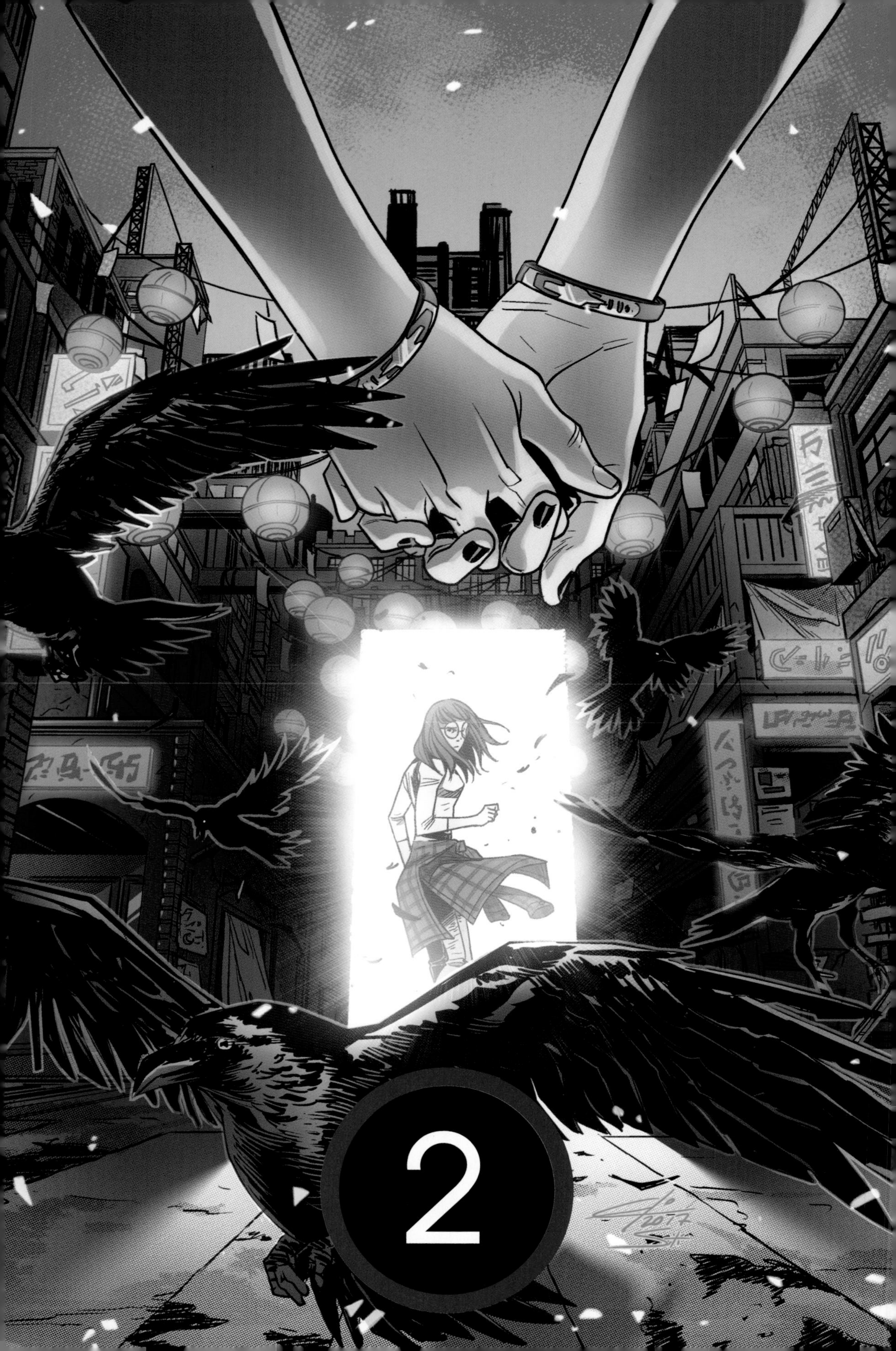
2

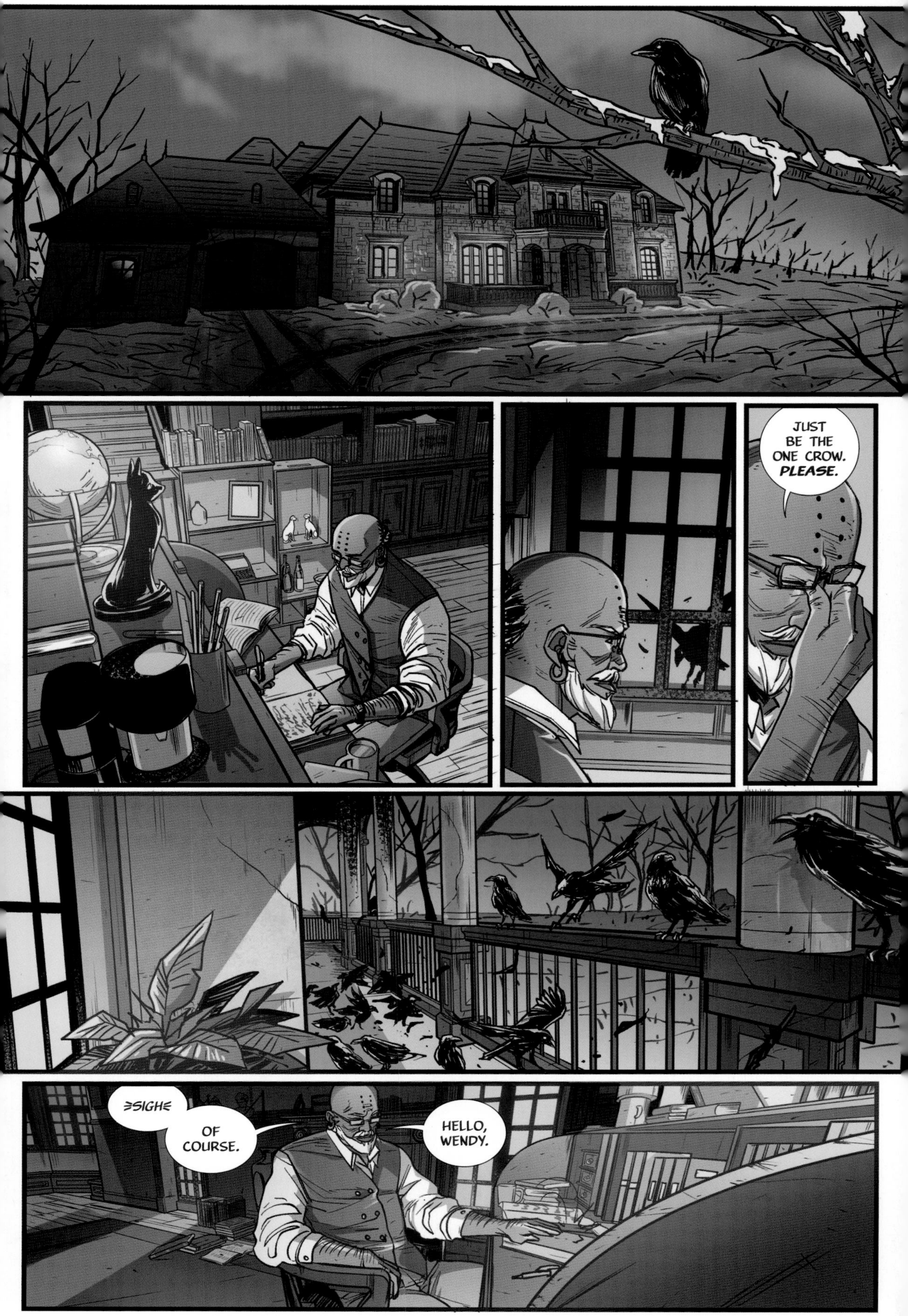
JUST BE THE ONE CROW. PLEASE.
=SIGH=
OF COURSE.
HELLO, WENDY.

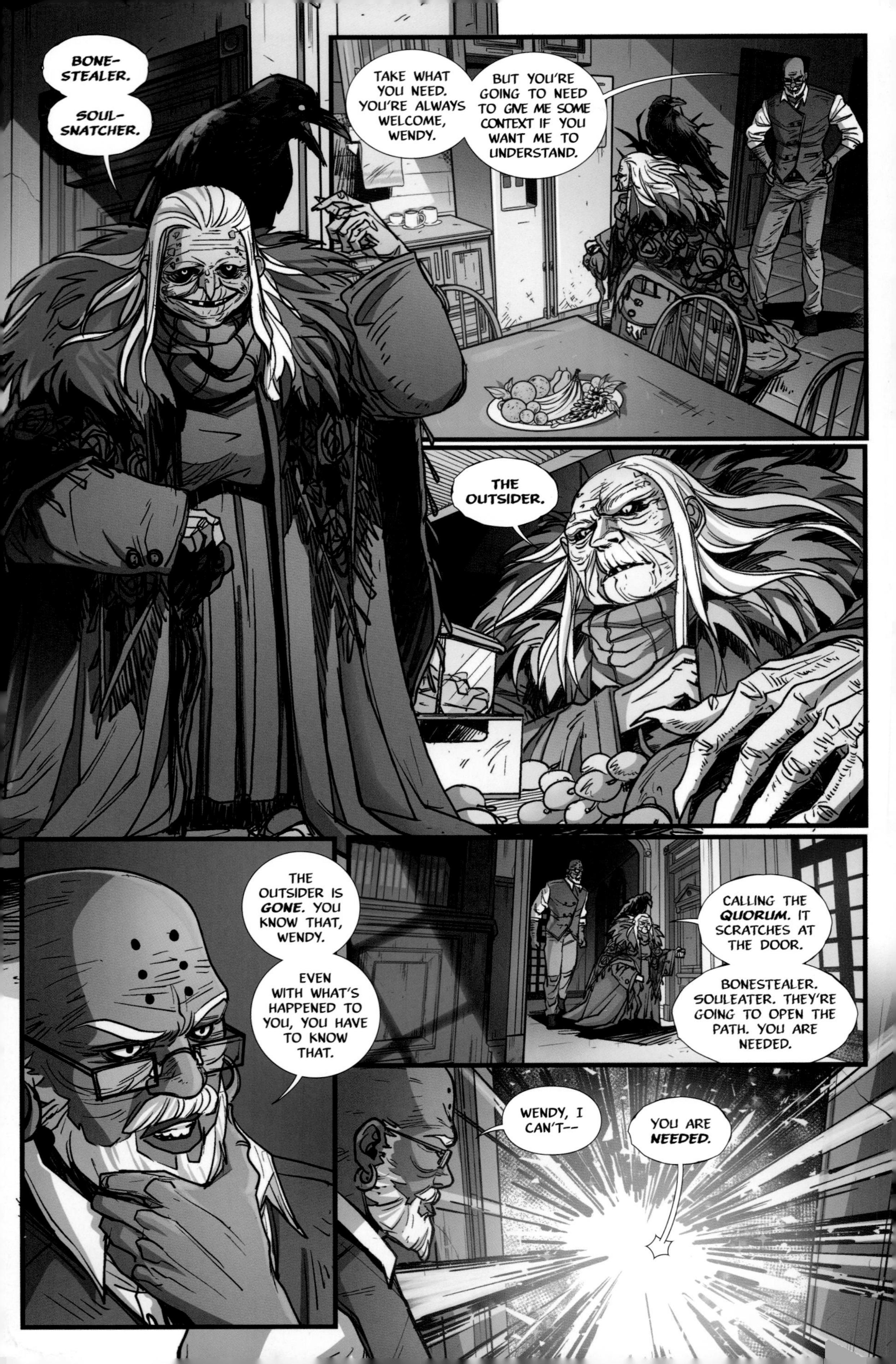
BONE-STEALER.
SOUL-SNATCHER.
TAKE WHAT YOU NEED. YOU'RE ALWAYS WELCOME, WENDY.
BUT YOU'RE GOING TO NEED TO GIVE ME SOME CONTEXT IF YOU WANT ME TO UNDERSTAND.
THE OUTSIDER.
THE OUTSIDER IS **GONE**. YOU KNOW THAT, WENDY.
EVEN WITH WHAT'S HAPPENED TO YOU, YOU HAVE TO KNOW THAT.
CALLING THE **QUORUM**. IT SCRATCHES AT THE DOOR.
BONESTEALER. SOULEATER. THEY'RE GOING TO OPEN THE PATH. YOU ARE NEEDED.
WENDY, I CAN'T--
YOU ARE **NEEDED.**

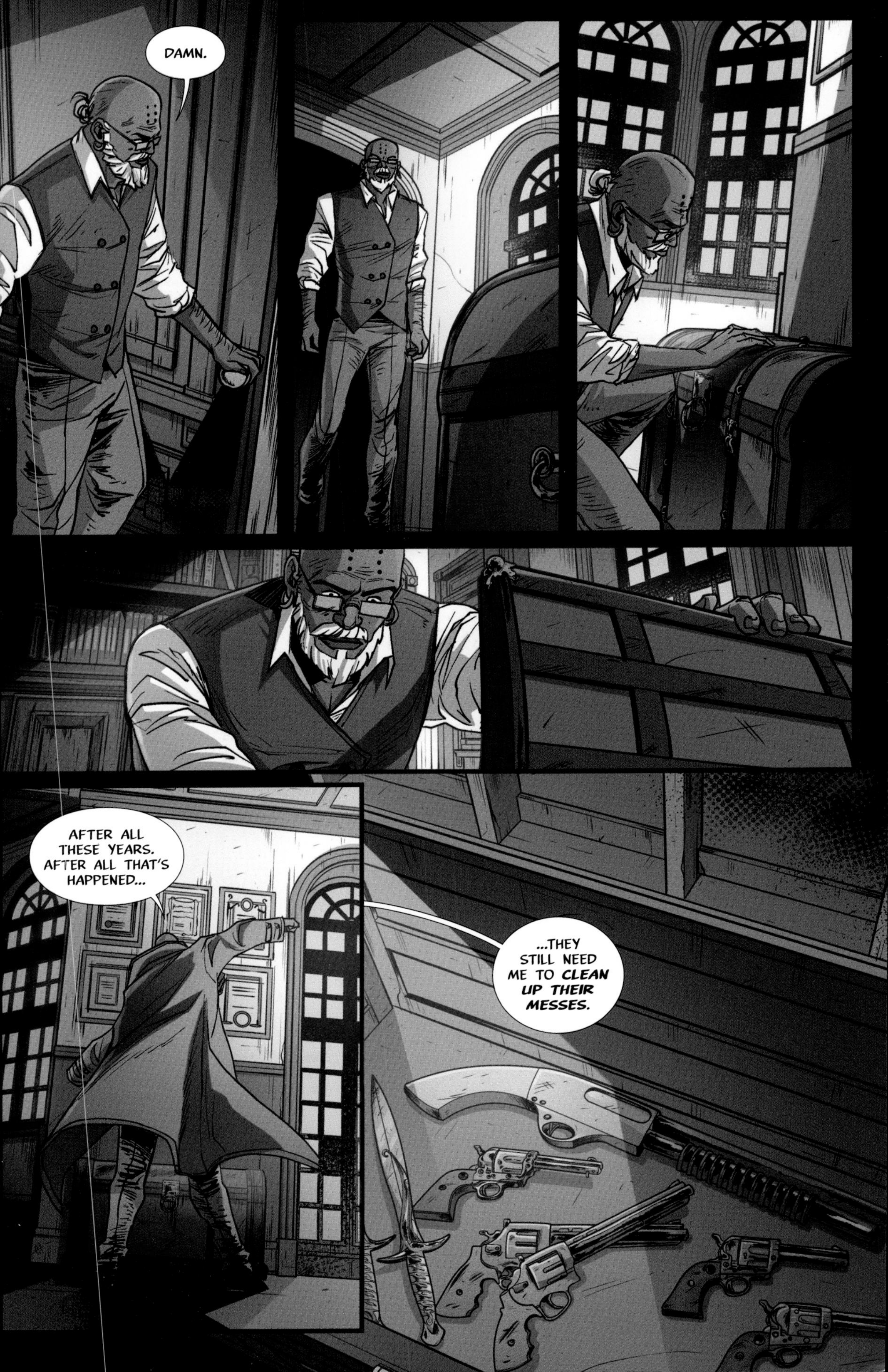
DAMN.
AFTER ALL THESE YEARS. AFTER ALL THAT'S HAPPENED...
...THEY STILL NEED ME TO CLEAN UP THEIR MESSES.

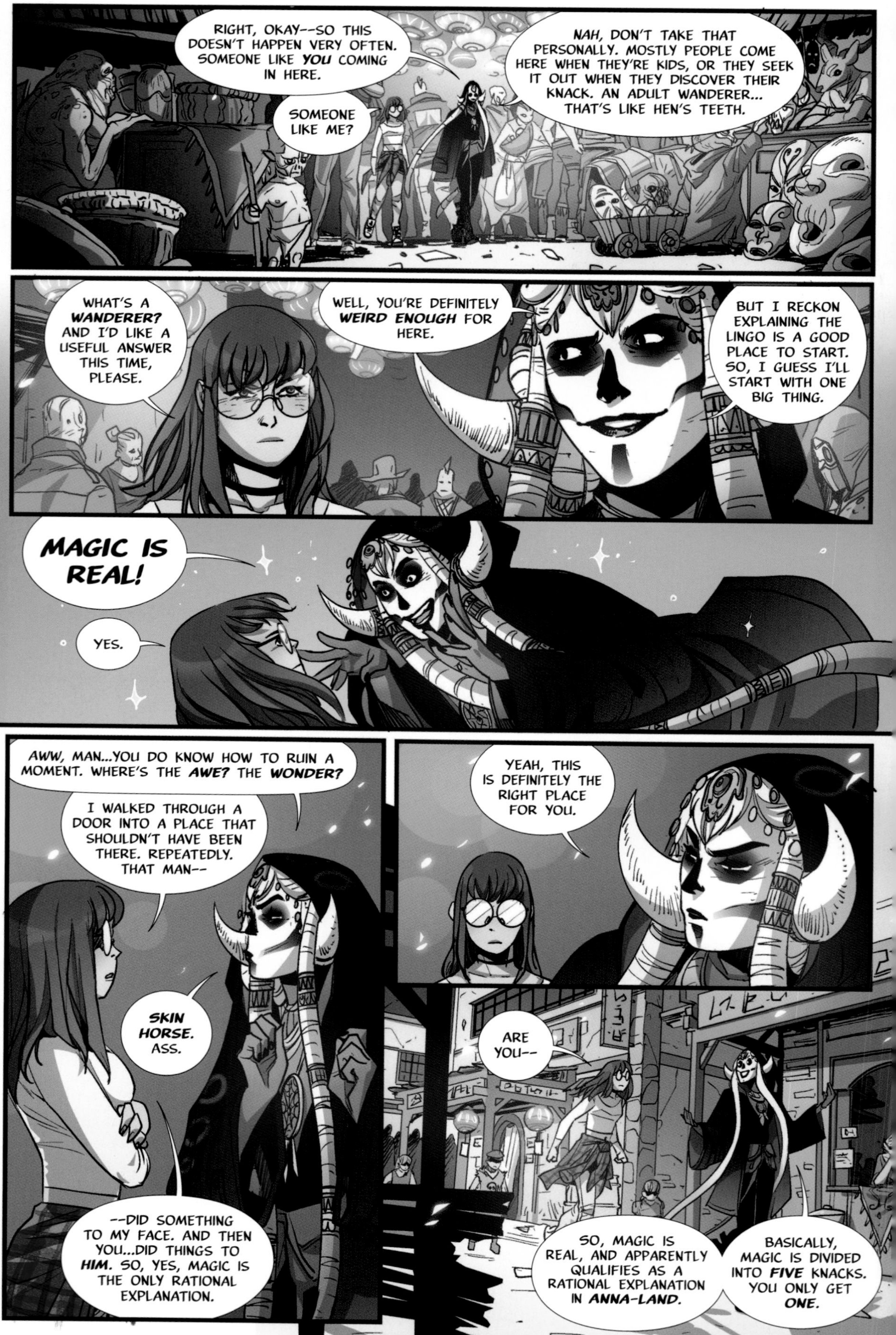
RIGHT, OKAY--SO THIS DOESN'T HAPPEN VERY OFTEN. SOMEONE LIKE YOU COMING IN HERE.
SOMEONE LIKE ME?
NAH, DON'T TAKE THAT PERSONALLY. MOSTLY PEOPLE COME HERE WHEN THEY'RE KIDS, OR THEY SEEK IT OUT WHEN THEY DISCOVER THEIR KNACK. AN ADULT WANDERER... THAT'S LIKE HEN'S TEETH.
WHAT'S A WANDERER? AND I'D LIKE A USEFUL ANSWER THIS TIME, PLEASE.
WELL, YOU'RE DEFINITELY WEIRD ENOUGH FOR HERE.
BUT I RECKON EXPLAINING THE LINGO IS A GOOD PLACE TO START. SO, I GUESS I'LL START WITH ONE BIG THING.
MAGIC IS REAL!
YES.
AWW, MAN...YOU DO KNOW HOW TO RUIN A MOMENT. WHERE'S THE AWE? THE WONDER?
I WALKED THROUGH A DOOR INTO A PLACE THAT SHOULDN'T HAVE BEEN THERE. REPEATEDLY. THAT MAN--
SKIN HORSE. ASS.
--DID SOMETHING TO MY FACE. AND THEN YOU...DID THINGS TO HIM. SO, YES, MAGIC IS THE ONLY RATIONAL EXPLANATION.
YEAH, THIS IS DEFINITELY THE RIGHT PLACE FOR YOU.
ARE YOU--
SO, MAGIC IS REAL, AND APPARENTLY QUALIFIES AS A RATIONAL EXPLANATION IN ANNA-LAND.
BASICALLY, MAGIC IS DIVIDED INTO FIVE KNACKS. YOU ONLY GET ONE.

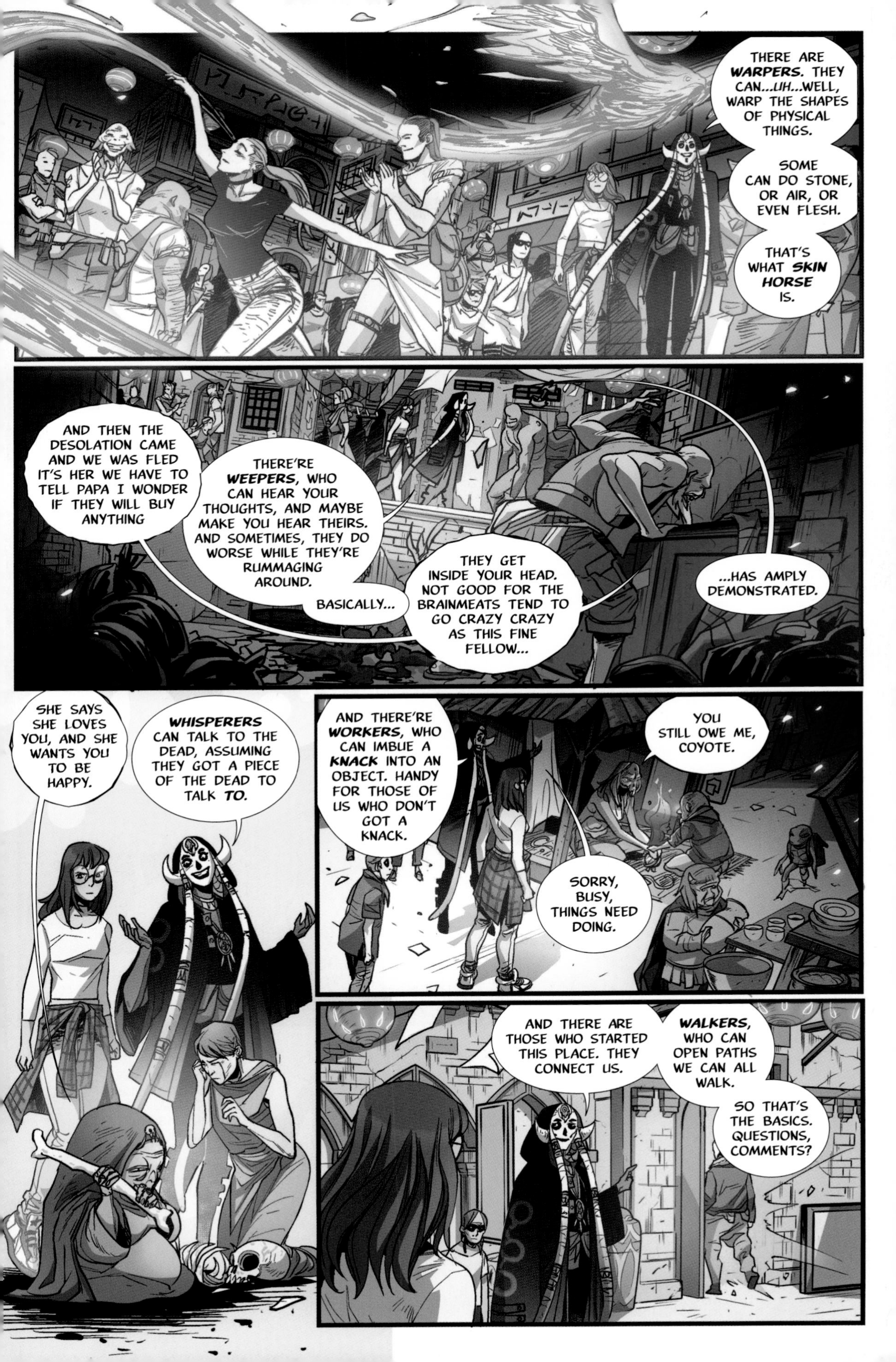
THERE ARE WARPERS. THEY CAN...UH...WELL, WARP THE SHAPES OF PHYSICAL THINGS.
SOME CAN DO STONE, OR AIR, OR EVEN FLESH.
THAT'S WHAT SKIN HORSE IS.
AND THEN THE DESOLATION CAME AND WE WAS FLED IT'S HER WE HAVE TO TELL PAPA I WONDER IF THEY WILL BUY ANYTHING
THERE'RE WEEPERS, WHO CAN HEAR YOUR THOUGHTS, AND MAYBE MAKE YOU HEAR THEIRS. AND SOMETIMES, THEY DO WORSE WHILE THEY'RE RUMMAGING AROUND.
BASICALLY...
THEY GET INSIDE YOUR HEAD. NOT GOOD FOR THE BRAINMEATS TEND TO GO CRAZY CRAZY AS THIS FINE FELLOW...
...HAS AMPLY DEMONSTRATED.
SHE SAYS SHE LOVES YOU, AND SHE WANTS YOU TO BE HAPPY.
WHISPERERS CAN TALK TO THE DEAD, ASSUMING THEY GOT A PIECE OF THE DEAD TO TALK TO.
AND THERE'RE WORKERS, WHO CAN IMBUE A KNACK INTO AN OBJECT. HANDY FOR THOSE OF US WHO DON'T GOT A KNACK.
YOU STILL OWE ME, COYOTE.
SORRY, BUSY, THINGS NEED DOING.
AND THERE ARE THOSE WHO STARTED THIS PLACE. THEY CONNECT US.
WALKERS, WHO CAN OPEN PATHS WE CAN ALL WALK.
SO THAT'S THE BASICS. QUESTIONS, COMMENTS?

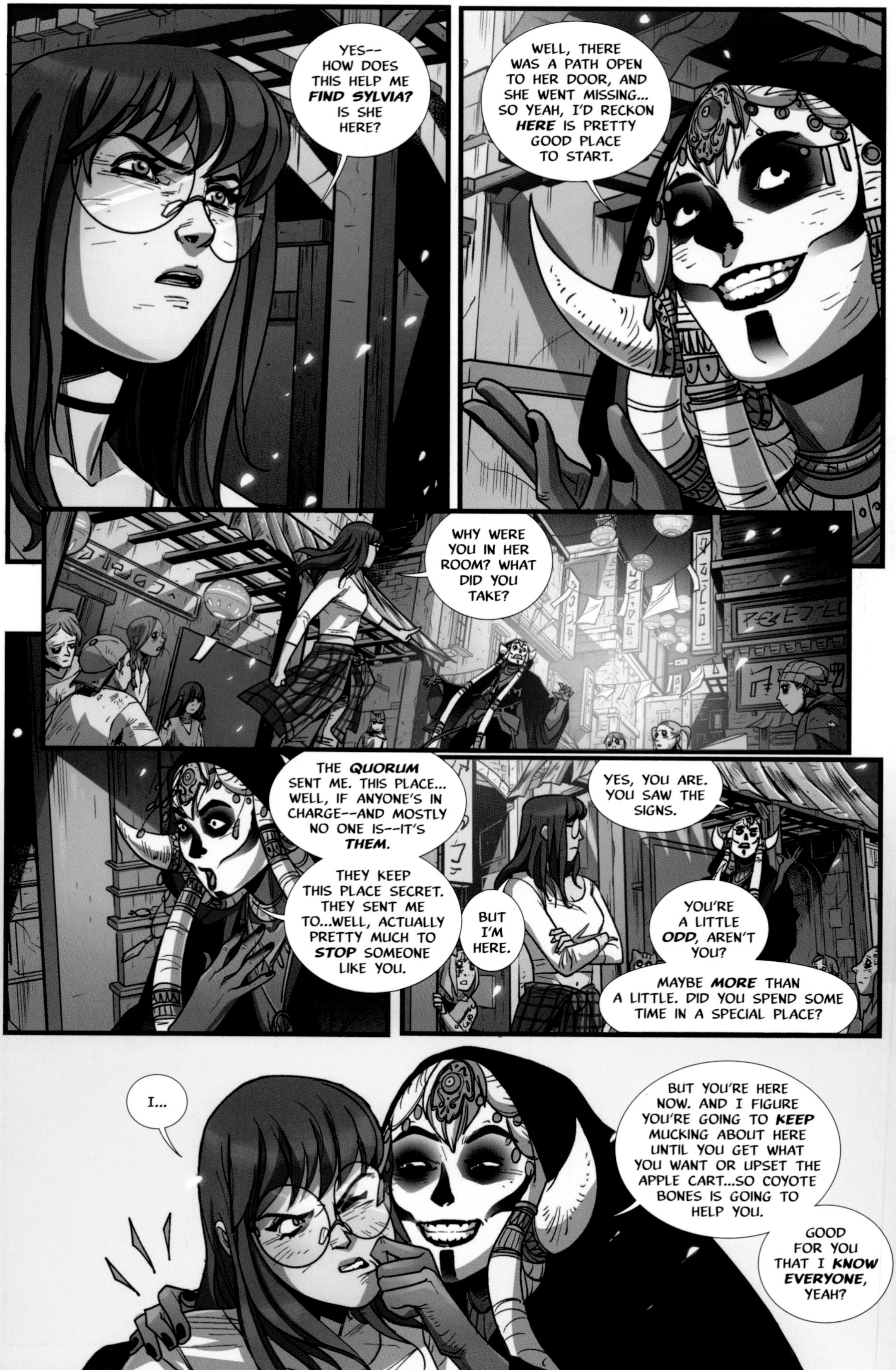
YES-- HOW DOES THIS HELP ME FIND SYLVIA? IS SHE HERE?
WELL, THERE WAS A PATH OPEN TO HER DOOR, AND SHE WENT MISSING... SO YEAH, I'D RECKON HERE IS PRETTY GOOD PLACE TO START.
WHY WERE YOU IN HER ROOM? WHAT DID YOU TAKE?
THE QUORUM SENT ME. THIS PLACE... WELL, IF ANYONE'S IN CHARGE--AND MOSTLY NO ONE IS--IT'S THEM.
THEY KEEP THIS PLACE SECRET. THEY SENT ME TO...WELL, ACTUALLY PRETTY MUCH TO STOP SOMEONE LIKE YOU.
BUT I'M HERE.
YES, YOU ARE. YOU SAW THE SIGNS.
YOU'RE A LITTLE ODD, AREN'T YOU?
MAYBE MORE THAN A LITTLE. DID YOU SPEND SOME TIME IN A SPECIAL PLACE?
I...
BUT YOU'RE HERE NOW. AND I FIGURE YOU'RE GOING TO KEEP MUCKING ABOUT HERE UNTIL YOU GET WHAT YOU WANT OR UPSET THE APPLE CART...SO COYOTE BONES IS GOING TO HELP YOU.
GOOD FOR YOU THAT I KNOW EVERYONE, YEAH?

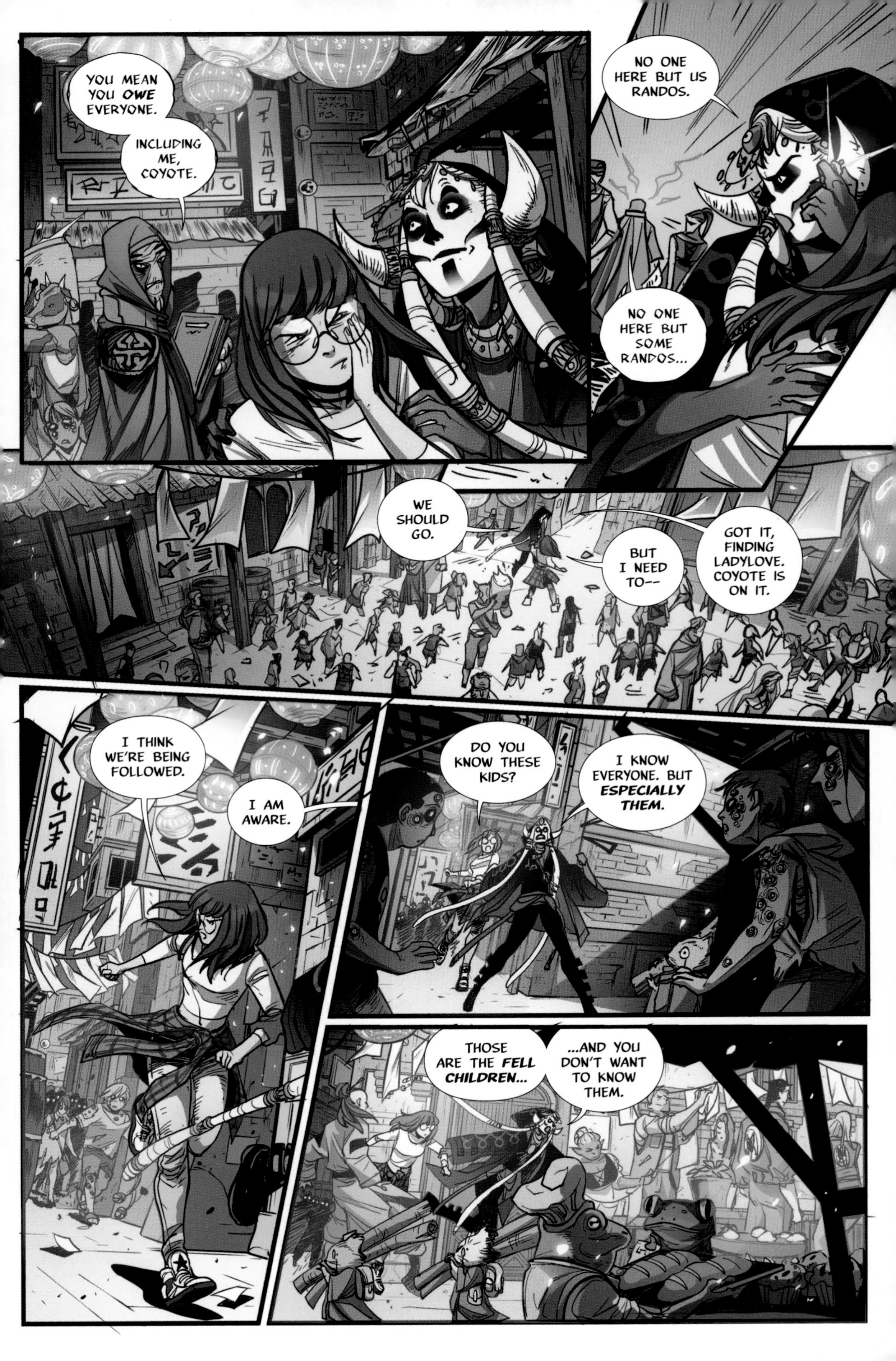
YOU MEAN YOU OWE EVERYONE.
INCLUDING ME, COYOTE.
NO ONE HERE BUT US RANDOS.
NO ONE HERE BUT SOME RANDOS...
WE SHOULD GO.
BUT I NEED TO--
GOT IT, FINDING LADYLOVE. COYOTE IS ON IT.
I THINK WE'RE BEING FOLLOWED.
I AM AWARE.
DO YOU KNOW THESE KIDS?
I KNOW EVERYONE. BUT ESPECIALLY THEM.
THOSE ARE THE FELL CHILDREN...
...AND YOU DON'T WANT TO KNOW THEM.

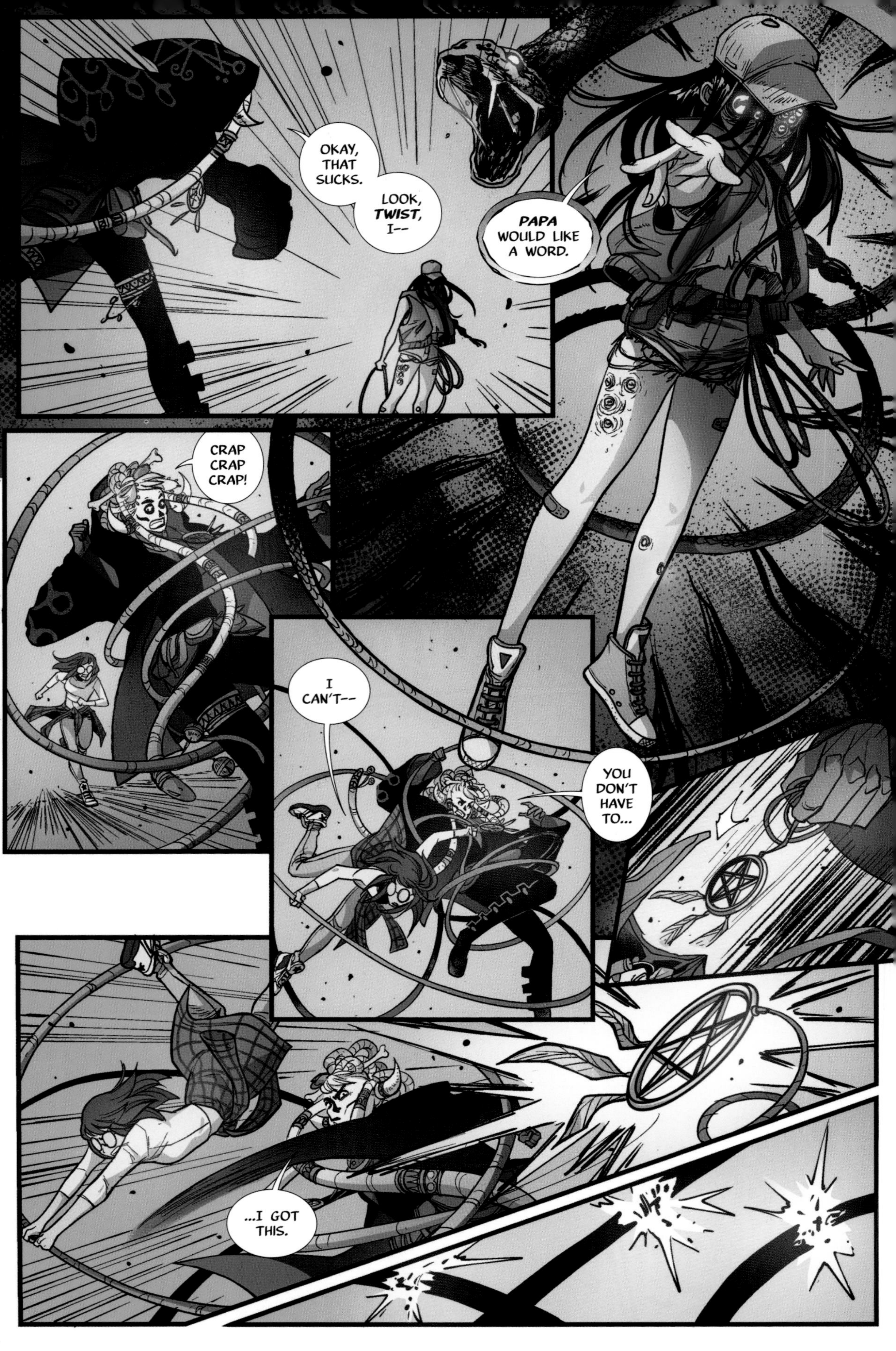
OKAY, THAT SUCKS.
LOOK, TWIST, I--
PAPA WOULD LIKE A WORD.
CRAP CRAP CRAP!
I CAN'T--
YOU DON'T HAVE TO...
...I GOT THIS.

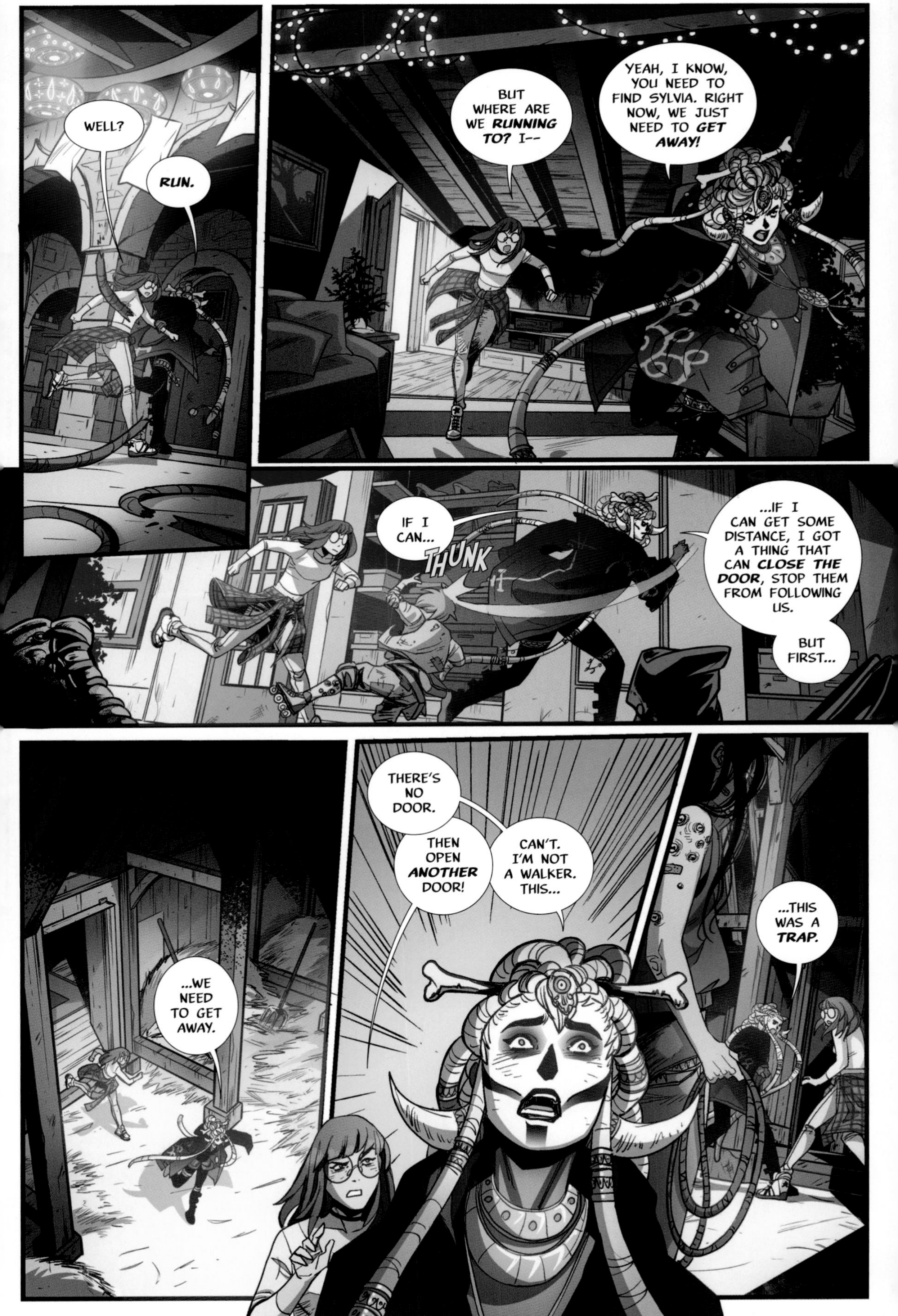
WELL?
RUN.
BUT WHERE ARE WE RUNNING TO? I--
YEAH, I KNOW, YOU NEED TO FIND SYLVIA. RIGHT NOW, WE JUST NEED TO GET AWAY!
IF I CAN...
THUNK
...IF I CAN GET SOME DISTANCE, I GOT A THING THAT CAN CLOSE THE DOOR, STOP THEM FROM FOLLOWING US.
BUT FIRST...
...WE NEED TO GET AWAY.
THERE'S NO DOOR.
THEN OPEN ANOTHER DOOR!
CAN'T. I'M NOT A WALKER. THIS...
...THIS WAS A TRAP.

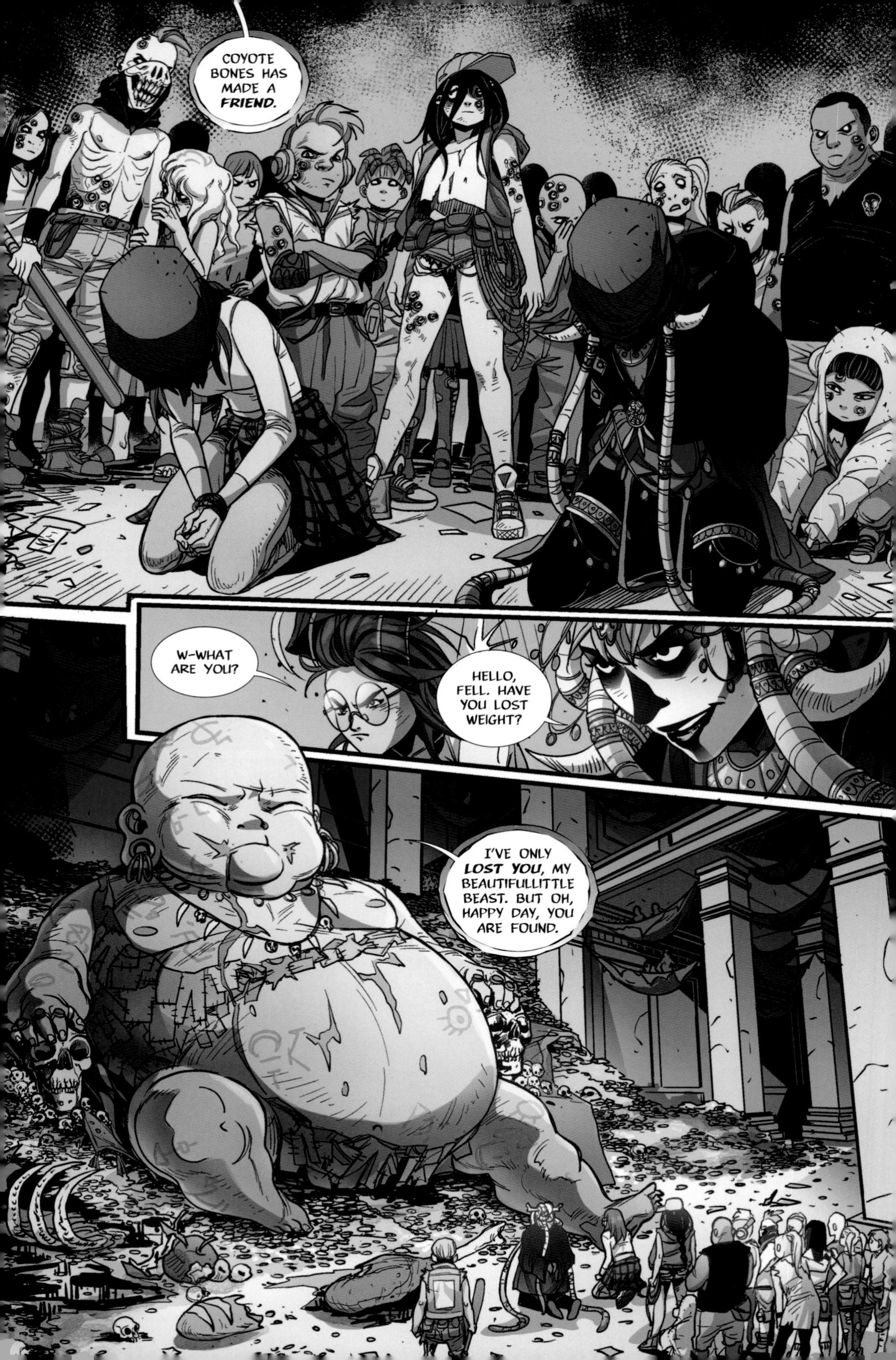
COYOTE BONES HAS MADE A **FRIEND.**
W-WHAT ARE YOU?
HELLO, FELL. HAVE YOU LOST WEIGHT?
I'VE ONLY **LOST YOU,** MY BEAUTIFULLITTLE BEAST. BUT OH, HAPPY DAY, YOU ARE FOUND.

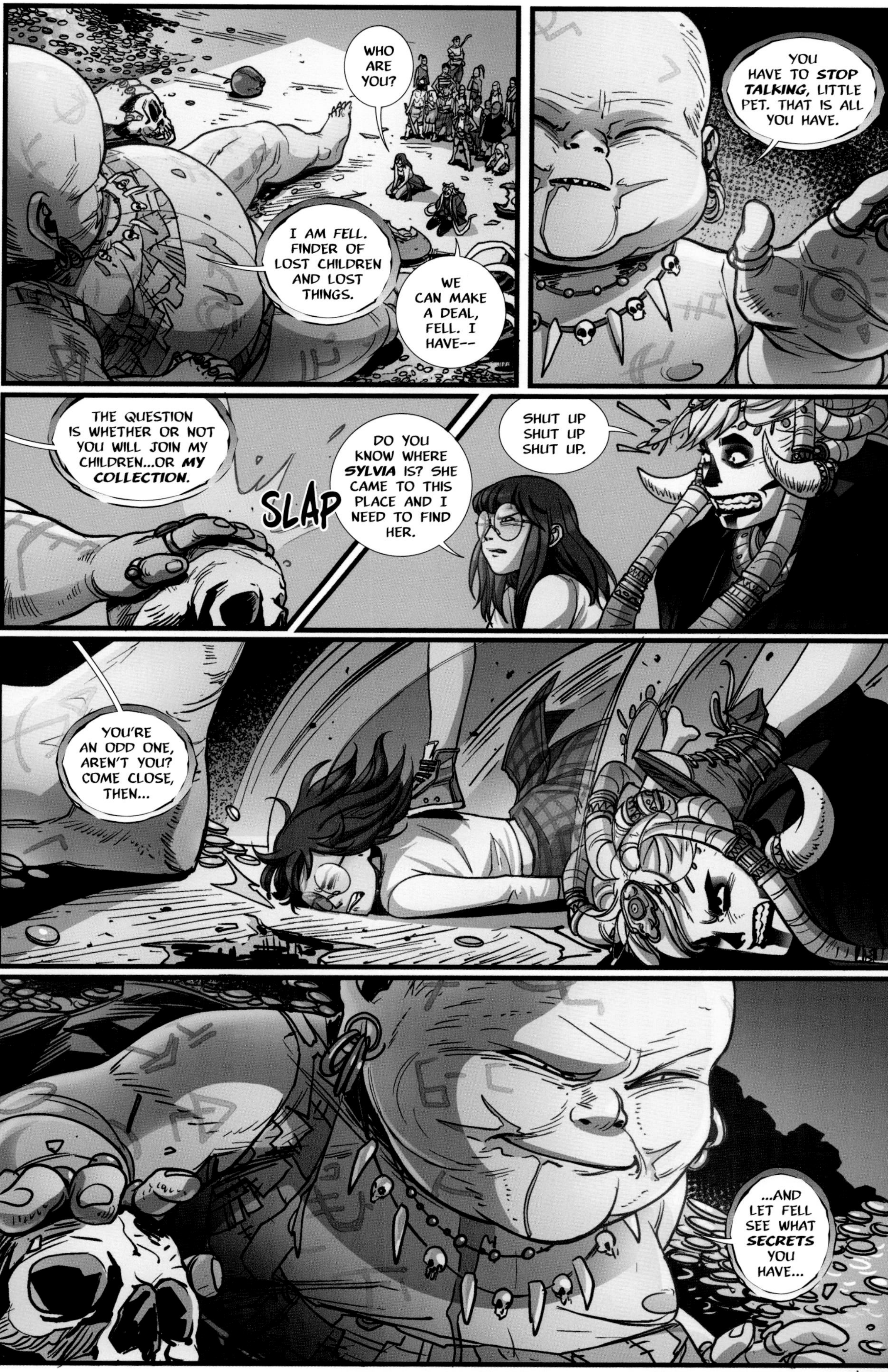
WHO ARE YOU?
I AM FELL. FINDER OF LOST CHILDREN AND LOST THINGS.
WE CAN MAKE A DEAL, FELL. I HAVE--
YOU HAVE TO STOP TALKING, LITTLE PET. THAT IS ALL YOU HAVE.
THE QUESTION IS WHETHER OR NOT YOU WILL JOIN MY CHILDREN...OR MY COLLECTION.
SLAP
DO YOU KNOW WHERE SYLVIA IS? SHE CAME TO THIS PLACE AND I NEED TO FIND HER.
SHUT UP SHUT UP SHUT UP.
YOU'RE AN ODD ONE, AREN'T YOU? COME CLOSE, THEN...
...AND LET FELL SEE WHAT SECRETS YOU HAVE...

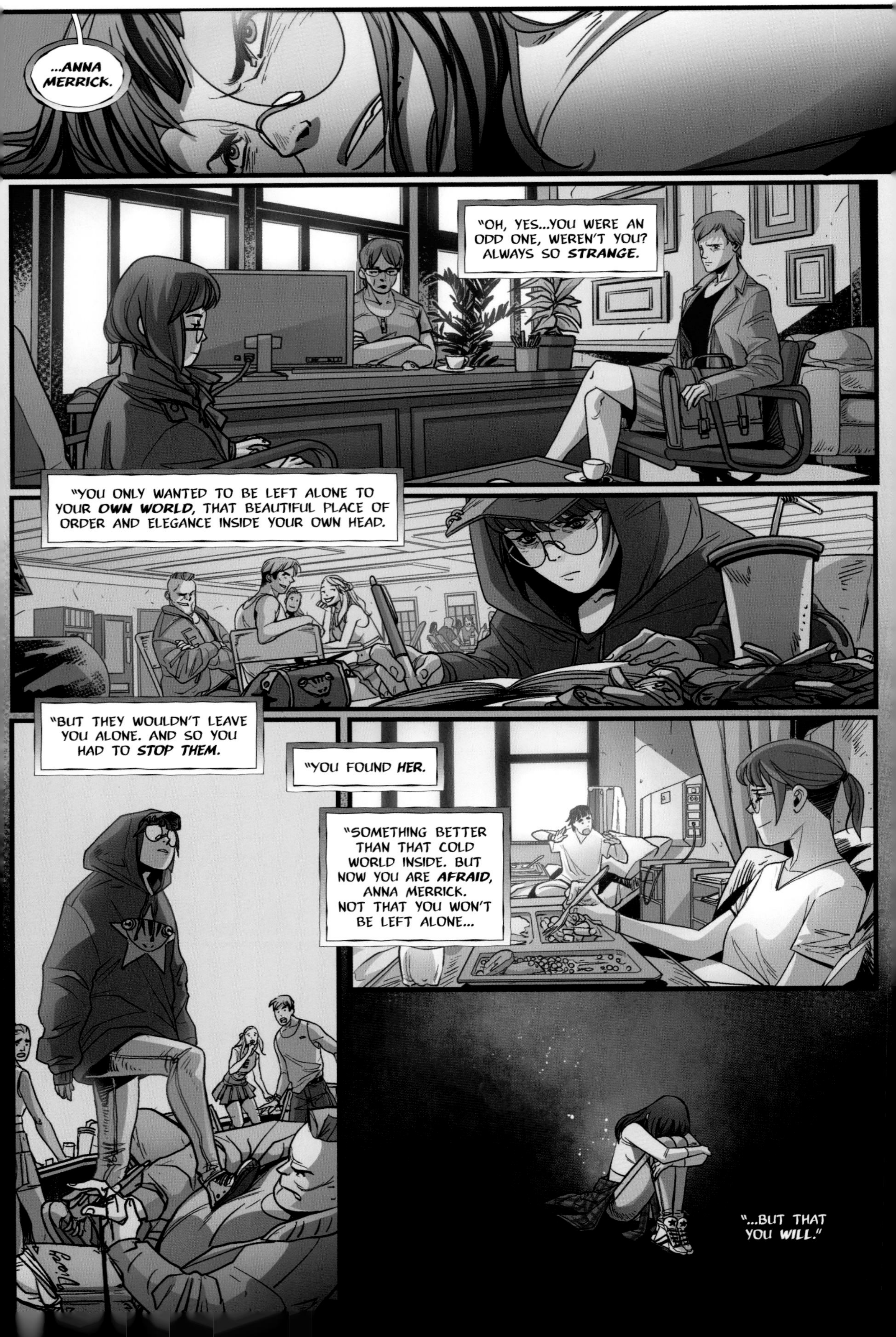
...ANNA MERRICK.
"OH, YES...YOU WERE AN ODD ONE, WEREN'T YOU? ALWAYS SO **STRANGE.**
"YOU ONLY WANTED TO BE LEFT ALONE TO YOUR **OWN WORLD,** THAT BEAUTIFUL PLACE OF ORDER AND ELEGANCE INSIDE YOUR OWN HEAD.
"BUT THEY WOULDN'T LEAVE YOU ALONE. AND SO YOU HAD TO **STOP THEM.**
"YOU FOUND **HER.**
"SOMETHING BETTER THAN THAT COLD WORLD INSIDE. BUT NOW YOU ARE **AFRAID,** ANNA MERRICK. NOT THAT YOU WON'T BE LEFT ALONE...
"...BUT THAT YOU **WILL.**"

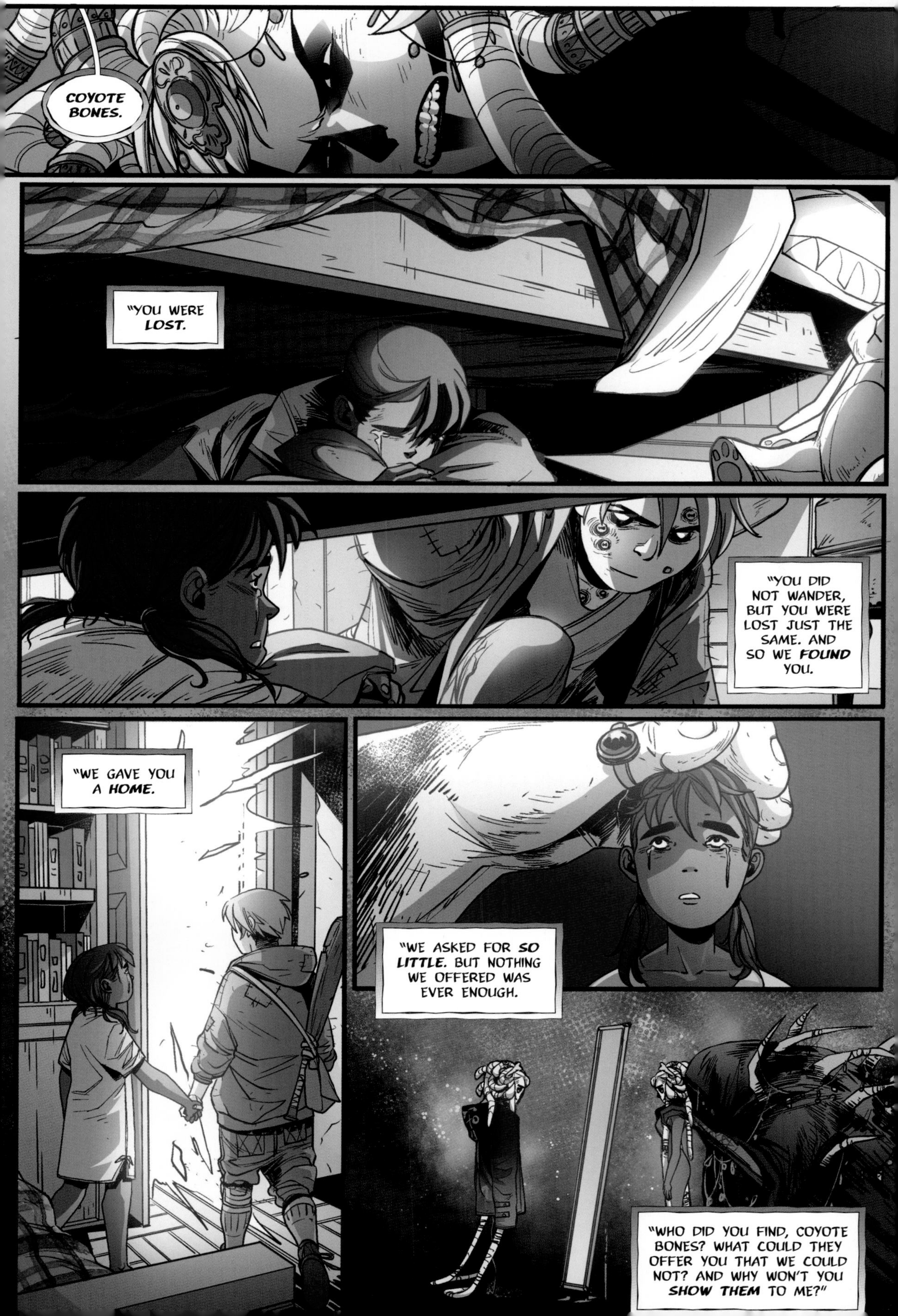
COYOTE BONES.
"YOU WERE LOST.
"YOU DID NOT WANDER, BUT YOU WERE LOST JUST THE SAME. AND SO WE FOUND YOU.
"WE GAVE YOU A HOME.
"WE ASKED FOR SO LITTLE. BUT NOTHING WE OFFERED WAS EVER ENOUGH.
"WHO DID YOU FIND, COYOTE BONES? WHAT COULD THEY OFFER YOU THAT WE COULD NOT? AND WHY WON'T YOU SHOW THEM TO ME?"

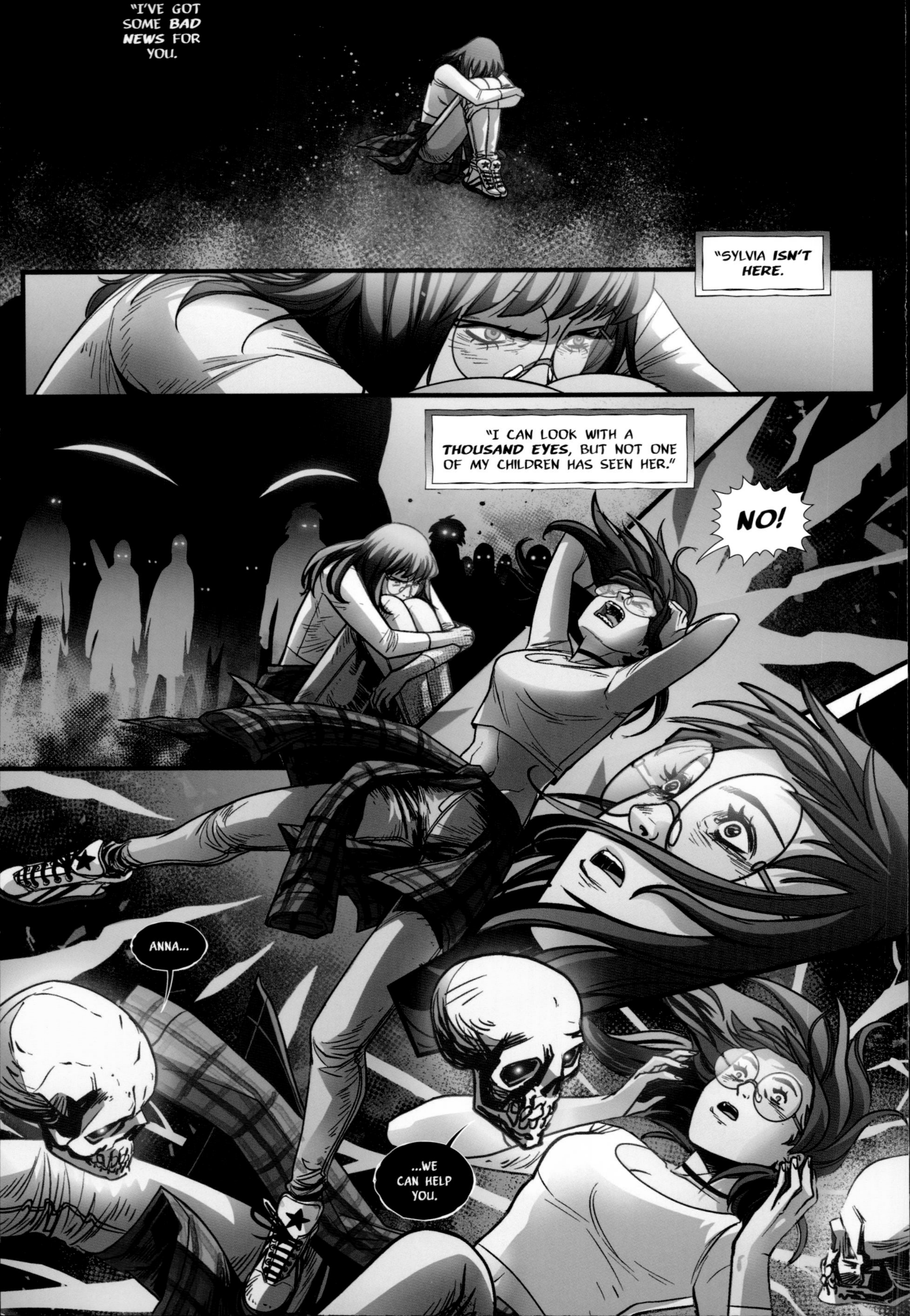
"I'VE GOT SOME BAD NEWS FOR YOU.
"SYLVIA ISN'T HERE.
"I CAN LOOK WITH A THOUSAND EYES, BUT NOT ONE OF MY CHILDREN HAS SEEN HER."
NO!
ANNA...
...WE CAN HELP YOU.

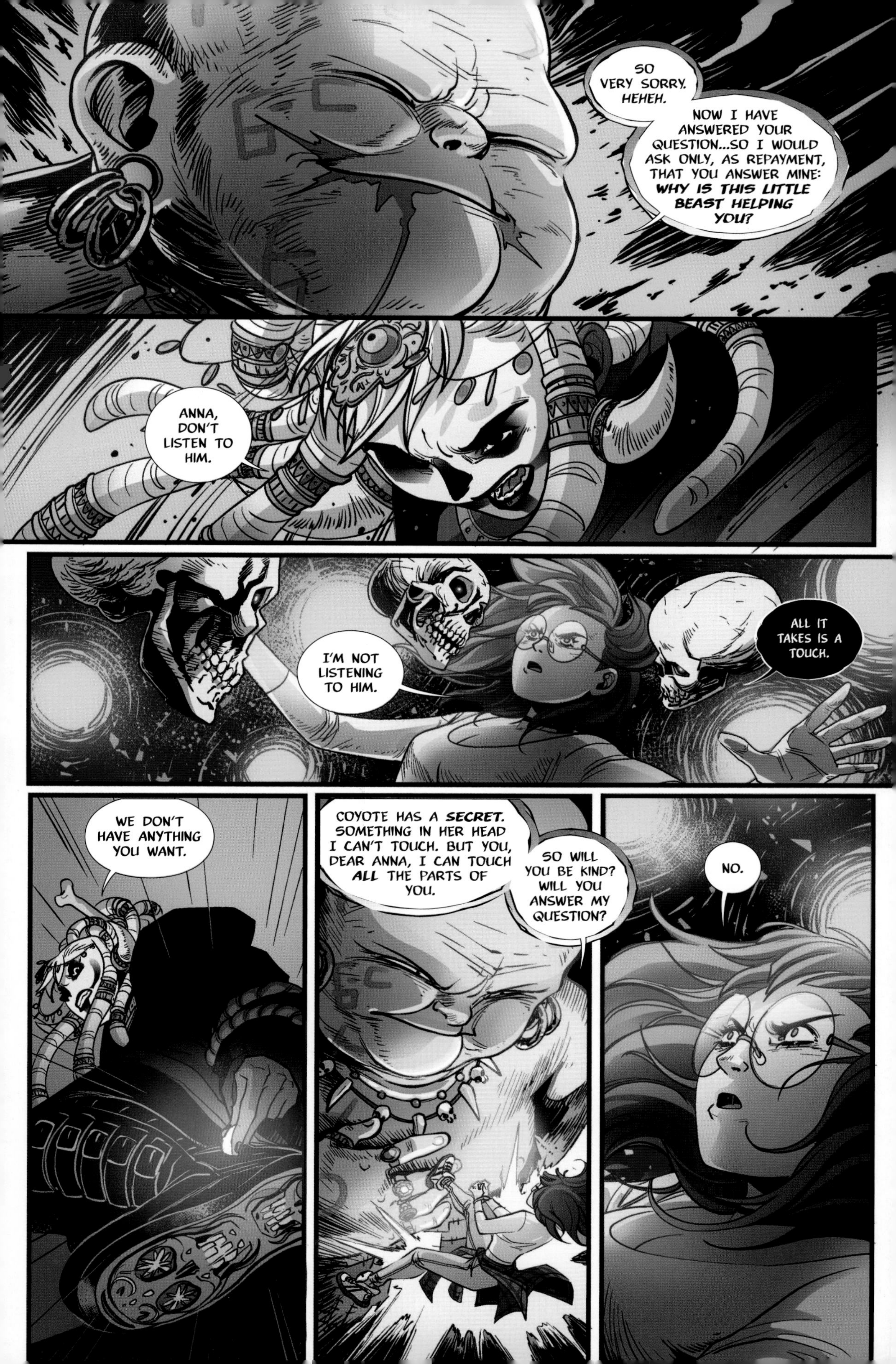
SO VERY SORRY. HEHEH.
NOW I HAVE ANSWERED YOUR QUESTION...SO I WOULD ASK ONLY, AS REPAYMENT, THAT YOU ANSWER MINE: **WHY IS THIS LITTLE BEAST HELPING YOU?**
ANNA, DON'T LISTEN TO HIM.
I'M NOT LISTENING TO HIM.
ALL IT TAKES IS A TOUCH.
WE DON'T HAVE ANYTHING YOU WANT.
COYOTE HAS A **SECRET.** SOMETHING IN HER HEAD I CAN'T TOUCH. BUT YOU, DEAR ANNA, I CAN TOUCH **ALL** THE PARTS OF YOU.
SO WILL YOU BE KIND? WILL YOU ANSWER MY QUESTION?
NO.

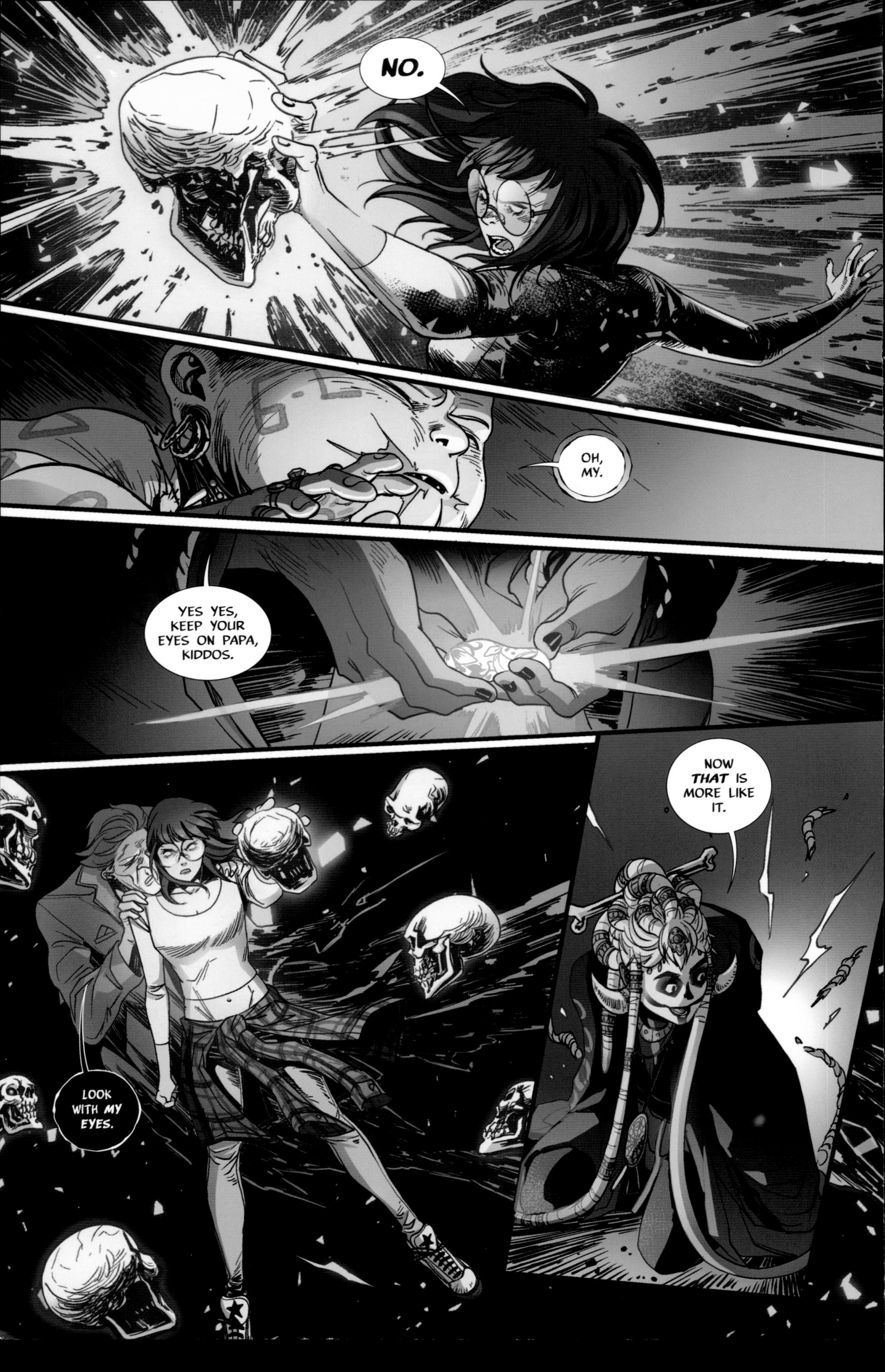
NO.
OH, MY.
YES YES, KEEP YOUR EYES ON PAPA, KIDDOS.
NOW THAT IS MORE LIKE IT.
LOOK WITH MY EYES.

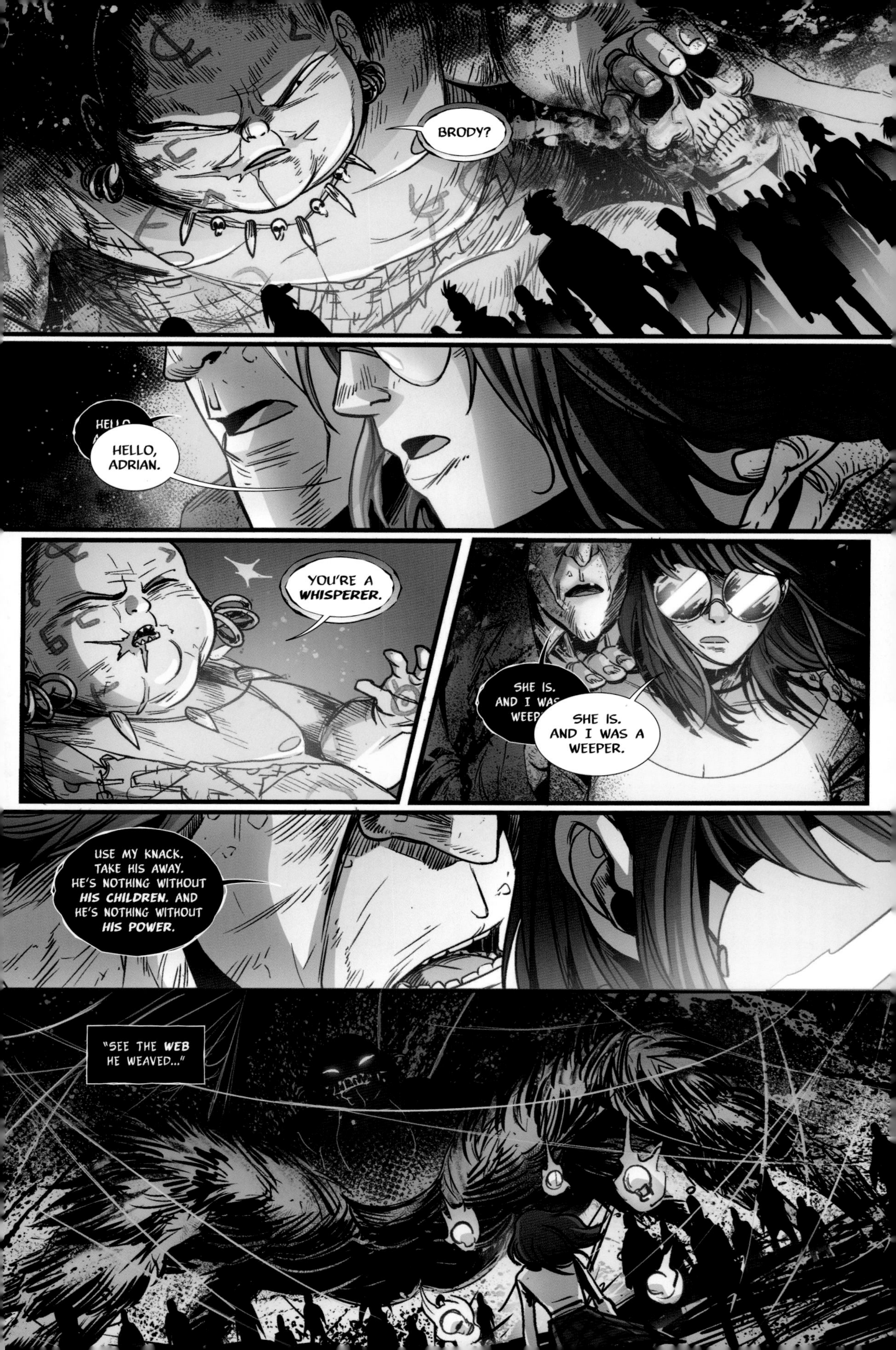
BRODY?
HELLO, ADRIAN.
YOU'RE A **WHISPERER.**
SHE IS. AND I WAS A WEEPER.
USE MY KNACK. TAKE HIS AWAY. HE'S NOTHING WITHOUT **HIS CHILDREN.** AND HE'S NOTHING WITHOUT **HIS POWER.**
"SEE THE **WEB** HE WEAVED..."

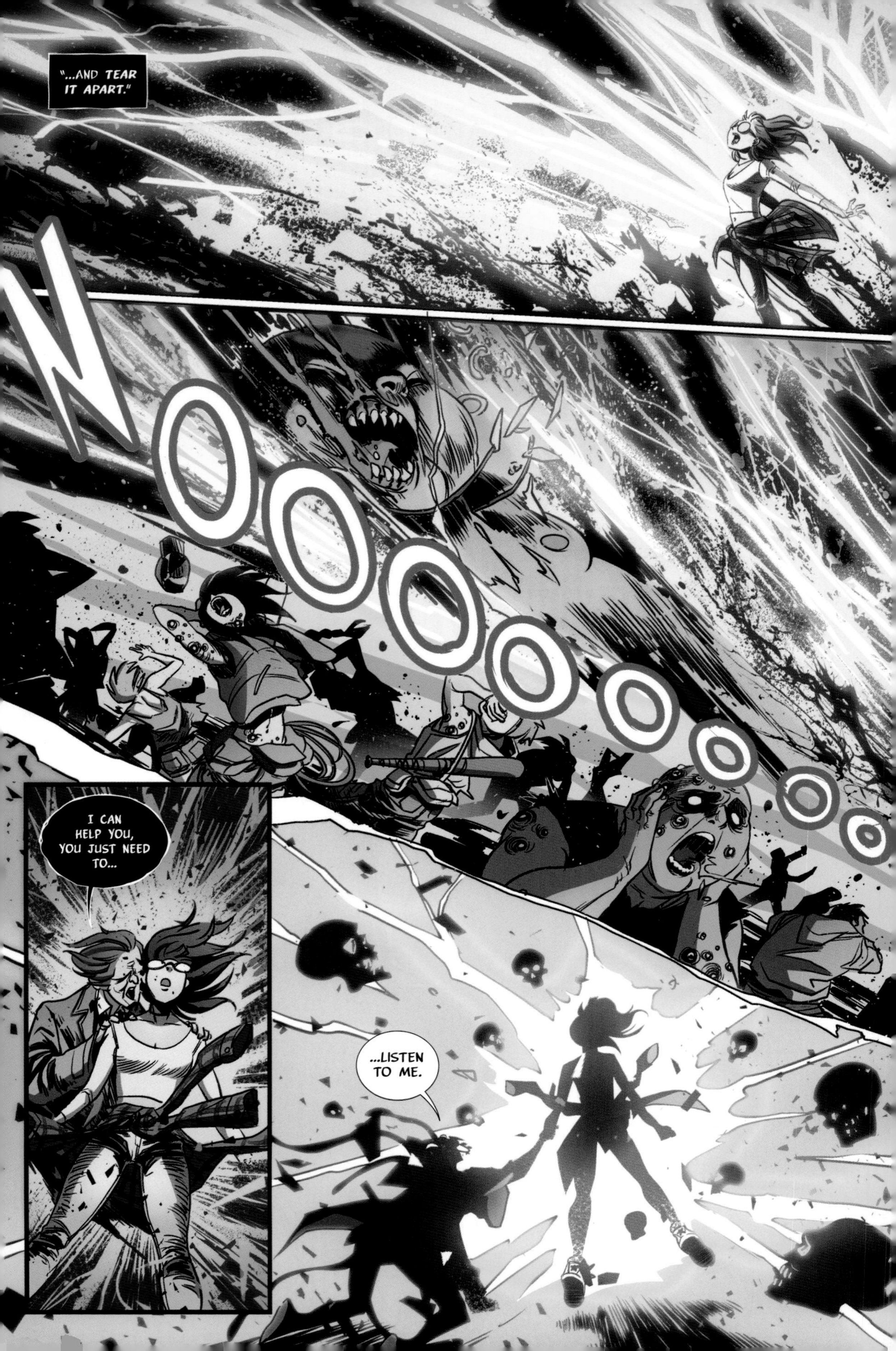
"...AND TEAR IT APART."
ZWOOOOOOOOOOO
I CAN HELP YOU, YOU JUST NEED TO...
...LISTEN TO ME.

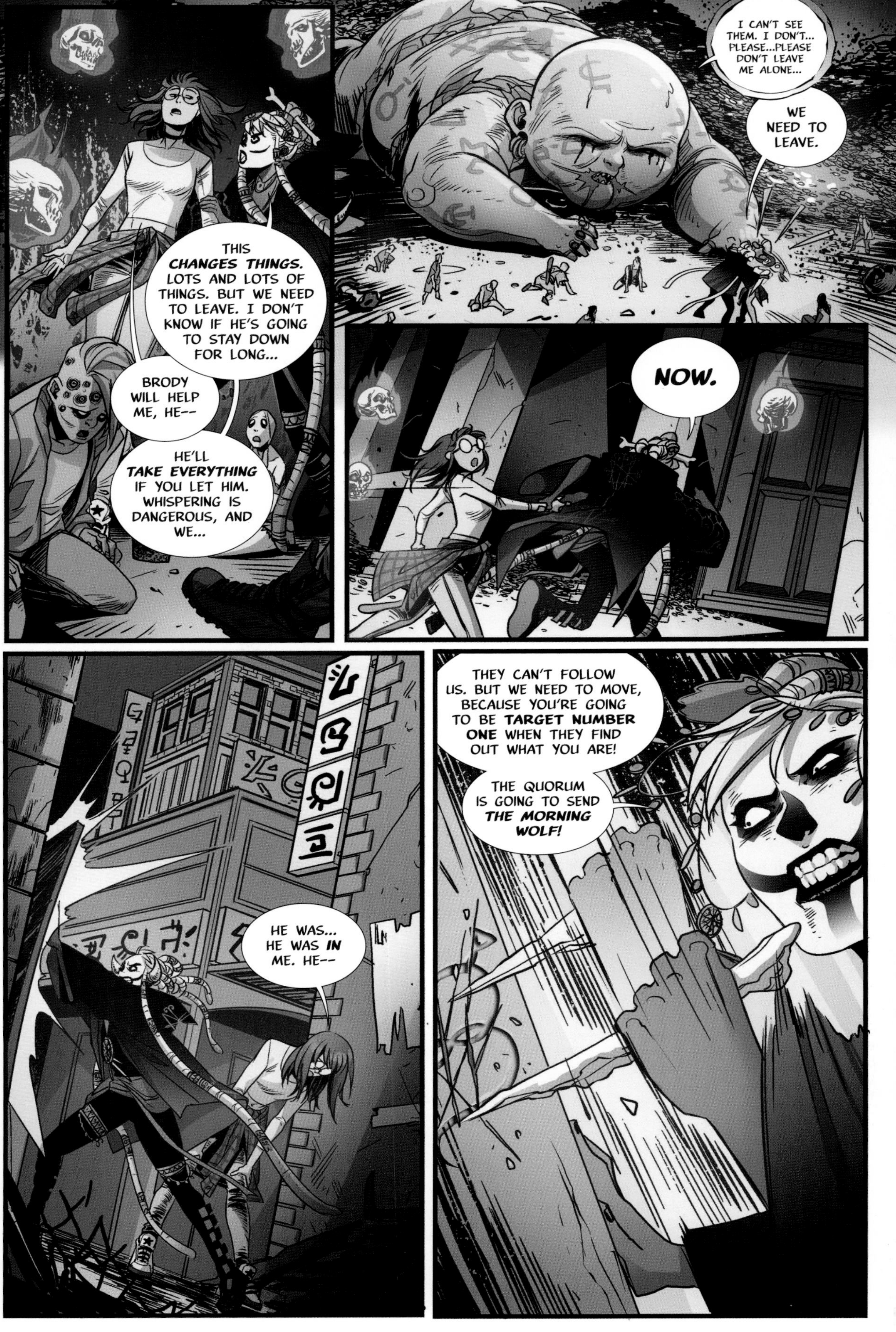
THIS **CHANGES THINGS.** LOTS AND LOTS OF THINGS. BUT WE NEED TO LEAVE. I DON'T KNOW IF HE'S GOING TO STAY DOWN FOR LONG...
BRODY WILL HELP ME, HE--
HE'LL ***TAKE EVERYTHING*** IF YOU LET HIM. WHISPERING IS DANGEROUS, AND WE...
I CAN'T SEE THEM. I DON'T... PLEASE...PLEASE DON'T LEAVE ME ALONE...
WE NEED TO LEAVE.
NOW.
HE WAS... HE WAS **IN** ME. HE--
THEY CAN'T FOLLOW US. BUT WE NEED TO MOVE, BECAUSE YOU'RE GOING TO BE **TARGET NUMBER ONE** WHEN THEY FIND OUT WHAT YOU ARE!
THE QUORUM IS GOING TO SEND ***THE MORNING WOLF!***

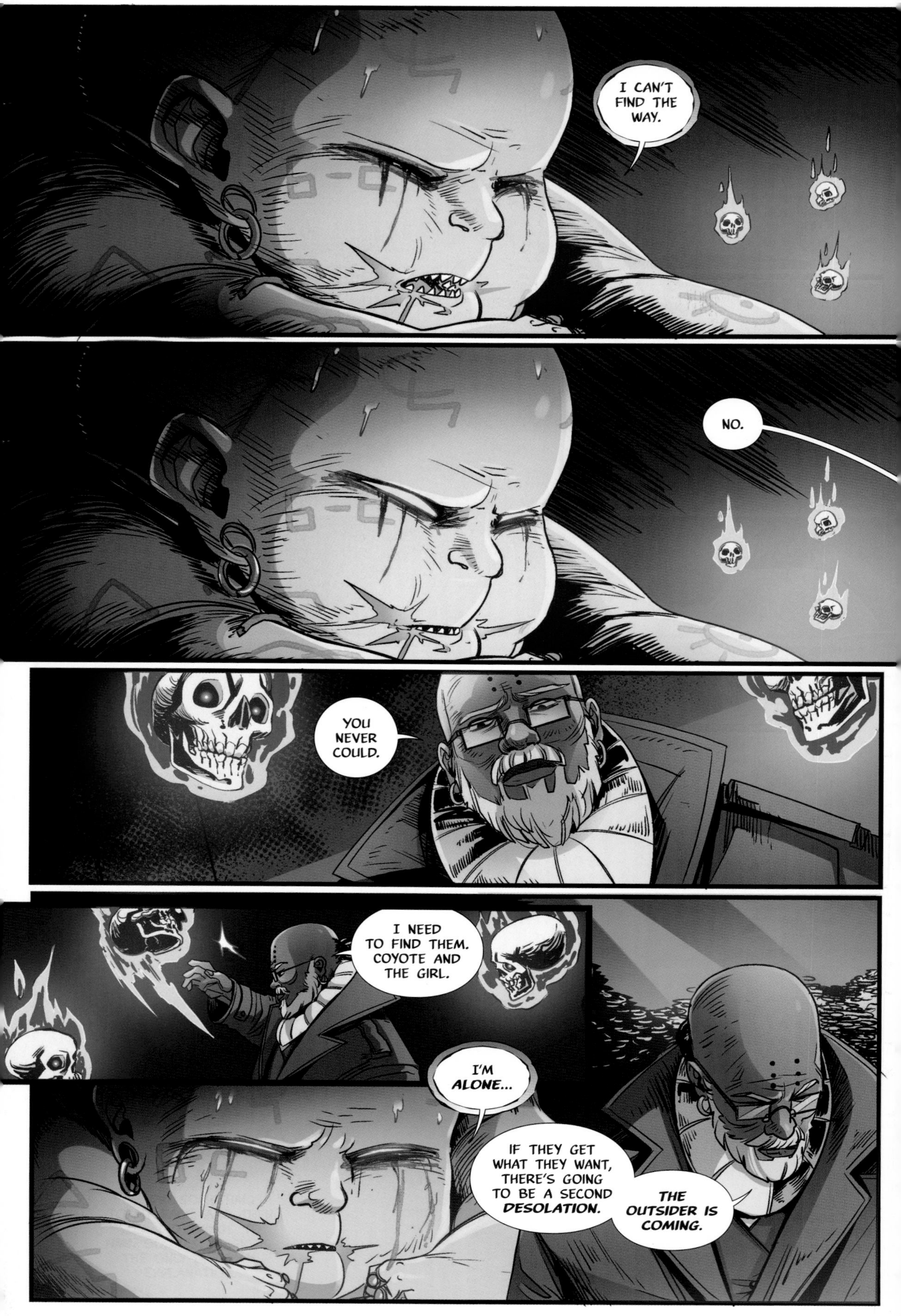
I CAN'T FIND THE WAY.
NO.
YOU NEVER COULD.
I NEED TO FIND THEM. COYOTE AND THE GIRL.
I'M *ALONE...*
IF THEY GET WHAT THEY WANT, THERE'S GOING TO BE A SECOND *DESOLATION.*
THE OUTSIDER IS COMING.

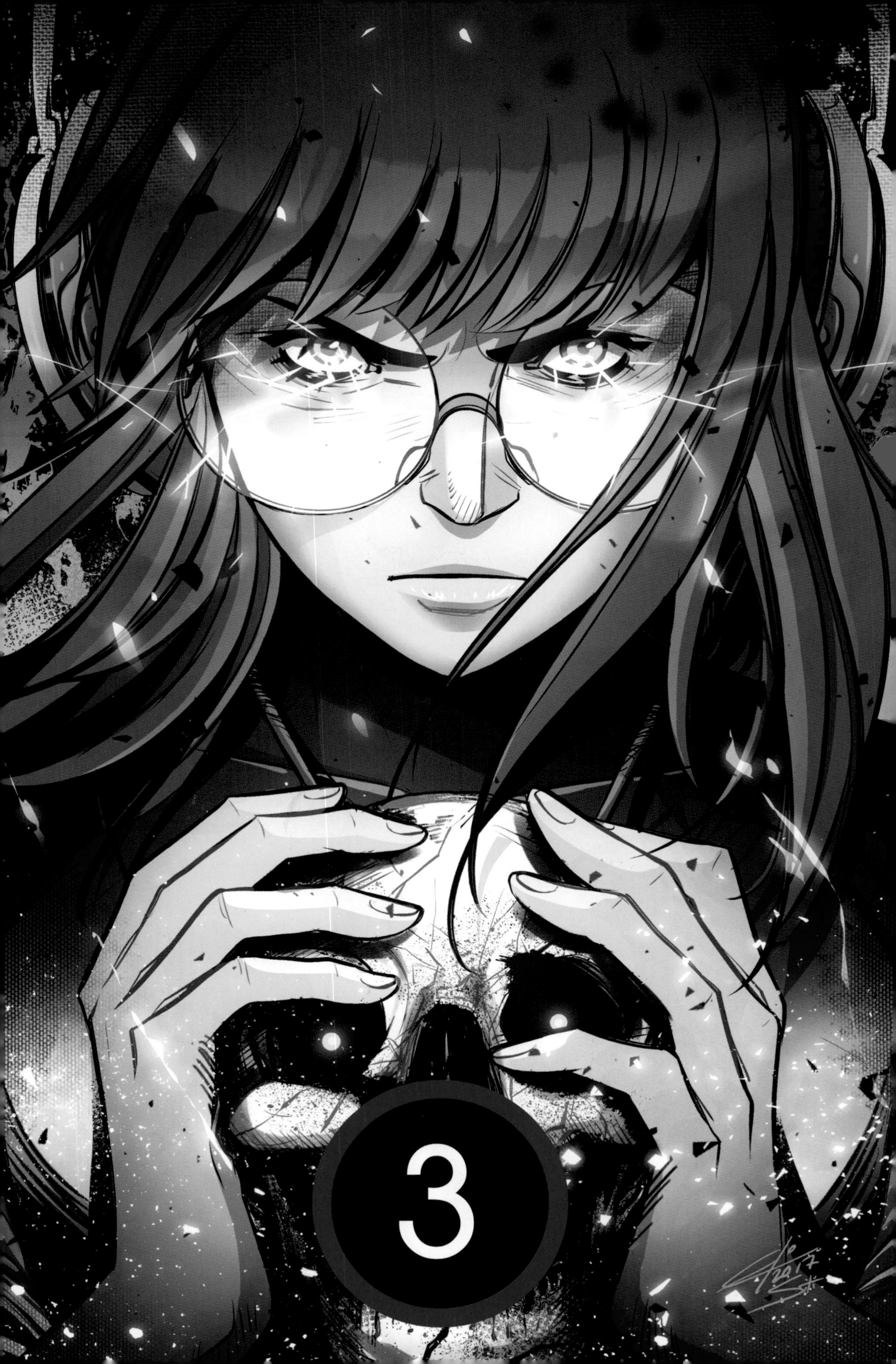
3

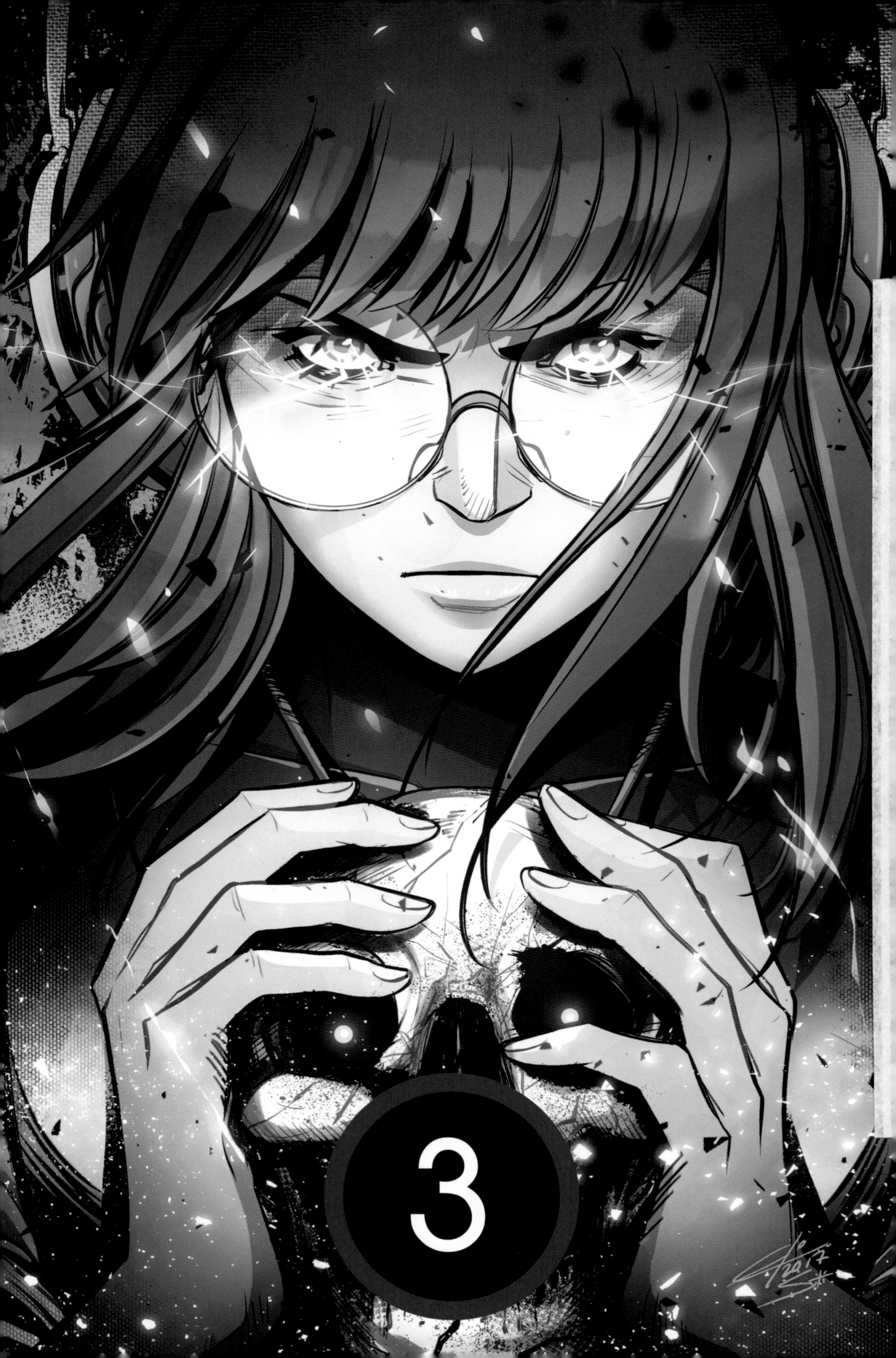
3

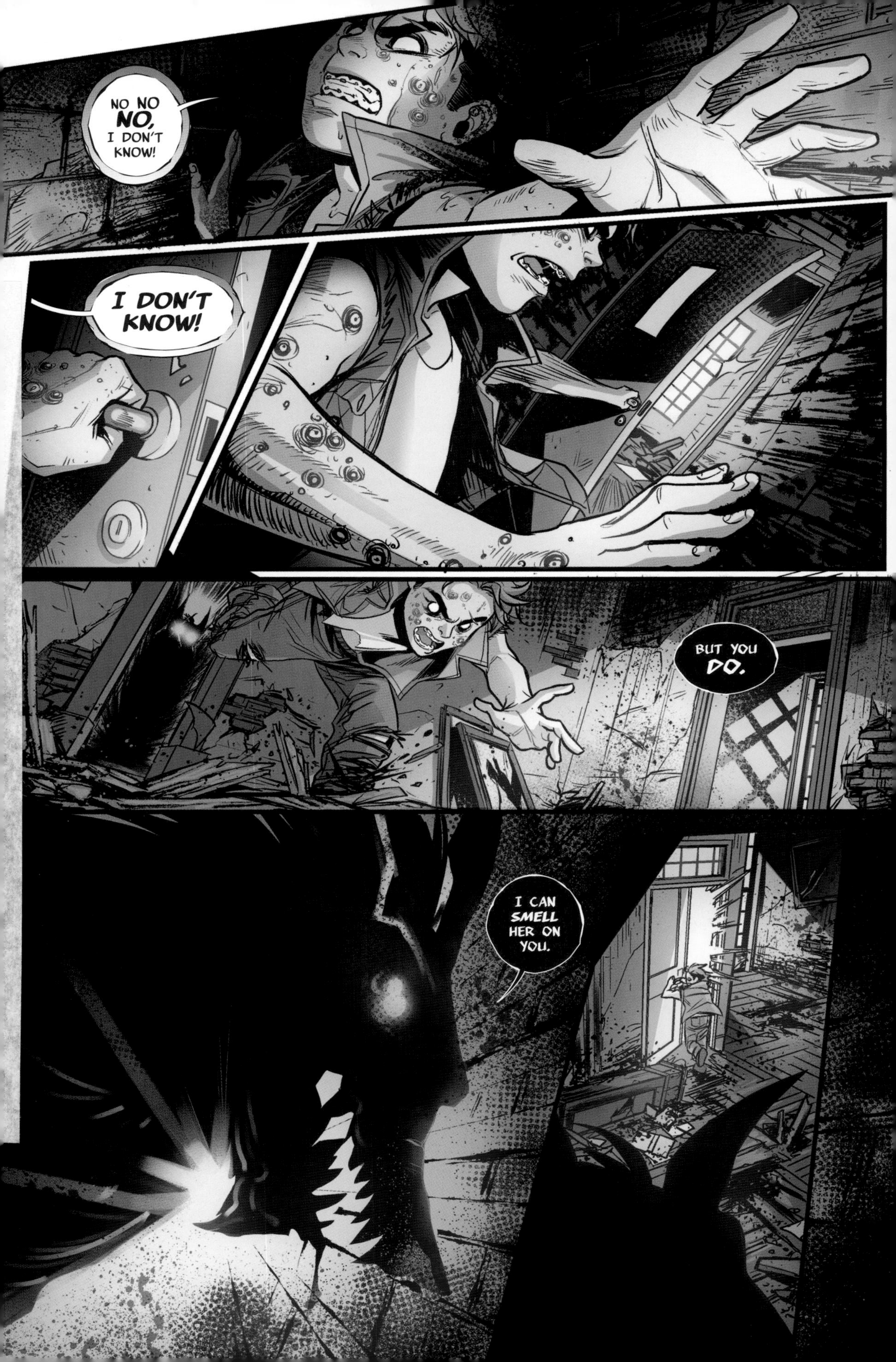
NO NO **NO,** I DON'T KNOW!
I DON'T KNOW!
BUT YOU **DO.**
I CAN **SMELL** HER ON YOU.

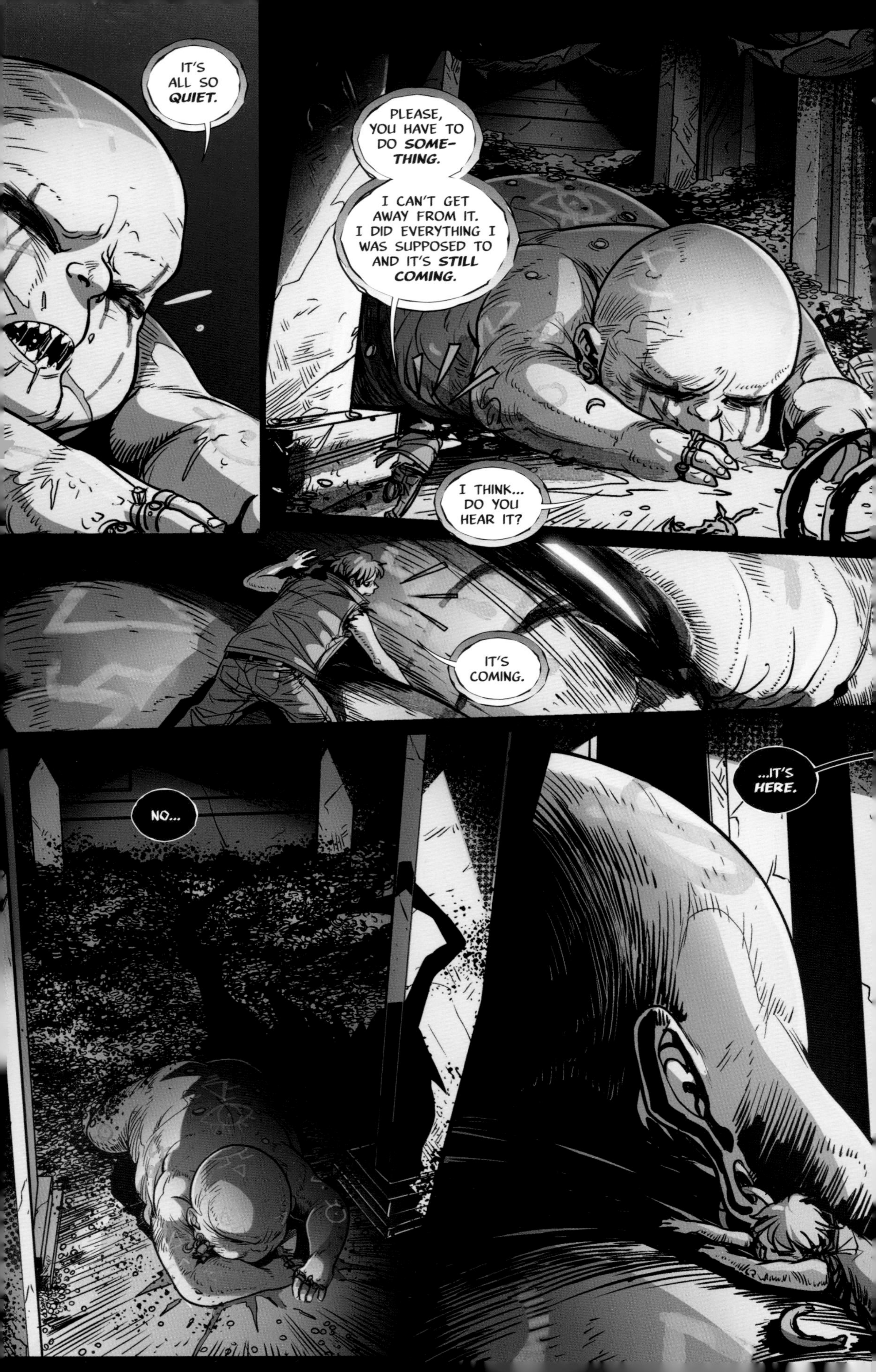
IT'S ALL SO QUIET.
PLEASE, YOU HAVE TO DO SOME-THING.
I CAN'T GET AWAY FROM IT. I DID EVERYTHING I WAS SUPPOSED TO AND IT'S STILL COMING.
I THINK... DO YOU HEAR IT?
IT'S COMING.
NO...
...IT'S HERE.

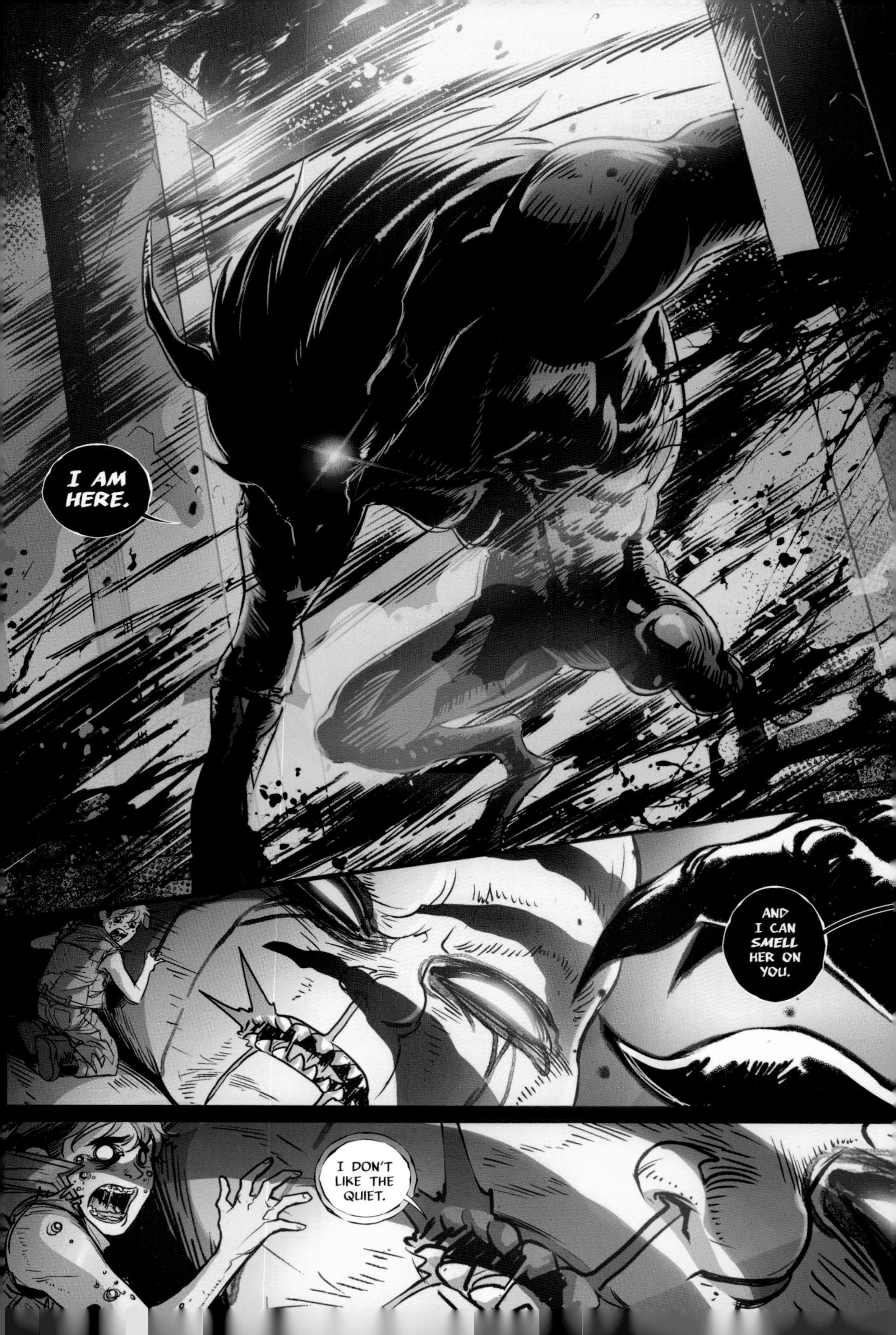
I AM HERE.
AND I CAN SMELL HER ON YOU.
I DON'T LIKE THE QUIET.

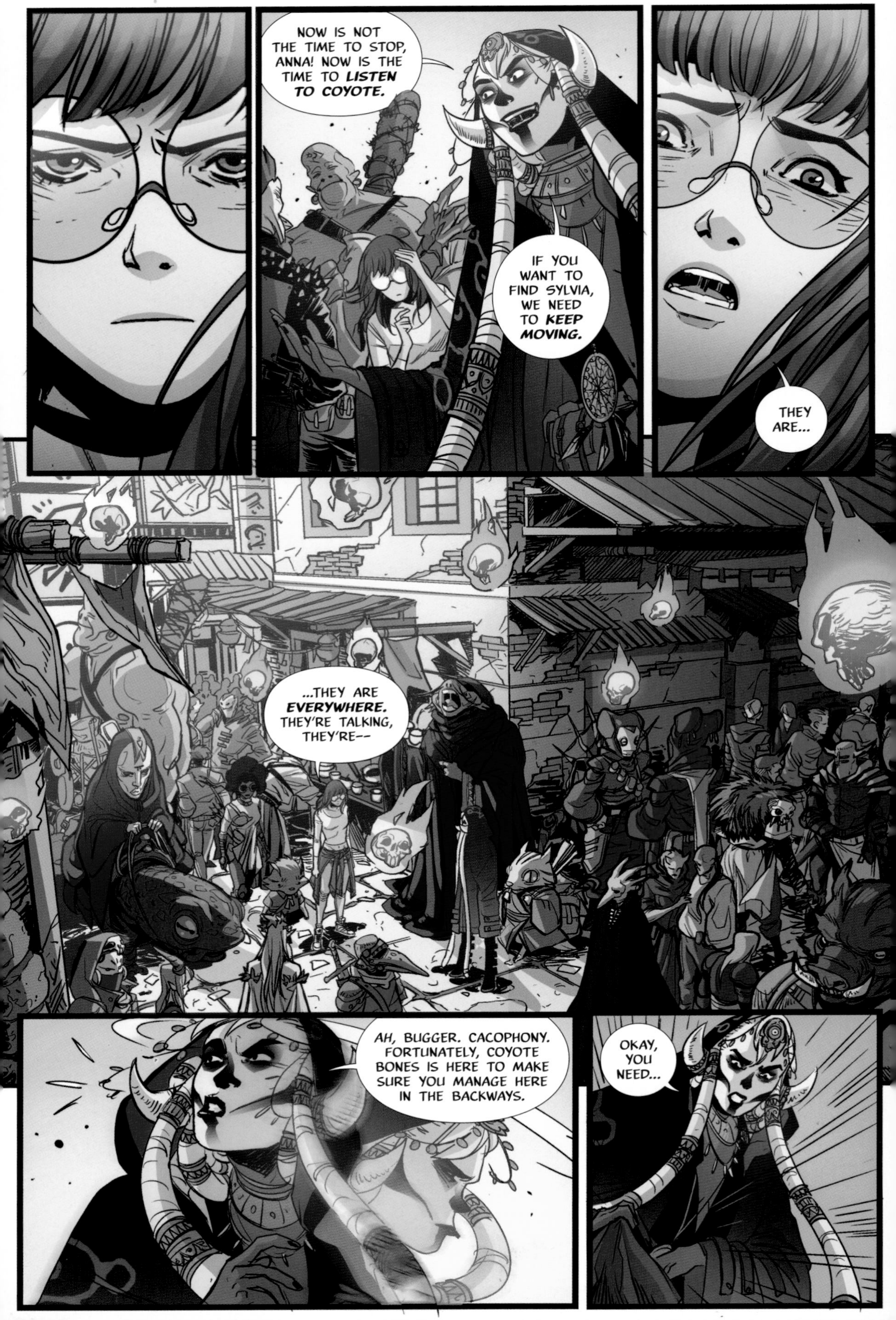
NOW IS NOT THE TIME TO STOP, ANNA! NOW IS THE TIME TO LISTEN TO COYOTE.
IF YOU WANT TO FIND SYLVIA, WE NEED TO KEEP MOVING.
THEY ARE...
...THEY ARE EVERYWHERE. THEY'RE TALKING, THEY'RE--
AH, BUGGER. CACOPHONY. FORTUNATELY, COYOTE BONES IS HERE TO MAKE SURE YOU MANAGE HERE IN THE BACKWAYS.
OKAY, YOU NEED...

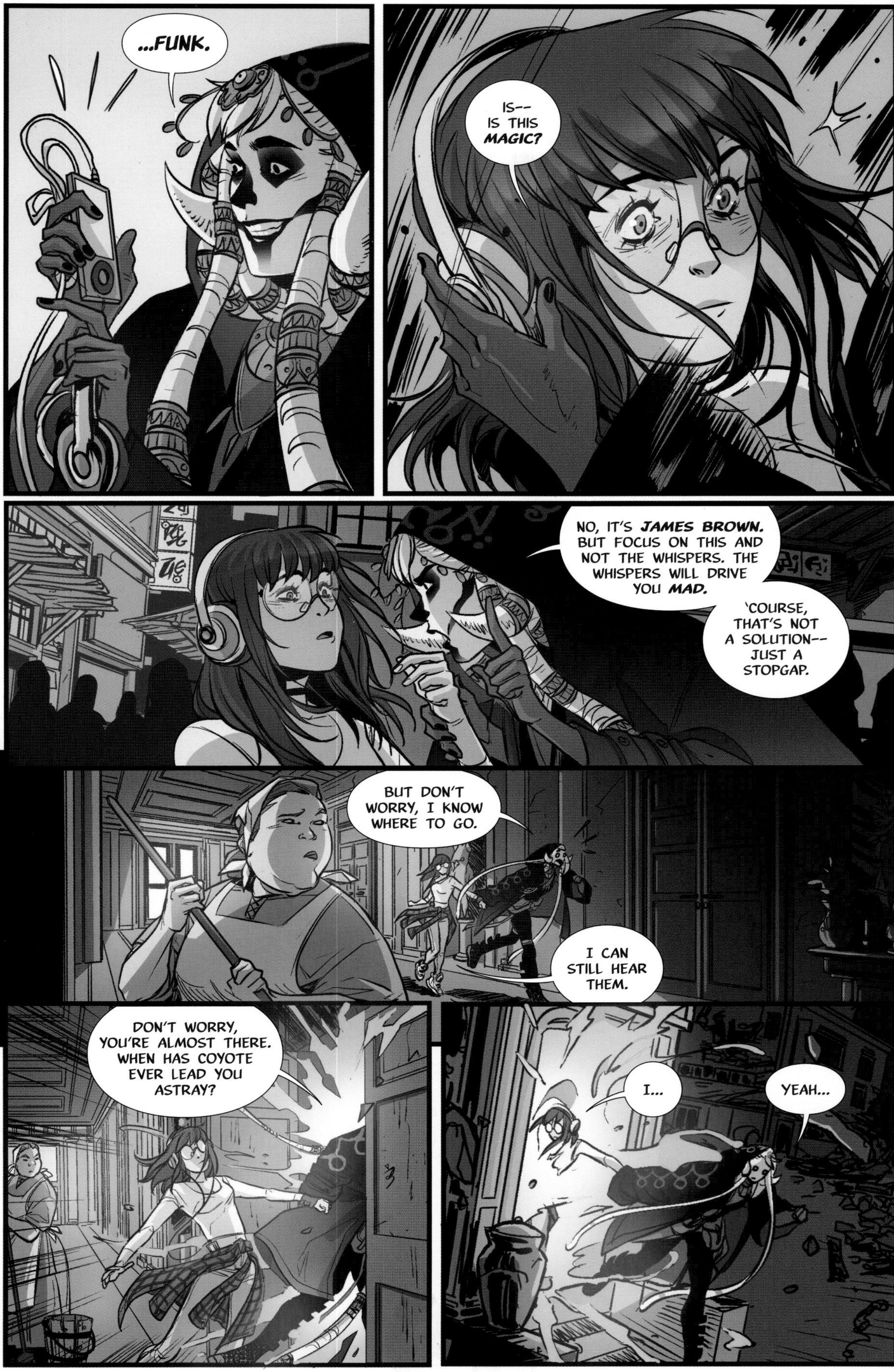
...FUNK.
IS--
IS THIS MAGIC?
NO, IT'S JAMES BROWN. BUT FOCUS ON THIS AND NOT THE WHISPERS. THE WHISPERS WILL DRIVE YOU MAD.
'COURSE, THAT'S NOT A SOLUTION-- JUST A STOPGAP.
BUT DON'T WORRY, I KNOW WHERE TO GO.
I CAN STILL HEAR THEM.
DON'T WORRY, YOU'RE ALMOST THERE. WHEN HAS COYOTE EVER LEAD YOU ASTRAY?
I...
YEAH...

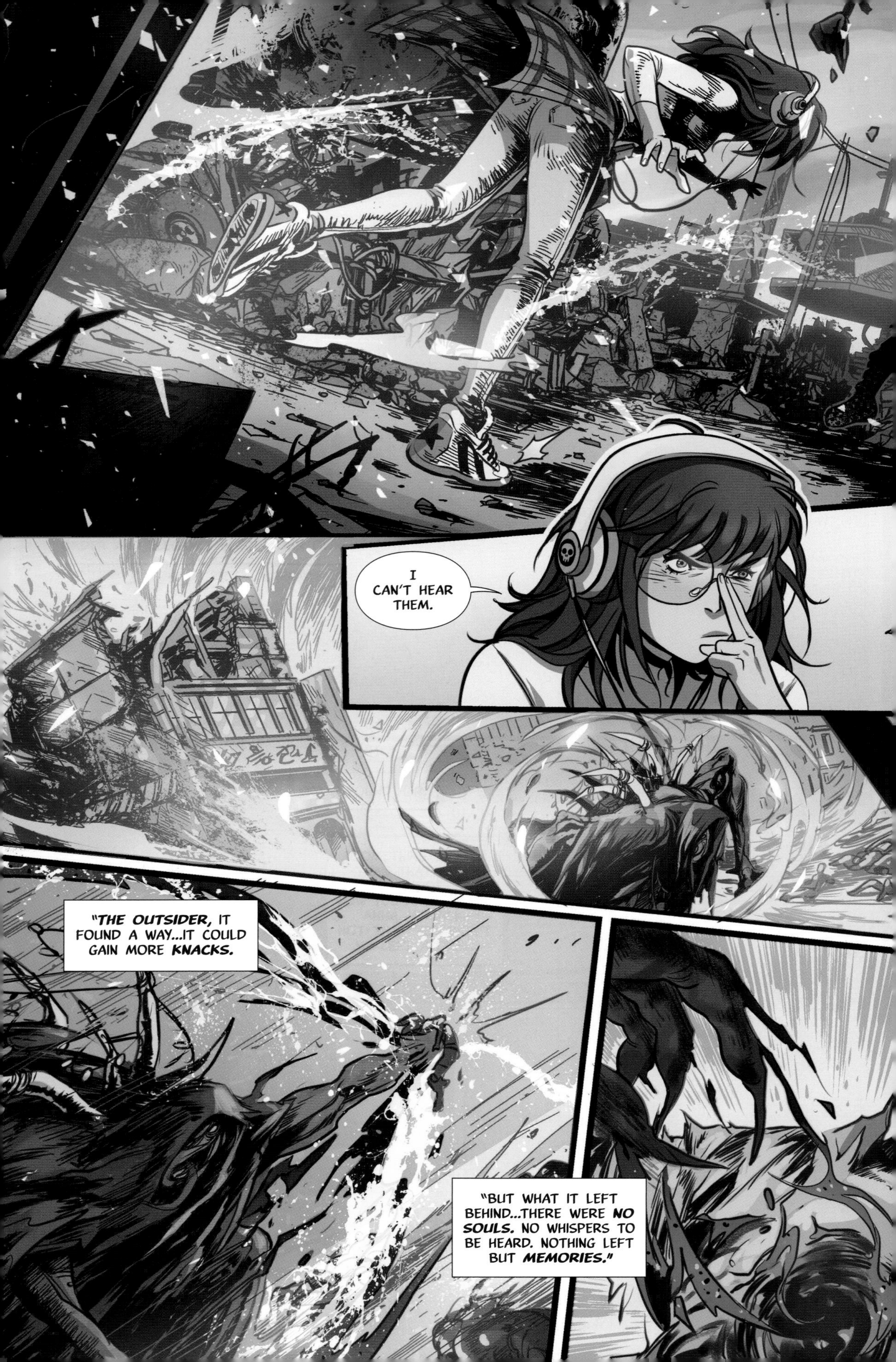
I CAN'T HEAR THEM.
"THE OUTSIDER, IT FOUND A WAY...IT COULD GAIN MORE KNACKS.
"BUT WHAT IT LEFT BEHIND...THERE WERE NO SOULS. NO WHISPERS TO BE HEARD. NOTHING LEFT BUT MEMORIES."

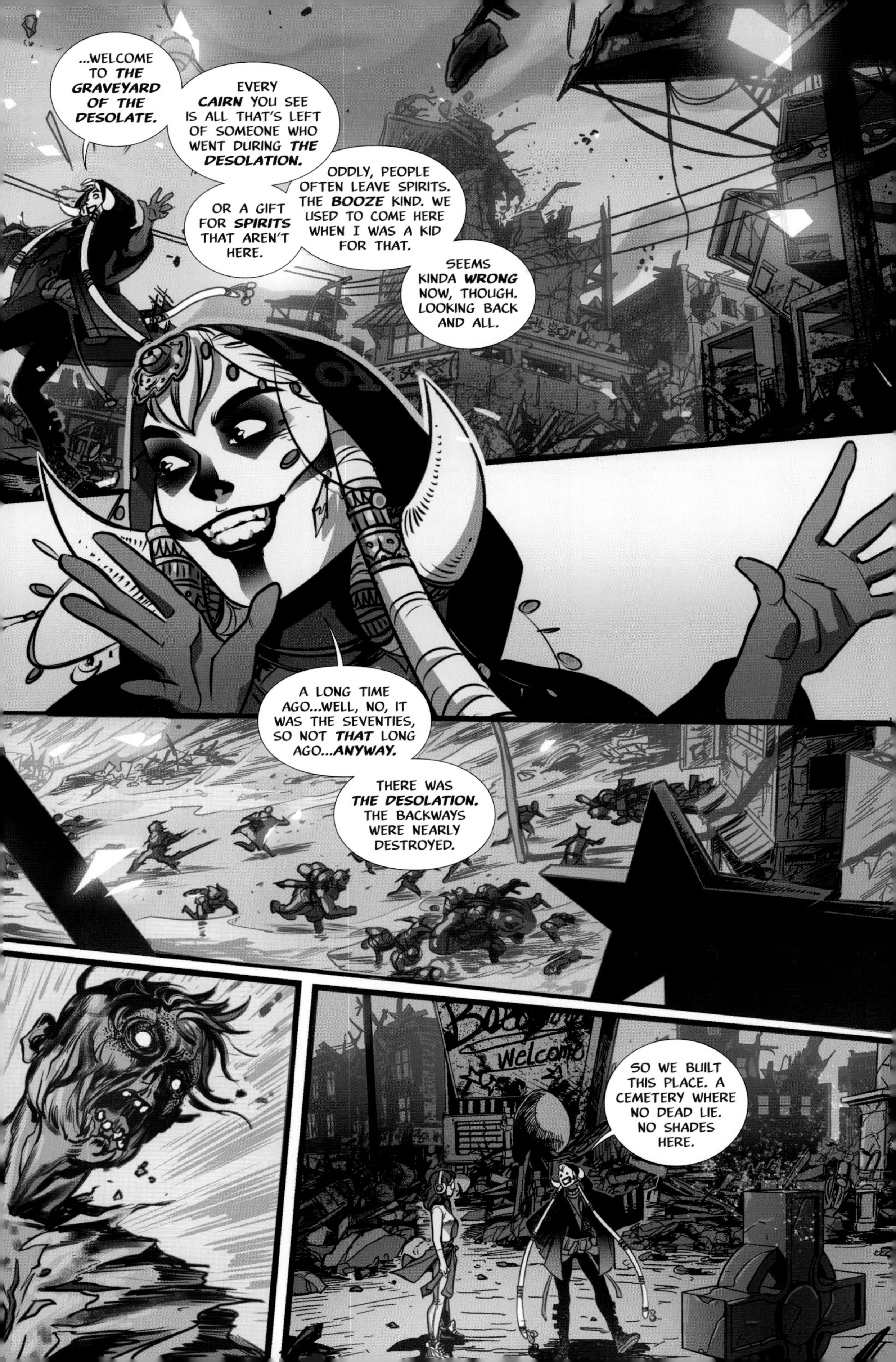
...WELCOME TO THE GRAVEYARD OF THE DESOLATE.
EVERY CAIRN YOU SEE IS ALL THAT'S LEFT OF SOMEONE WHO WENT DURING THE DESOLATION.
OR A GIFT FOR SPIRITS THAT AREN'T HERE.
ODDLY, PEOPLE OFTEN LEAVE SPIRITS. THE BOOZE KIND. WE USED TO COME HERE WHEN I WAS A KID FOR THAT.
SEEMS KINDA WRONG NOW, THOUGH. LOOKING BACK AND ALL.
A LONG TIME AGO...WELL, NO, IT WAS THE SEVENTIES, SO NOT THAT LONG AGO...ANYWAY.
THERE WAS THE DESOLATION. THE BACKWAYS WERE NEARLY DESTROYED.
Welcome
SO WE BUILT THIS PLACE. A CEMETERY WHERE NO DEAD LIE. NO SHADES HERE.

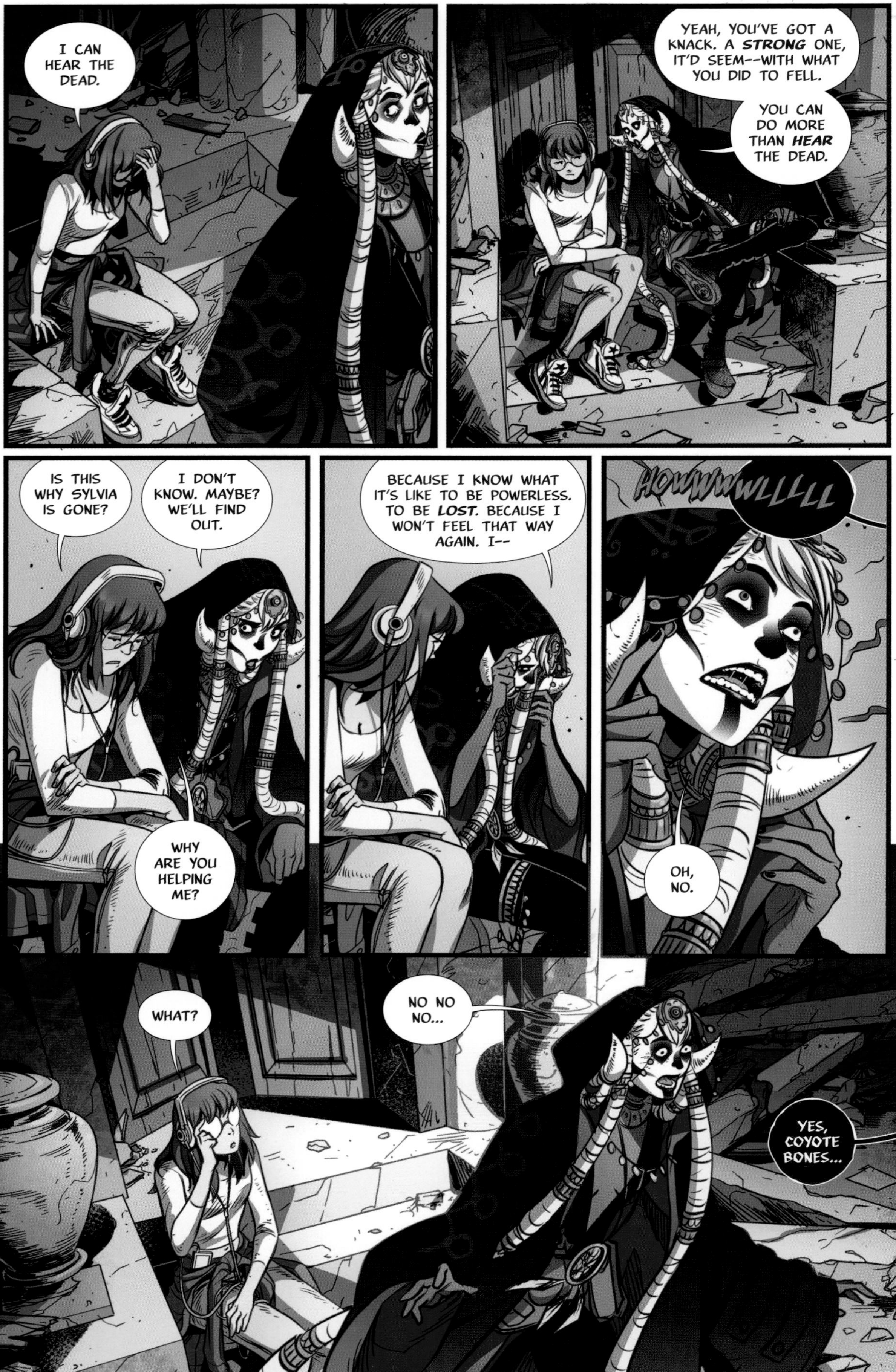
I CAN HEAR THE DEAD.
YEAH, YOU'VE GOT A KNACK. A STRONG ONE, IT'D SEEM--WITH WHAT YOU DID TO FELL.
YOU CAN DO MORE THAN HEAR THE DEAD.
IS THIS WHY SYLVIA IS GONE?
I DON'T KNOW. MAYBE? WE'LL FIND OUT.
WHY ARE YOU HELPING ME?
BECAUSE I KNOW WHAT IT'S LIKE TO BE POWERLESS. TO BE LOST. BECAUSE I WON'T FEEL THAT WAY AGAIN. I--
HOWWWWLLLLL
OH, NO.
WHAT?
NO NO NO...
YES, COYOTE BONES...

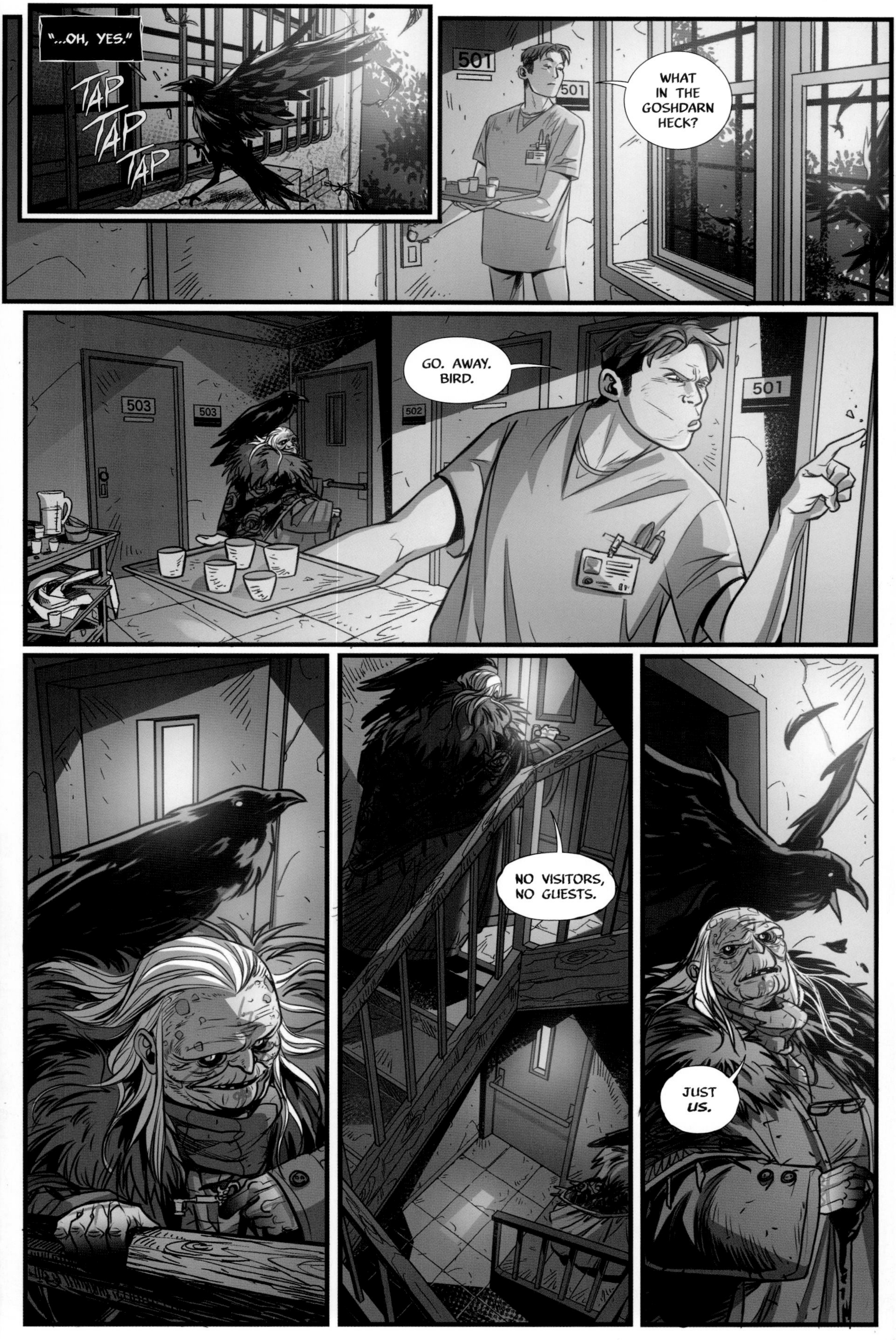
"...OH, YES."
TAP
TAP
TAP
501
501
WHAT IN THE GOSHDARN HECK?
503
503
502
501
GO. AWAY. BIRD.
NO VISITORS, NO GUESTS.
JUST US.

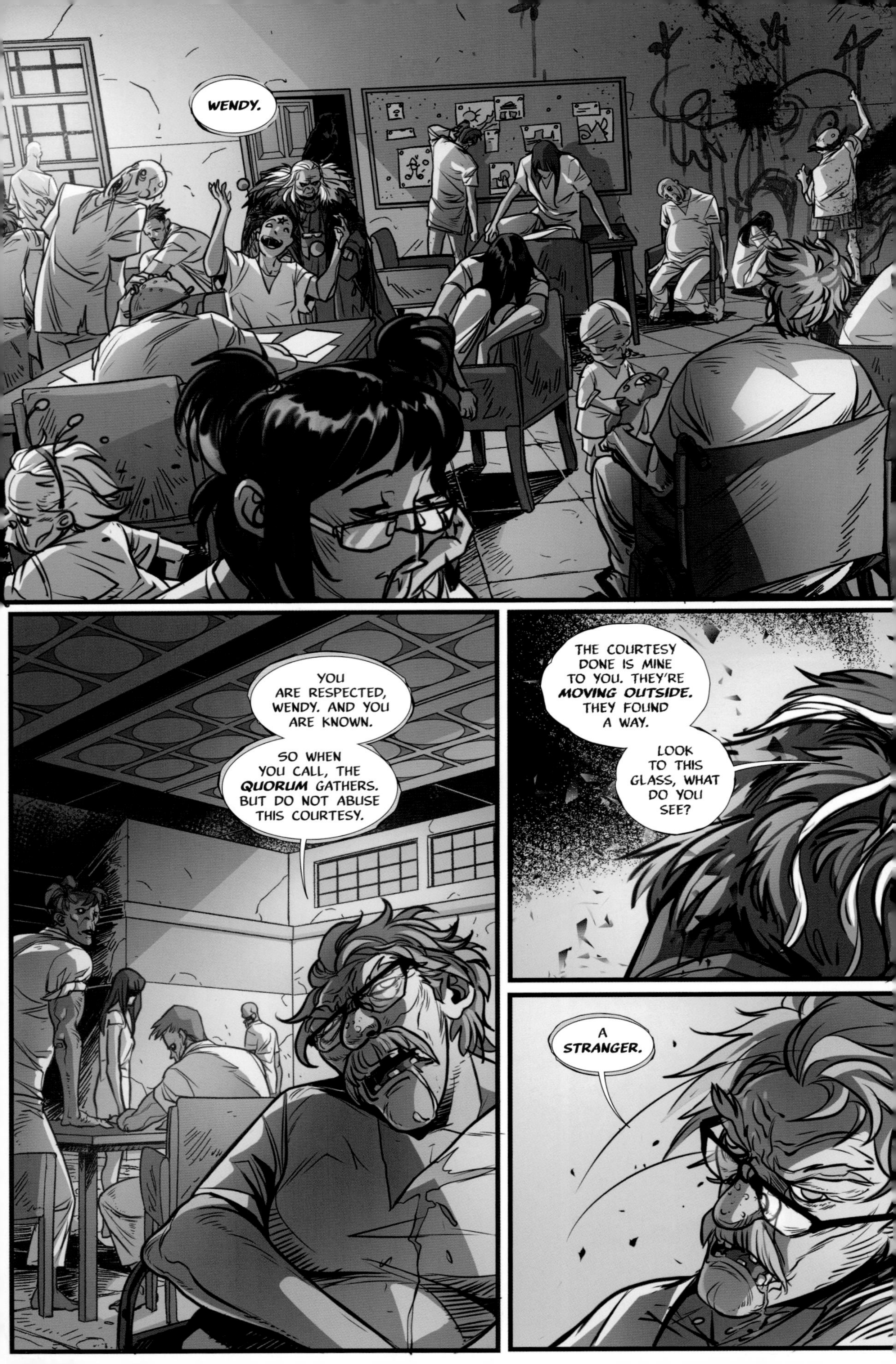
WENDY.
YOU ARE RESPECTED, WENDY. AND YOU ARE KNOWN.
SO WHEN YOU CALL, THE QUORUM GATHERS. BUT DO NOT ABUSE THIS COURTESY.
THE COURTESY DONE IS MINE TO YOU. THEY'RE MOVING OUTSIDE. THEY FOUND A WAY.
LOOK TO THIS GLASS, WHAT DO YOU SEE?
A STRANGER.

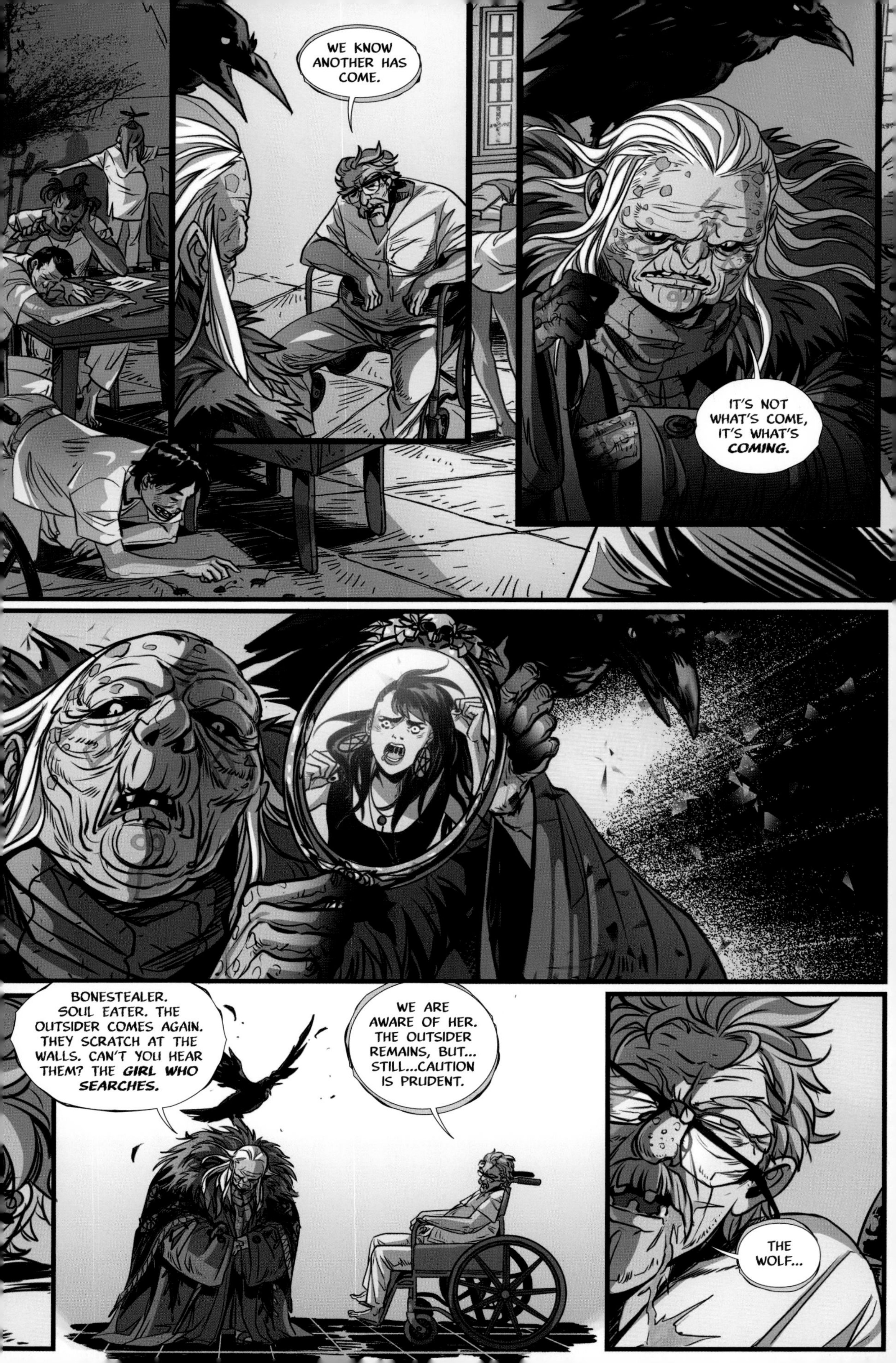
WE KNOW ANOTHER HAS COME.
IT'S NOT WHAT'S COME, IT'S WHAT'S **COMING.**
BONESTEALER. SOUL EATER. THE OUTSIDER COMES AGAIN. THEY SCRATCH AT THE WALLS. CAN'T YOU HEAR THEM? THE ***GIRL WHO SEARCHES.***
WE ARE AWARE OF HER. THE OUTSIDER REMAINS, BUT... STILL...CAUTION IS PRUDENT.
THE WOLF...

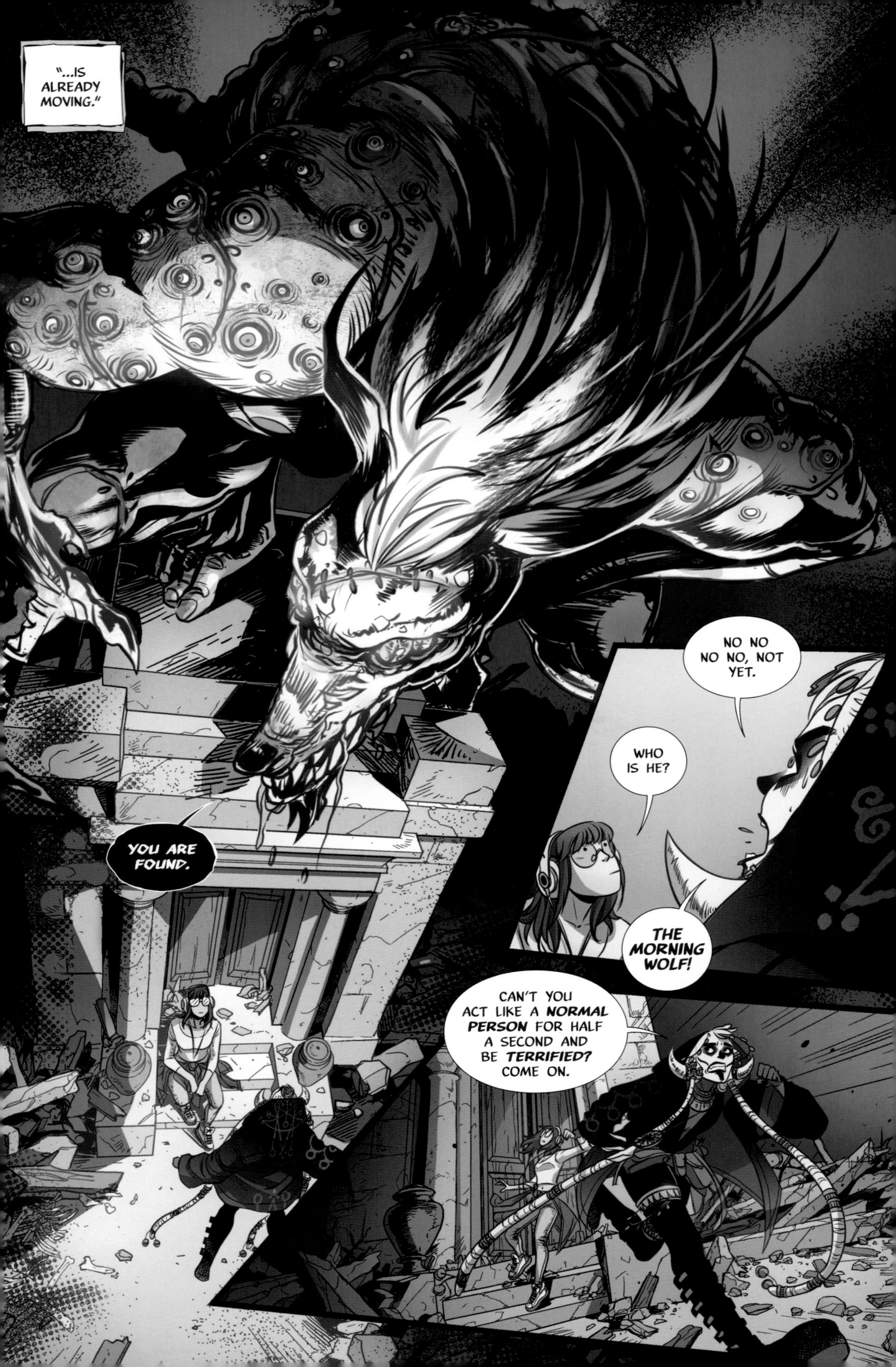
"...IS ALREADY MOVING."
YOU ARE FOUND.
NO NO NO NO, NOT YET.
WHO IS HE?
THE MORNING WOLF!
CAN'T YOU ACT LIKE A NORMAL PERSON FOR HALF A SECOND AND BE TERRIFIED? COME ON.

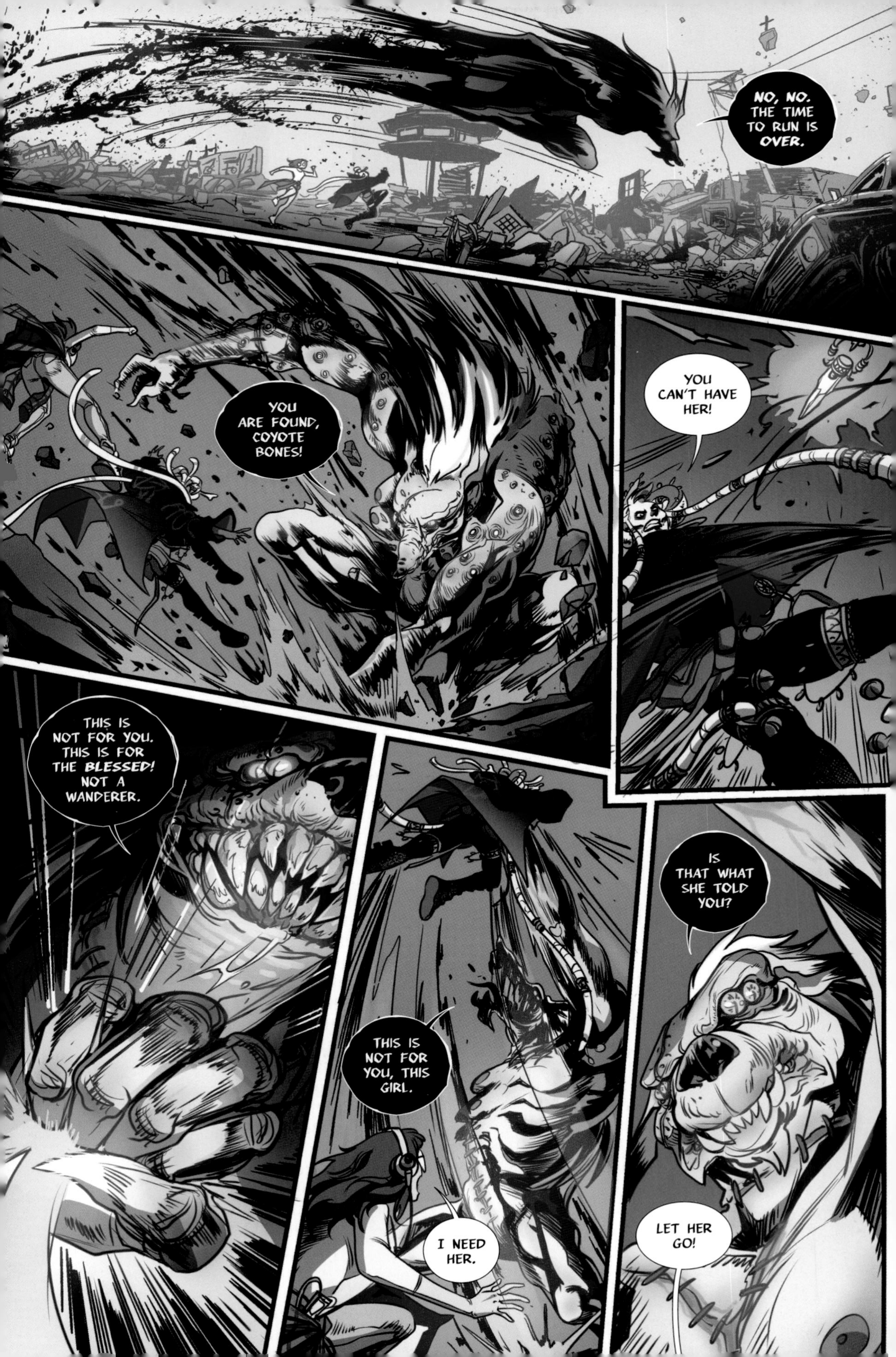
NO, NO. THE TIME TO RUN IS OVER.
YOU ARE FOUND, COYOTE BONES!
YOU CAN'T HAVE HER!
THIS IS NOT FOR YOU. THIS IS FOR THE BLESSED! NOT A WANDERER.
THIS IS NOT FOR YOU, THIS GIRL.
I NEED HER.
IS THAT WHAT SHE TOLD YOU?
LET HER GO!

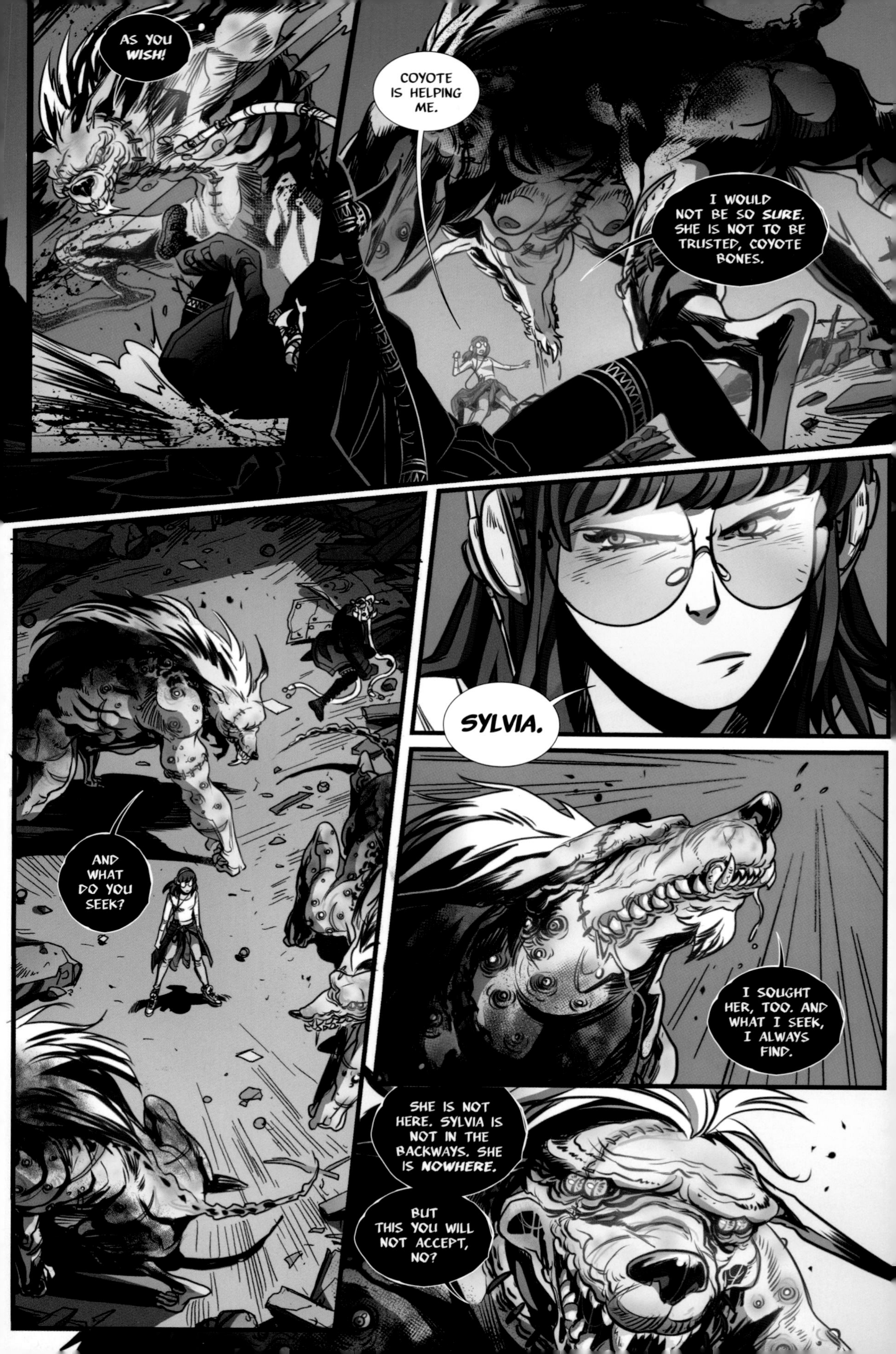
AS YOU WISH!
COYOTE IS HELPING ME.
I WOULD NOT BE SO SURE. SHE IS NOT TO BE TRUSTED, COYOTE BONES.
AND WHAT DO YOU SEEK?
SYLVIA.
I SOUGHT HER, TOO. AND WHAT I SEEK, I ALWAYS FIND.
SHE IS NOT HERE. SYLVIA IS NOT IN THE BACKWAYS. SHE IS NOWHERE.
BUT THIS YOU WILL NOT ACCEPT, NO?

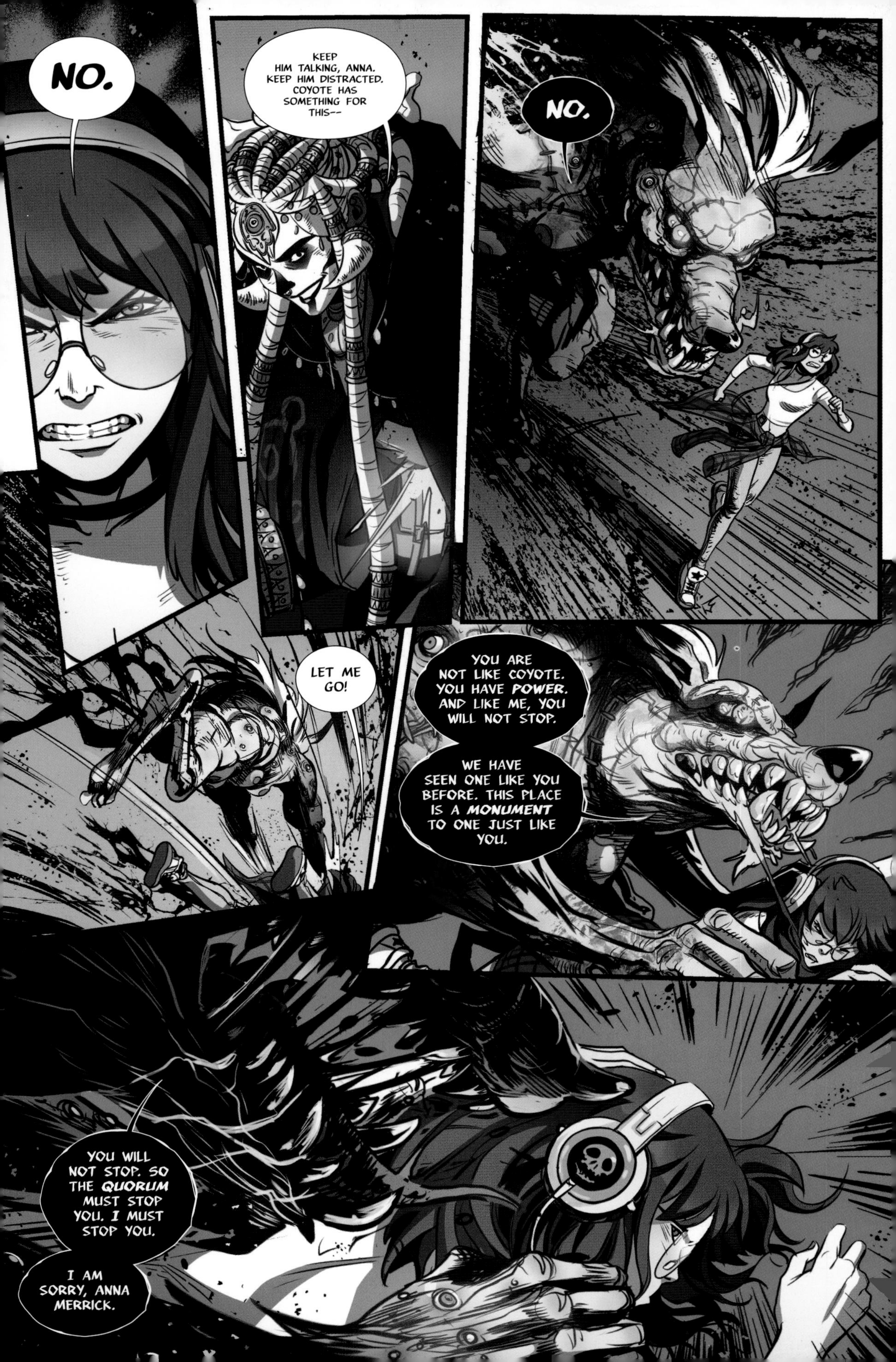
NO.
KEEP HIM TALKING, ANNA. KEEP HIM DISTRACTED. COYOTE HAS SOMETHING FOR THIS--
NO.
LET ME GO!
YOU ARE NOT LIKE COYOTE. YOU HAVE POWER. AND LIKE ME, YOU WILL NOT STOP.
WE HAVE SEEN ONE LIKE YOU BEFORE. THIS PLACE IS A MONUMENT TO ONE JUST LIKE YOU.
YOU WILL NOT STOP. SO THE QUORUM MUST STOP YOU. I MUST STOP YOU.
I AM SORRY, ANNA MERRICK.

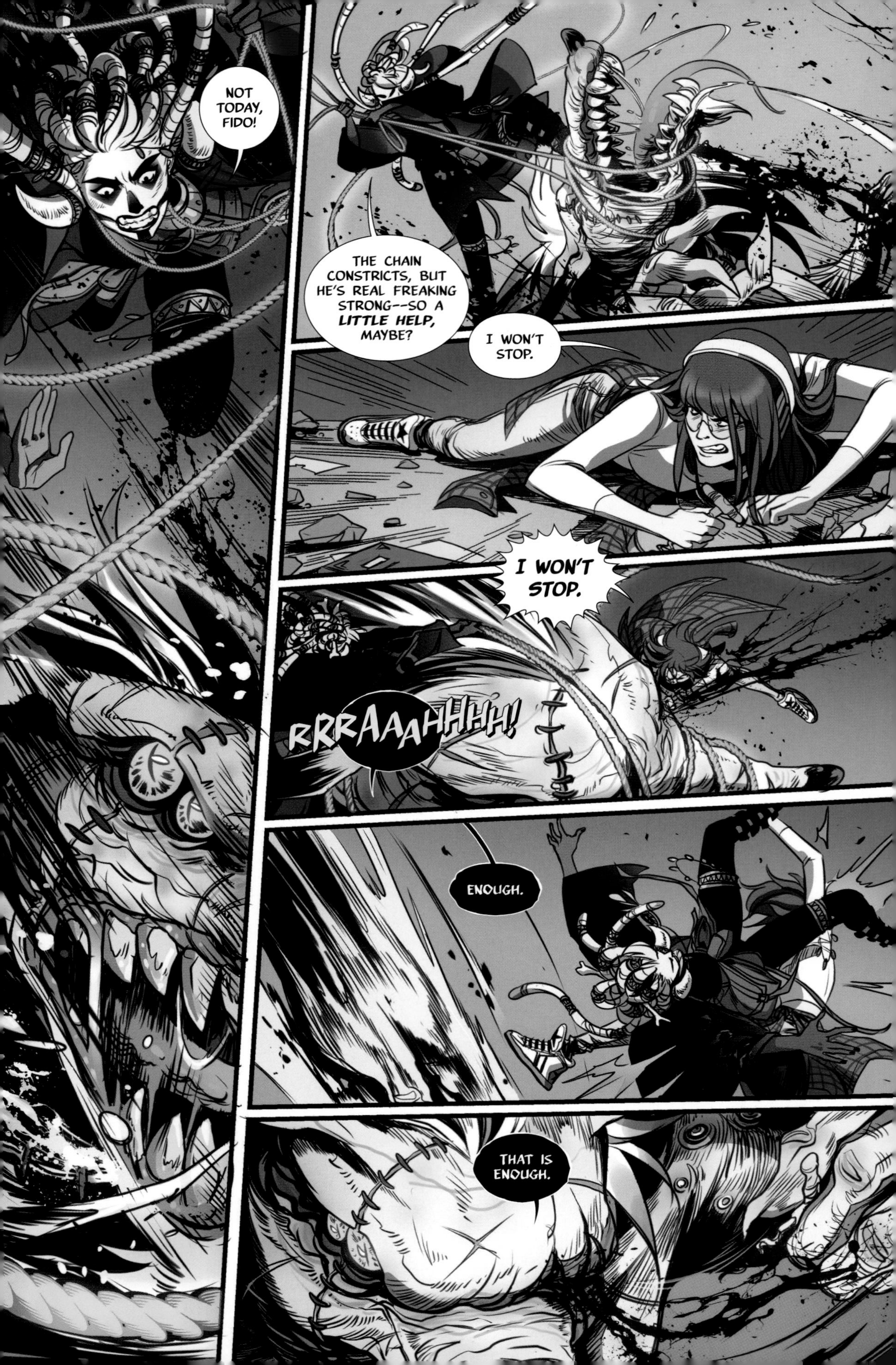
NOT TODAY, FIDO!
THE CHAIN CONSTRICTS, BUT HE'S REAL FREAKING STRONG--SO A LITTLE HELP, MAYBE?
I WON'T STOP.
I WON'T STOP.
RRRAAAAHHHH!
ENOUGH.
THAT IS ENOUGH.

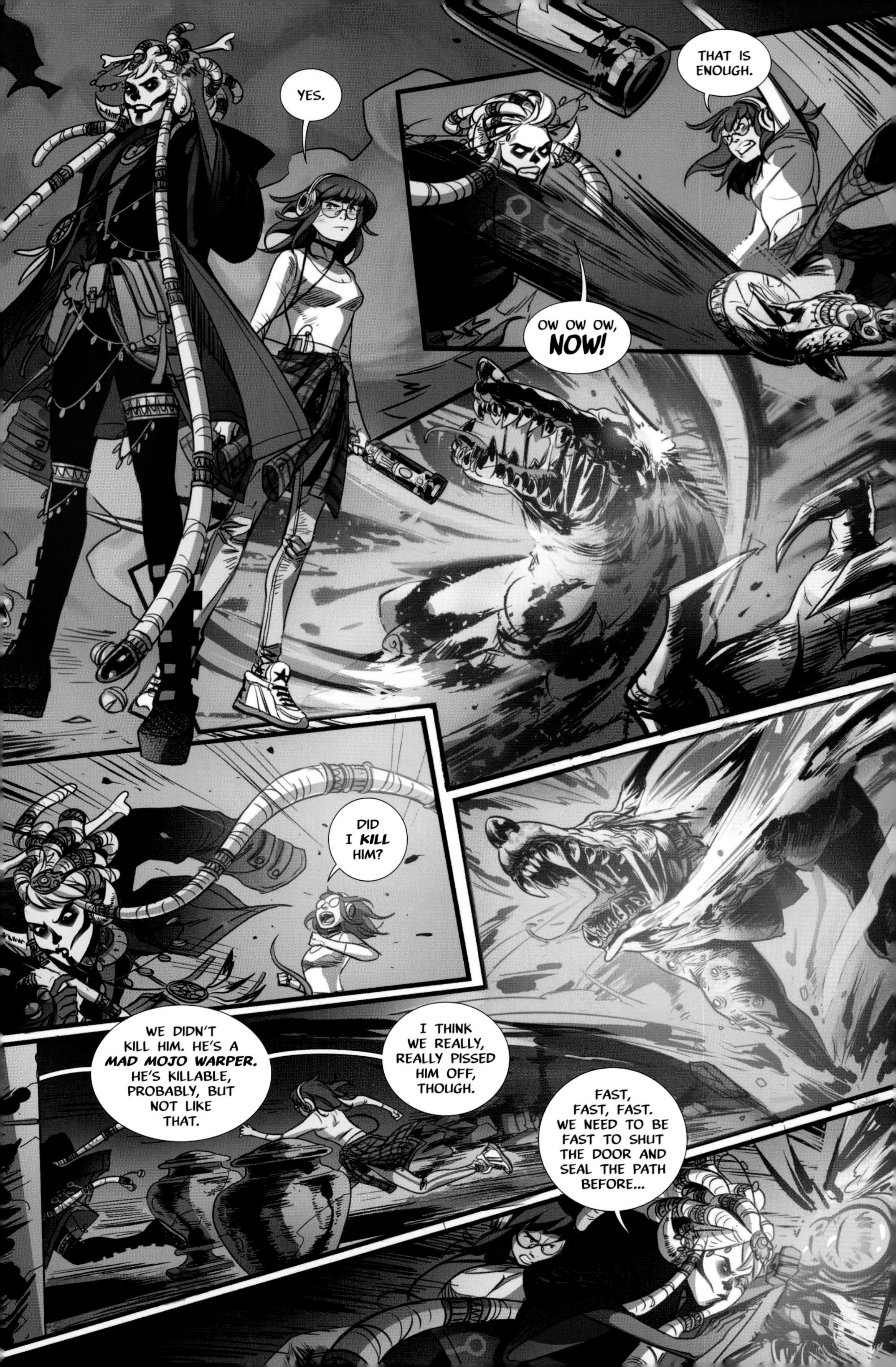
YES.
THAT IS ENOUGH.
OW OW OW, **NOW!**
DID I **KILL** HIM?
WE DIDN'T KILL HIM. HE'S A ***MAD MOJO WARPER.*** HE'S KILLABLE, PROBABLY, BUT NOT LIKE THAT.
I THINK WE REALLY, REALLY PISSED HIM OFF, THOUGH.
FAST, FAST, FAST. WE NEED TO BE FAST TO SHUT THE DOOR AND SEAL THE PATH BEFORE...

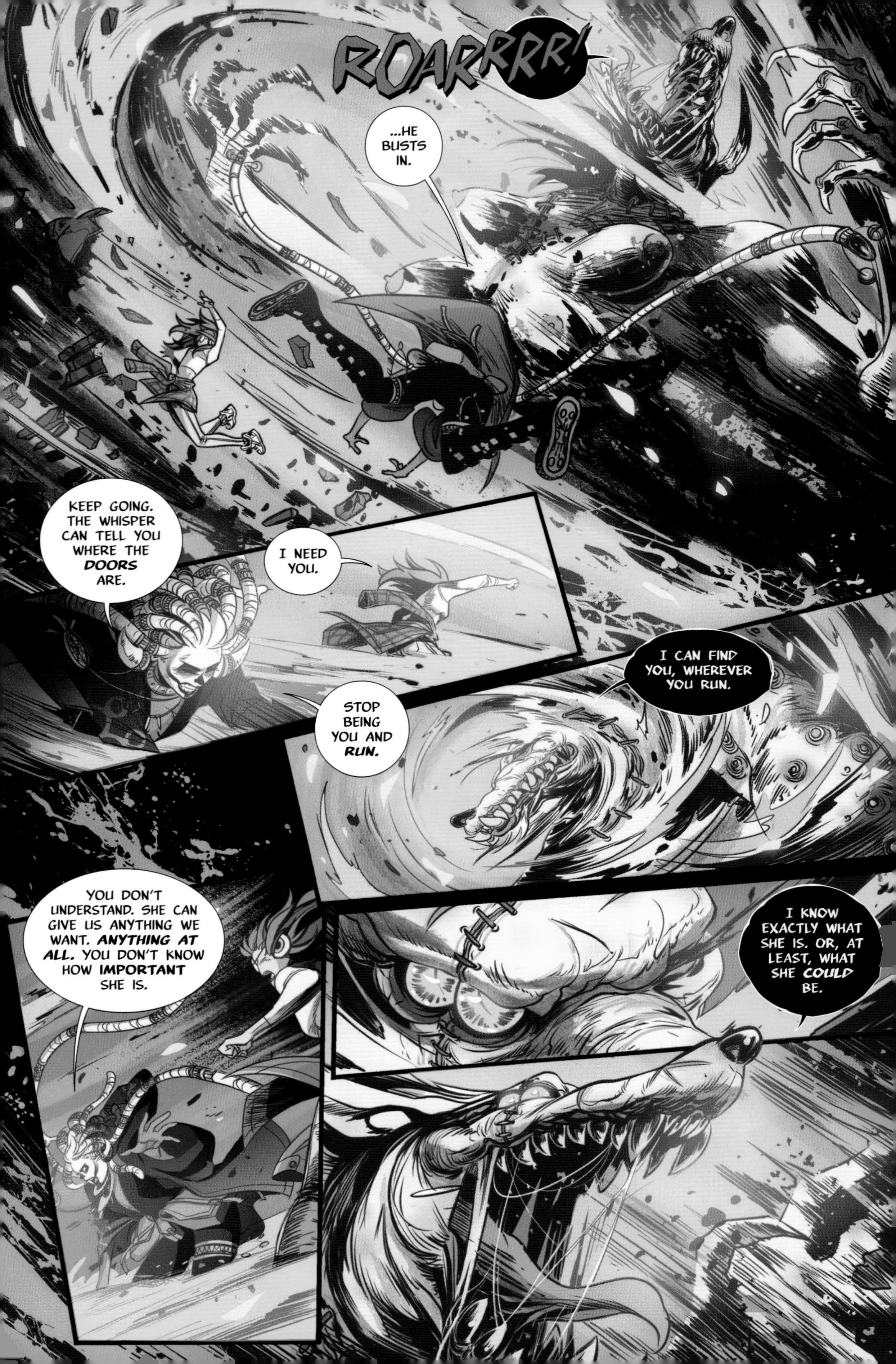
ROARRRR!
...HE BUSTS IN.
KEEP GOING. THE WHISPER CAN TELL YOU WHERE THE DOORS ARE.
I NEED YOU.
I CAN FIND YOU, WHEREVER YOU RUN.
STOP BEING YOU AND RUN.
YOU DON'T UNDERSTAND. SHE CAN GIVE US ANYTHING WE WANT. ANYTHING AT ALL. YOU DON'T KNOW HOW IMPORTANT SHE IS.
I KNOW EXACTLY WHAT SHE IS. OR, AT LEAST, WHAT SHE COULD BE.

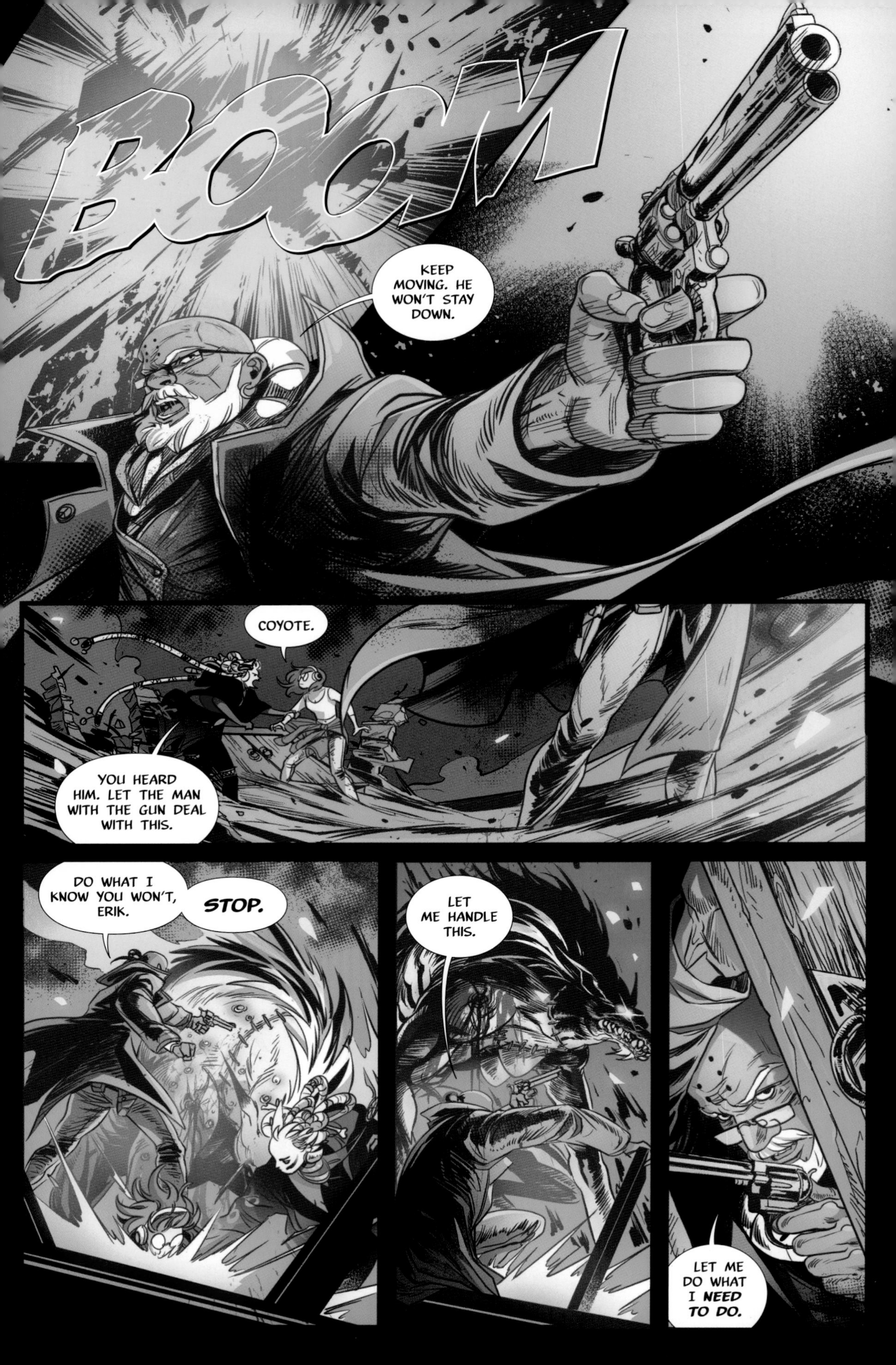
BOOM
KEEP MOVING. HE WON'T STAY DOWN.
COYOTE.
YOU HEARD HIM. LET THE MAN WITH THE GUN DEAL WITH THIS.
DO WHAT I KNOW YOU WON'T, ERIK.
STOP.
LET ME HANDLE THIS.
LET ME DO WHAT I NEED TO DO.

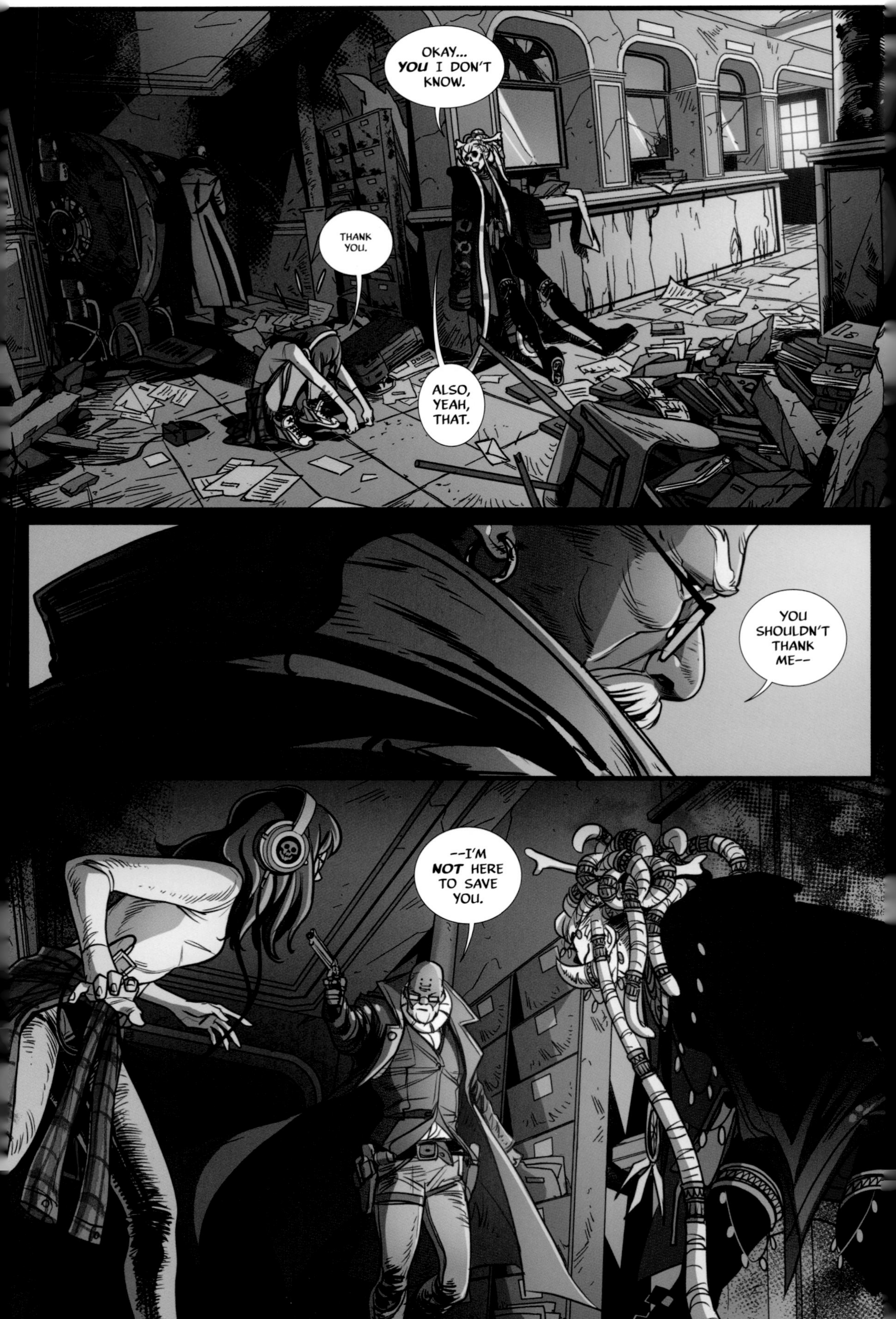
OKAY... **YOU** I DON'T KNOW.
THANK YOU.
ALSO, YEAH, THAT.
YOU SHOULDN'T THANK ME--
--I'M **NOT** HERE TO SAVE YOU.

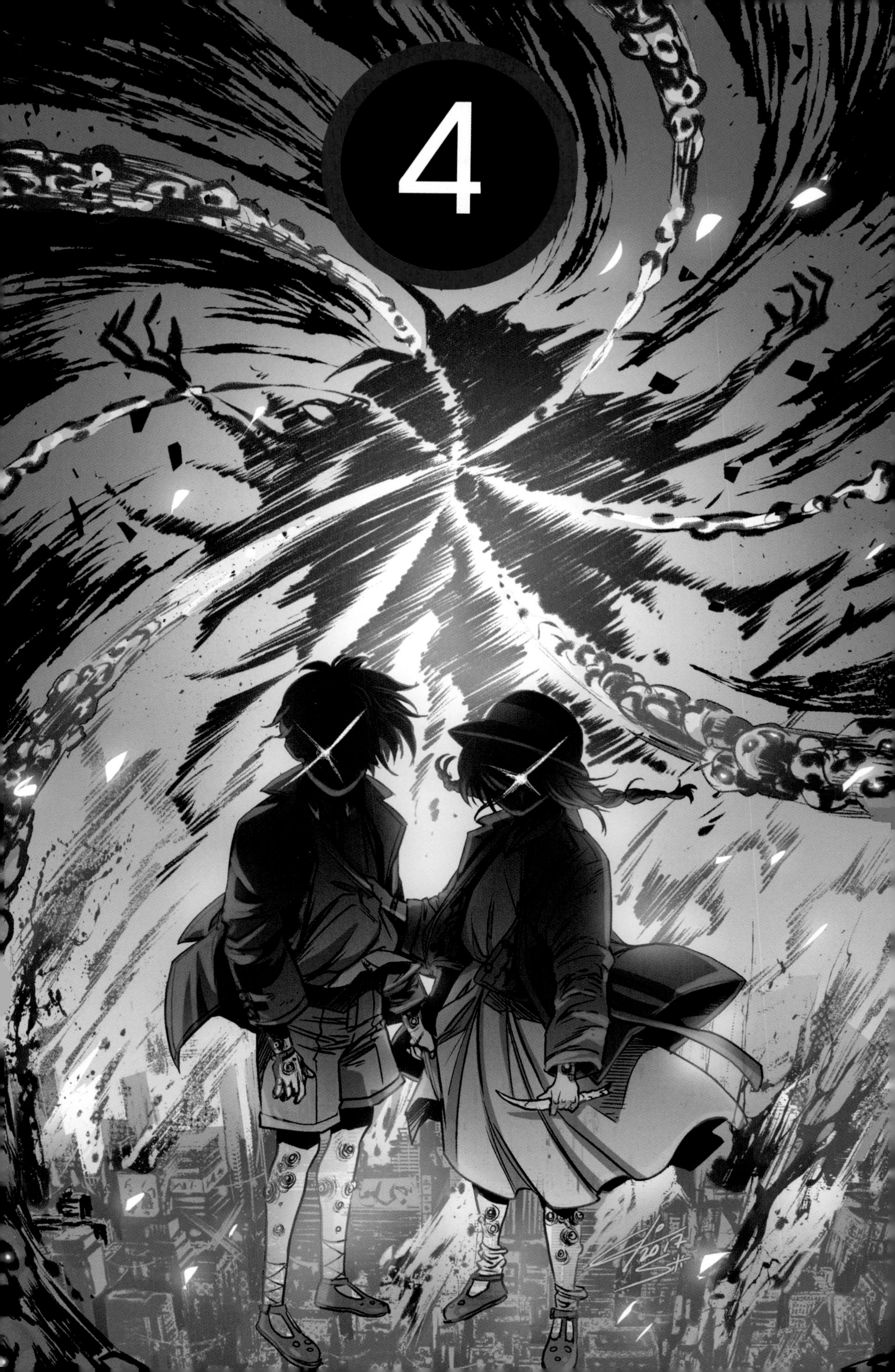
4

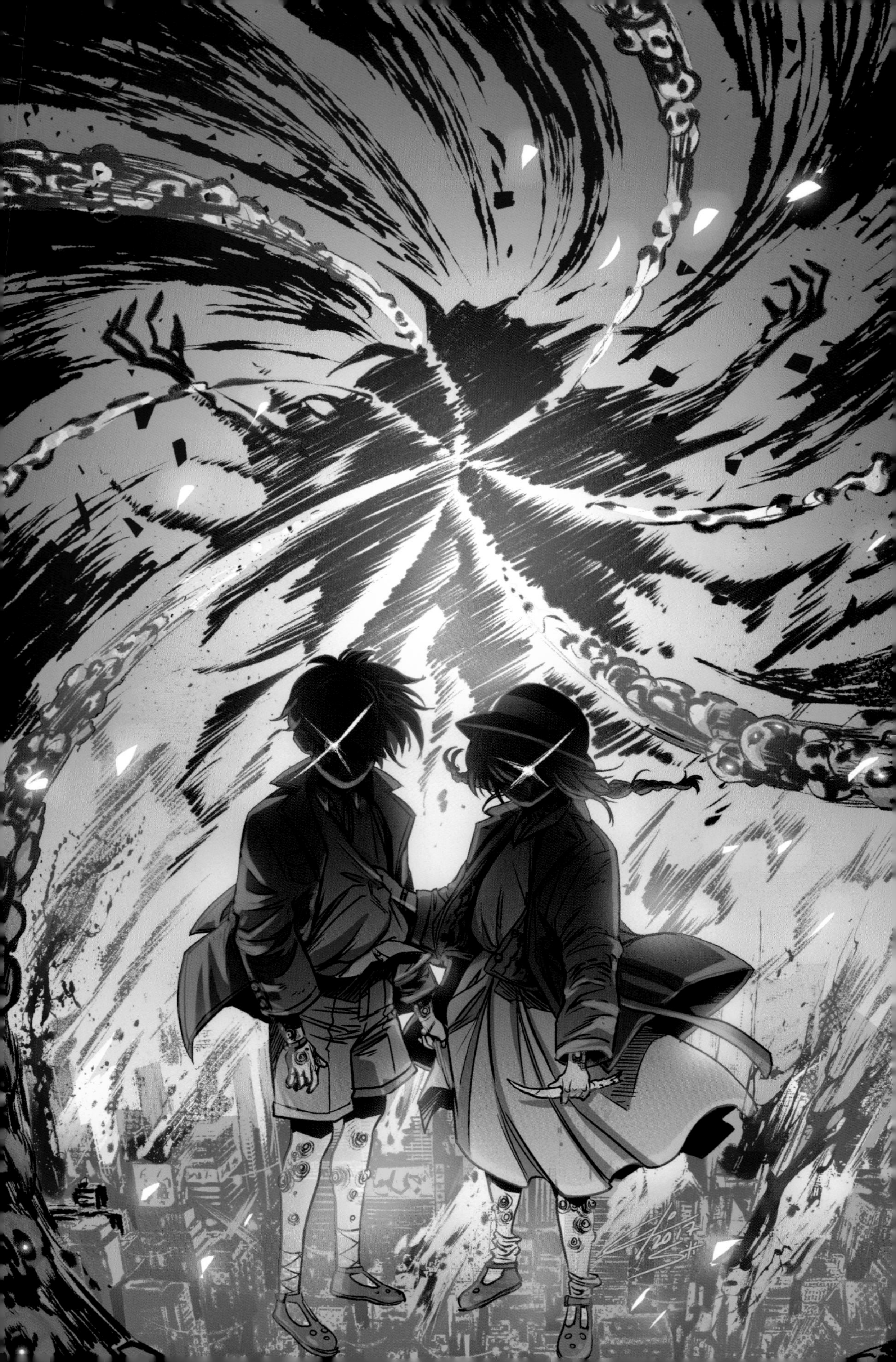

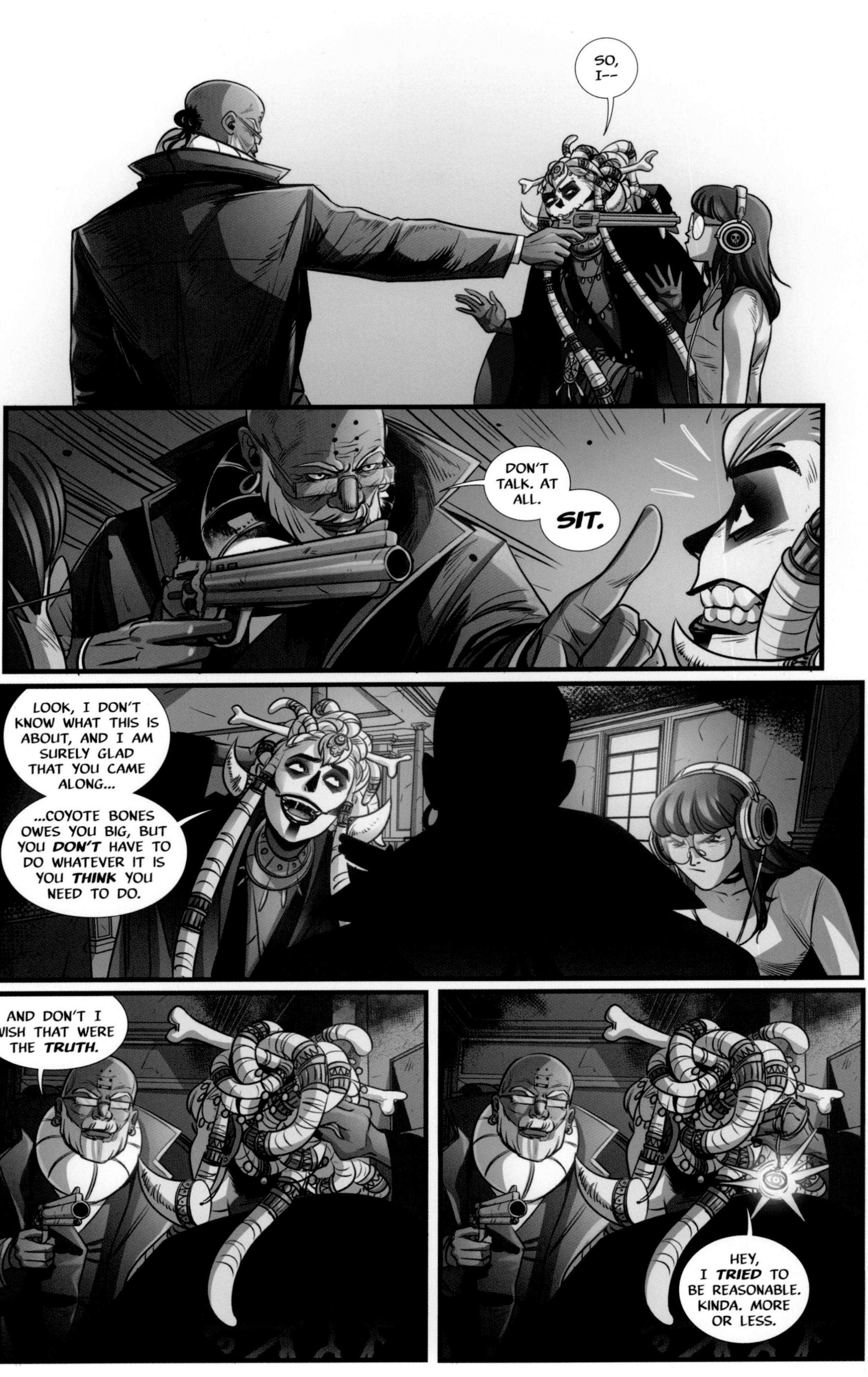
SO, I--
DON'T TALK. AT ALL.
SIT.
LOOK, I DON'T KNOW WHAT THIS IS ABOUT, AND I AM SURELY GLAD THAT YOU CAME ALONG...
...COYOTE BONES OWES YOU BIG, BUT YOU DON'T HAVE TO DO WHATEVER IT IS YOU THINK YOU NEED TO DO.
AND DON'T I WISH THAT WERE THE TRUTH.
HEY, I TRIED TO BE REASONABLE. KINDA. MORE OR LESS.

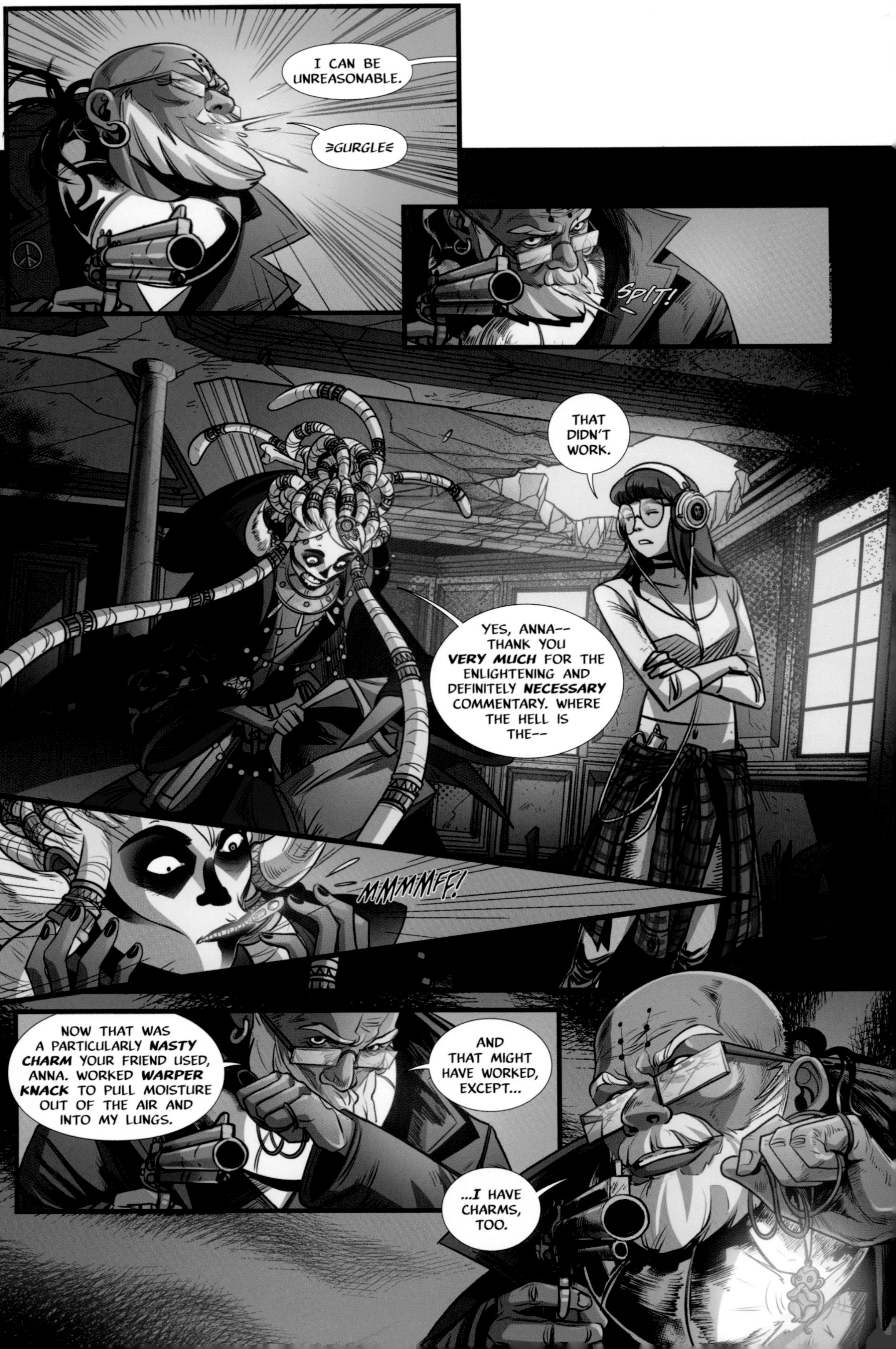
I CAN BE UNREASONABLE.
≡GURGLE≡
SPIT!
THAT DIDN'T WORK.
YES, ANNA-- THANK YOU VERY MUCH FOR THE ENLIGHTENING AND DEFINITELY NECESSARY COMMENTARY. WHERE THE HELL IS THE--
MMMMFF!
NOW THAT WAS A PARTICULARLY NASTY CHARM YOUR FRIEND USED, ANNA. WORKED WARPER KNACK TO PULL MOISTURE OUT OF THE AIR AND INTO MY LUNGS.
AND THAT MIGHT HAVE WORKED, EXCEPT...
...I HAVE CHARMS, TOO.

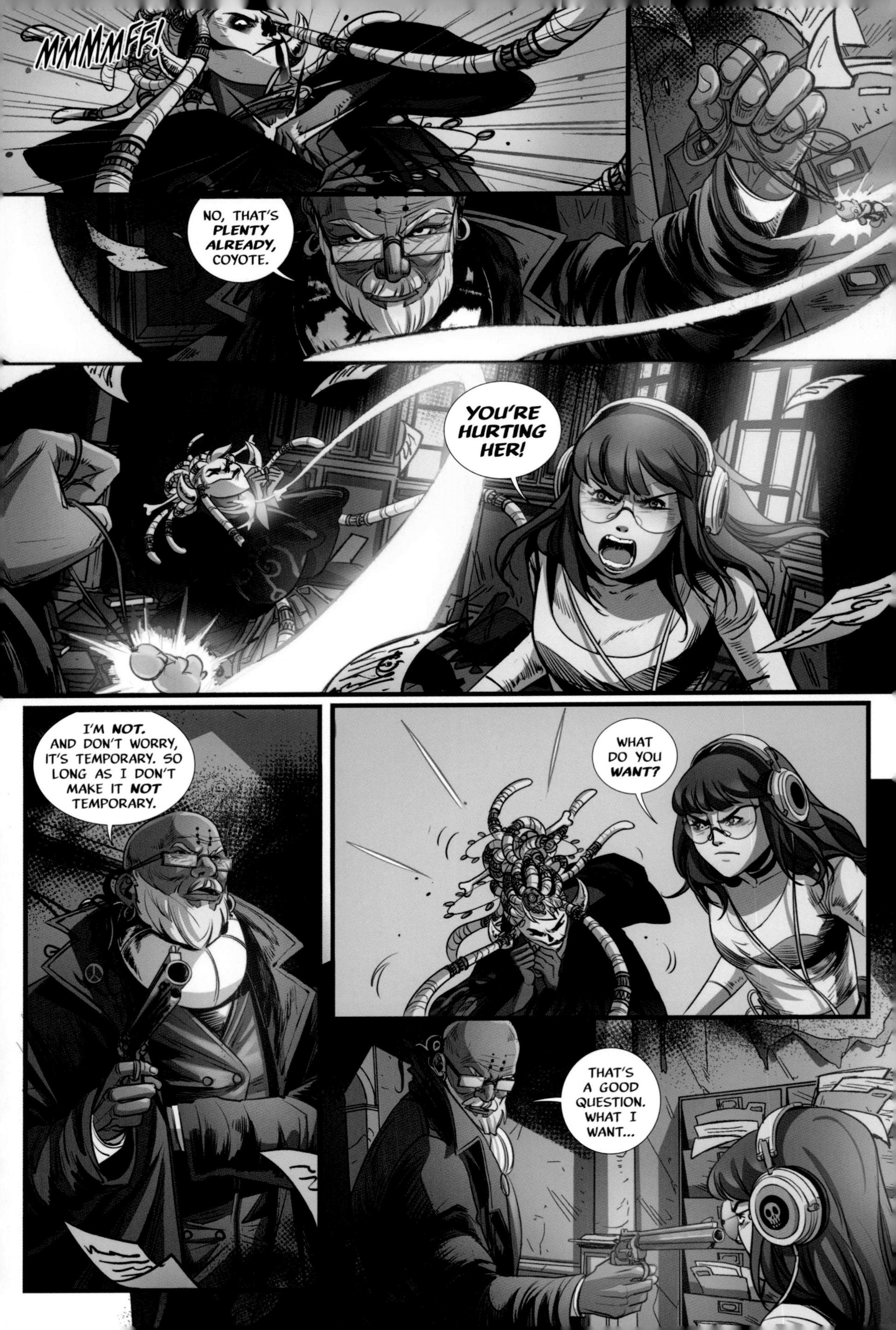
MMMMFF!
NO, THAT'S PLENTY ALREADY, COYOTE.
YOU'RE HURTING HER!
I'M NOT. AND DON'T WORRY, IT'S TEMPORARY. SO LONG AS I DON'T MAKE IT NOT TEMPORARY.
WHAT DO YOU WANT?
THAT'S A GOOD QUESTION. WHAT I WANT...

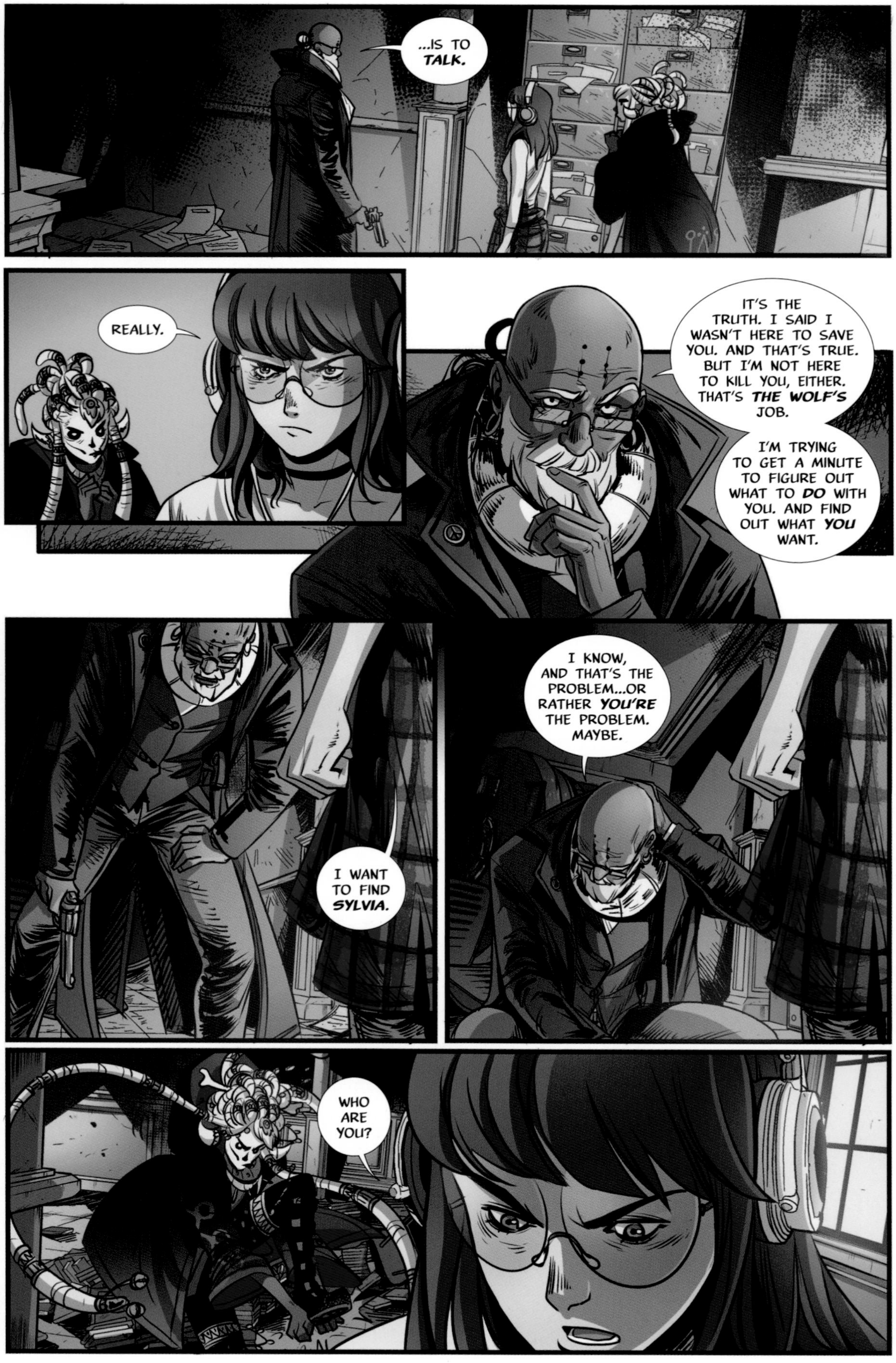
...IS TO TALK.
REALLY.
IT'S THE TRUTH. I SAID I WASN'T HERE TO SAVE YOU. AND THAT'S TRUE. BUT I'M NOT HERE TO KILL YOU, EITHER. THAT'S THE WOLF'S JOB.
I'M TRYING TO GET A MINUTE TO FIGURE OUT WHAT TO DO WITH YOU. AND FIND OUT WHAT YOU WANT.
I WANT TO FIND SYLVIA.
I KNOW, AND THAT'S THE PROBLEM...OR RATHER YOU'RE THE PROBLEM. MAYBE.
WHO ARE YOU?

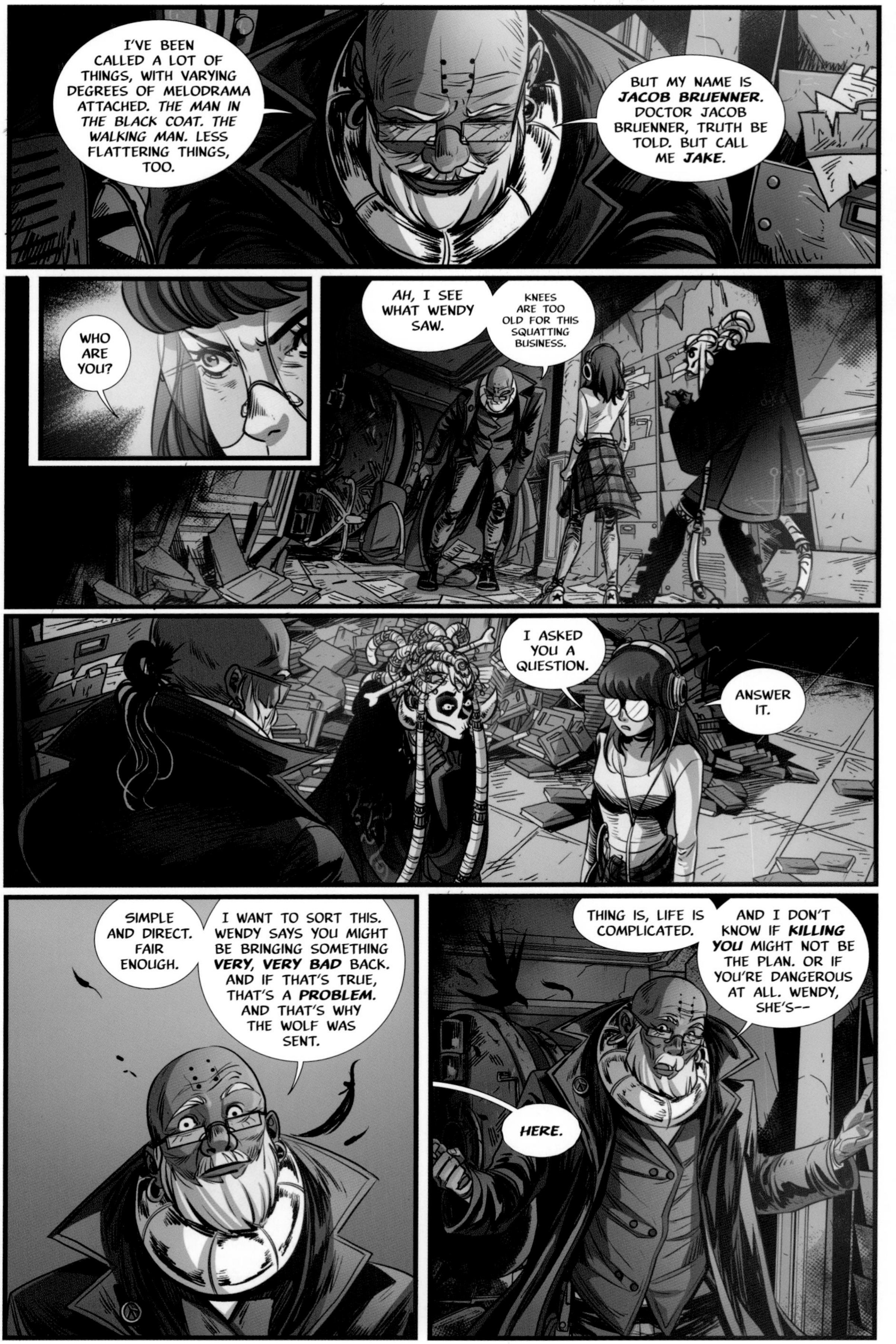
I'VE BEEN CALLED A LOT OF THINGS, WITH VARYING DEGREES OF MELODRAMA ATTACHED. *THE MAN IN THE BLACK COAT. THE WALKING MAN.* LESS FLATTERING THINGS, TOO.
BUT MY NAME IS ***JACOB BRUENNER.*** DOCTOR JACOB BRUENNER, TRUTH BE TOLD. BUT CALL ME ***JAKE.***
WHO ARE YOU?
AH, I SEE WHAT WENDY SAW.
KNEES ARE TOO OLD FOR THIS SQUATTING BUSINESS.
I ASKED YOU A QUESTION.
ANSWER IT.
SIMPLE AND DIRECT. FAIR ENOUGH.
I WANT TO SORT THIS. WENDY SAYS YOU MIGHT BE BRINGING SOMETHING ***VERY, VERY BAD*** BACK. AND IF THAT'S TRUE, THAT'S A ***PROBLEM.*** AND THAT'S WHY THE WOLF WAS SENT.
THING IS, LIFE IS COMPLICATED.
AND I DON'T KNOW IF ***KILLING YOU*** MIGHT NOT BE THE PLAN. OR IF YOU'RE DANGEROUS AT ALL. WENDY, SHE'S--
HERE.

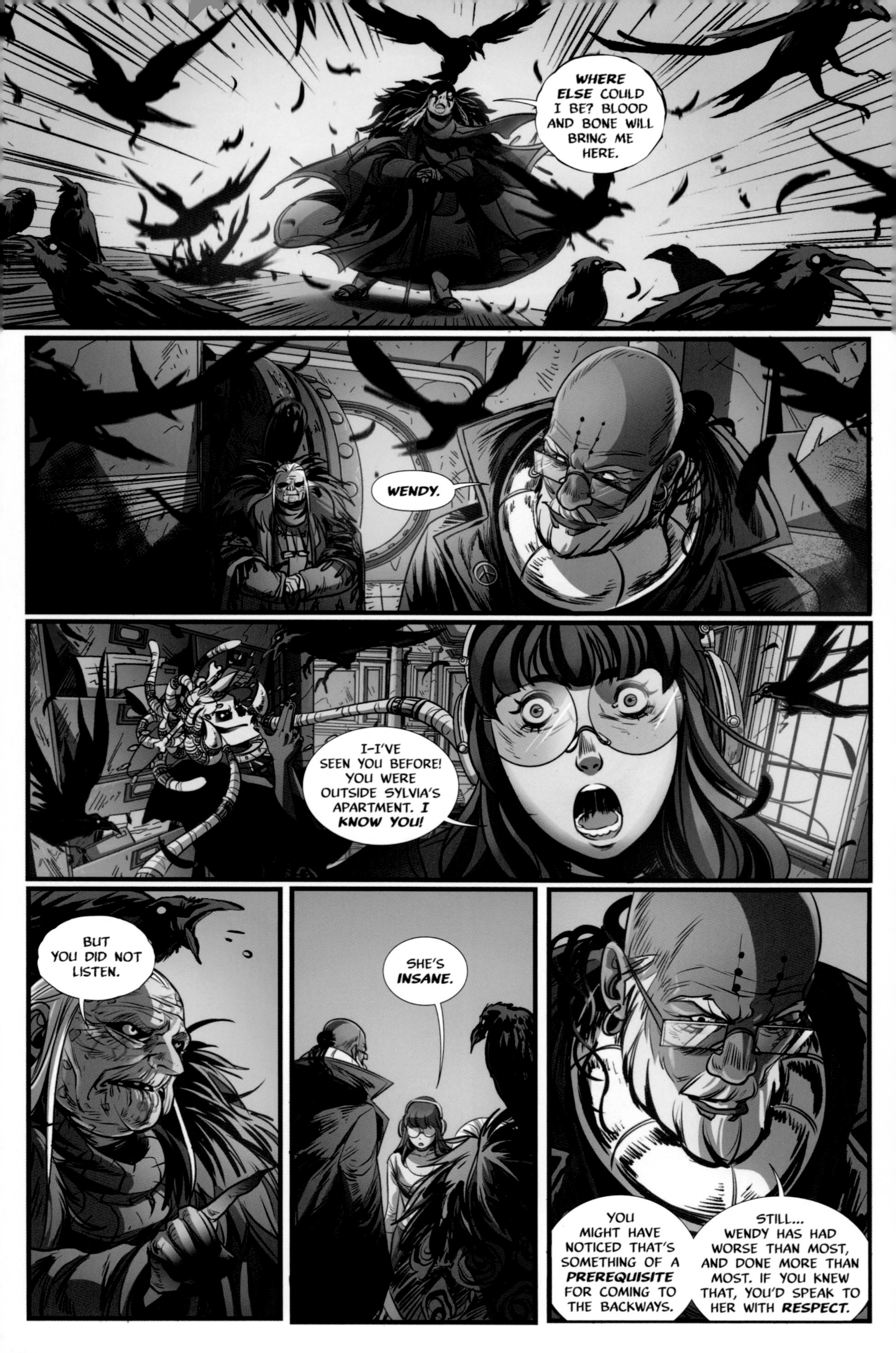
WHERE ELSE COULD I BE? BLOOD AND BONE WILL BRING ME HERE.
WENDY.
I-I'VE SEEN YOU BEFORE! YOU WERE OUTSIDE SYLVIA'S APARTMENT. I KNOW YOU!
BUT YOU DID NOT LISTEN.
SHE'S INSANE.
YOU MIGHT HAVE NOTICED THAT'S SOMETHING OF A PREREQUISITE FOR COMING TO THE BACKWAYS.
STILL... WENDY HAS HAD WORSE THAN MOST, AND DONE MORE THAN MOST. IF YOU KNEW THAT, YOU'D SPEAK TO HER WITH RESPECT.

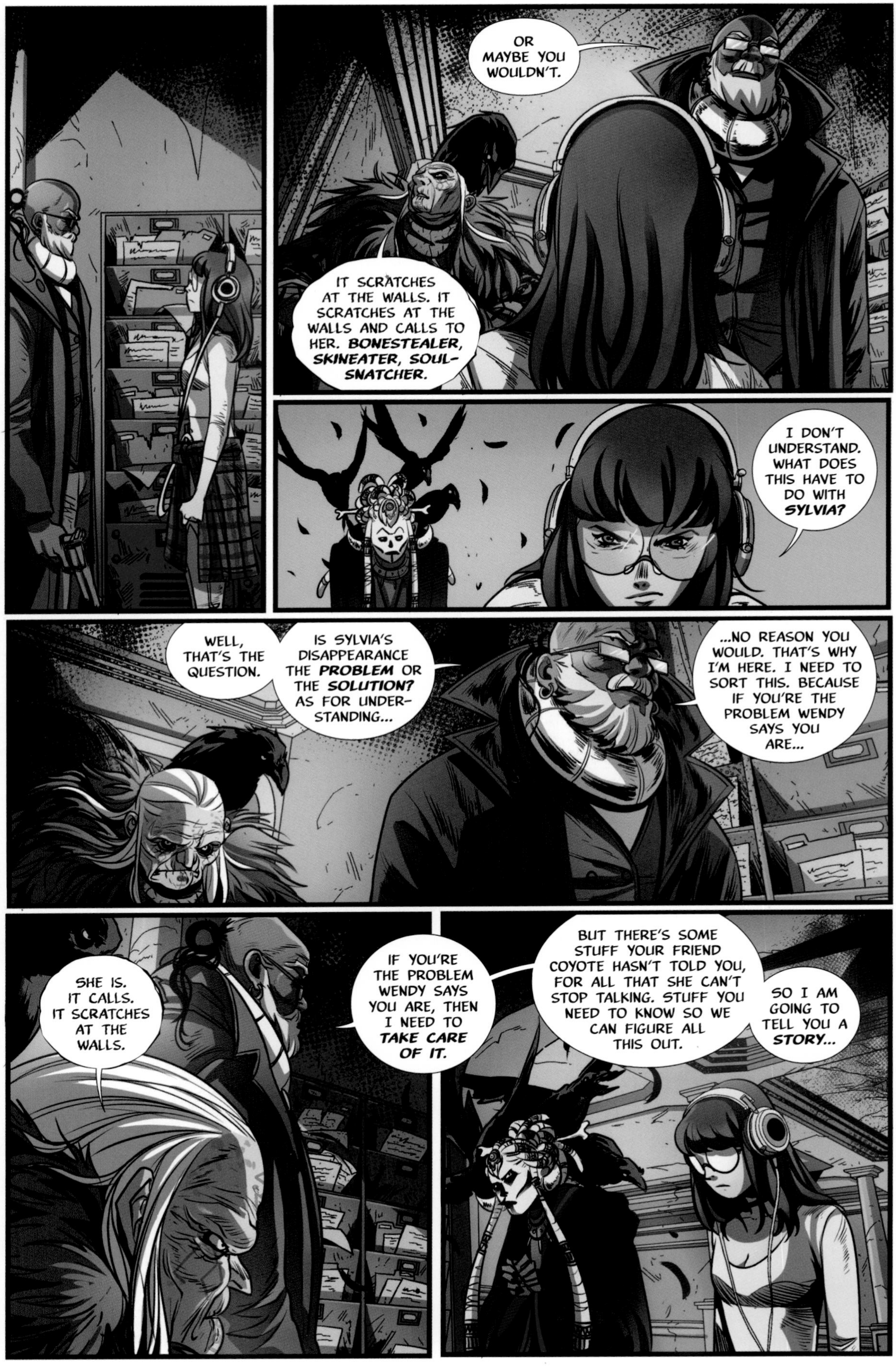
OR MAYBE YOU WOULDN'T.
IT SCRATCHES AT THE WALLS. IT SCRATCHES AT THE WALLS AND CALLS TO HER. **BONESTEALER, SKINEATER, SOUL-SNATCHER.**
I DON'T UNDERSTAND. WHAT DOES THIS HAVE TO DO WITH **SYLVIA?**
WELL, THAT'S THE QUESTION.
IS SYLVIA'S DISAPPEARANCE THE **PROBLEM** OR THE **SOLUTION?** AS FOR UNDER-STANDING...
...NO REASON YOU WOULD. THAT'S WHY I'M HERE. I NEED TO SORT THIS. BECAUSE IF YOU'RE THE PROBLEM WENDY SAYS YOU ARE...
SHE IS. IT CALLS. IT SCRATCHES AT THE WALLS.
IF YOU'RE THE PROBLEM WENDY SAYS YOU ARE, THEN I NEED TO **TAKE CARE OF IT.**
BUT THERE'S SOME STUFF YOUR FRIEND COYOTE HASN'T TOLD YOU, FOR ALL THAT SHE CAN'T STOP TALKING. STUFF YOU NEED TO KNOW SO WE CAN FIGURE ALL THIS OUT.
SO I AM GOING TO TELL YOU A **STORY...**

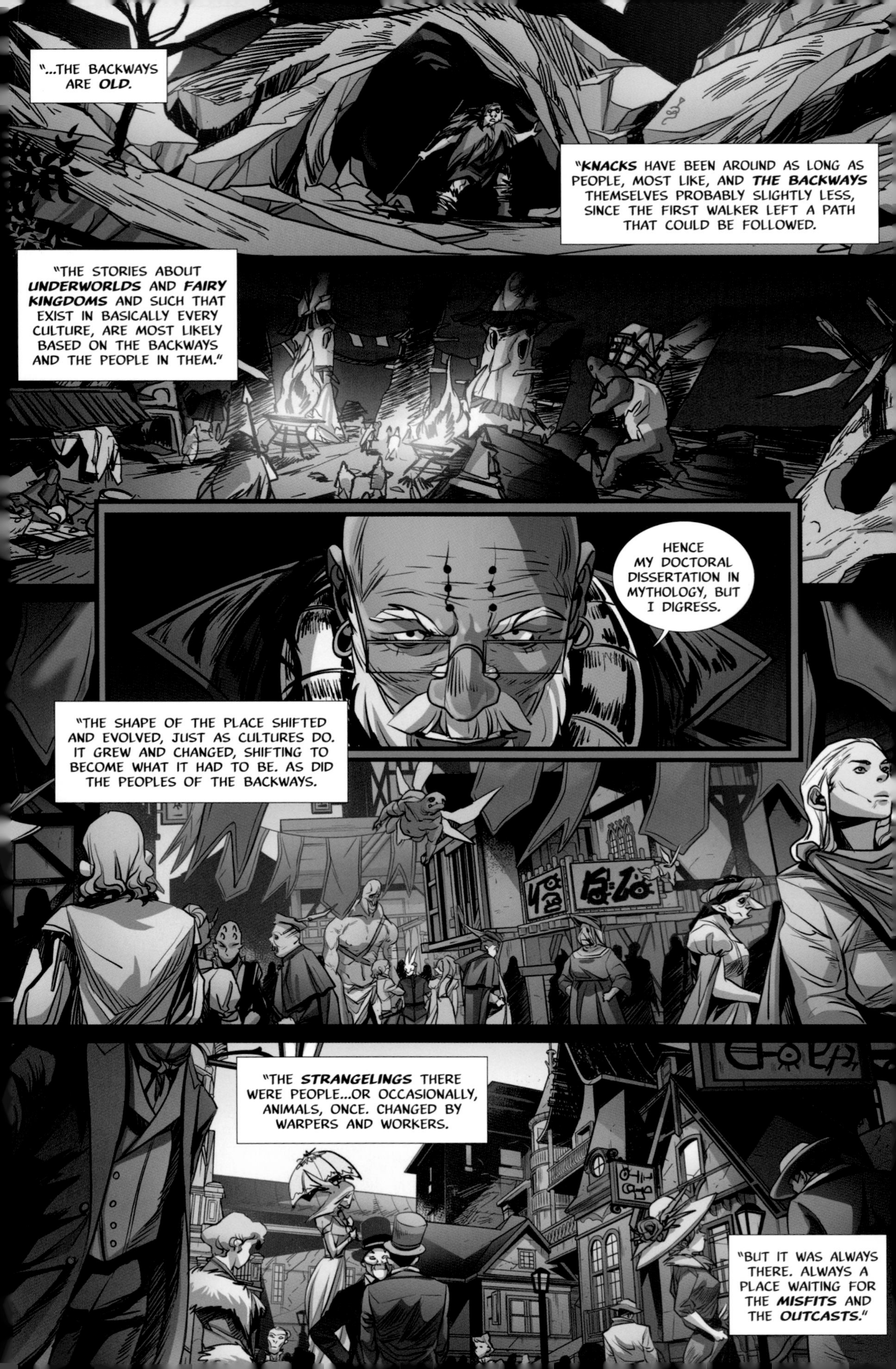
"...THE BACKWAYS ARE OLD.
"KNACKS HAVE BEEN AROUND AS LONG AS PEOPLE, MOST LIKE, AND THE BACKWAYS THEMSELVES PROBABLY SLIGHTLY LESS, SINCE THE FIRST WALKER LEFT A PATH THAT COULD BE FOLLOWED.
"THE STORIES ABOUT UNDERWORLDS AND FAIRY KINGDOMS AND SUCH THAT EXIST IN BASICALLY EVERY CULTURE, ARE MOST LIKELY BASED ON THE BACKWAYS AND THE PEOPLE IN THEM."
HENCE MY DOCTORAL DISSERTATION IN MYTHOLOGY, BUT I DIGRESS.
"THE SHAPE OF THE PLACE SHIFTED AND EVOLVED, JUST AS CULTURES DO. IT GREW AND CHANGED, SHIFTING TO BECOME WHAT IT HAD TO BE. AS DID THE PEOPLES OF THE BACKWAYS.
"THE STRANGELINGS THERE WERE PEOPLE...OR OCCASIONALLY, ANIMALS, ONCE. CHANGED BY WARPERS AND WORKERS.
"BUT IT WAS ALWAYS THERE. ALWAYS A PLACE WAITING FOR THE MISFITS AND THE OUTCASTS."

"AND THERE WAS **ONE RULE.** WELL, ACTUALLY, IT APPEARS TO BE A LAW OF THE UNIVERSE.

"ONE PERSON, ONE KNACK. YOU MIGHT HAVE A STRONG KNACK OR A WEAK ONE, BUT WHAT YOU WERE **BORN** WITH WAS WHAT YOU **HAD.**

"NOW, AS COYOTE AND I HAVE AMPLY DEMONSTRATED, WORKERS AND THEIR CHARMS AND TOTEMS COULD HELP YOU GET AROUND THAT, BUT THE EFFECT WAS LIMITED.

"IT WAS **SELF-LIMITING.** THE BACKWAYS, LIKE ANY PLACE ELSE, HAD BAD PEOPLE, AND SOMETIMES THEY WERE EVEN **POWERFUL.**

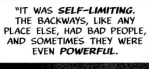

"HOWEVER, IT WAS ALWAYS MANAGEABLE. BECAUSE THERE WERE **LIMITS.**

"AND SO FOR A LONG TIME, FAR LONGER THAN WE PROBABLY HAD ANY RIGHT, THINGS WERE GOOD.

"UNTIL THEY **WEREN'T.**"

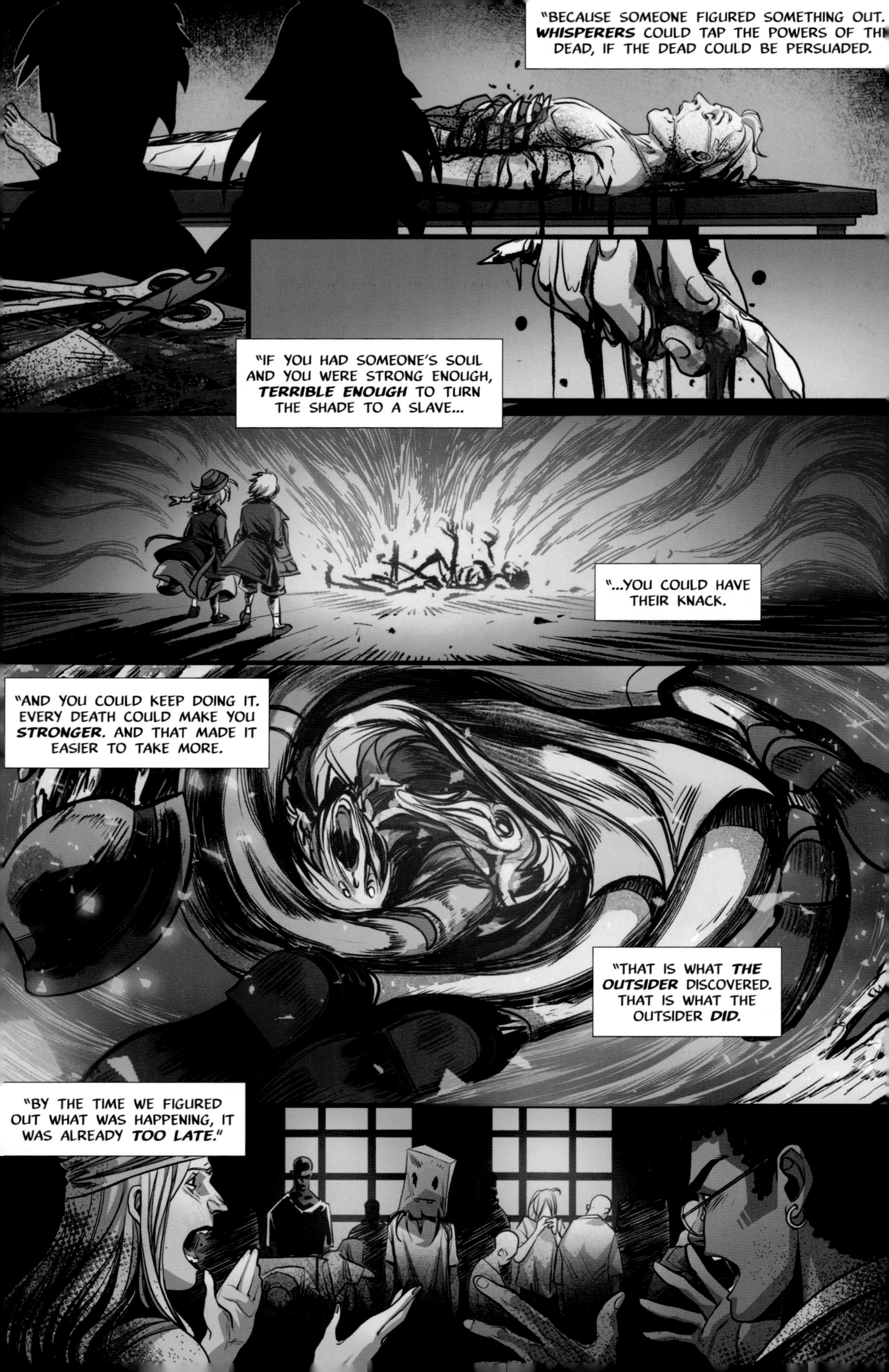
"BECAUSE SOMEONE FIGURED SOMETHING OUT. **WHISPERERS** COULD TAP THE POWERS OF THE DEAD, IF THE DEAD COULD BE PERSUADED.
"IF YOU HAD SOMEONE'S SOUL AND YOU WERE STRONG ENOUGH, ***TERRIBLE ENOUGH*** TO TURN THE SHADE TO A SLAVE...
"...YOU COULD HAVE THEIR KNACK.
"AND YOU COULD KEEP DOING IT. EVERY DEATH COULD MAKE YOU ***STRONGER***. AND THAT MADE IT EASIER TO TAKE MORE.
"THAT IS WHAT ***THE OUTSIDER*** DISCOVERED. THAT IS WHAT THE OUTSIDER ***DID***.
"BY THE TIME WE FIGURED OUT WHAT WAS HAPPENING, IT WAS ALREADY ***TOO LATE***."

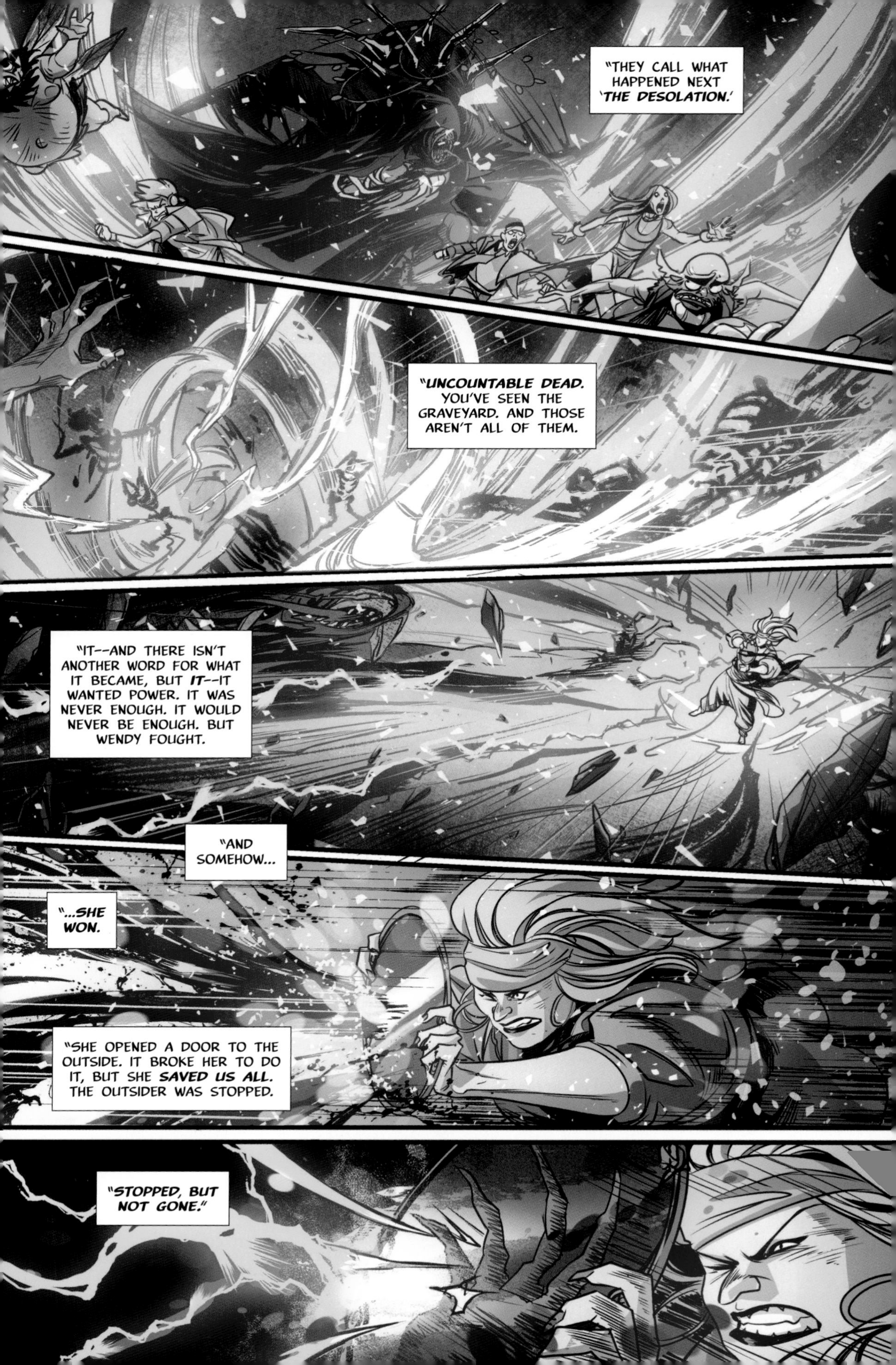
"THEY CALL WHAT HAPPENED NEXT 'THE DESOLATION.'
"UNCOUNTABLE DEAD. YOU'VE SEEN THE GRAVEYARD. AND THOSE AREN'T ALL OF THEM.
"IT--AND THERE ISN'T ANOTHER WORD FOR WHAT IT BECAME, BUT IT--IT WANTED POWER. IT WAS NEVER ENOUGH. IT WOULD NEVER BE ENOUGH. BUT WENDY FOUGHT.
"AND SOMEHOW...
"...SHE WON.
"SHE OPENED A DOOR TO THE OUTSIDE. IT BROKE HER TO DO IT, BUT SHE SAVED US ALL. THE OUTSIDER WAS STOPPED.
"STOPPED, BUT NOT GONE."

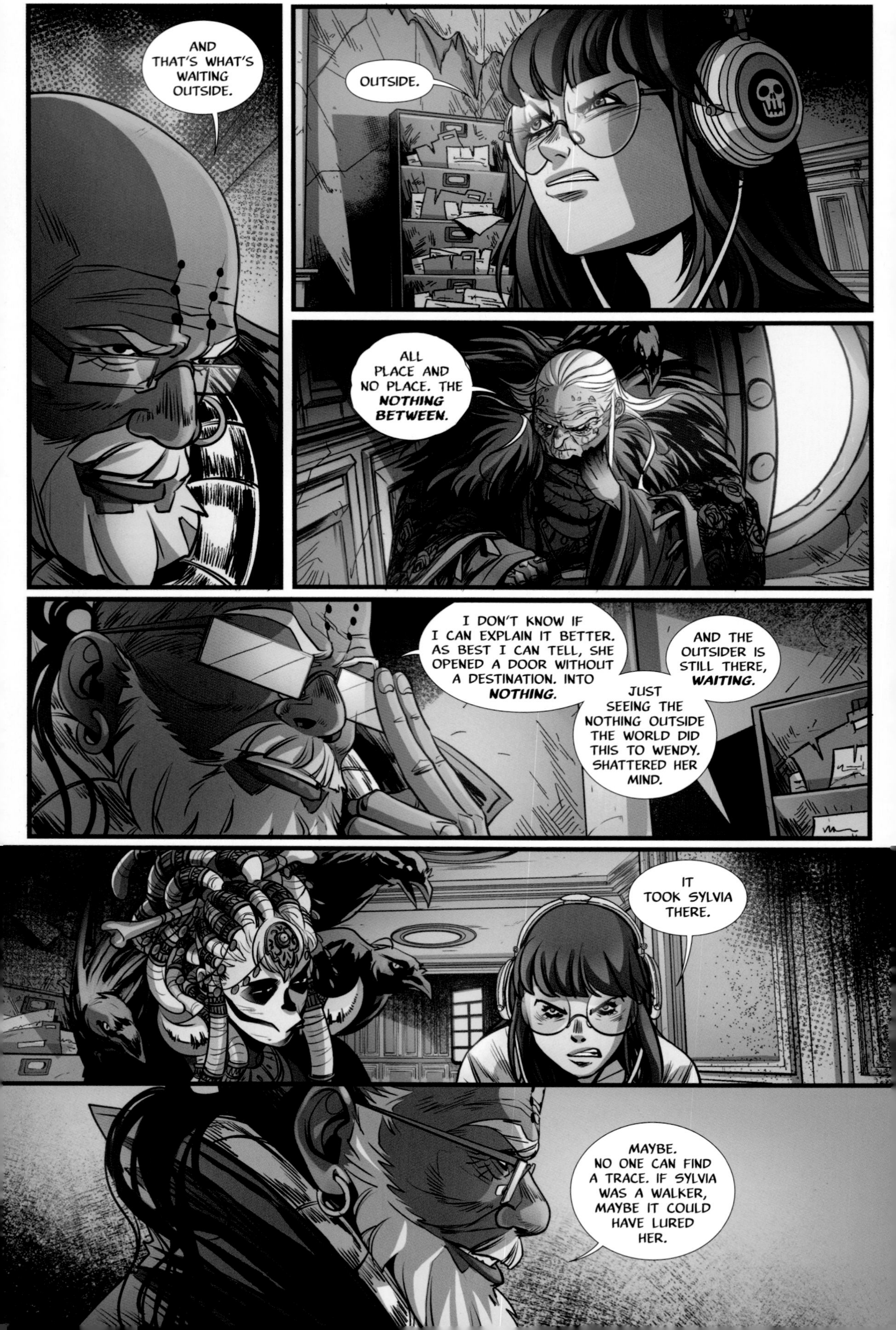
AND THAT'S WHAT'S WAITING OUTSIDE.
OUTSIDE.
ALL PLACE AND NO PLACE. THE **NOTHING BETWEEN.**
I DON'T KNOW IF I CAN EXPLAIN IT BETTER. AS BEST I CAN TELL, SHE OPENED A DOOR WITHOUT A DESTINATION. INTO ***NOTHING.***
AND THE OUTSIDER IS STILL THERE, ***WAITING.***
JUST SEEING THE NOTHING OUTSIDE THE WORLD DID THIS TO WENDY. SHATTERED HER MIND.
IT TOOK SYLVIA THERE.
MAYBE. NO ONE CAN FIND A TRACE. IF SYLVIA WAS A WALKER, MAYBE IT COULD HAVE LURED HER.

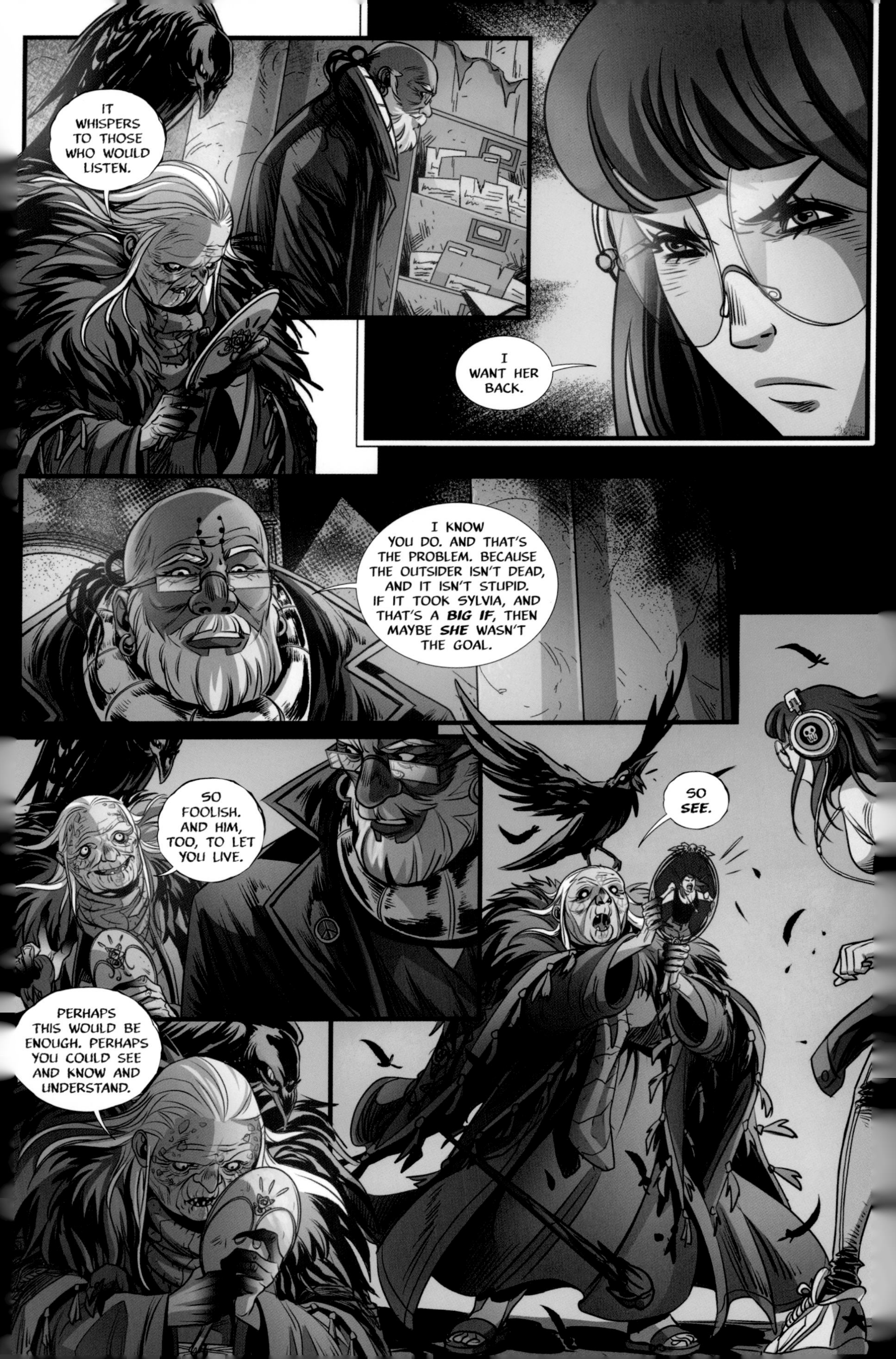
IT WHISPERS TO THOSE WHO WOULD LISTEN.
I WANT HER BACK.
I KNOW YOU DO. AND THAT'S THE PROBLEM. BECAUSE THE OUTSIDER ISN'T DEAD, AND IT ISN'T STUPID. IF IT TOOK SYLVIA, AND THAT'S A BIG IF, THEN MAYBE SHE WASN'T THE GOAL.
SO FOOLISH. AND HIM, TOO, TO LET YOU LIVE.
PERHAPS THIS WOULD BE ENOUGH. PERHAPS YOU COULD SEE AND KNOW AND UNDERSTAND.
SO SEE.

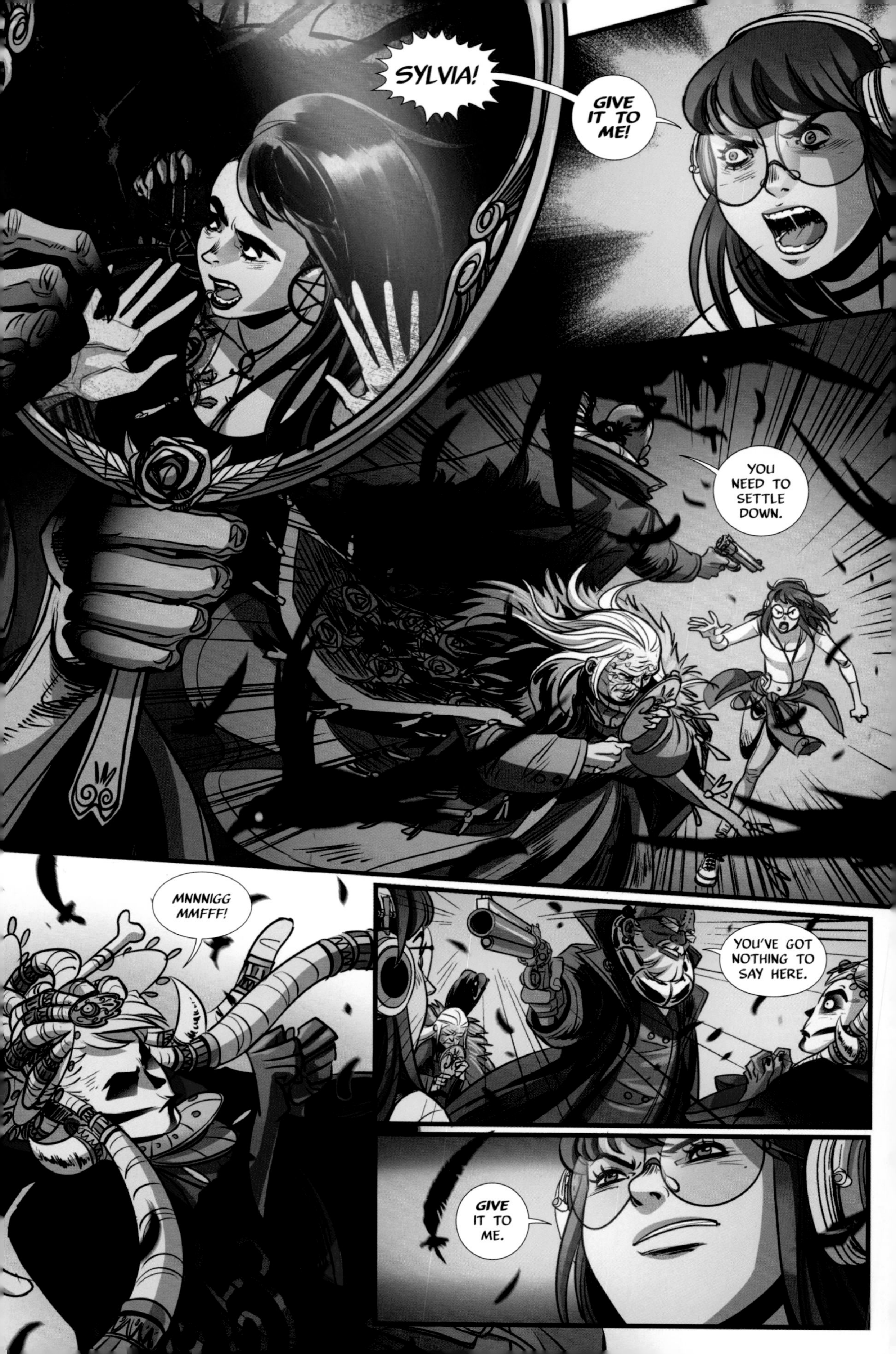
SYLVIA!
GIVE IT TO ME!
YOU NEED TO SETTLE DOWN.
MNNNIGG MMFFF!
YOU'VE GOT NOTHING TO SAY HERE.
GIVE IT TO ME.

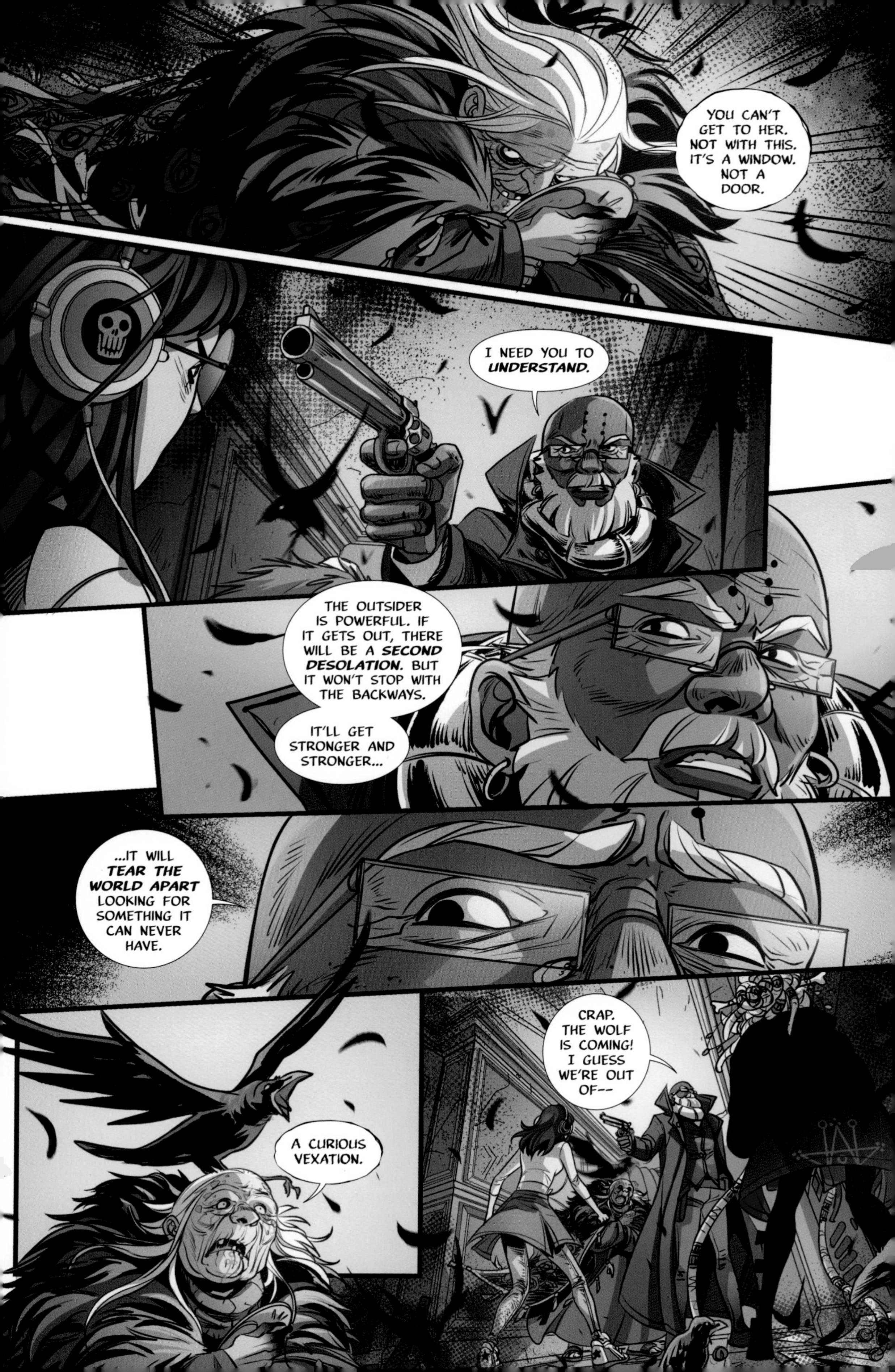
YOU CAN'T GET TO HER. NOT WITH THIS. IT'S A WINDOW. NOT A DOOR.
I NEED YOU TO UNDERSTAND.
THE OUTSIDER IS POWERFUL. IF IT GETS OUT, THERE WILL BE A SECOND DESOLATION. BUT IT WON'T STOP WITH THE BACKWAYS.
IT'LL GET STRONGER AND STRONGER...
...IT WILL TEAR THE WORLD APART LOOKING FOR SOMETHING IT CAN NEVER HAVE.
CRAP. THE WOLF IS COMING! I GUESS WE'RE OUT OF--
A CURIOUS VEXATION.

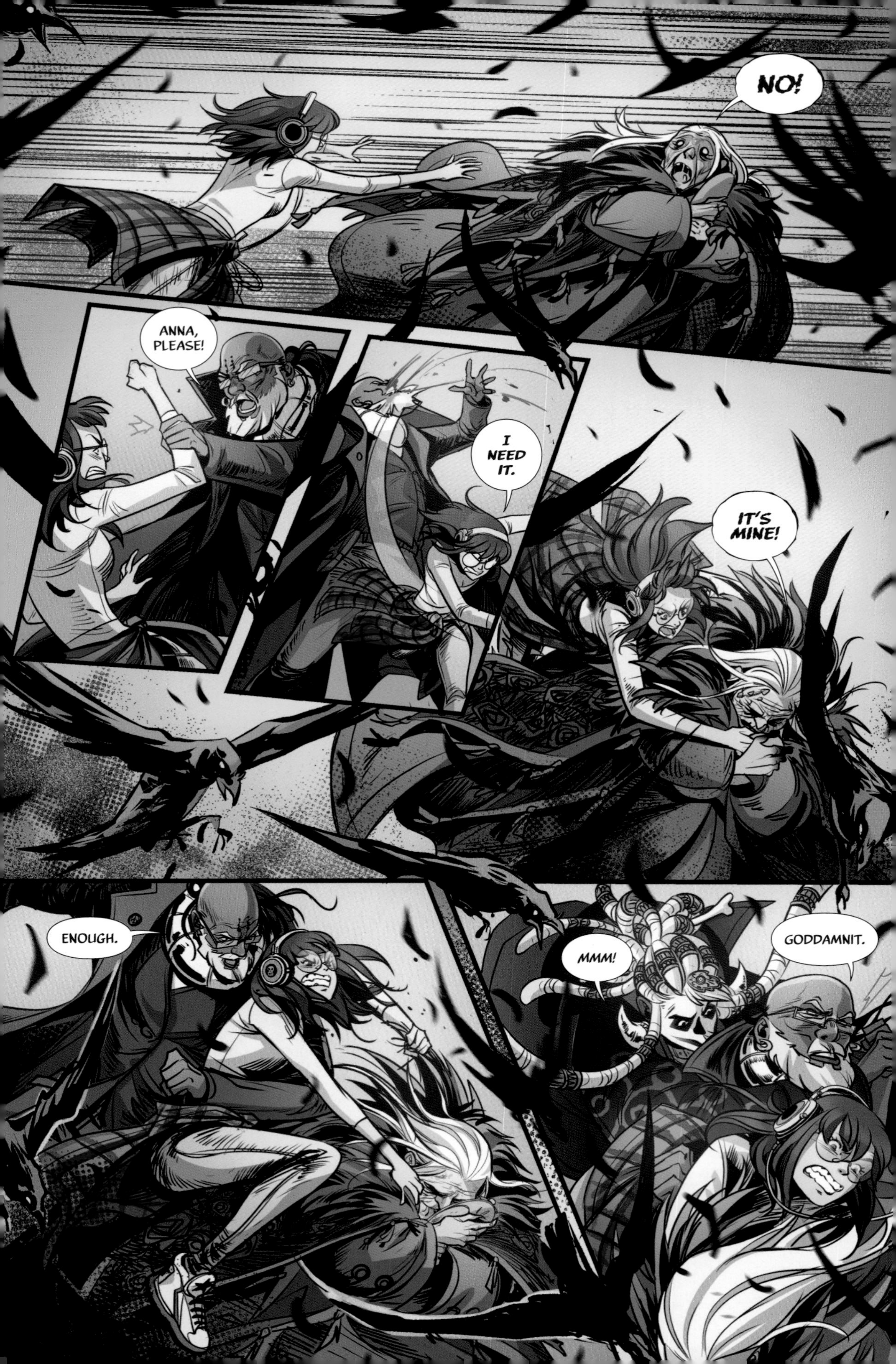
NO!
ANNA, PLEASE!
I NEED IT.
IT'S MINE!
ENOUGH.
MMM!
GODDAMNIT.

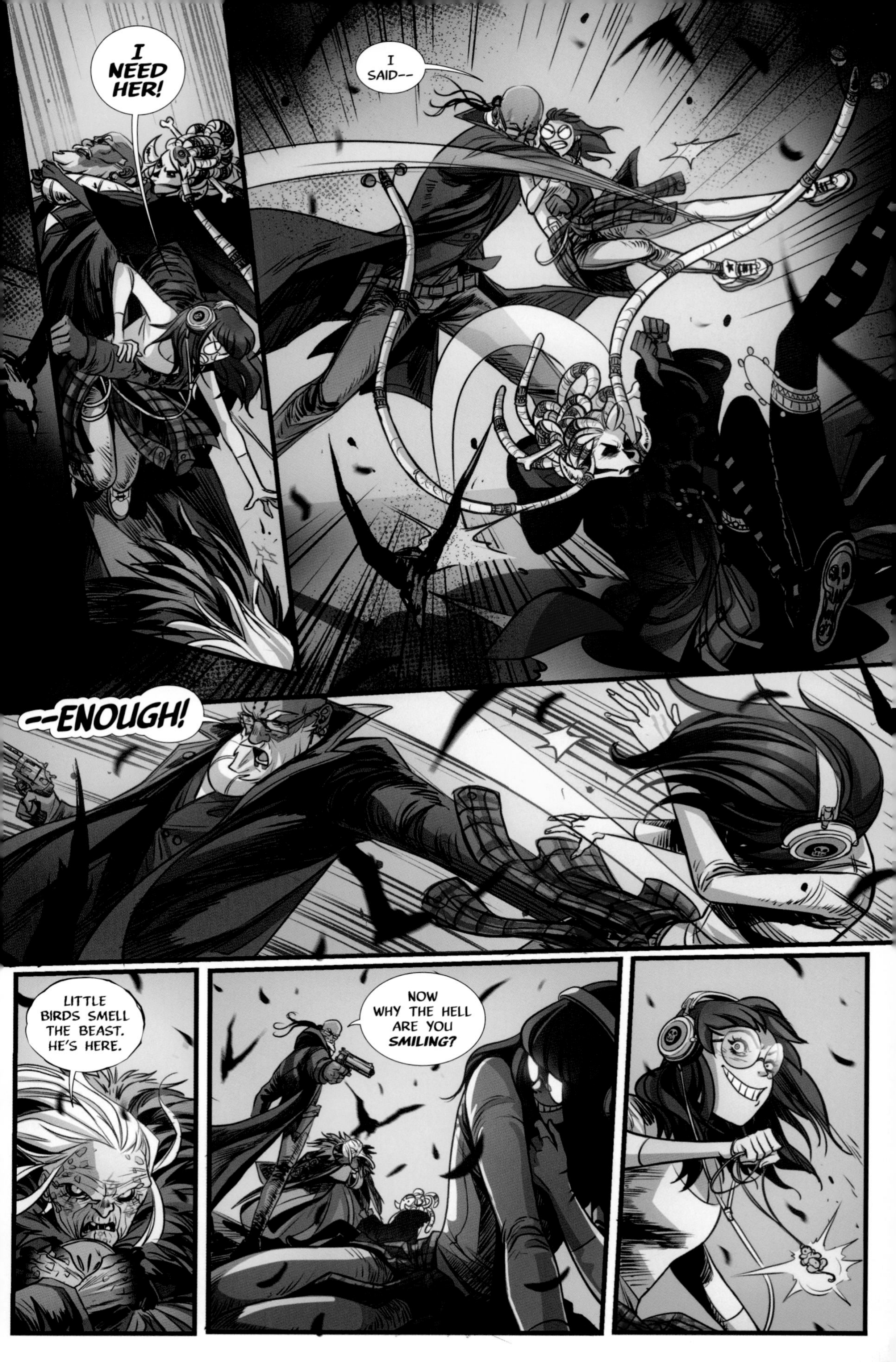
I NEED HER!
I SAID--
--ENOUGH!
LITTLE BIRDS SMELL THE BEAST. HE'S HERE.
NOW WHY THE HELL ARE YOU SMILING?

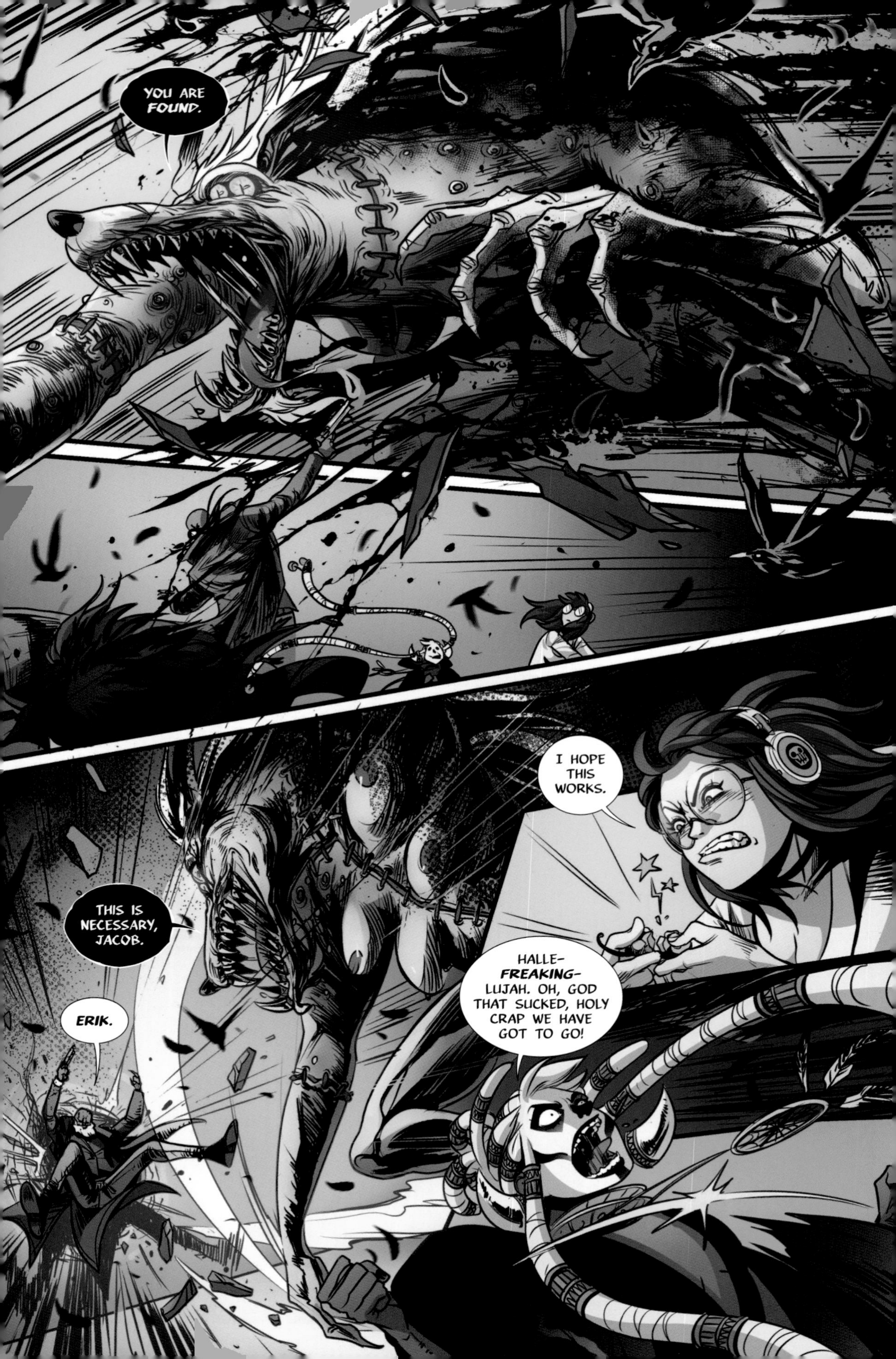
YOU ARE FOUND.
I HOPE THIS WORKS.
THIS IS NECESSARY, JACOB.
ERIK.
HALLE-FREAKING-LUJAH. OH, GOD THAT SUCKED, HOLY CRAP WE HAVE GOT TO GO!

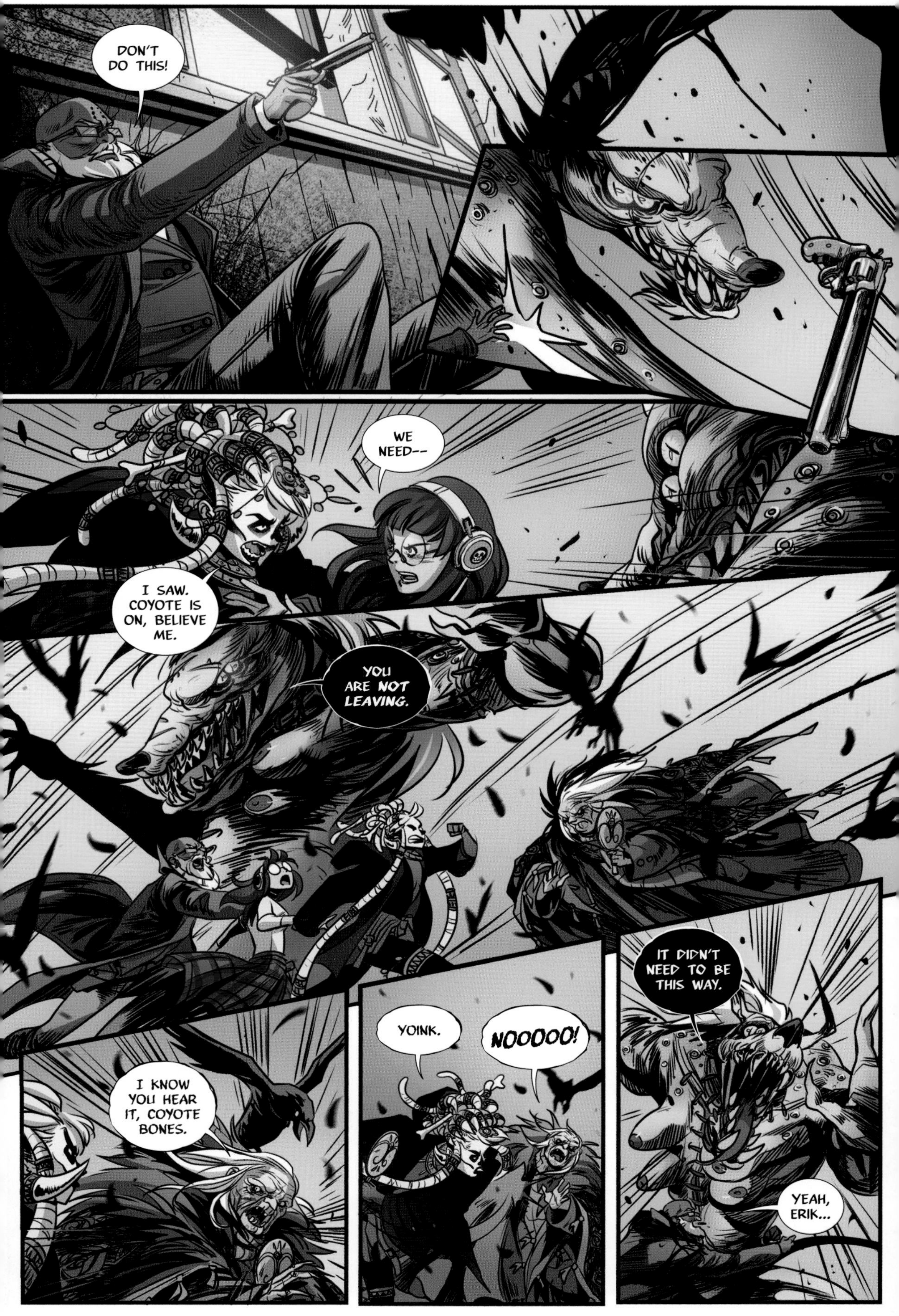
DON'T DO THIS!
WE NEED--
I SAW. COYOTE IS ON, BELIEVE ME.
YOU ARE NOT LEAVING.
I KNOW YOU HEAR IT, COYOTE BONES.
YOINK.
NOOOOO!
IT DIDN'T NEED TO BE THIS WAY.
YEAH, ERIK...

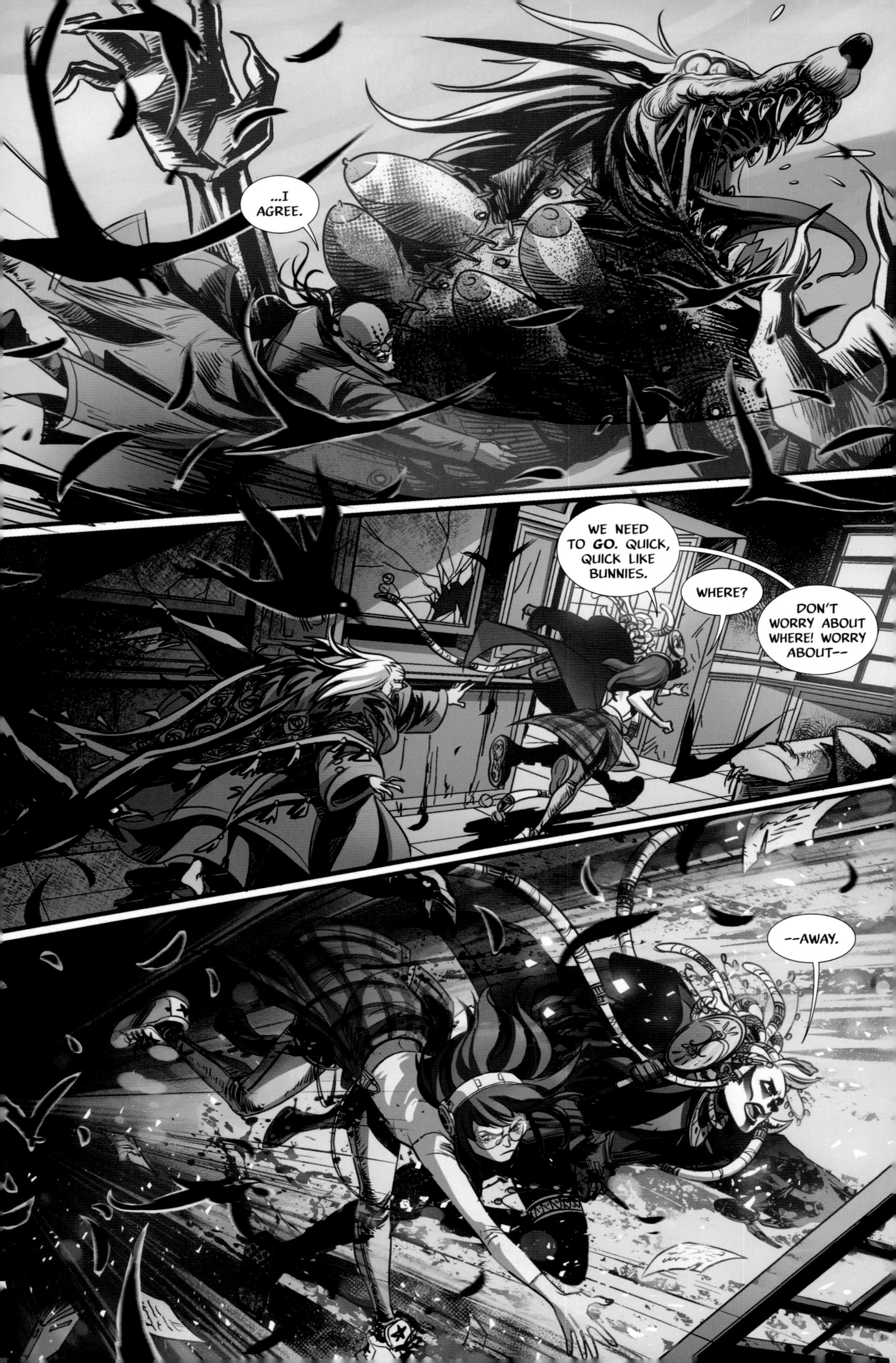
...I AGREE.
WE NEED TO GO. QUICK, QUICK LIKE BUNNIES.
WHERE?
DON'T WORRY ABOUT WHERE! WORRY ABOUT--
--AWAY.

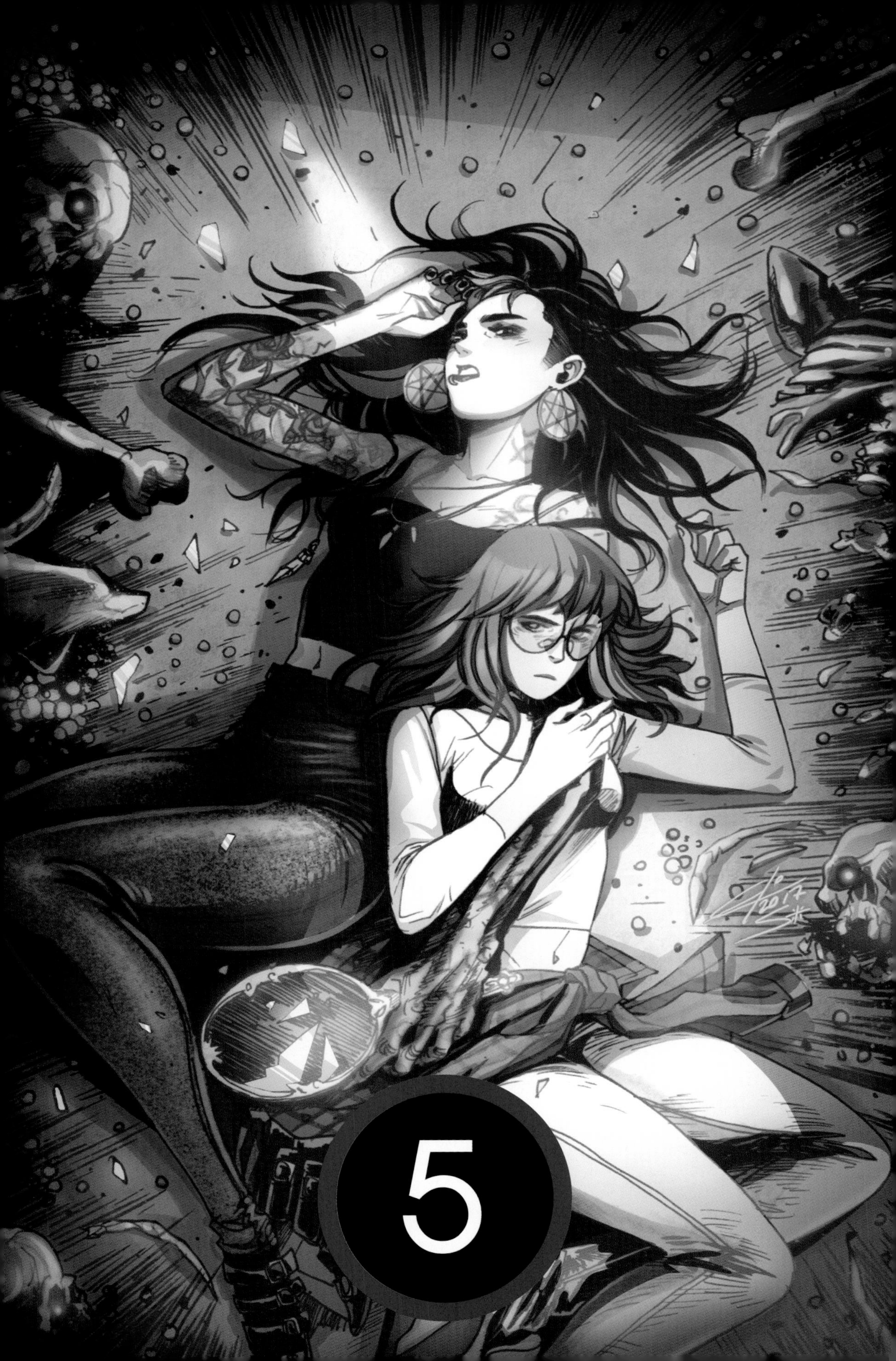
5

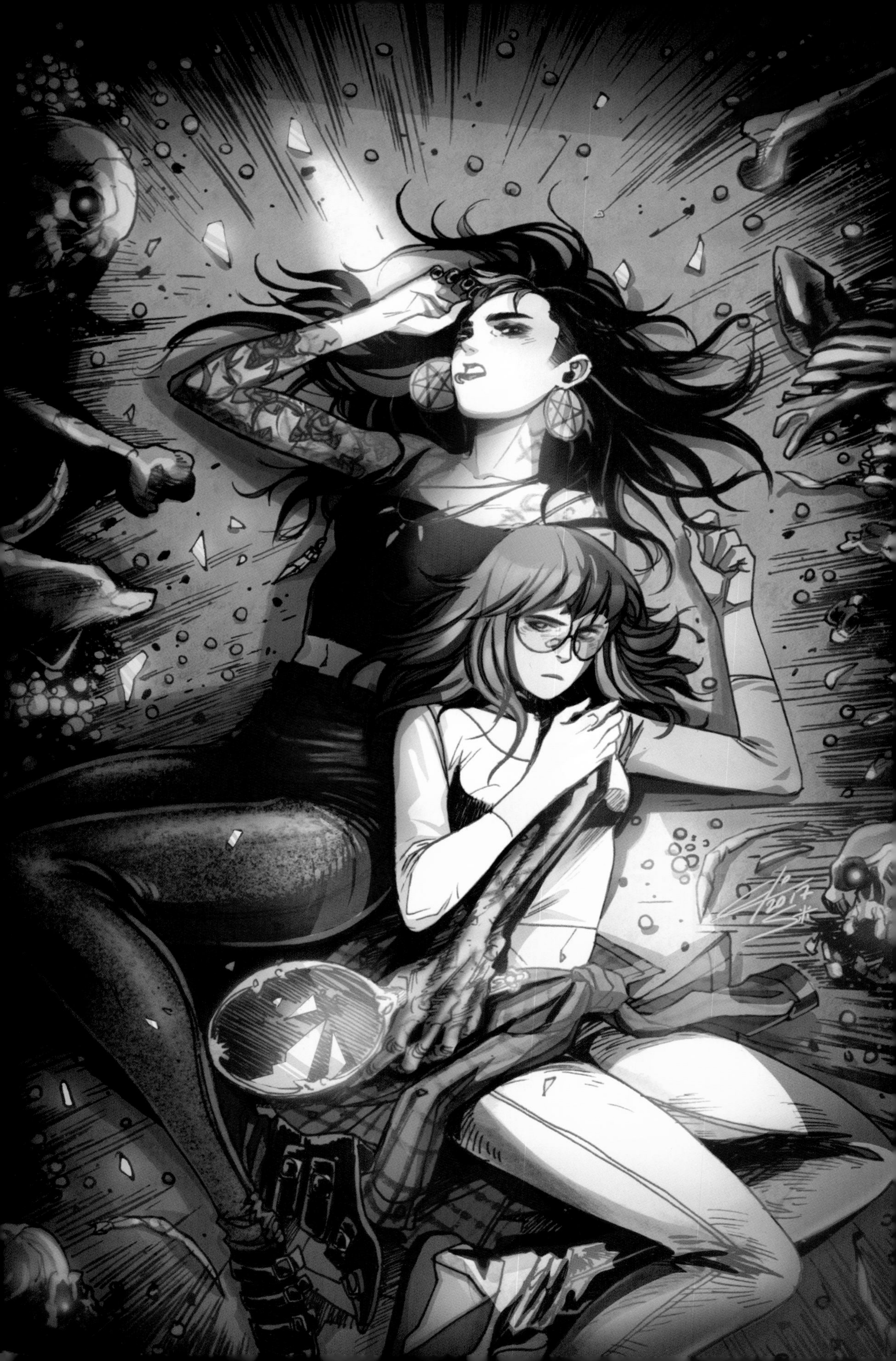

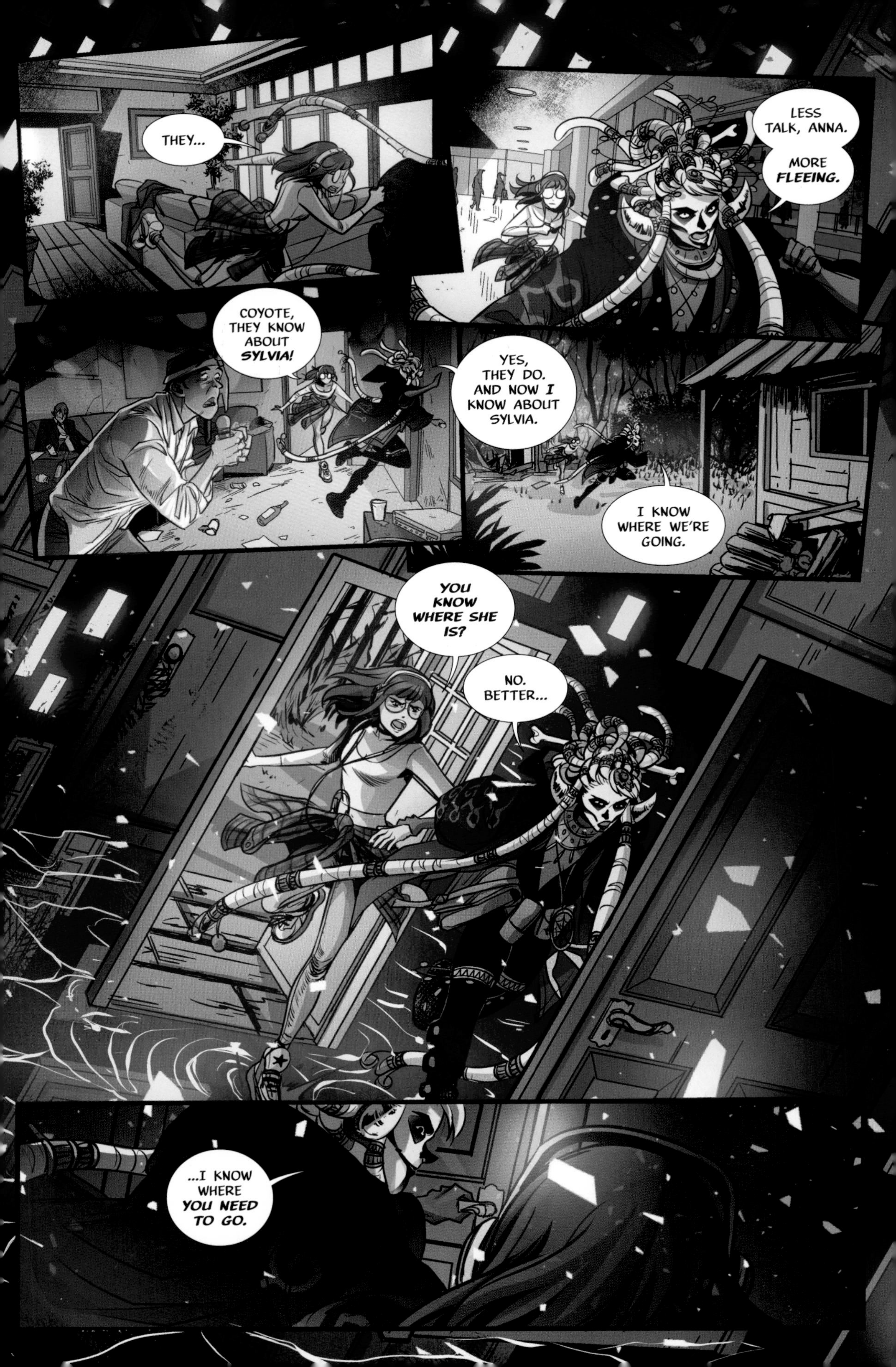
THEY...
LESS TALK, ANNA.
MORE FLEEING.
COYOTE, THEY KNOW ABOUT SYLVIA!
YES, THEY DO. AND NOW I KNOW ABOUT SYLVIA.
I KNOW WHERE WE'RE GOING.
YOU KNOW WHERE SHE IS?
NO. BETTER...
...I KNOW WHERE YOU NEED TO GO.

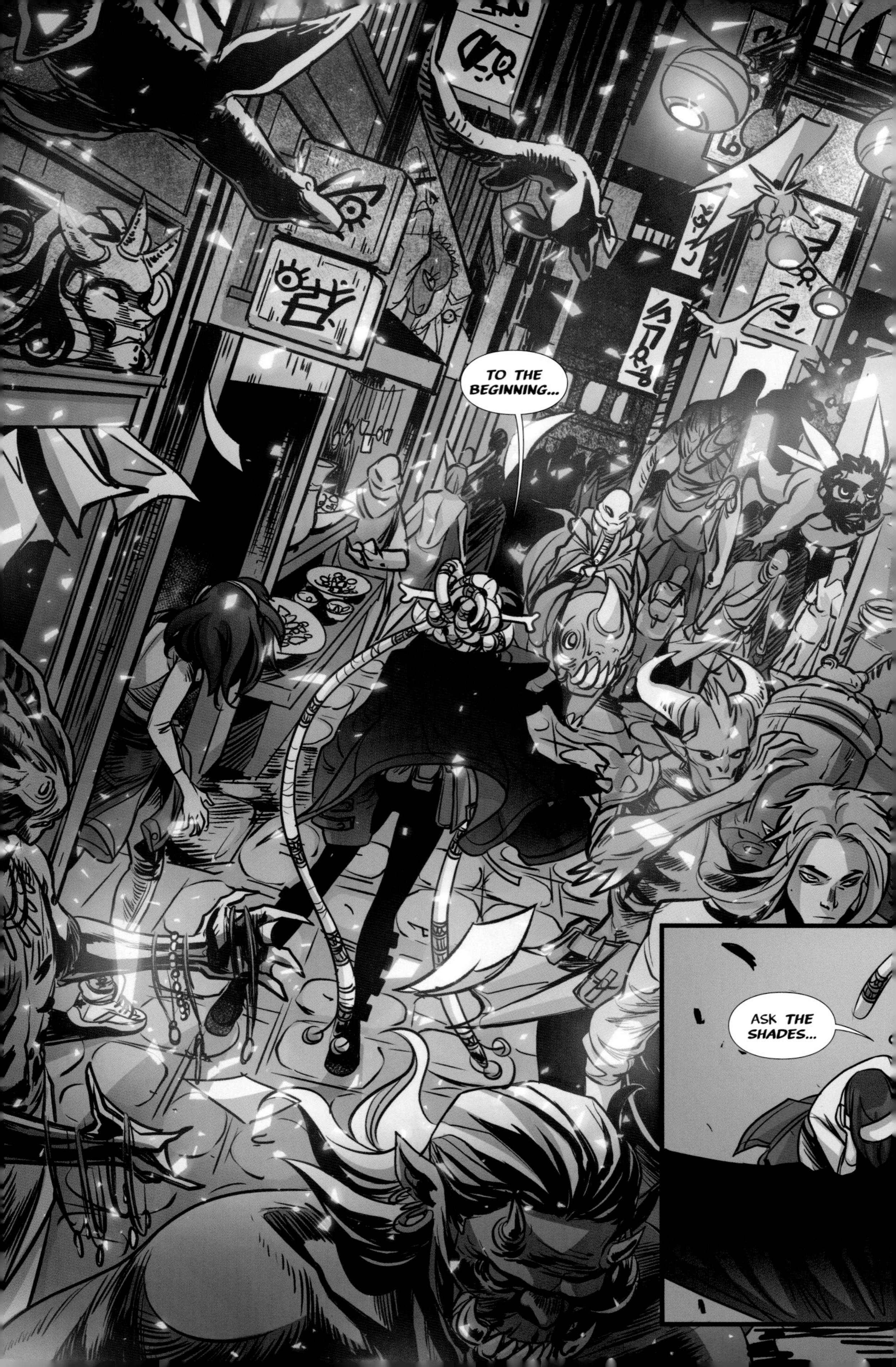
TO THE BEGINNING...
ASK THE SHADES...

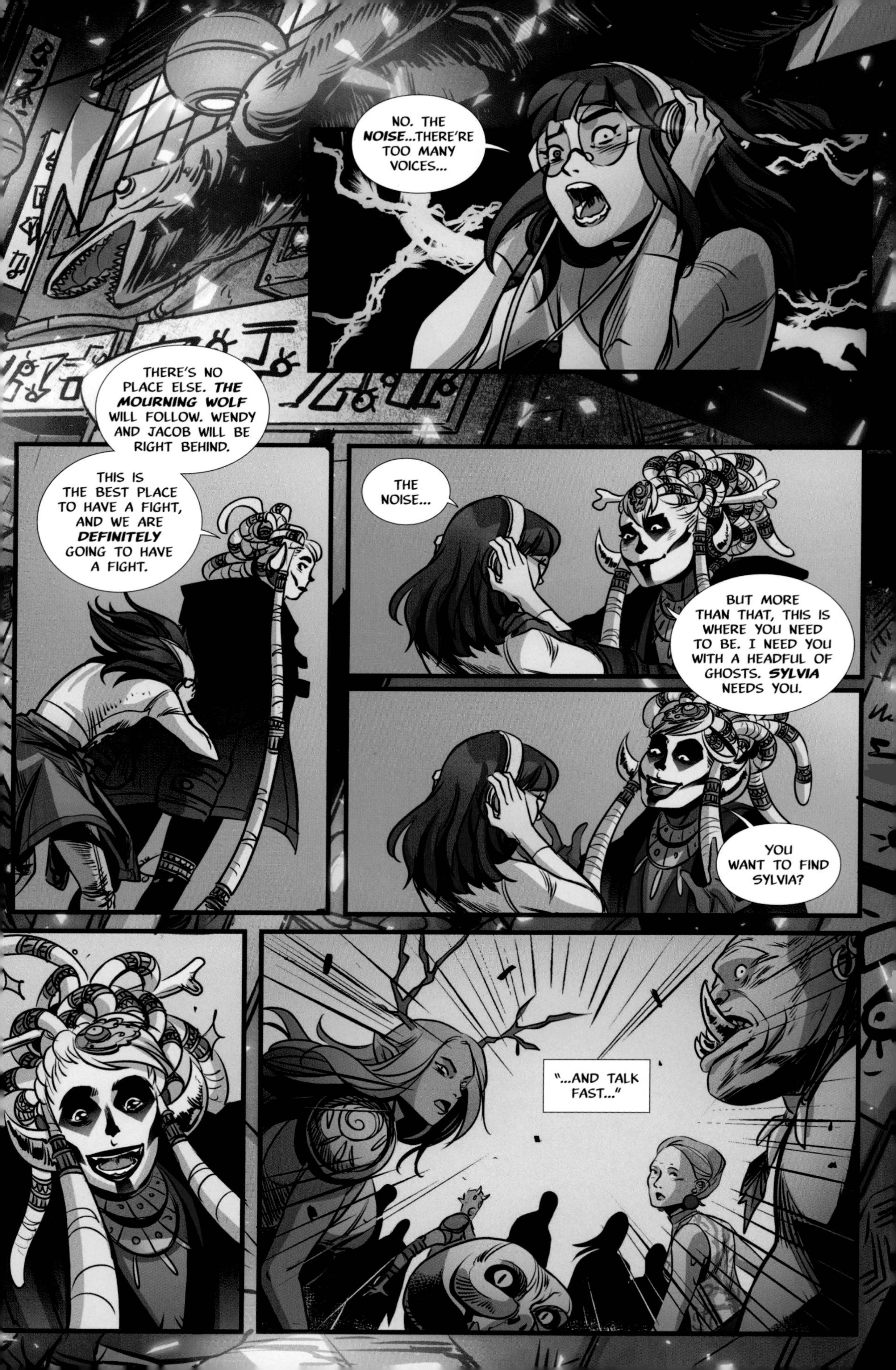
NO. THE NOISE...THERE'RE TOO MANY VOICES...
THERE'S NO PLACE ELSE. THE MOURNING WOLF WILL FOLLOW. WENDY AND JACOB WILL BE RIGHT BEHIND.
THIS IS THE BEST PLACE TO HAVE A FIGHT, AND WE ARE DEFINITELY GOING TO HAVE A FIGHT.
THE NOISE...
BUT MORE THAN THAT, THIS IS WHERE YOU NEED TO BE. I NEED YOU WITH A HEADFUL OF GHOSTS. SYLVIA NEEDS YOU.
YOU WANT TO FIND SYLVIA?
"...AND TALK FAST..."

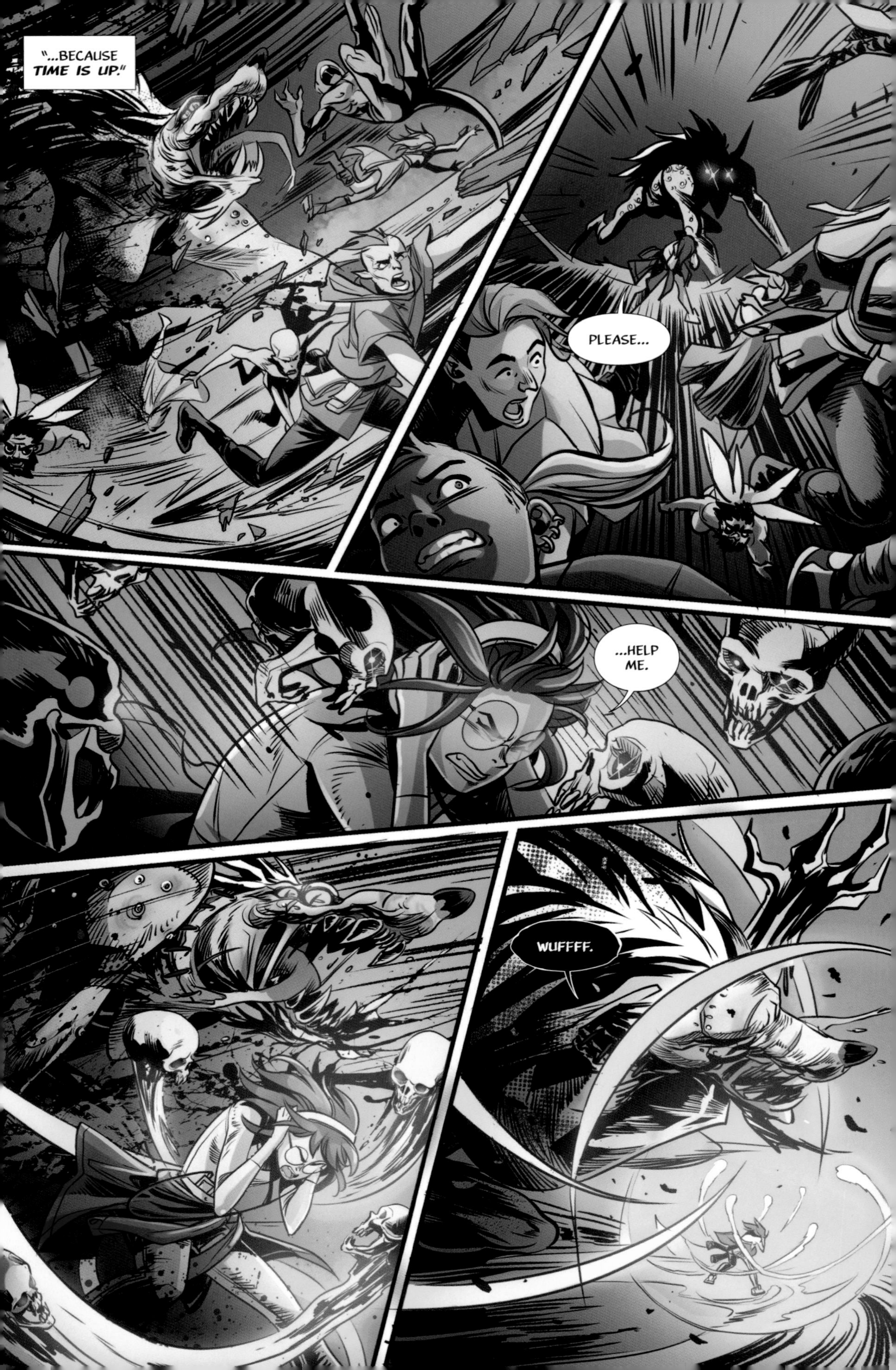
"...BECAUSE *TIME IS UP.*"
PLEASE...
...HELP ME.
WUFFFF.

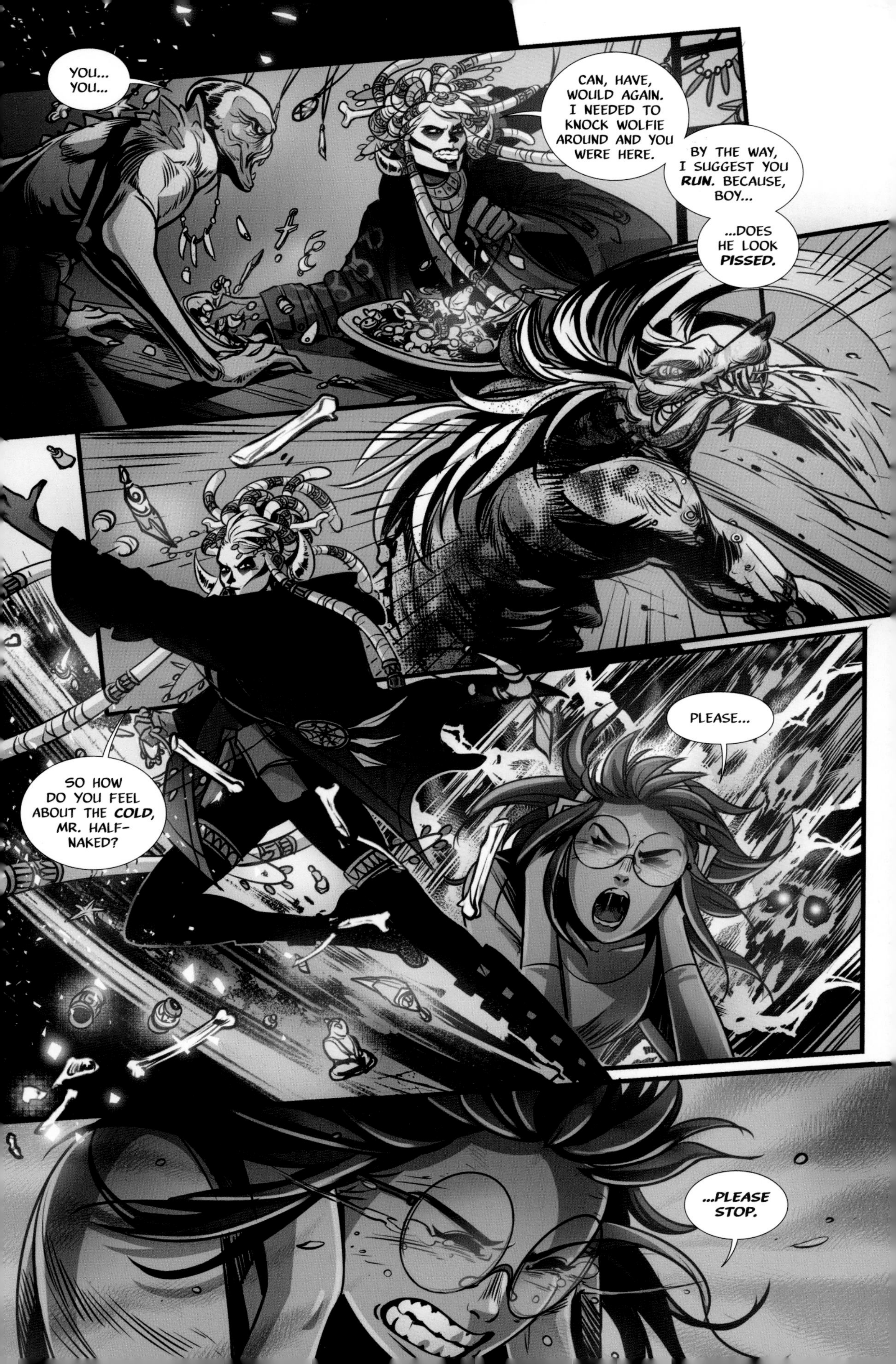
YOU... YOU...
CAN, HAVE, WOULD AGAIN. I NEEDED TO KNOCK WOLFIE AROUND AND YOU WERE HERE.
BY THE WAY, I SUGGEST YOU **RUN**. BECAUSE, BOY...
...DOES HE LOOK **PISSED.**
SO HOW DO YOU FEEL ABOUT THE **COLD**, MR. HALF-NAKED?
PLEASE...
...PLEASE STOP.

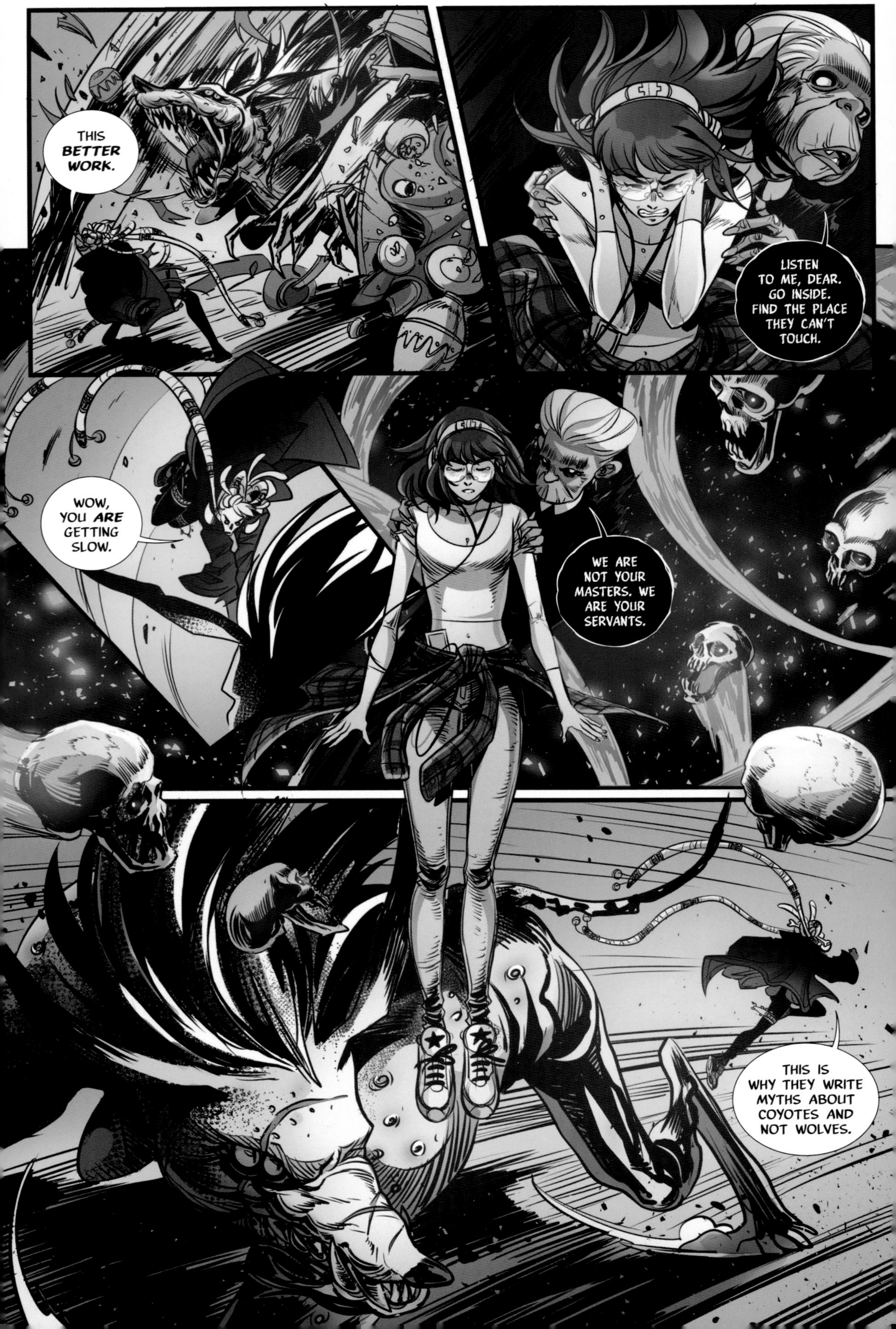

THIS BETTER WORK.
LISTEN TO ME, DEAR. GO INSIDE. FIND THE PLACE THEY CAN'T TOUCH.
WOW, YOU ARE GETTING SLOW.
WE ARE NOT YOUR MASTERS. WE ARE YOUR SERVANTS.
THIS IS WHY THEY WRITE MYTHS ABOUT COYOTES AND NOT WOLVES.

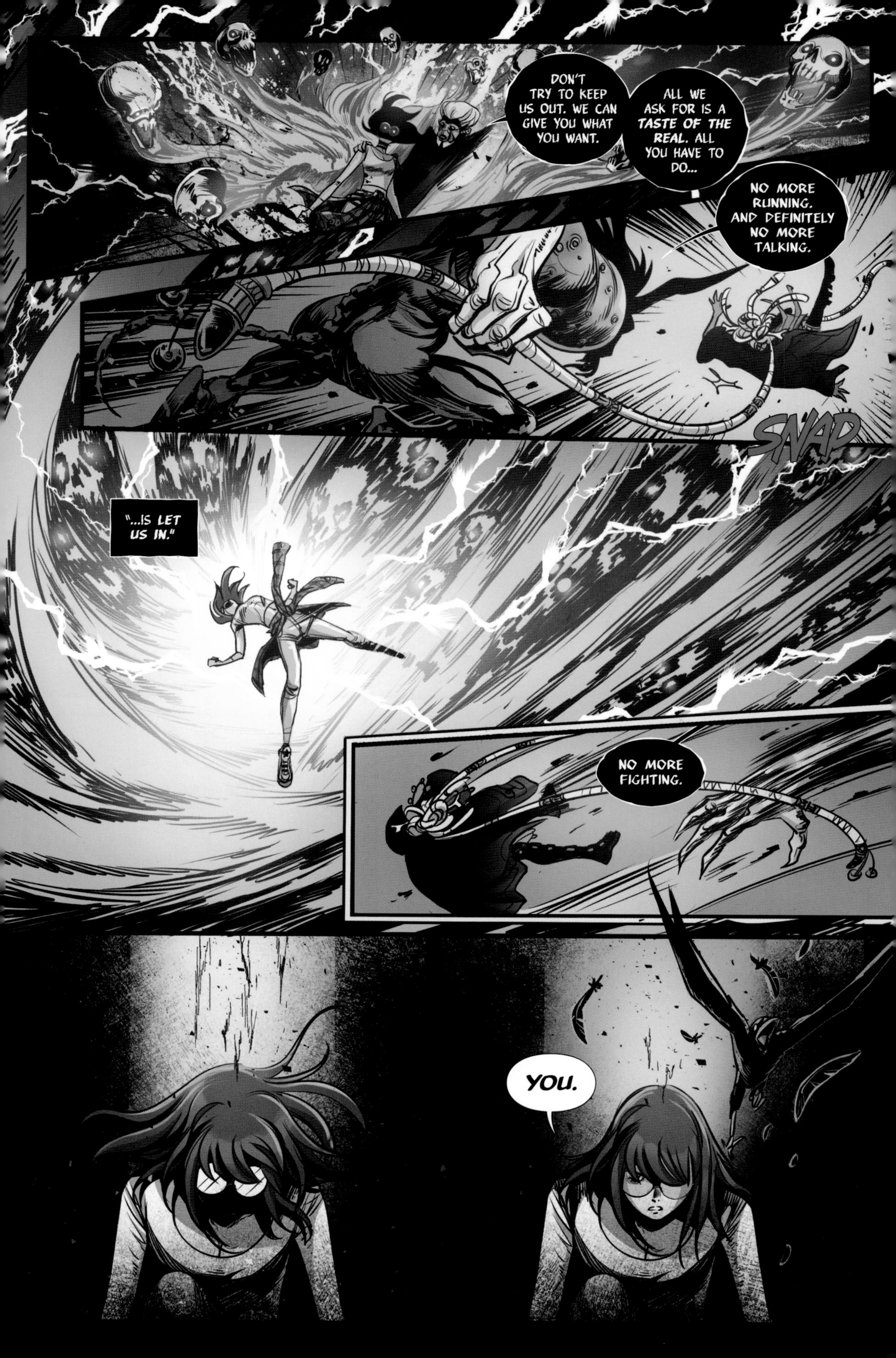
DON'T TRY TO KEEP US OUT. WE CAN GIVE YOU WHAT YOU WANT.
ALL WE ASK FOR IS A TASTE OF THE REAL. ALL YOU HAVE TO DO...
NO MORE RUNNING. AND DEFINITELY NO MORE TALKING.
SNAP
"...IS LET US IN."
NO MORE FIGHTING.
YOU.

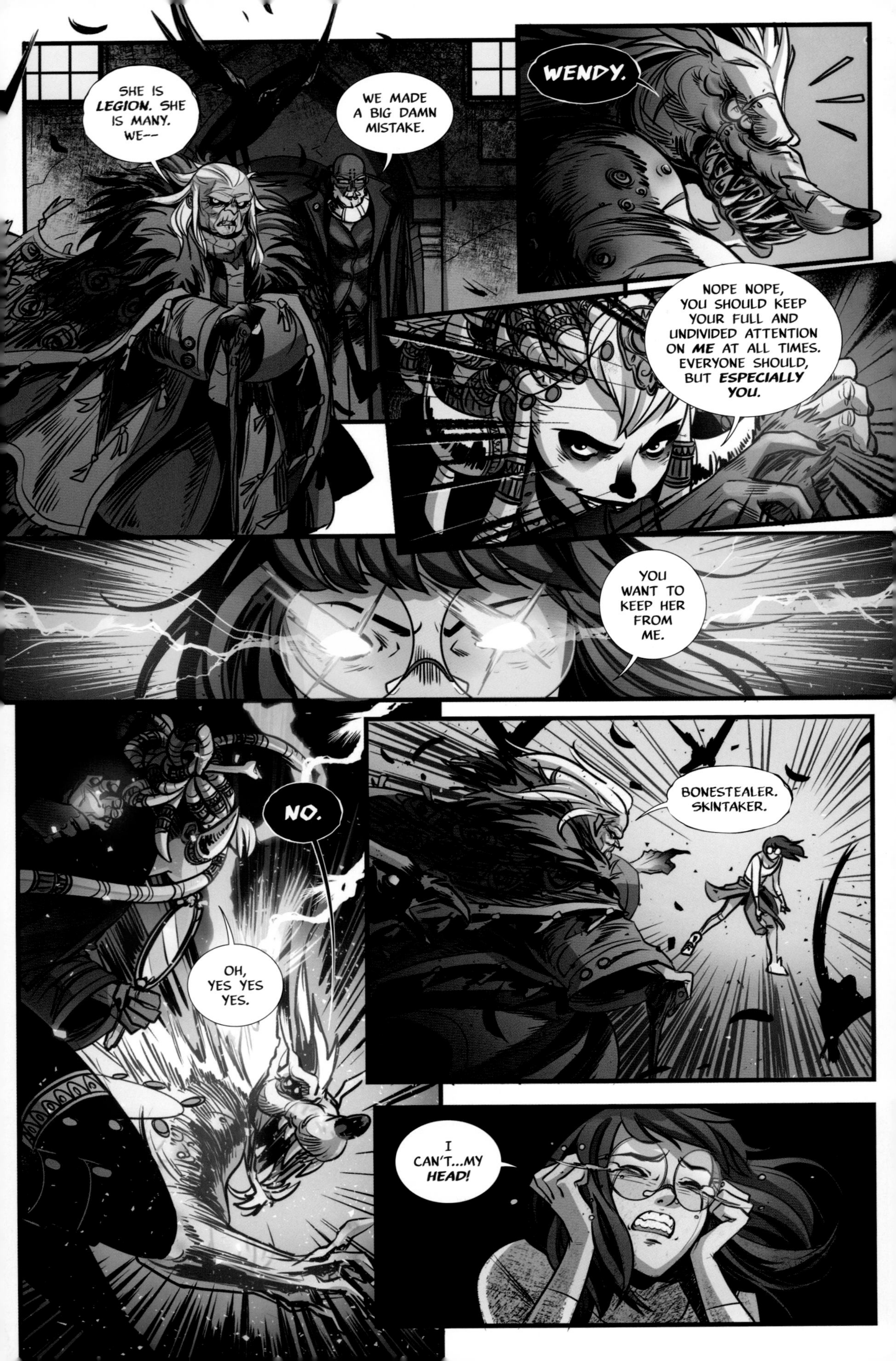
SHE IS LEGION. SHE IS MANY. WE--
WE MADE A BIG DAMN MISTAKE.
WENDY.
NOPE NOPE, YOU SHOULD KEEP YOUR FULL AND UNDIVIDED ATTENTION ON ME AT ALL TIMES. EVERYONE SHOULD, BUT ESPECIALLY YOU.
YOU WANT TO KEEP HER FROM ME.
NO.
OH, YES YES YES.
BONESTEALER. SKINTAKER.
I CAN'T...MY HEAD!

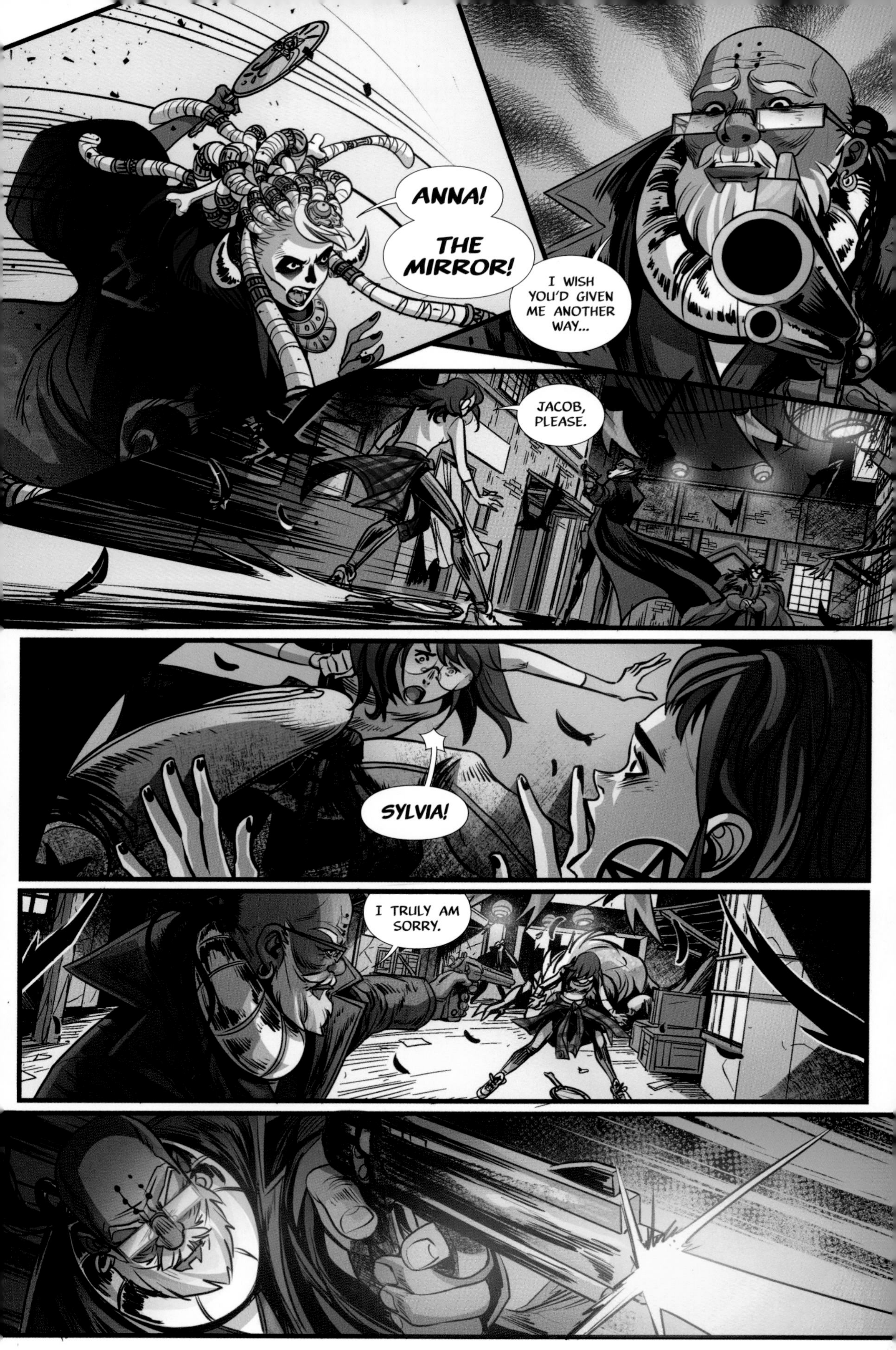
ANNA!
THE MIRROR!
I WISH YOU'D GIVEN ME ANOTHER WAY...
JACOB, PLEASE.
SYLVIA!
I TRULY AM SORRY.

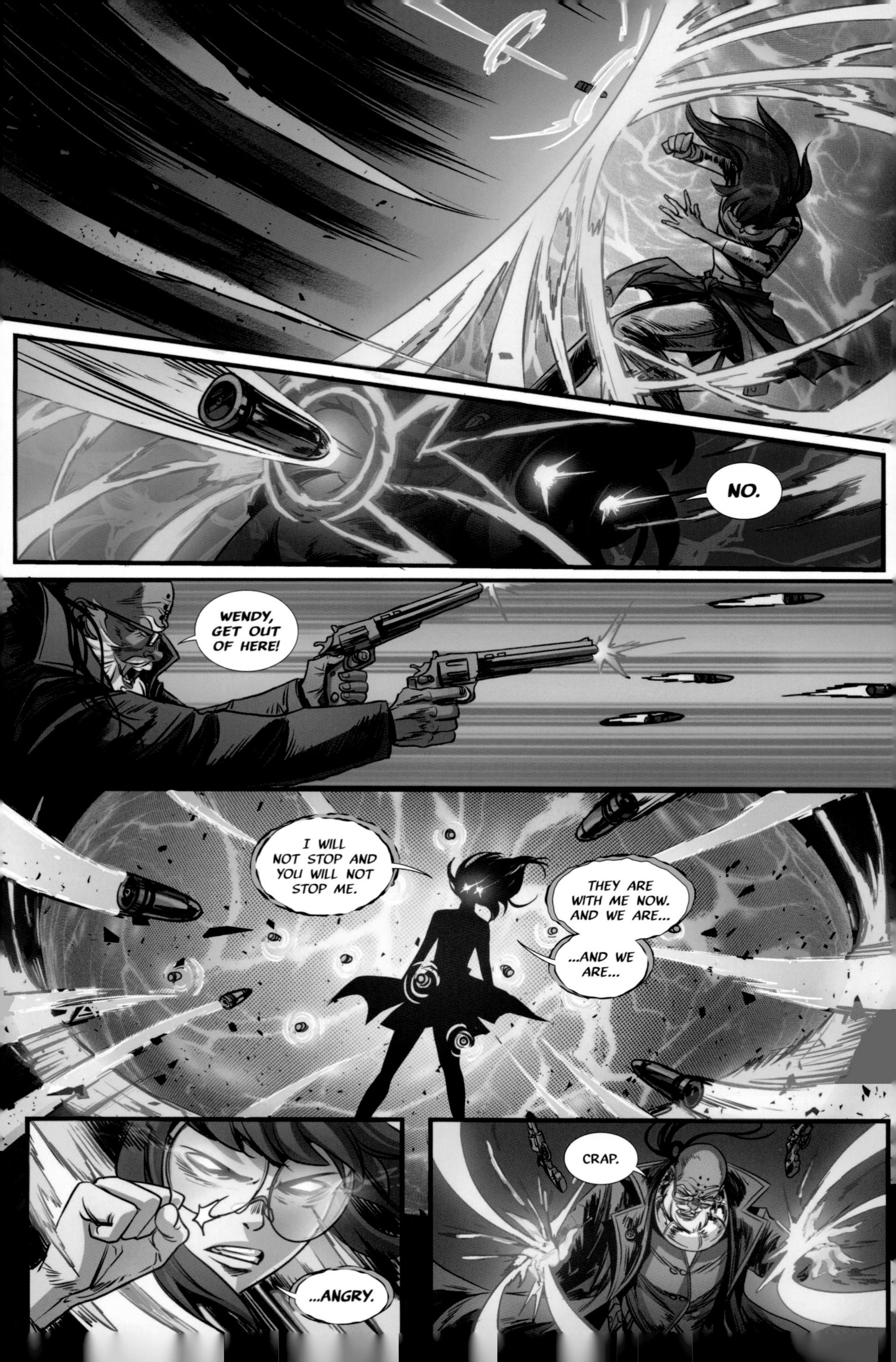

NO.
WENDY, GET OUT OF HERE!
I WILL NOT STOP AND YOU WILL NOT STOP ME.
THEY ARE WITH ME NOW. AND WE ARE...
...AND WE ARE...
...ANGRY.
CRAP.

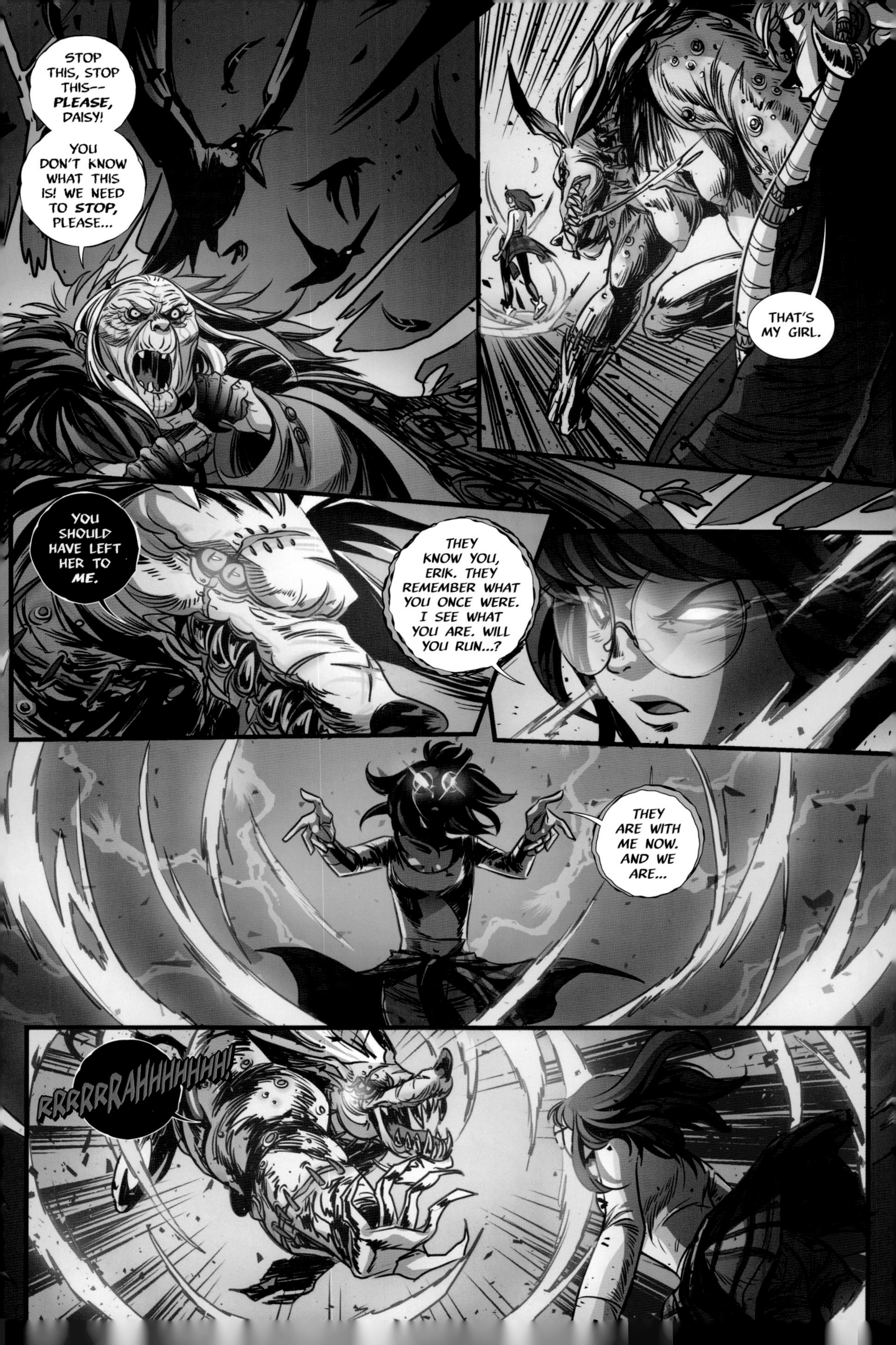
STOP THIS, STOP THIS-- PLEASE, DAISY!
YOU DON'T KNOW WHAT THIS IS! WE NEED TO STOP, PLEASE...
THAT'S MY GIRL.
YOU SHOULD HAVE LEFT HER TO ME.
THEY KNOW YOU, ERIK. THEY REMEMBER WHAT YOU ONCE WERE. I SEE WHAT YOU ARE. WILL YOU RUN...?
THEY ARE WITH ME NOW. AND WE ARE...
RRRRRRAHHHHHHH!

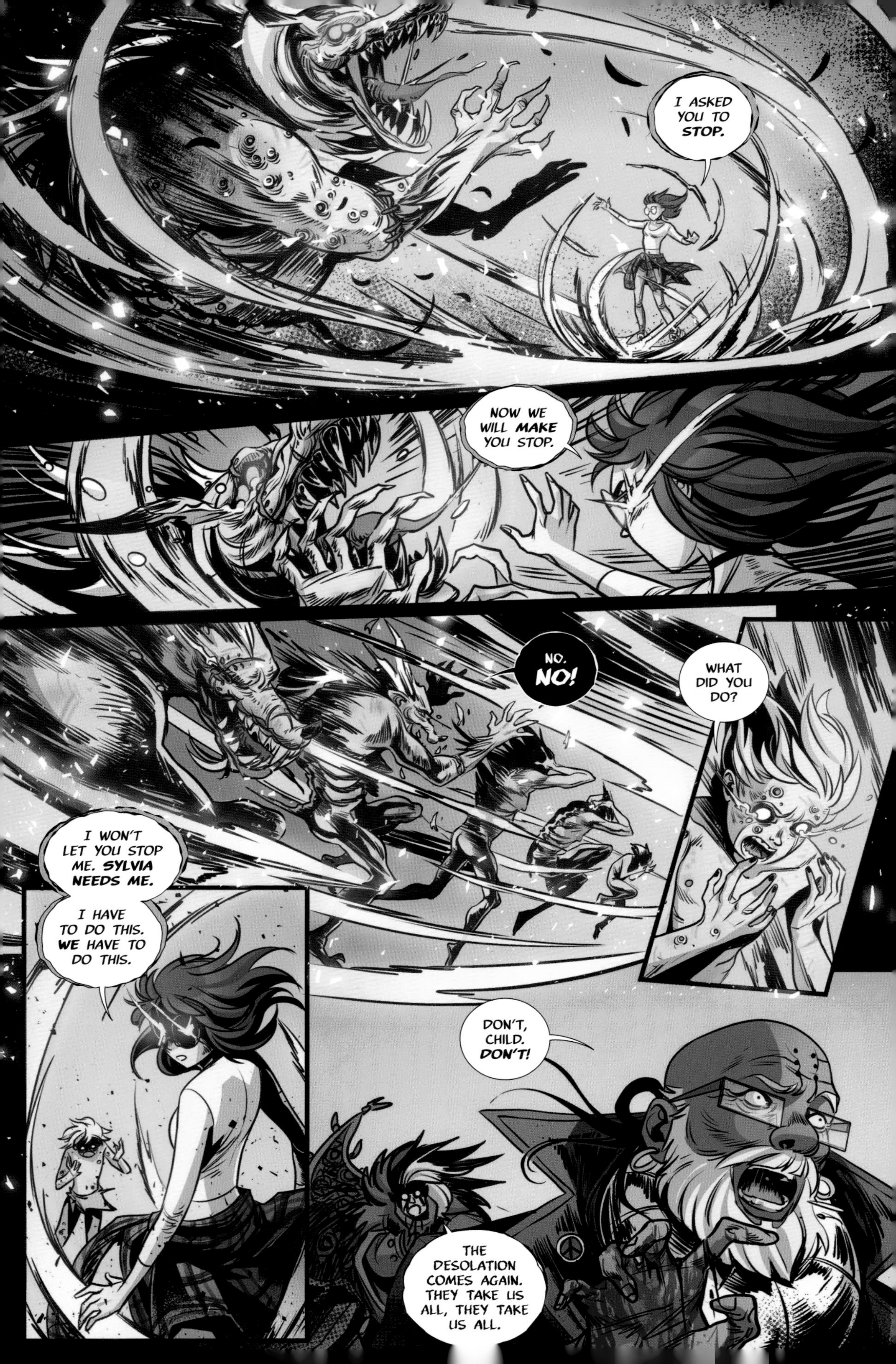
I ASKED YOU TO STOP.
NOW WE WILL MAKE YOU STOP.
NO. NO!
WHAT DID YOU DO?
I WON'T LET YOU STOP ME. SYLVIA NEEDS ME.
I HAVE TO DO THIS. WE HAVE TO DO THIS.
DON'T, CHILD. DON'T!
THE DESOLATION COMES AGAIN. THEY TAKE US ALL, THEY TAKE US ALL.

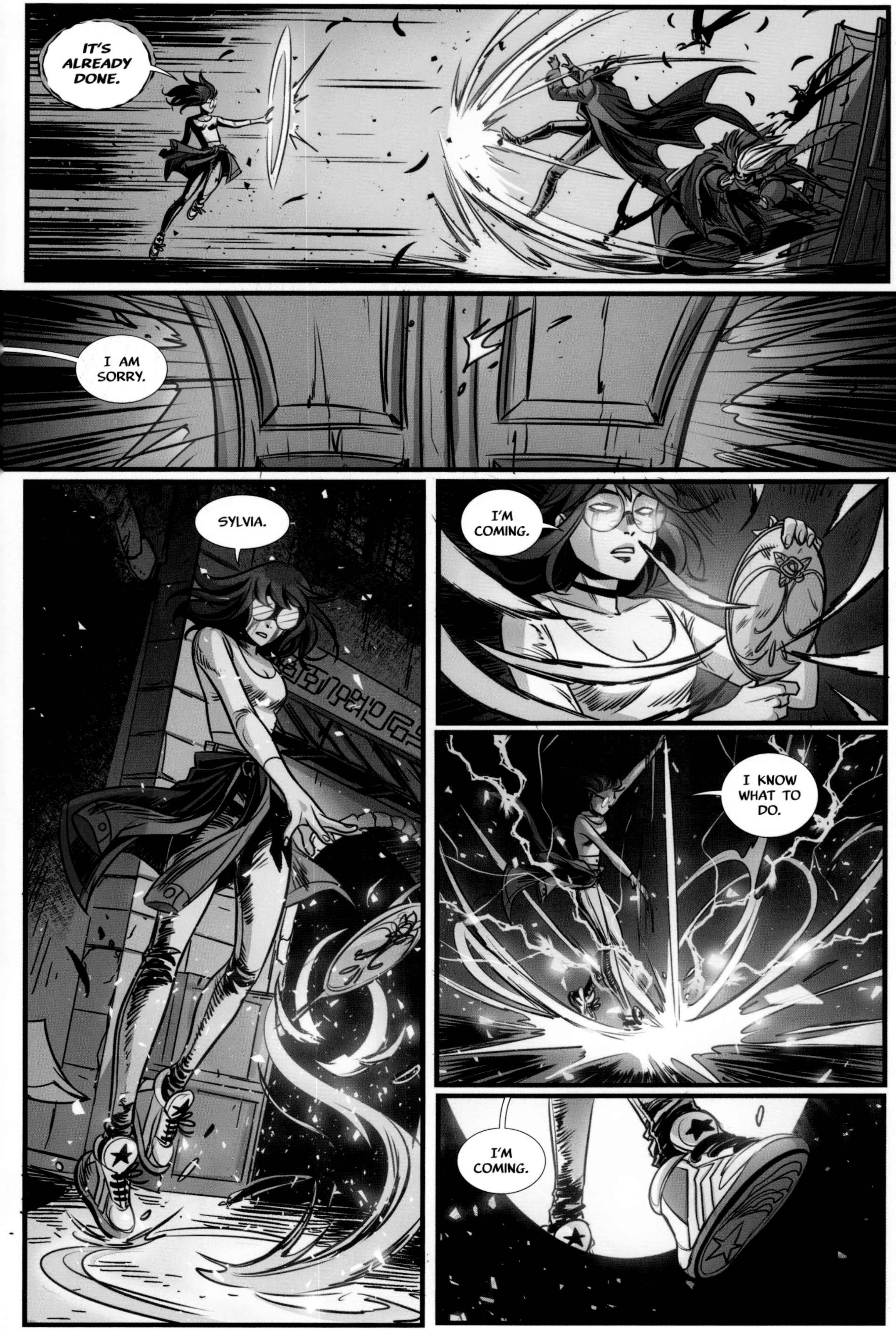
IT'S ALREADY DONE.
I AM SORRY.
SYLVIA.
I'M COMING.
I KNOW WHAT TO DO.
I'M COMING.

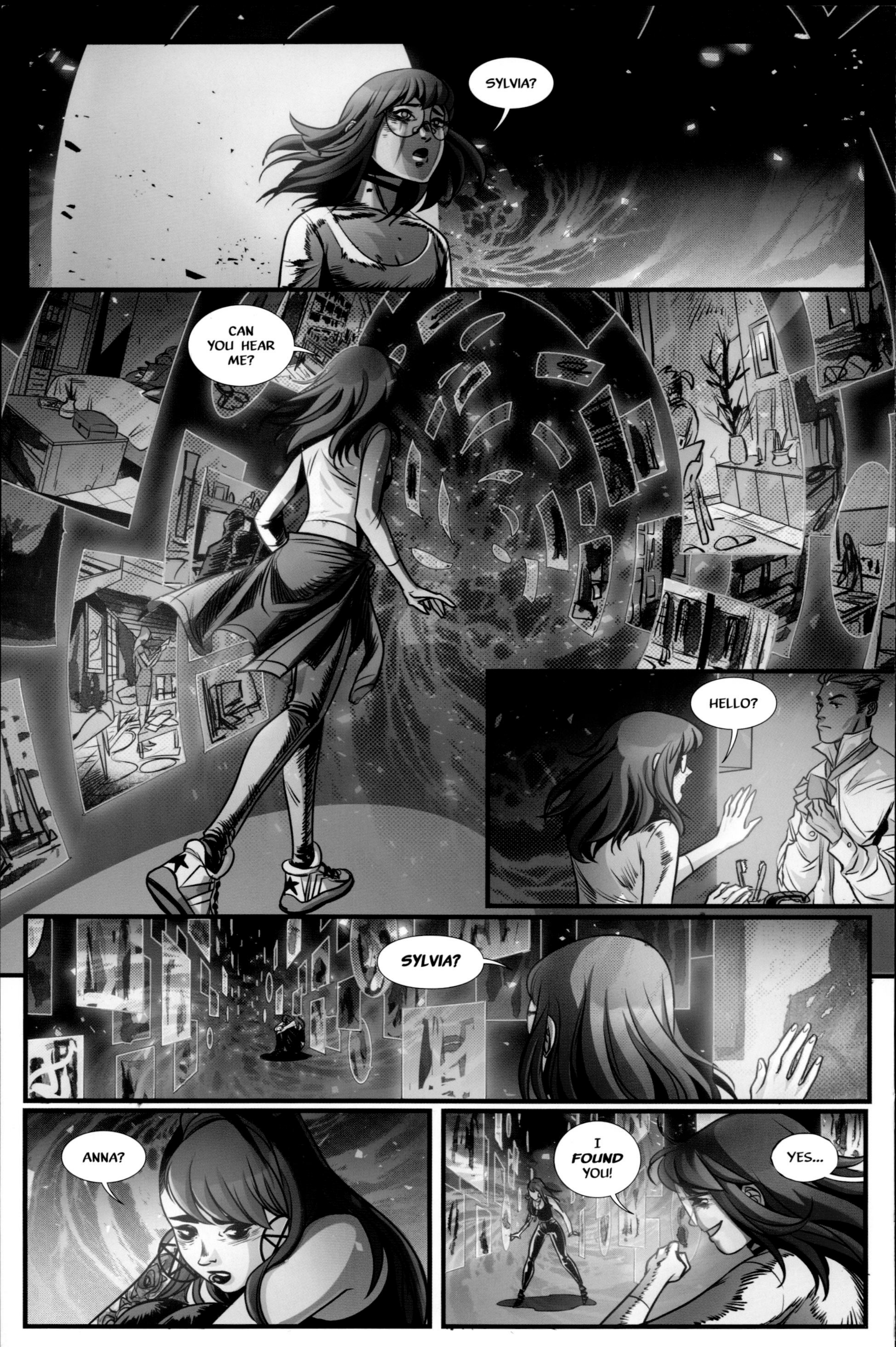
SYLVIA?
CAN YOU HEAR ME?
HELLO?
SYLVIA?
ANNA?
I FOUND YOU!
YES...

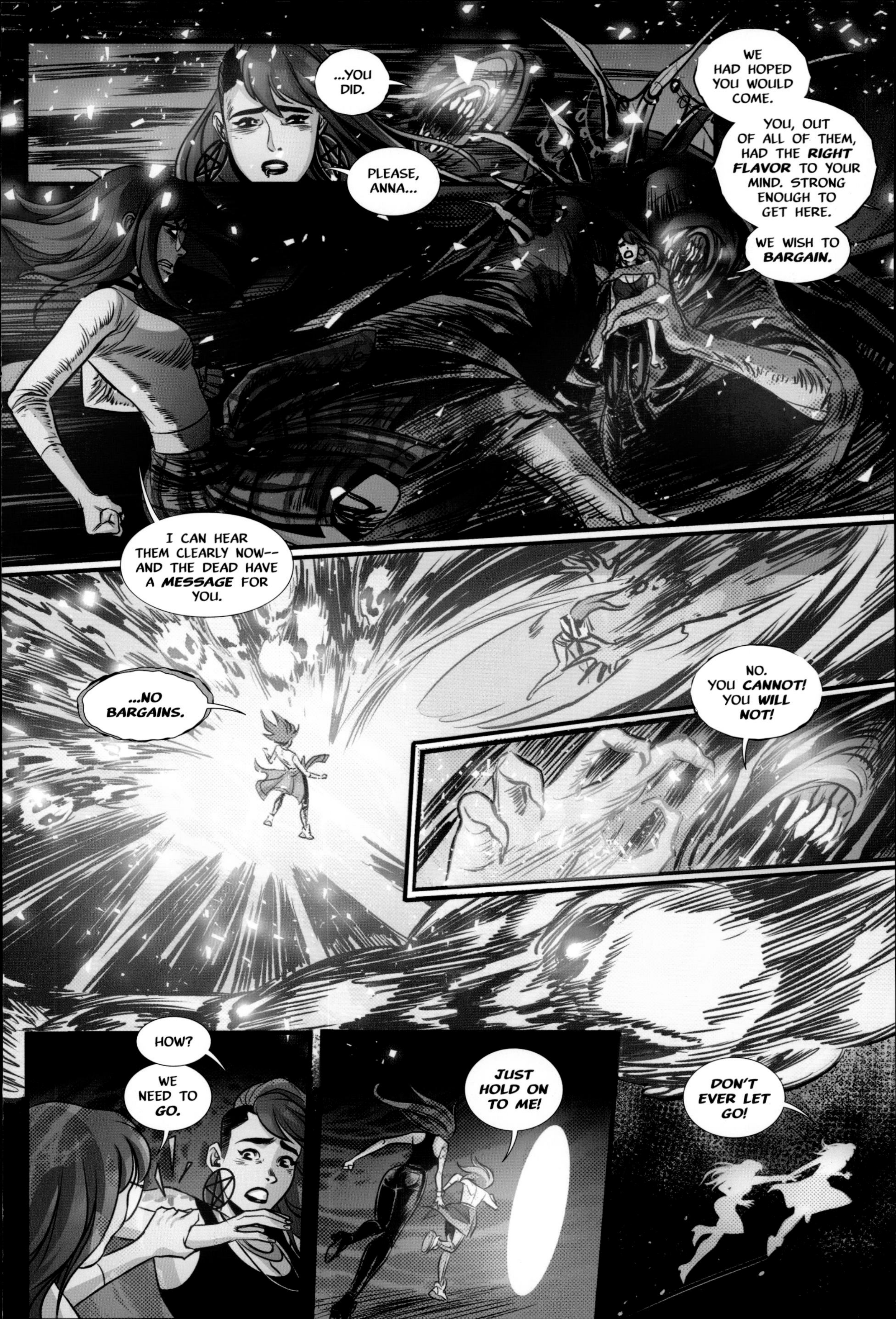
...YOU DID.
PLEASE, ANNA...
WE HAD HOPED YOU WOULD COME.
YOU, OUT OF ALL OF THEM, HAD THE RIGHT FLAVOR TO YOUR MIND. STRONG ENOUGH TO GET HERE.
WE WISH TO BARGAIN.
I CAN HEAR THEM CLEARLY NOW-- AND THE DEAD HAVE A MESSAGE FOR YOU.
...NO BARGAINS.
NO. YOU CANNOT! YOU WILL NOT!
HOW?
WE NEED TO GO.
JUST HOLD ON TO ME!
DON'T EVER LET GO!

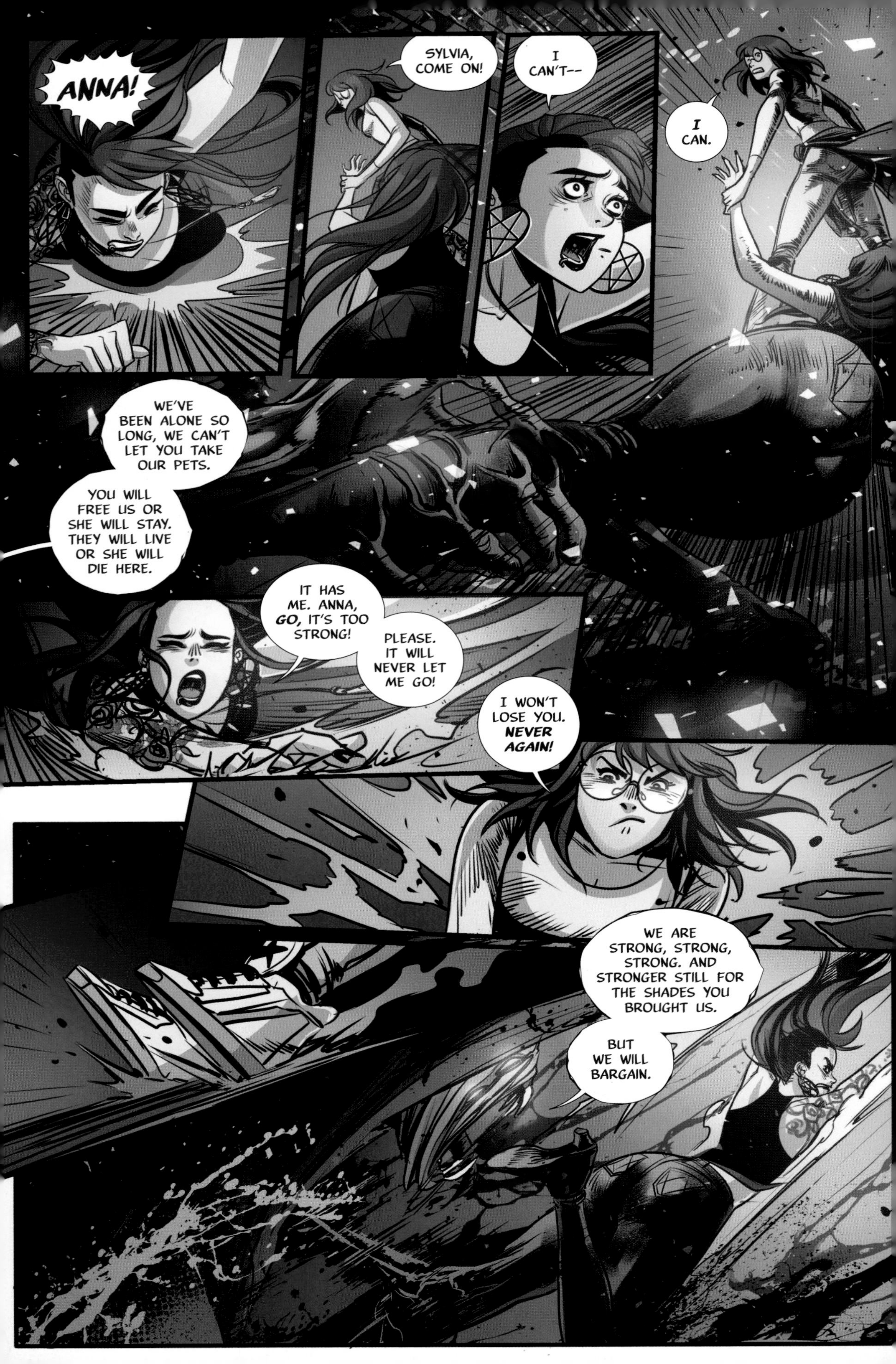
ANNA!
SYLVIA, COME ON!
I CAN'T--
I CAN.
WE'VE BEEN ALONE SO LONG, WE CAN'T LET YOU TAKE OUR PETS.
YOU WILL FREE US OR SHE WILL STAY. THEY WILL LIVE OR SHE WILL DIE HERE.
IT HAS ME. ANNA, GO, IT'S TOO STRONG!
PLEASE. IT WILL NEVER LET ME GO!
I WON'T LOSE YOU. NEVER AGAIN!
WE ARE STRONG, STRONG, STRONG. AND STRONGER STILL FOR THE SHADES YOU BROUGHT US.
BUT WE WILL BARGAIN.

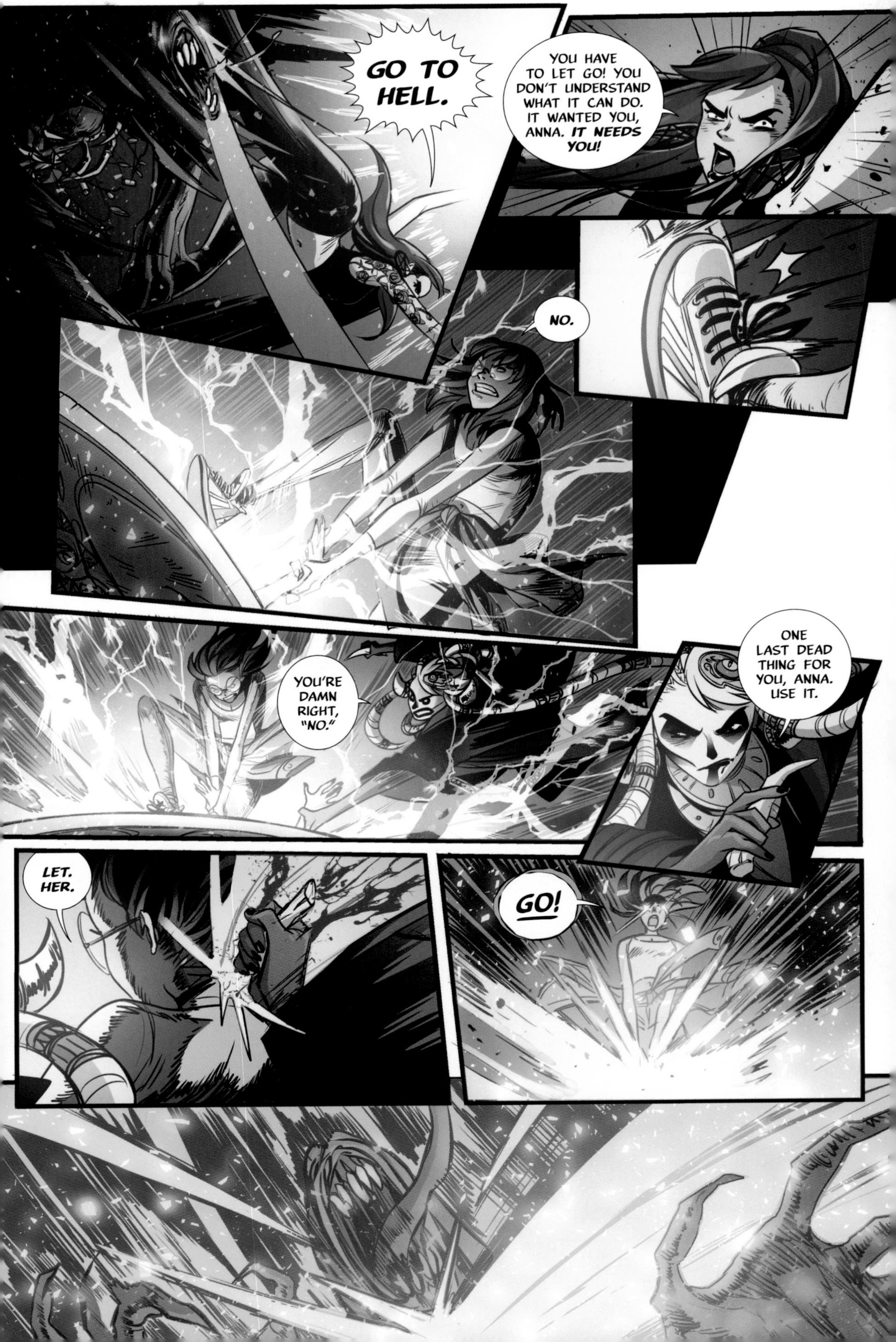
GO TO HELL.
YOU HAVE TO LET GO! YOU DON'T UNDERSTAND WHAT IT CAN DO. IT WANTED YOU, ANNA. IT NEEDS YOU!
NO.
YOU'RE DAMN RIGHT, "NO."
ONE LAST DEAD THING FOR YOU, ANNA. USE IT.
LET. HER.
GO!

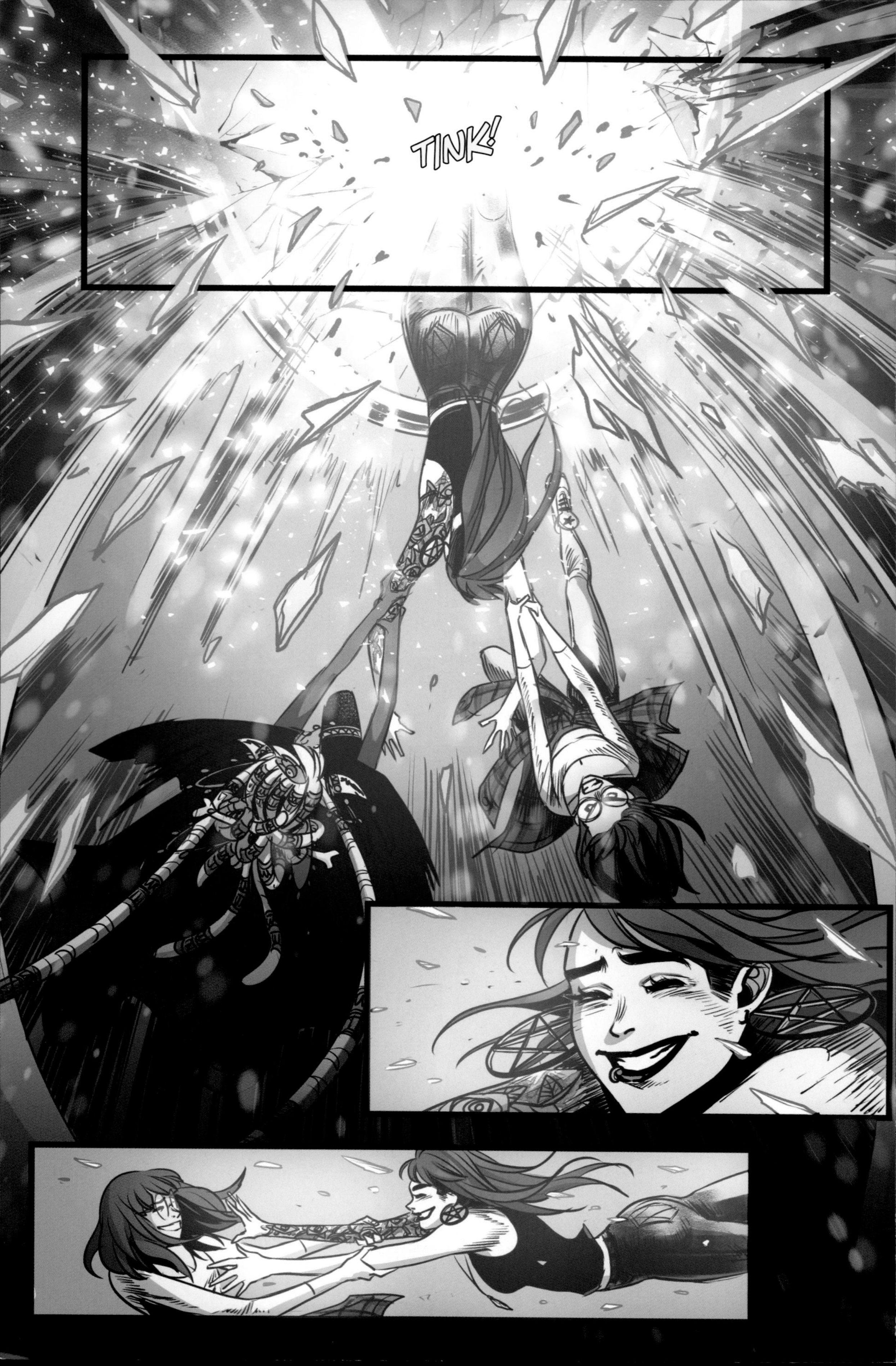
TINK!

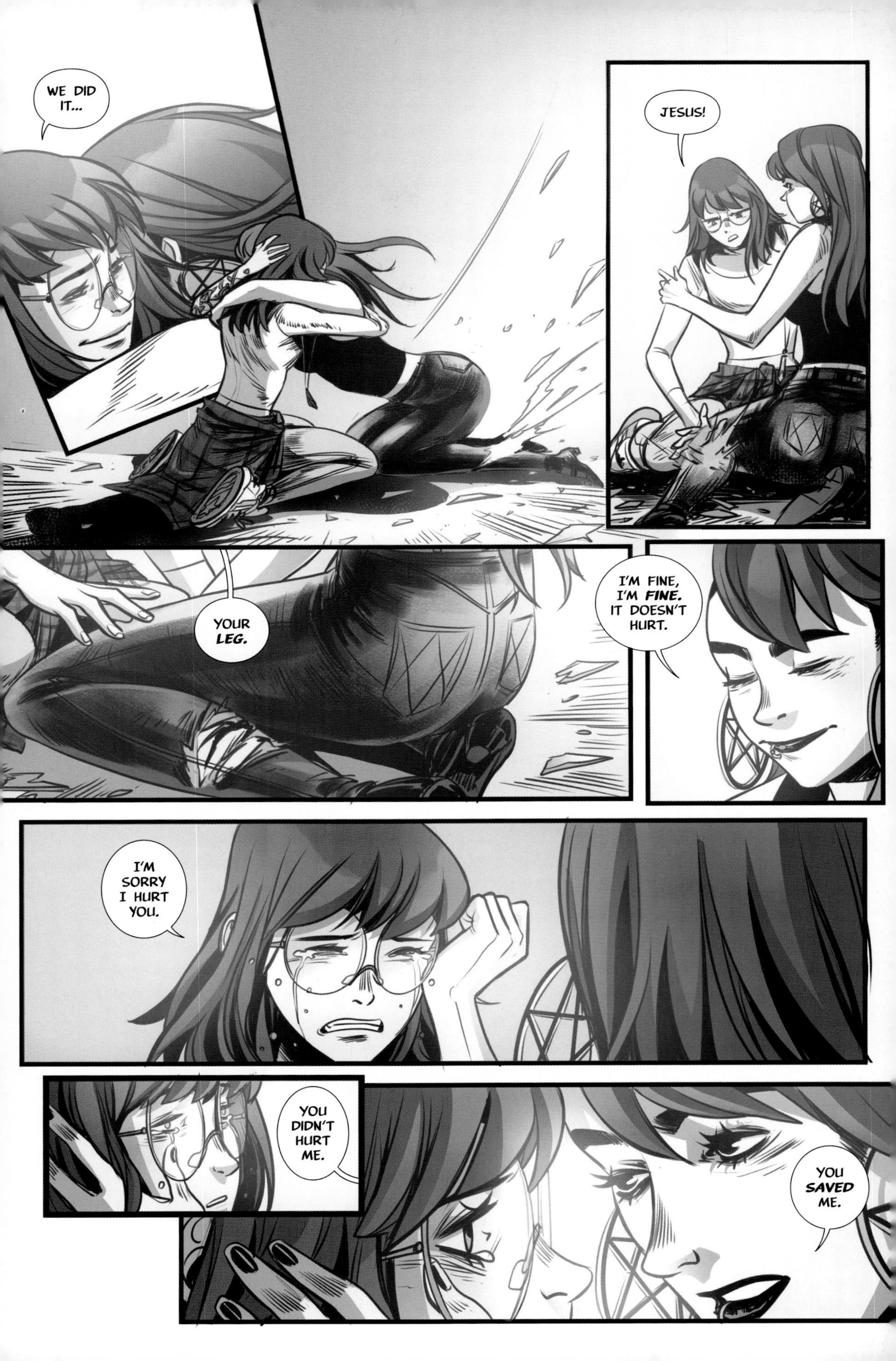
WE DID IT...
JESUS!
YOUR LEG.
I'M FINE, I'M FINE. IT DOESN'T HURT.
I'M SORRY I HURT YOU.
YOU DIDN'T HURT ME.
YOU SAVED ME.

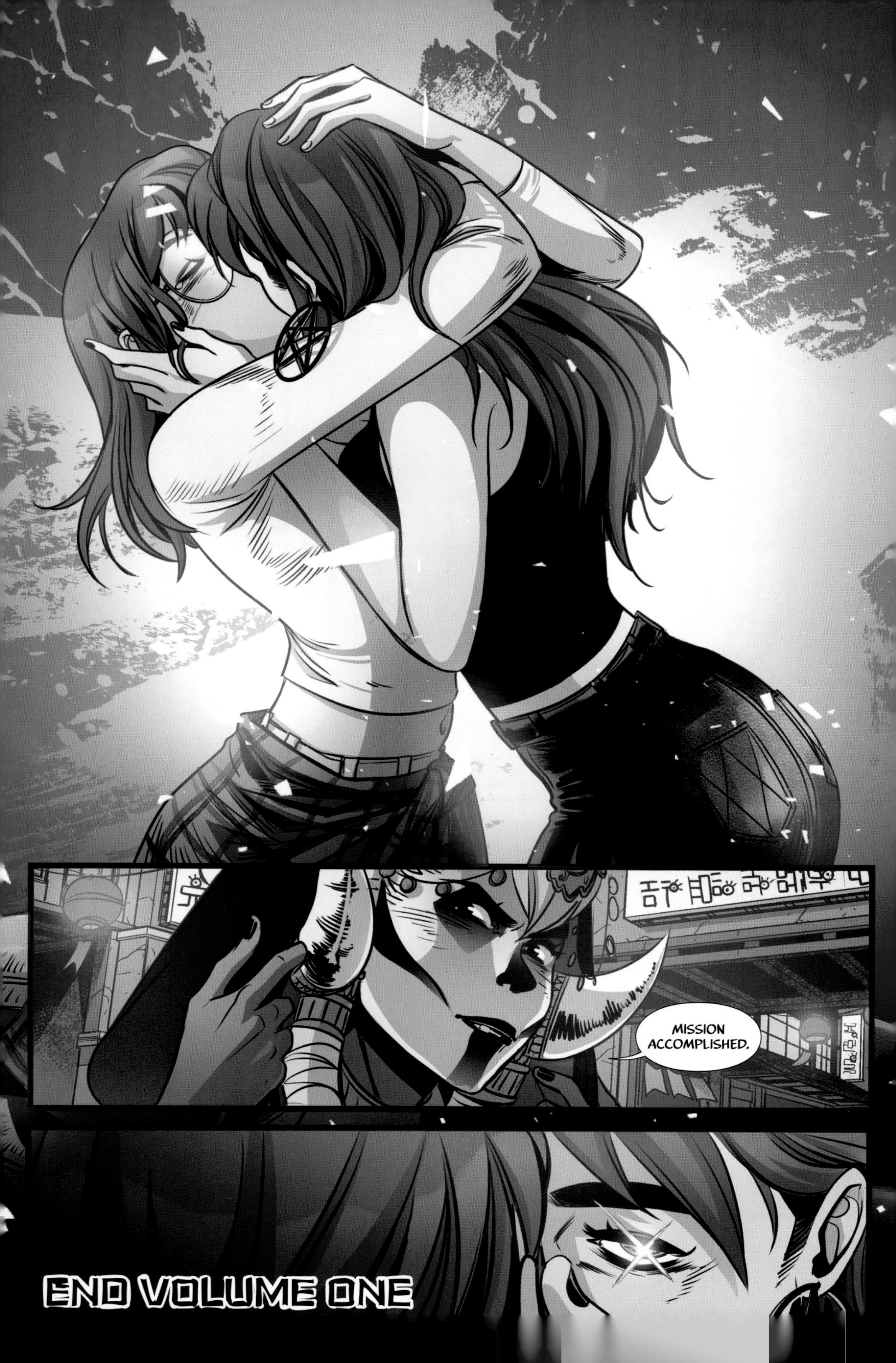
MISSION ACCOMPLISHED.
END VOLUME ONE

BACKWAYS™

COVER GALLERY

AFTERSHOCK™

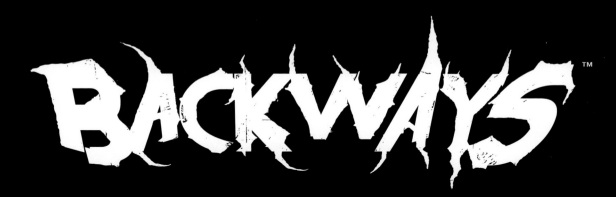

Issue 1
MIKE ROOTH
The Comic Mint variant cover

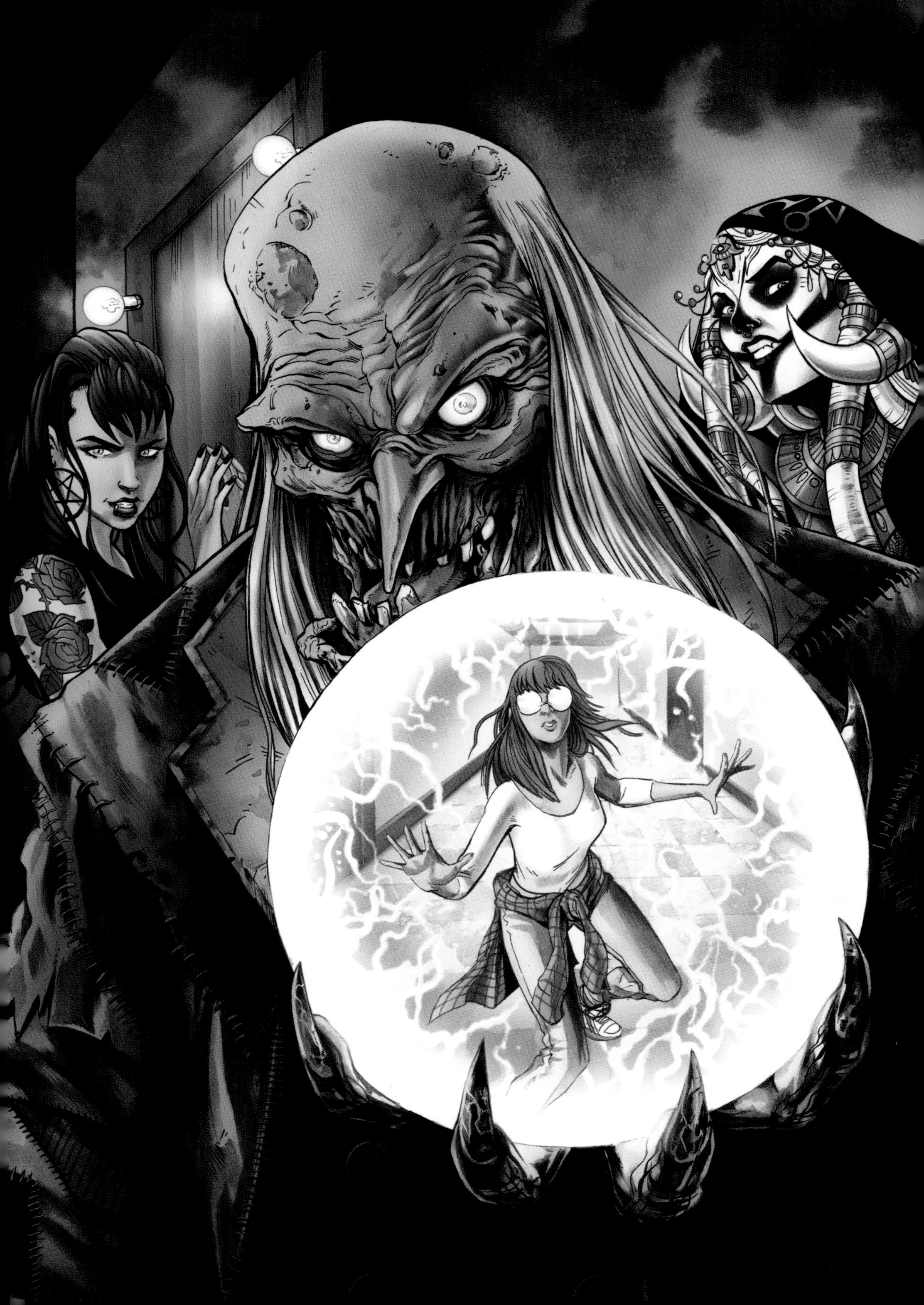

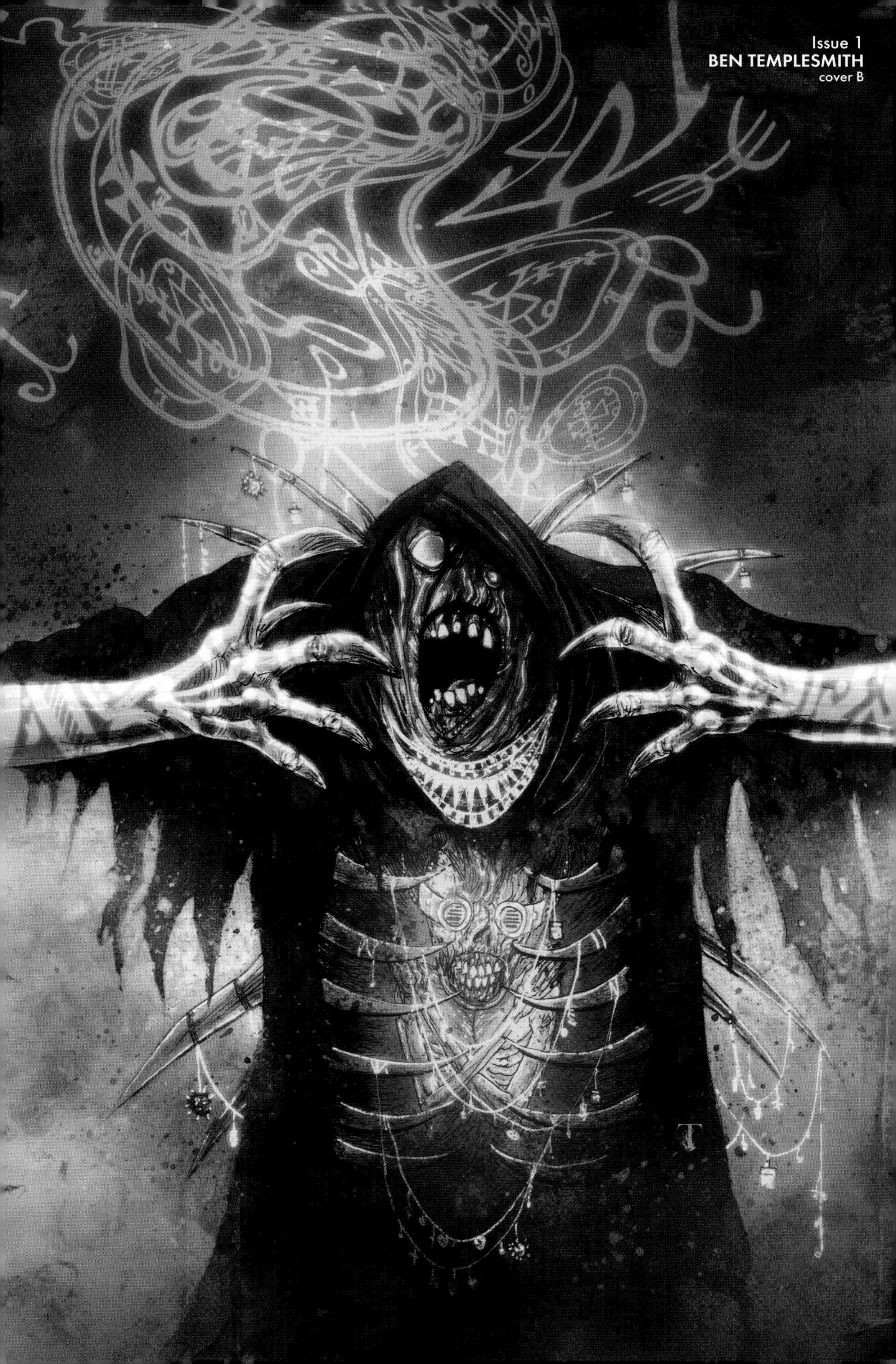

Issue 1
BEN TEMPLESMITH
cover B

Issue 1
ERIKA ROOTH
The Comic Mint variant cover

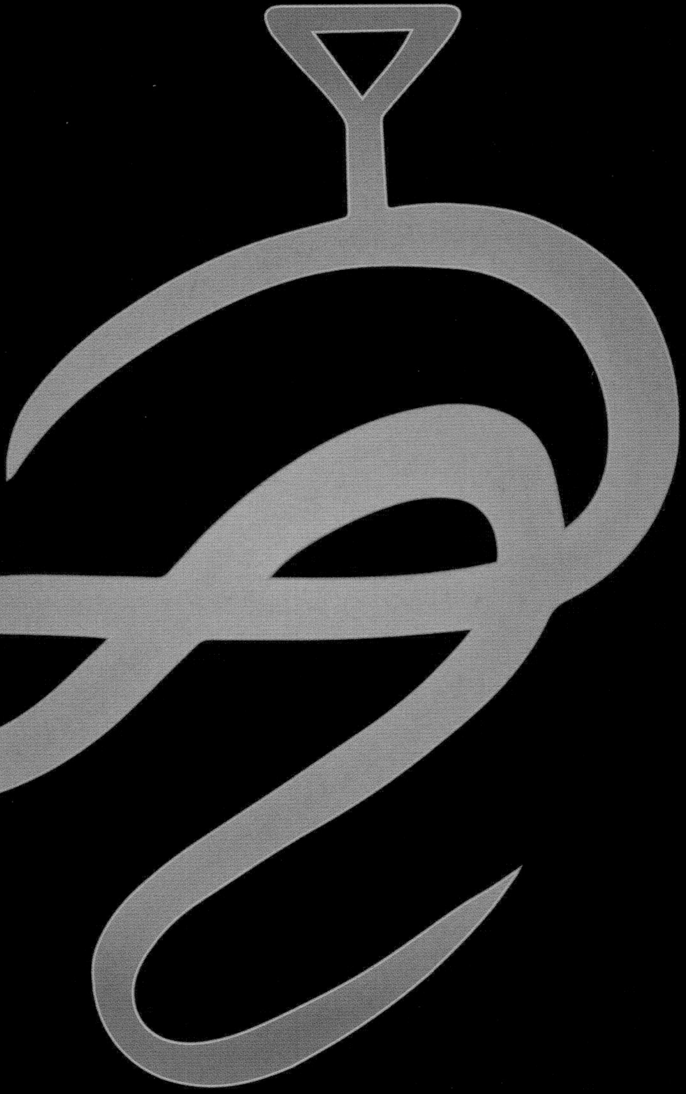

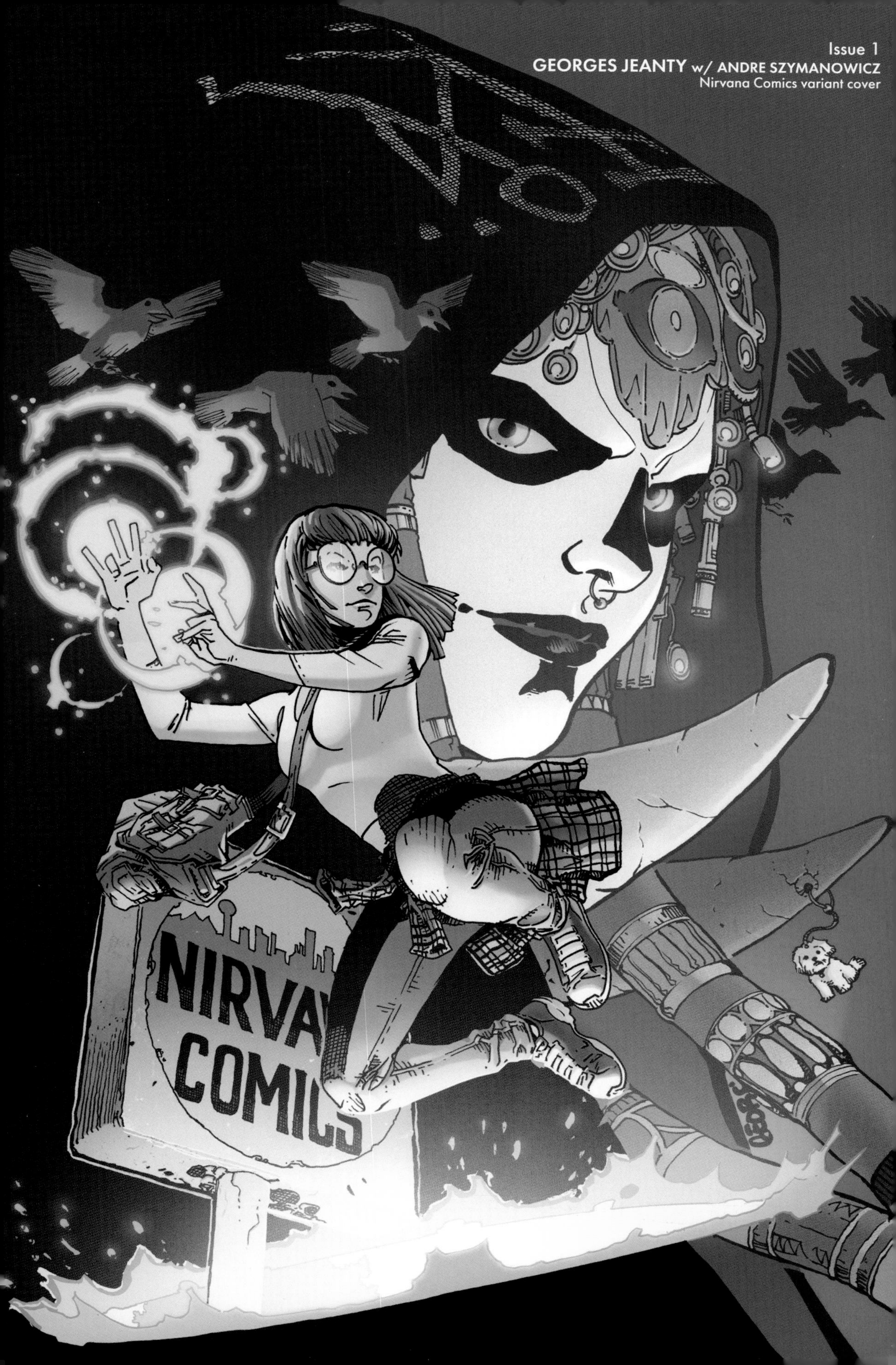
COMICS

Issue 1
GEORGES JEANTY w/ **ANDRE SZYMANOWICZ**
Nirvana Comics variant cover

BACKWAYS™

sketchbook

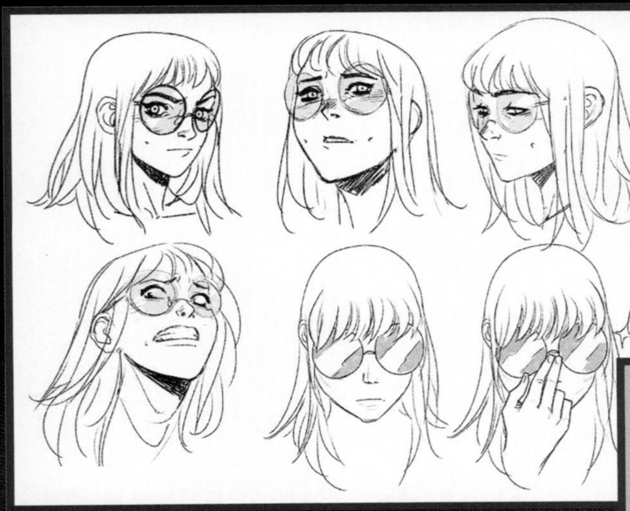

ANNA

Artist Eleonora Carlini brings our heroes and the colorful inhabitants of the BACKWAYS to life!

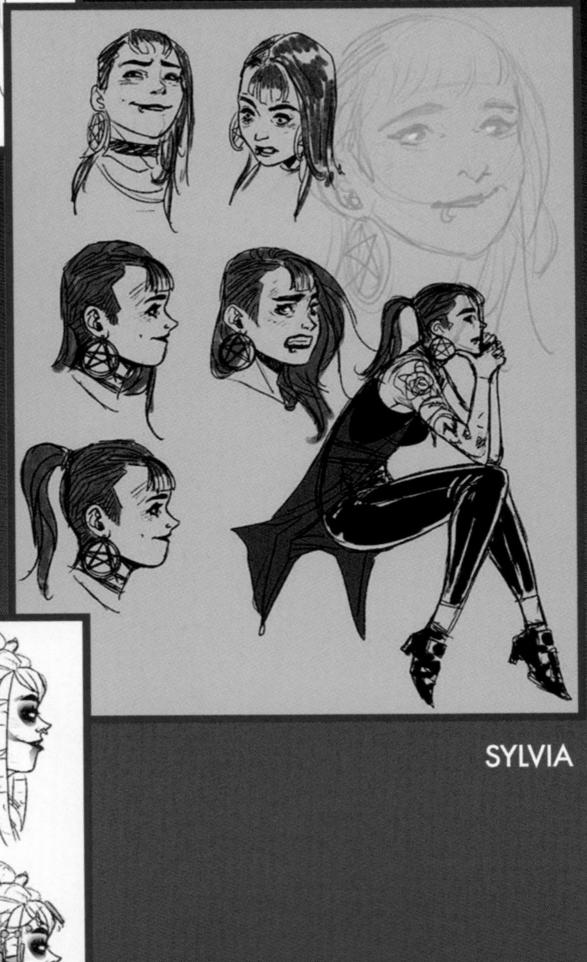

SYLVIA

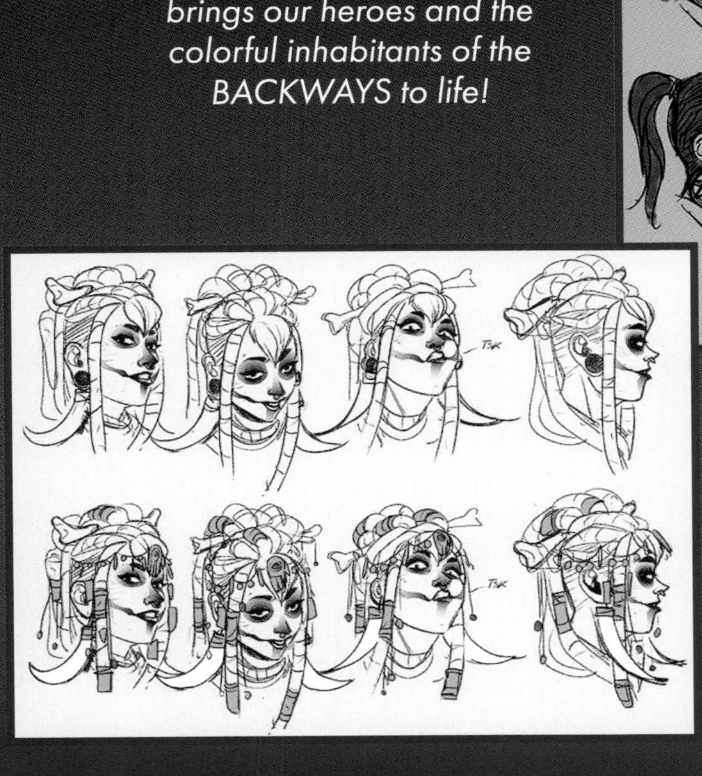

COYOTE BONES

BACKWAYS™

heroes

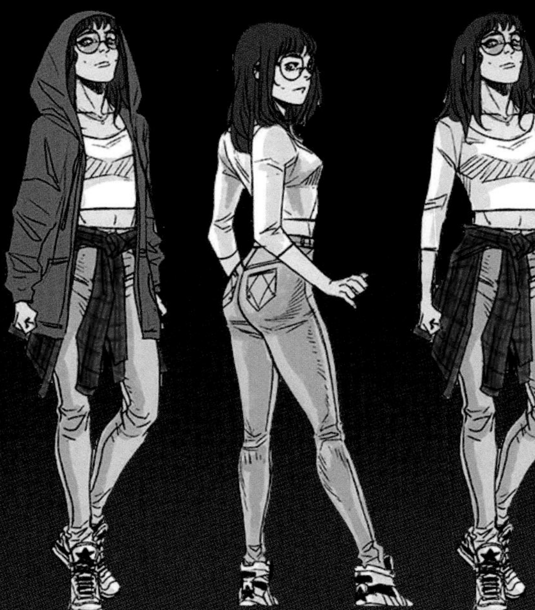

ANNA

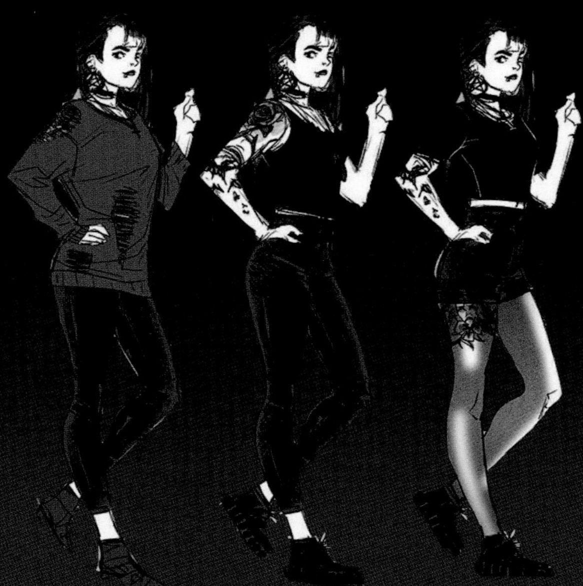

SYLVIA

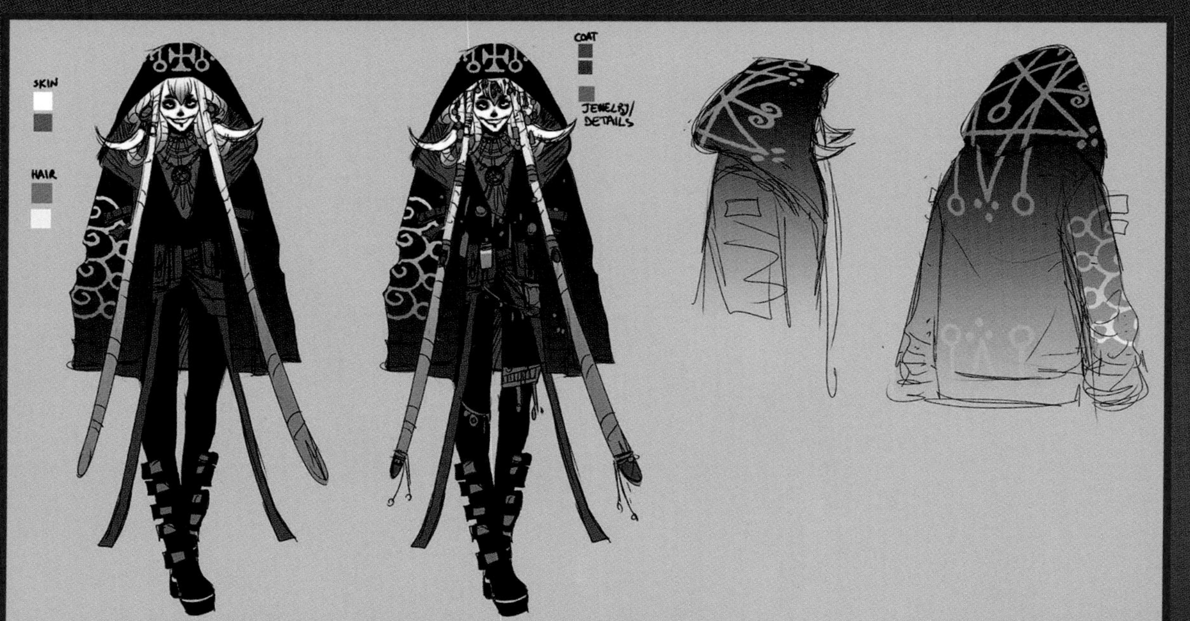
SKIN
HAIR
COAT
JEWELRY/
DETAILS

COYOTE BONES

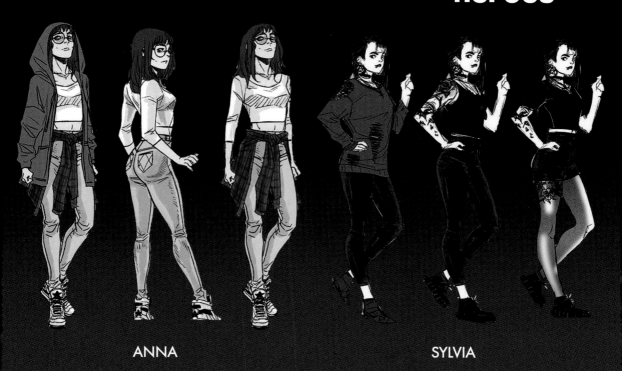

BACKWAYS™

villains

THE OUTSIDER

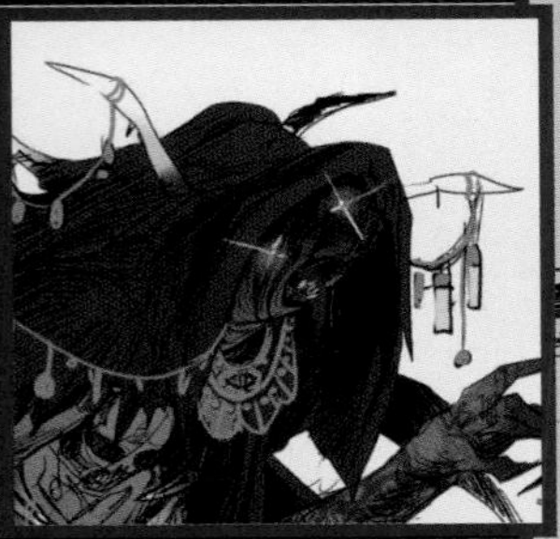

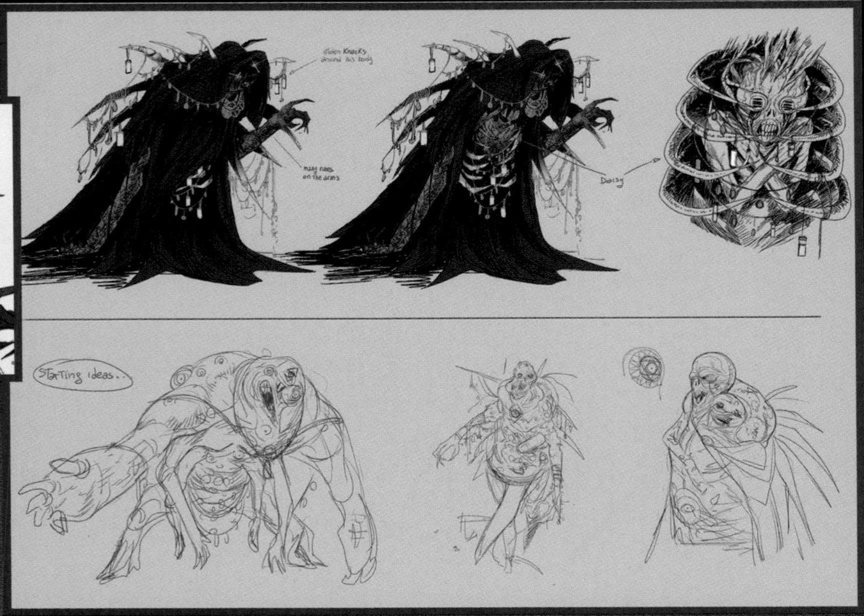

Stolen Knacks around his body
many robes on the arms
Daisy
Starting ideas...

SKIN HORSE

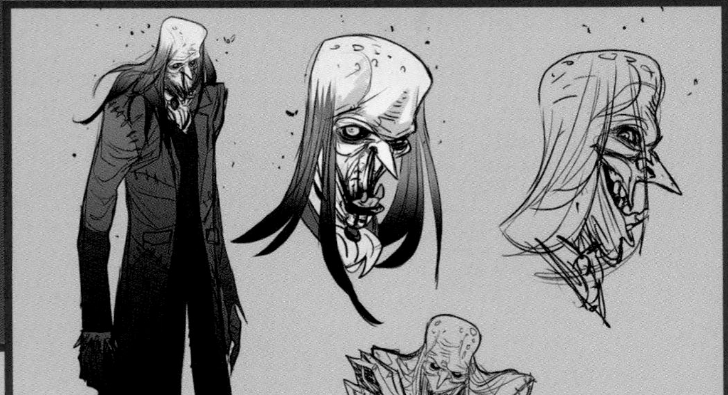

SKIN HORSE

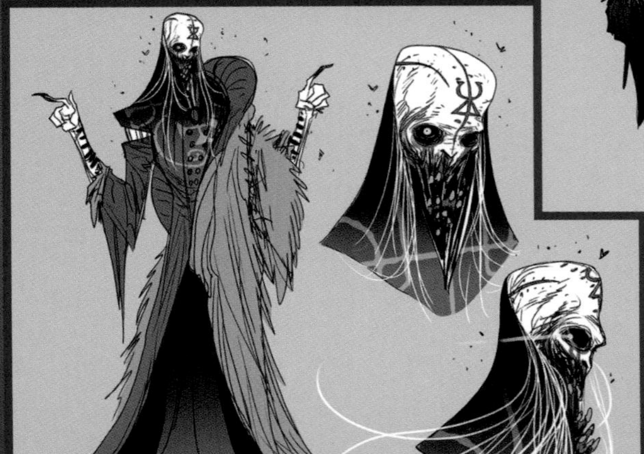

BACKWAYS™

myth & magic

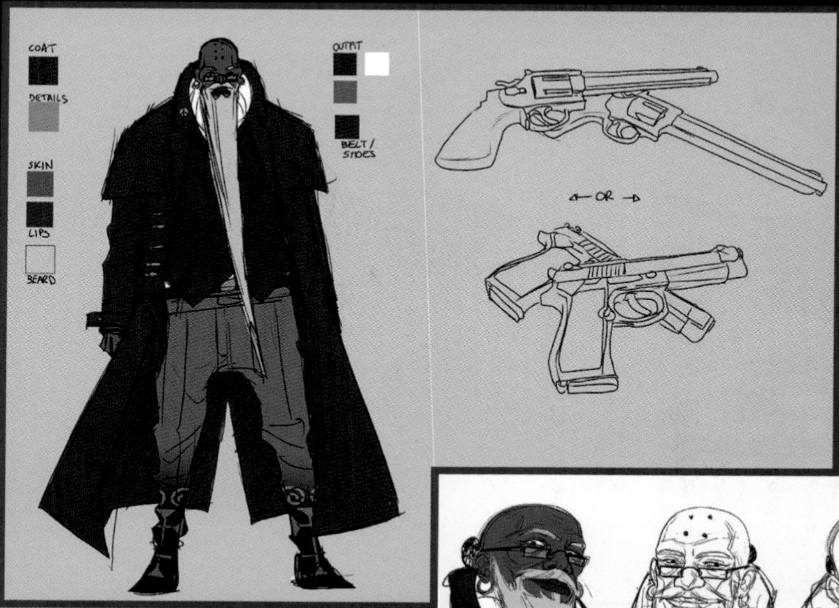

COAT
DETAILS
SKIN
LIPS
BEARD
OUTFIT
BELT / SHOES
OR

JACOB

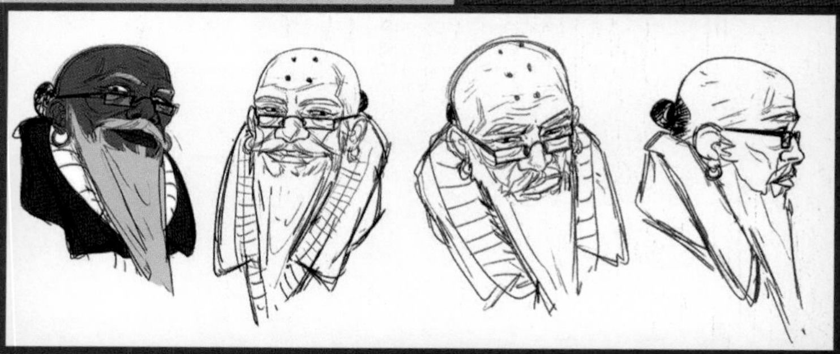

OLD WENDY

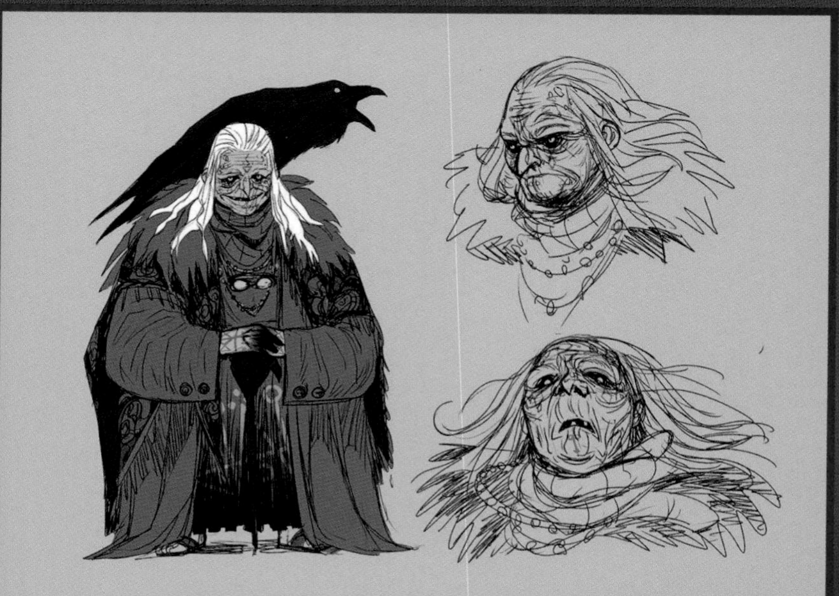

script by
JUSTIN JORDAN

BACKWAYS™
#1

PAGES
22 & 23
PROCESS

The Backways
Issue One
Justin Jordan

Page Twenty Two/Twenty Three

Panel One – Inset on Anna's face. Her eyes widen and this does actually seem to impress her.

Panel Two – The splash. Coyote gestures sweepingly, smiles. The Backways Bazarre. Basically, this is one of the central meeting places of the Backways. It's a huge space, which is full of people trading all kinds of things. There are a bunch of Backways residents here, some of whom have been warped by the warpers into flesh no longer entirely human. Likewise, some of the animals have been created through magic. A couple of children are pointing at Coyote and one is whispering into another's ear.

                        COYOTE
            This is the Backways, sister. All the hidden
            places, the forgotten places, sewn together
            in a nation of our own design. This is where
            magic lives. Where people with Knacks can
            bend the world.

                        COYOTE
            This is home of wanderers and wonders.
            Workers and weepers. This is the ground zero
            for weird, Anna, and if you want to find
            your friend, this is where we start.

End Issue One

inks by
ELEONORA CARLINI

colors by
SILVIA TIDEI

BACKWAYS

JUSTIN JORDAN writer
🐦 @justin_jordan

Justin Jordan broke into comics with *The Strange Talent of Luther Strode* with Tradd Moore at Image. Since then, he's written two more *Strode* series for Image, as well as *Dead Body Road* with Matteo Scalera and *Spread* with Kyle Strahm. He's recently written the creator-owned series *Deep State* and *John Flood* for BOOM! He rebooted *Shadowman* for Valiant and *Team 7* for DC's New 52. His other works have included *The Adventures of Superman*, *Deathstroke*, *Superboy* and, most recently, a two-year run on *Green Lantern: New Guardians*. He lives in very rural Pennsylvania with a cat named Tom Waits. Who is a girl. And adorable.

ELEONORA CARLINI artist
🐦 @eloelo

An Italian artist, Eleonora graduated from Rome's Institute of Arts with a degree in fashion and the art of costume making. She then combined her expertise in designing textures and patterns with an early childhood love for fables and storytelling, and decided to start her career as a professional comics artist. She worked for several years illustrating comics for various Italian publishers, then in 2014 Eleonora expanded her career with *Grimm Tales of Terror* for Zenescope Entertainment and *Doctor Who* for Titan Comics. More recently, she has worked for DC Comics on various titles like *Batgirl*, *Green Arrow*, *Harley Quinn* and *Suicide Squad*. BACKWAYS is her first collaboration with AfterShock Comics!

SILVIA TIDEI colorist

Silvia is an Italian illustrator who attended the International School of Comics in Rome. Teaching herself how to color comics, she soon found work on the *Vegas* short story from the French publication *Lanfeust Magazine*. At the same time, she created and worked as co-writer and colorist on the heavily award-nominated Italian trilogy *Hadez*, published by Dentiblù Editions. AfterShock is proud to welcome Silvia into their creative family with her work on BACKWAYS!

MARSHALL DILLON letterer
🐦 @MarshallDillon

A comic book industry veteran, Marshall got his start in 1994, in the midst of the indy comic boom. Over the years, he's been everything from an independent self-published writer to an associate publisher working on properties like *G.I. Joe*, *Voltron* and *Street Fighter*. He's done just about everything except draw a comic book, and worked for just about every publisher except the "big two." Primarily a father and letterer these days, he also dabbles in old-school paper and dice RPG game design. You can catch up with Marshall at firstdraftpress.net.